A MYSTERY NOVEL

DAVID HARRY

DEDICATION

To my wife Mary. I couldn't do it without you.

LOCATION

The events described in this book are centered on South Padre Island, an island in the Gulf of Mexico separated from Texas by the Laguna Madre. A two and a half mile causeway separates Port Isabel on the mainland with the island. Every year the island is host to spring breakers kicking back from their studies in mid-March and to Winter Texans who migrate south to keep warm in the winter months. Despite what you might read in my books, SPI remains a safe and extremely friendly place to live, work, or vacation. Come on down. The sun, sand, and surf await you.

DISCLAIMER

Everything in this book, except for the establishments listed and a few local folks, is fictitious. The words spoken by any of the locals are, of course, also fictional.

SOUTH PADRE ISLAND
ESTABLISHMENTS FREQUENTED BY

JIMMY REDSTONE AND ANGELLA MARTINEZ

Café Kranzler
Gabriella's
Groovi Smoothi
Hannah's House

Island Dog Wash
Laguna Bob's
Origins Recovery Center
Paragraphs on Padre
Pier 19

Sea Ranch
southpadretv.tv
South Padre Island Convention Center
Ted's

Turtle Rescue
UT Pan American Coastal Studies

Please stop by and tell them Jimmy and Angella sent you.

ONE

It is difficult to miss brightly colored parachutes as they float to earth. I couldn't take my eyes away from the two orange ones with broad white stripes being buffeted by the wind into snake-like trajectories almost directly above us.

Angella and I were walking north on the South Padre Island beach enjoying the cool water of the Gulf of Mexico gently rolling over our bare feet. The chutes were flying offshore heading for a landing just ahead of us.

It was late March, and with the craziness of Spring Break behind us, we were relaxing before Angella's belated birthday celebration which was planned for later in the day. My arm was around Angella's waist, and given the events of the recent past, I might be forgiven for holding on tighter than normal. My emotions were still too raw to take anything for granted.

"Ever do that, Jimmy?" Angella asked, nodding in the direction of the colorful chutes framed perfectly against the deep-blue cloudless sky.

"Not for recreation," I responded.

"I forgot you were an Army Ranger. Did you jump often?"

"Often enough to last a lifetime." It wasn't so much the jumping, but the follow-up operations on the ground after landing that produced the troubling memories. The less I thought about that time in my life the better.

Angella, sensing my reluctance to elaborate, asked, "Where'd they come from? I mean I didn't hear a plane."

"With the surf, I'm not surprised. Dropped upwind somewhere back there," I replied, pointing south down the beach in the direction we had come. Glancing back, I noticed a third all blue chute separated from the others by what looked to be two or three minutes. It was higher than the others, but descending faster.

"There seems to be two people on each," Angella commented, "I see four legs dangling."

"Probably an instructor and a tourist. I'm told an outfit called Skydive South Padre Island runs jumping sessions over there at *Clayton's*," I said, pointing toward a section of the beach marked with red cones.

"It would be fun to watch them land up close. Come on!" Angella broke into an easy sprint, her long legs gracefully moving, sand flying from beneath her feet.

Indeed, a group of people had gathered just south of *Clayton's Beach Bar,* a local watering hole featuring great burgers, beer and good music. During Spring Break, volleyball, and an amped-up stage had been the main non-drinking attractions. The biggest attraction, of course, was the availability of the opposite sex———everyone was there for a great time with activities seemingly running twenty-four-seven. During the day, crop-duster planes, their engines droning in rebellion, struggled south against the wind, trailing banners promoting activities like *Schlitterbahn*

Water Park and encouraging the safe consumption of *Captain Morgan* rum. Of course, condom ads were also in evidence.

"I was right," Angella called back to me. "There *are* two in the harness. The passenger seems to be screaming."

We arrived at the landing site just as the first passenger's flaming orange sneakers touched the sand just ahead of the instructor's more practical jump boots. A helper began gathering in the orange nylon chute before it even had a chance to flutter onto the beach. The instructor was a woman I vaguely recognized, but could not immediately place. The passenger, also female, was smiling broadly and yelling something in what I took to be French. She freed herself of the harness and began jumping up and down, embracing several on-lookers, all presumably family or friends. Kisses were abundant and it wasn't fifteen seconds before a margarita appeared in her hand.

"It never ceases to amaze me how this island revolves around alcohol," Angella, a former South Padre Island cop, commented. "Booze goes down like water."

"Staff of life," I commented. "You'd think they'd been weaned on the stuff right from their mother's breast."

"You just proved Freud's thesis. You're ogling the young talent. That behavior doesn't become you."

"Who's og———"

The rest of my pathetic response was thankfully drowned out by a cheer that erupted when the second parachute landed. A tall, slender guy, wearing bright plaid shorts, a ball cap will a Kansas Jayhawk emblazoned on the front, and a T-shirt showing both the U. S. and French flags, broke free of the harness and raced over to hug the French woman. Their kiss lasted significantly longer than a platonic relationship kiss and held the promise of continued activity. An old bald guy yelled for them to take a room.

While all eyes were on the loving couple, the blue chute landed slightly off-target a short way up the beach. The riders were quickly engulfed in a sea of blue nylon.

"Something's wrong, Jimmy," Angella said, interrupting my observation of the festivities. "No one came out from under the chute and I don't see anyone from here going to help."

I trailed Angella as she ran toward the billowing nylon. The landing site was actually further away than it had first appeared. It took us a full minute, maybe slightly longer, to reach the downed parachute.

Several people arrived at the scene before us and were standing around looking puzzled. I grabbed an edge of the flimsy material, intent on taming the chute.

Angella ducked underneath. "Jimmy," she cried a few seconds later, "he's injured." Then she added, "I'm not getting a pulse."

"Grab those straps," I called in the direction of the onlookers, "and pull!" I pointed north. The wind would help clear the area in that direction.

Immediately, two men and a teenage girl ran forward. I yelled, "Call nine-one-one. Tell them we have a man down on the beach just north of *Clayton's*."

When he didn't respond, I asked, "Do you speak English?"

He shook his head. "Who speaks English?" I yelled into the wind.

The teenage girl waved her hand.

"Call nine-one-one," I repeated for her benefit. "Tell them we have a man down on the beach just north of *Clayton's*."

She immediately produced a cell phone and began dialing.

I turned back to help with the chute, and the blue nylon came clear of where Angella was trying to breathe life into the comatose body.

"So where's the instructor?" I yelled. "I don't see anyone else here."

"Maybe this guy jumped alone," Angella responded, between breaths. "A single?"

I had clearly seen four dangling legs when the big blue chute had passed overhead. "I'm positive there were two. I'll check the dunes."

I expected to see someone on or behind the dunes, perhaps suffering a broken leg———or worse———from the botched landing.

But no one was there, not even the harness the second person had been riding in.

Returning to the beach, I found Angella still bent over the prone body. "Nothing up there," I reported. "I'll check if anybody went north to the beach access."

I immediately spotted footprints leading away from the landing site. I followed the trail north and lost the footprints in the parking lot of the county beach access road.

I returned to where Angella was working on the still not moving body. She called, "No pulse and he's not breathing. I'll continue resuscitating until the medics arrive, but I'm getting nothing."

My assumption was that the instructor———or at least the person riding in the dominant position———was the one who had disappeared. In truth, however, all we really knew was that one person was missing and judging from Angella's assessment, the other was dead———or well on his way.

TWO

"**B**oots," I exclaimed. "Why boots? And why me?" We were at *Pier 19* celebrating Angella's birthday, albeit a little over two months late. So why was I receiving a present? "Who are they from?"

I glanced over at Tiny foolishly anticipating that he'd provide a reason why he had hand carried cowboy boots from the nation's capital to Texas; proverbial ice to Eskimos kind of thing. Tiny, a supposedly married man, was again playing me, this time by flirting with Angella's sister, Jayme, the cast on her broken arm having been recently removed. Jayme had arrived last evening and the celebration actually began the instant she stepped foot out of the car. She has no idea Tiny is a CIA operative posing as a Secret Service Agent working directly for the President. I doubt if Jayme would miss a beat even if she knew the full truth.

Jayme, a civilian, had been picked up at a bar and literally dragged into our last assignment as a decoy for her look-alike sister. The ruse had proven effective. Tiny, before he disappeared back to Washington——or wherever undercover CIA agents hide——covered up what really happened. He concocted a story about how Angella's house in Port Isabel had been used for a SEAL training mission. As for the drugs found in Jayme's system, his explanation was simple. The SEALs screwed up.

This was but one more example of the many falsehoods I had witnessed where fabricating reality is second nature to Tiny, and presumably a prerequisite to becoming a CIA agent.

Tiny had come down to South Padre Island ostensibly to attend Angella's party. My agitation came from the simple fact that Tiny was our babysitter when Angella and I were on a mission. Right now we were on leave and I knew all too well that Tiny or more accurately, the people he worked for, never did anything without a purpose. I also knew all too well that Tiny's presence on the island didn't bode well for Angella and I.

"Hey, Tiny," I called to the almost seven footer, "are the boots from you?" The boots were hand-stitched crocodile with my initials inlaid within a map of Texas. "These puppies must have set you back several paychecks. What gives?"

"Didn't want you to pout," he winked, "what with Angella receiving all the gifts."

"You've made up better cover stories than that," I called to him. "You're having an off day. Rewind and start again."

"If you must know," Tiny confessed with another wink, "they came from McNaughton. She said you needed to clean up your act."

"What's that supposed to mean?"

"I suppose she's tired of seeing you with those ratty boots."

I had three pairs of boots I wore interchangeably. All made for me by the same boot maker——and all identical. Looking down, I had to admit Tiny——or Cindy McNaughton——had a valid point; the pair I was wearing was beyond scruffy. The others were no better. My bad.

"Did I hear you mention Mommy Long Legs?" Angella said, suddenly appearing next to Tiny. "Those gorgeous boots came from her? I should have known. I have a birthday, and Jimmy gets the presents——from a beautiful woman, no less. What should I make of that?"

"Hey, don't shoot the messenger," Tiny replied, waving his beer bottle in my direction. "I'm just following orders from the General."

Angella frowned. She had never trusted Lucinda Westminster McNaughton, retired Marine General and the person who seems to coordinate domestic terrorism threats for the President. In fact, Cindy, or Mommy Long Legs, as Angella calls her, is very much behind Angella. I would go so far as to say that McNaughton directed the operation that saved Angella's life a few months back.

McNaughton was certainly well-connected, leading to my speculation that she was still on the government payroll. Judging from the way Tiny kowtows around her, I surmise she's CIA as well.

"So Madam General had boots custom made for you! How'd she do it without your cooperation?" Angella wasn't letting go of the thread——at least not without a good hard yank.

"How the hell should I know?" I replied, trying not to give her an opening. "She must have used existing molds. I certainly didn't know anything about it."

"Try them on," Tiny suggested, "let's see if she got it right."

In fact, they fit perfectly and felt like I had slipped a glove over my feet. I said as much.

"Does Cindy ever get anything wrong?" Angella commented, seemingly upset at how well the boots fit.

"Hey, Angella," Tiny said, "Can't leave you out. Don't go any-where." He turned and left the room, heading toward the parking lot.

Angella threw me a glance, as if to say, What the hell's that about? Instead of continuing on the theme of McNaughton, she kissed me on the cheek and said, "Help me with my sister. She's got it on for Tiny. That's a major formula for disaster."

His or hers? I thought, but withheld comment. "He's mar-ried," I replied, stalling for time. "And not her type."

"Tried that. She says at this point she doesn't care what the hell type he is and that storm flags are flying. This port is as good as the next."

"Her sayings are mixed up."

"That's not the point. The point is, she's about to make a fool of herself."

"She's old enough———"

"What are you two love-birds huddling about?" Jayme said, holding a Bud in one hand and a birthday cookie in the other. "This is your party, Sis, have fun. You're way too serious. Here, take the beer. I'll fetch a fresh one. You look like you need it."

Jayme was holding the bottle at an alarming angle and when I reached out to straighten it, she pulled the bottle back. "Hey, the offer is for Ange. Get your own, big guy."

"Thanks, Sis, but I've had about as much as I'm going to."

"If you insist," Jayme said, tipping her head back and empty-ing the contents down her throat. Swallowing hard, she said, "What'd you do with Tiny?" She nodded in the direction of the door. "He's fun. Ange, you took the wrong one." Jayme looked at me, her eyes refusing to focus. "With all due respect, Mr. Texas Ranger. Don't take that the wrong way."

"Jayme, he's...not for you. He's———"

"Married. You've told me several times, Sis. Hell, all the good ones are married. You married, Jimmy?"

"Of course he's not——"

"Let the man answer for himself! I want to see how he handles it. I'll judge for myself."

"Jayme!" Angella snapped, "That's un——"

"I'm long divorced," I replied. "Been so for years. It's a matter of public record, if you care to follow up."

Jayme studied me for several seconds and then pronounced, "I really like Tiny. He's fun. But I think he's hiding something. Everyone down here is hiding something. The SEALs didn't give me drugs. Some guy you call Snow did. The SEALs weren't training either, if you want my opinion. They came to your house to save you——not me."

"That's enough Jayme," Angella snapped, her eyes narrowing as they did when she was angry. You've had more to drink than——"

"Maybe so, Sis. But I know enough to call bullshit on your cover story. You and the Ranger are up to…up to…something. I just haven't figured it all out yet. A few more beers and I'll have it worked out."

"A few more beers and you'll be laid out," Angella said, glancing around, obviously looking to see who she could trust to cut her sister off for the night.

"Drum roll, everybody!" Tiny called from the doorway. When he had everyone's attention, he announced, "Got a gift here for the belle of the ball. Birthday gift to Angella Martinez from a secret admirer."

"Secret admirer," Jayme repeated, "sounds delicious. Jimmy, you should be so jealous."

Angella looked at me and I shrugged. One thing was certain; the gift was not from me.

Tiny brought a large gift-wrapped package out from behind his massive back and said, "Here, Angella, for you." He handed the package to Angella.

Indeed, the tag said, "Happy birthday, Angella. From your Secret Admirer."

"Are you going to tell us who this secret admirer is?" I asked, "Or do we just guess?"

"That's up to the admirer, I suppose," Angella responded, her neck turning red all the way to her ears.

"Do I have something to worry about?" I asked, getting into the fun. "Are you holding back on me?"

"Not to worry, Ranger Redstone," Jayme called, "I'm available."

The look Angella shot her sister was at least R-rated. I suspected there was a history here I was not yet privy to. Perhaps, I never would be. The truth is I was better off not knowing.

Angella focused her attention on the packaging and gently ripped the tape away, trying to preserve the gorgeous paper. Removing the gift-wrapping exposed a second layer of brown paper that Angella tore into. A moment later she held up a box.

Jayme yelled, "Shake it."

I wasn't sure if she meant the box or Angella's well-proportioned body. This was not the time or place to find out. But I did note that Jayme's moveable parts were indeed moving in a manner that I suppose she believed was seductive.

Playing along, Angella dutifully shook the box. Hearing nothing unusual, she opened it, revealing paper wound tightly around something having the form of a boot.

"Ah," Angella exclaimed, "this appears to be boot night."

She quickly unwound the paper, revealing that the form was indeed a pair of boots apparently made from the same crocodile skin as mine. Angella's boots did not have inlaid initials, but instead there was a design of South Padre Island magnificently hand-carved on the boot sides.

"Oh, my God!" Angella said, "I can't believe this! Thank you to my Secret Admirer——or whomever!"

"Put them on," I encouraged. "Mine feel sensational."

"But why did she——"

"You're assuming it was McNaughton," I said. "They could be from Tiny."

"I wouldn't be happy if you spent this much on me——and you know it. So it wasn't you. And frankly, who the hell else could afford something like this?"

"Lots of folks," I chided, "but unfortunately we don't know many of them."

Angella sat and allowed me to pull the boots on for her. Her reaction was the same as mine had been. "These fit...like...like they were poured onto my feet! Thank you Secret Admirer, whoever you are."

"I'll drink to that," Jayme called out. "Hear, hear! My bottle is empty. Tiny, my dear, would you——"

"Another Bud?" Tiny asked.

"Switch her to club soda," Angella replied. "Or water."

"You're not my keeper, baby sister. "Never mind. I'll get my own." She marched toward the corner where the private bar had been set up.

Tiny, observing the tension, said, "I'll take it from here. No worries, Ange. She'll get home safely, I promise."

"It's not the alcohol I'm worried about, Tiny. That's the least of it. Alcohol she can handle."

"What then?"

"You, big guy. You. Kapish?"

"We're on the same side, remember. I'll tuck her in safe-n-sound."

"That's exactly what——"

"Then I'm coming over to your condo. We've things to discuss," Tiny interrupted.

"Tonight? This is my birthday celebra——"

"See you in an hour. Business. Brew a pot of coffee. Kapish?"

THREE

"What the hell's so important it couldn't wait 'till morning?" I called to Tiny, who was walking slowly back to the den from the kitchen, trying diligently not to dribble coffee on the floor. He had filled his mug to the brim and was now paying the price. "Midnight on Angella's birthday party night hardly seems appropriate. You could have briefed us earlier instead of spending your time hitting on Jayme."

"What ever happened to southern hospitality? The lady was enjoying herself and why not? All business and no fun...you know how it is."

"You're a married man, for goodness sake," Angella again reminded him. "The last thing in the world Jayme needs is to get mixed up with you——or with whatever brought you down here."

"You know, Ange,"Tiny said, his eyes turning cold for a brief instant, "if I didn't know better, I'd say you didn't trust me." He paused, the sparkle returning to his face. "It's a bit late now for distrust, I would think. But if you have something to get on the table, now would be the time."

"It's just that…that Jayme's vulnerable, and you're———" Angella glanced at me, and receiving no help, said, "you're…let's just say, glib with the language."

"In my line of work———and in yours as well, I might add———glib keeps you alive. The truth serves no one well. All you need to know———and know deep in your soul———is that I have your back. And not only when it's convenient. I have your back all the time."

"I don't doubt———"

Tiny cut Angella off with a wave of the hand. "Of course you have doubts. But you are alive———both of you. You may choose to believe you've managed alone, but the truth is otherwise. Your lives depend upon me being there for you and I haven't, and I won't, let you down. And I won't compromise your sister. It's part of the…shall we say…act. You can't imagine how many eyes are watching. Some friendly, most are not. It's the world we now live in. For better or worse, the three of us are joined." His face set hard, this time all trace of levity gone. "You want me reassigned just say the word and I'll be gone from your lives. But I assure you, I'm the best the country has to offer you." Tiny may be lots of things, but we've never known him to be a braggart.

"No," Angella said, "I'm———"

"Be certain. You two are about to become engaged in a highly dangerous and critical mission. Perhaps the most dangerous of your lives. Super sensitive, high profile to both sides. You want another handler, you got it."

This time Angella said nothing, but again looked toward me.

Tiny, following her lead, said, "Jimmy, you also. What's your take? Say the word and I'll disappear."

In our last mission, when it looked bleak for Angella, Tiny was there for us every step of the way. He had been rock solid. "I do share Angella's concern. You never give us all the facts and what facts you do give us …shall we say…are heavily filtered."

"For your benefit. Understand something. Even if I wanted to, it would be impossible to feed you everything the government knows. There is just too much pouring in by the minute. It's a wonder we ever get it sorted properly. And, frankly, I can't always vouch for us getting it right. In fact, I know damn well we screw up all too often. But, and this is critical for you to know, I do my level best to give you what you need, when you need it. Overload is a distinct possibility."

This is a debate Angella and I would love to have with Tiny, but my suspicion is that he is right. So it was senseless to continue. "Just be sure we're not given false information. Can we ask that much of you?"

"The only promise I can and will make is to protect your back. Beyond that, I can't promise a thing."

"Well, thanks at least for being honest."

"You want me or someone else? We don't have time to change before the briefing. But tomorrow we can bring in someone new if you prefer. You need to be comfortable. Both of you."

I glanced at Angella who seemed to be nodding. "I'm okay if Angella's okay," I said, unintentionally throwing her under the bus.

"Let's move on," Angella said. "I thought we were on a short fuse here."

"I take it that means you trust me," Tiny said.

"That means let's move on," Angella snapped back. "I don't see what good it does to debate something we have no real control

over. Time will work this out. Give me five minutes to get comfortable and we can get started."

In fact, Angella was back in less than three minutes, having
changed into jeans and an old brown SPI Police work shirt, a rem-
nant from her brief stint on the local police force. She had put
her boots back on and to say they were stunning is an understate-
ment.

"So, Tiny," I said, turning to the big guy who had settled into
my lounge chair, "are you going to brief us, or is this just a way to
interrupt our personal time?"

"I come bearing presents, like a springtime Santa, and this is
the welcome I receive."

"They weren't your gifts, I might add. Or perhaps they were.
Get on with it."

"Santa's just the messenger as well. But everyone loves the
old gent."

"I hate to break it to you big guy, but you're no Santa."

"Whatever. The important thing is you're now on assignment."

"I figured as much when you flew down," Angella commented, letting him know we hadn't been fooled by his coming
all this way for a birthday party. "The boots were a peace-offering.
I get that. Now get on with it."

Tiny took a long swallow of coffee before saying, "As you both
know full well, your pal Snow received safe-passage in exchange
for letting you live. The idea was to follow him and see who all
he worked with. Round them all up together type of operation."

"So," I said, "tell us something we don't know."

"So, he never contacted any of the usual suspects. Kept his
nose clean. Didn't go to Mexico, nothing we expected him to do."

"Sounds like good news to me," I said, when Tiny settled back to work some more on his coffee. "Obviously I'm missing something."

"Last month he landed a job. A real job with a real company. The company's called, PanAm Pharma. Goes by PAP. Stock exchange listed. Sales in the billions. He's head of logistics."

Angella leaned forward. "That's what he did for the Mexican drug lord Santiago. Only then he transported illegal drugs north. He's moving up——or possibly down——the food chain. That's the American way. But getting a job with a criminal record makes——"

"Record was wiped clean when we allowed him to run free," Tiny added.

"Who's this PAP company? What do they do?" I asked.

"PAP's a prescription drug manufacturer of high end, exotic medications. Like for chemotherapy. They also manufacture leading-edge antibiotics for rare disease control."

"This couldn't wait until morning?" Angella said. "Sometimes I wonder about you Tiny."

"Hear me out. The returns on investment are huge. A hundred thousand invested in the heroin trade returns twenty-thousand a day. That's good money and you know how much of that goes on. Figure this. That same amount, a hundred thousand, invested in counterfeit pharmaceuticals returns four-hundred-fifty thousand a day. We're talking real money now."

"You think this PAP company is into counterfeit drugs?"

"Not for me to think. I'm the messenger. I'm just providing information. I ask you, though, what the hell qualifications does Snow have to be in charge of logistics for PAP? His resume can't very well say he expedited drugs for a Mexican drug lord.

He was hired for something and I doubt if that something can be found in a printed job description at company headquarters."

"The punch line?" I said, tired of chasing the bait.

"Snow escaped from surveillance two days ago."

"So how's that our problem?"Angella asked, again leaning forward, this time tension forming across her forehead. "Last I was told Jimmy and I work for Homeland Security. This sounds like FBI. Or possibly ATF. Maybe even the U. S. Marshall Service."

"Assume for a moment that a terrorist infected the population with a virus. I'm thinking a smallpox virus. We would need to inoculate folks with a vaccine. Lots of folks. What if the vaccine were counterfeit and ineffective? That could wipe a country out before we realized what was going on."

"Smallpox is essentially non-existent," I said, recalling a documentary I had watched a year or so back. "That means there's only a small amount of vaccine being stockpiled. Every few years someone puts out a movie about mutant drugs running wild. I don't like those movies and I certainly don't like where this is going any better."

"I was posing a hypothetical situation with the smallpox,"Tiny replied. "But what if a counterfeit antibiotic were to allow some bacterial infection to take hold? Maybe even enhance the bacteria, then what would happen? Again, by the time we realized the situation, a lot of people would have died."

"Are you telling us a terrorist operation is under way?"

"I'm telling you Interpol is very much concerned. Snow being hired——and then disappearing from our radar——has everyone on the edge of their seats. Got our respective bosses worried."

"So why us?" Angella asked. "And why in the middle of the night?"

"You worked out the satellite frequency stuff. D.C. is impressed. Apparently some of these drugs are tracked using radio frequency identification. The word frequency in that sentence triggered your name. Also, understand there is some connection between PAP and some company you investigated a few years ago, Jimmy. Couple that with your knowledge of Snow, and you two drew the short straw."

"Why tonight?" I pressed. "What's the bloom'n hurry?"

"You're scheduled to talk with Interpol at eight GMT."

"That's seven hours from now," Angella said, standing as if she planned to head down the hall to the bedroom. "You could have woken us at six."

"Interpol agents are in London. Call's an hour from now."

"They couldn't have waited a few hours?"

"Travel plans don't allow it, I'm afraid," Tiny said, refusing to elaborate.

"Are we taking the call here?" I asked. "Nothing's secure."

"The military is working on it as we speak. We'll use my cell for a camera and your TV as we've done in the past. That works for our purposes."

"Now I'll take that coffee," I said. "Angella, you want me to pour for you?"

"No thanks. Tiny got my attention. I'm wide awake."

FOUR

A t exactly two in the morning, with the help of the coffee, I managed to sit up straight in my chair. Angella now wore a blue blazer over a white blouse, more appropriate for a mid-day meeting in an office than for a late night video-conference from our condo. At Angella's insistence, I reluctantly substituted a blue shirt for the multi-color, flower-splashed, island shirt I had worn to the party.

"Lights, camera, action!" Tiny exclaimed, just before he touched a strange-looking icon on his cell phone. Tiny then positioned himself behind the lens as he always did on video calls.

To my surprise, the first image to appear on the screen was that of FBI Deputy Director Chris Kagan. There was no love lost between us. Our previous encounters have been rocky at best. Kagan is the ultimate consensus guy. Nothing moves forward until the group is in agreement. I'm a staunch defender of one riot-one Ranger. Committees make me nuts.

"Good morning Agents Redstone and Martinez. Agent Martinez, it is especially good to see you looking well after your... shall we say...ordeal with Snow. I trust you have fully recovered from your...surgery."

Angella smiled what I have come to learn is her forced-pleasant smile. The one she reserves for bosses————and bores. "I have. Thank you for asking." Pausing a beat she added, "And thanks for supporting my rescue." In fact, as we later learned from the post-operational debriefing, Kagan had only reluctantly gone along with allowing Snow to have his freedom. And only after McNaughton had used her influence with the President.

"Don't mention it," he replied, his expression of what passed for friendship not changing. "You two did a rather good job in a particularly messy situation. The war games became a tad disrupted, but nothing we couldn't patch up. Military got some egg on its face. Goes with the bloody territory. Hey, great boots."

"Thanks," Angella said. "Birthday present."

"From Redstone?"

"From a secret admirer. That's all I can tell you."

Kagan didn't immediately respond.

I was remaining out of this. Anything I said was certain to cause more friction between Kagan and myself.

"As you by now know," Kagan began when no one spoke, "Snow has disappeared from our surveillance. The short story is we have reason to believe he's involved with a company called PanAm Pharma. I believe you've been briefed."

"We have," Angella replied.

"Counterfeit medications are a serious problem. Evidence suggests counterfeit medications are being coordinated to effect mass deaths. We don't yet know if the medications themselves will be used to spark an epidemic of some sort————or if some other mechanism will be used to trigger an outbreak and the altered medications used to fuel mass deaths."

"Excuse me," I said, "but you're Deputy Director of the FBI. Why are you———"

"I happen to also serve as Director of the USNCB."

I glanced at Angella. Her eyebrows bounced, indicating she also didn't know what he was talking about.

Before I could ask, Kagan continued, "That's our coordinating agency charged with cooperating with Interpol. I trust you do know what Interpol is, Agent Redstone."

"I've not had the pleasure of working with them, but yes, I do know who they are and generally what they do."

"Then you understand they are mostly a coordinating agency. These days terrorist activities, by their very nature, consume most of their band-width. Because counterfeit pharmaceuticals are international in nature, Interpol has them high on its priority list. In a moment I'm going to bridge your counterparts at Interpol, Agent Lillie Holland and Agent Barrington Plevin III. Agent Plevin was formerly with Scotland Yard. I had the pleasure of serving with Agent Holland for many years at MI Nine. I'll let them outline the situation. She's the senior operator on this investigation. I'll drop off, but keep in mind your liaison is as it's been in the past, through Tiny. Any confusion on that?"

"Not from me," I said, guessing Kagan had been listening to our earlier conversation with Tiny. He was also referring to the fact that I had used retired Marine General Cindy McNaughton to get around his obstructions.

"And you, Agent Martinez? Any problems?"

"None," Angella responded, the forced pleasant smile still on her face.

"I must remind you Agent Redstone, not to turn this into a one-man operation, so to speak. This is international in nature and sensitive negotiations are on-going at this very moment. One false step and it can spell disaster. You are not to go rogue on us as is your propensity." He cleared his throat. "Am I quite clear?"

"Clear," I replied, knowing anything else I said would trigger another tirade.

"Just to elaborate," Kagan said, showing no sign of easing up, "counterfeit drug trafficking is international, with several countries blaming the other, while denying they are involved. It's a diplomatic mess. Wars have begun over far less. Let me assure you of that."

"We will do our best," I pledged.

"Well then, I'll take you at your word. Keep in mind the diplomatic sensitivities are my last words to you." Kagan, still preserving his own version of a friendly face, said, "Have a pleasant night."

The video image immediately switched from Kagan to two people who were the mirror image of Angella and me, with Lillie Holland being several years older than Plevin.

"Sorry to rouse you at this hour," Holland said, her British voice clipped and proper. "Director Kagan suggested it would not be a problem. As I'm sure he told you, I'm Lille Holland and my partner is Barrington Plevin."

"I'm Jimmy Redstone. Angella Martinez is my partner. Pleased to meet you. We've been briefed, but let's start at the beginning, if you will."

"Thank you both for being so gracious. Call me Lil if you prefer. Barrington goes by BP. Counterfeit pharma has been our concern for a while now. We have reason to believe something major is about to occur. In fact, it's more than a suspicion. We have snippets of hard facts, but nothing is at all clear. The gravitas seems to point to medications being transported——and most likely tampered with at some point. I understand a person known to you has recently been hired to facilitate their movement for PAP. A man by the name of Snow."

"We indeed know Snow," I replied. Kagan personally vouched for these folks, so it was permissible to give them information. However, my natural inclination is to impart as little as I can until I'm comfortable. And right now I'm anything but comfortable. Despite Kagan's admonition, I intend to follow my natural instincts. "Where do we fit into this?" I asked. "I've no experience with medication smuggling——or whatever is going on."

"Mr. Redstone——"

"Call me Jimmy."

"Jimmy, as you know, all we, as Interpol can do is observe—— and take notes so to speak. We have no authority to do anything other than investigate. Actual on-the-ground operations must be handled through locals."

"Angella and I are it. We're the locals. Is that what I'm hearing?"

"Please allow me to assure you of one thing. Your selection was not random."

That didn't surprise me, but just the fact that Snow disappeared and we knew Snow wasn't enough. "Can you elaborate a bit more? We'd like to know what's expected of us."

"The desire is for Interpol to Red Card this guy Snow, the one you are both familiar with. Interpol can't do so unless there is an active arrest warrant issued in the requesting country."

"Pardon me," Angella asked, "Red Tag?"

"Red Card. Wanted for arrest. Any Interpol member country is authorized to hold a person if Interpol issues a Red Card.

That's where you come in. We need you to obtain evidence of criminal activity. Once you do that, we will attend to the Red Card."

"I'm still missing something here. You're saying a warrant has not been issued, yet we are to find reason to issue a warrant." Fact is, the U. S. government already has sufficient reasons——his own confession even——that he conspired to kill several people, cops among them. Yet they want Angella and me to ignore the existing evidence and find new reasons. This made no sense.

"I think the idea is for the two of you to find something he's done and obtain the warrant," Lil said.

"That will take a while," I replied, not letting on we knew of Snow's past confession. And I certainly didn't want to communicate how foolish this all sounded. Not yet, anyhow.

Angella, not being on the same page with me, said, "If Kagan is willing to use information from our previous encounter with him then there is really nothing for us to do. After all, he killed several people."

"Obviously, they don't need us for that," I commented, trying to move Angella onto a different track. "Let's perhaps begin with what is known. Would you, Lil or BP, care to elaborate on the information you have pertaining to medicals being involved in a terrorist plot? After all, isn't that what this is really about?"

Silence for several seconds. Then Holland said, "I recognize this is a secure line, but all the same, we…we're not comfortable proceeding in this manner. Perhaps when we are together. But for now let us just say that there are reports of a build-up of counterfeit medicals, let's call them CMs, in the field of Macrolides. One example is Erythromycin which is a medication used for respiratory tract infections. It's one of the drugs that can penetrate human cells. Around the world the drug is becoming less effective. Some of this is because the microbes are becoming immune to the medication. However, and let me caution you, this is mostly speculation, if the drug is being altered, then that could account for the reduced effectiveness. We just don't know."

"Can't the drugs be tested? Inspected?" Angella asked.

"Easy to say. Hard to do. Standard protocol calls for the medicine to be controlled at its production site. Once it leaves there, it is under tight security. Electronic tracking devices, the works."

"So what's the problem? Everything seems to be under control if you are monitoring the operations."

"That's just it. All highly circumstantial. For example, the employment of a known drug smuggler by a reputable pharmaceutical manufacturer is one fact that makes no legitimate sense. But, and I stress this, there is nothing wrong with hiring Snow, other than the optics are wrong."

"Why Mac...macro...what was that medication you spoke about?" I asked, trying to focus the discussion on tangible facts.

"Macrolides," BP said, speaking for the first time. "If a modified version is in circulation, and if it proliferates, we would be in serious trouble. Couple that with terrorists spreading microbes that attack breathing, such as S.pneumoniae, and large numbers of people, perhaps into the millions, perhaps higher, will die."

I remained confused. "Snow is working for PAP, a reputable pharma company. You think they are involved in CMs of this nature? Is there any evidence that PAP is doing anything improper?"

Holland responded, "PAP is not, to our knowledge involved in the mutant form of the CMs. Those are the ones that increase the problems. If PAP were to modify the drug in any way, we believe they would do so simply to distribute a cheaper form of

Erythromycin, perhaps with some impurities, perhaps with fewer efficacies, to low cost payers, such as your Medicare patients. We don't believe, not yet anyway, that PAP is involved with terrorist activities."

"Then, are you suggesting that Snow was hired to smuggle the degraded drugs into the country?"

"That we don't know. But he was hired for something, shall we say…off center. As you are aware, he has long-standing ties to criminal elements, some of which have been approached by known terrorist groups to help distribute the tainted medication." Holland paused, then added, her tone softer, "Look, Snow is just not the type of person a reputable company hires. Either PAP is running a scam, or…or…someone in a position of influence within PAP arranged to have Snow hired. In any event, a known drug runner in charge of transporting medications set the bells off in investigative circles in many countries."

We were going in circles. "Sounds as though we'll be working this together for a while. So what do you suggest as first steps?" I was not yet certain of where this was going. But I did know we had not yet been told the full truth as to why we had been selected for this assignment.

"We suggest you pick up Snow's trail. Retrace his movements. Interview PAP. We understand you had some previous involvement with a company that is linked to PAP. Build the investigation from the bottom up in traditional fashion. We will continue our work from this end on CM manufacturing. We'll be using this same hookup, say every other day."

"Works for us. Except, let's make it after lunch on your end," I suggested. "That makes it, what, eight in the morning here."

"Let's say two GMT. Nine in Texas, eight on the east coast."

"Works here," I said. Putting my nice guy smile on my face, I said, "Looking forward to working with you." I don't believe for a minute I fooled either of them. From the quick glance Angella flashed me, I certainly hadn't fooled her.

"Good night mates and sorry about the inconvenient time," Holland apologized again.

"Not as sorry as we are," I thought, as the video faded.

FIVE

"So when do we get the file on Snow?" I asked Tiny. "And where the hell is PAP's headquarters anyway?"

"Jimmy, let's pick this up in the morning," Angella said. "I'm beyond exhausted. Tiny, are you staying the night with us, or do you have your own place?" Angella started down the hall and then suddenly spun around. "And don't you dare say you're bunking with my sister!"

"It's really not your business, but if you must know, I'm over at Clayton's——alone." To ease the sudden tension, Tiny added, "Let's regroup at Ted's for breakfast. I didn't come all this way to miss out on the pecan pancakes. Ten work for you?"

"It's three-fifteen now. Make it eleven," I answered, hoping Angella would let her beef with Tiny lie.

"Eleven it is," Tiny replied, his infectious smile back where it belonged.

"I'm wired from the caffeine," I said. "You have the file? I need something to read while I come down."

"Just so happens, I e-mailed what I have for you a few hours ago. Decrypt with the key SNOW. Happy reading."

Angella rolled her eyes and headed for the bedroom. Before the door closed, she called to Tiny, "I trust you'll stay away from Jayme."

I locked up behind Tiny, changed into sweats, and fired up my laptop. There wasn't much on Snow that I already didn't know. FBI agent Fred Dickerson had been assigned to meet Snow's SWA flight when it landed at Houston's Hobby Airport from Dallas. Snow caught a cab and Dickerson, using his own car, followed them toward downtown. The cab drove directly to MD Anderson Hospital and parked at the back of the cab line. Dickerson approached the driver and found no passenger. Interrogation revealed that the passenger had slipped out just after they had turned a corner several blocks from the hospital. The driver had been given a hundred dollar bill and told to go to Anderson.

Snow was gone.

I didn't have to concern myself with issuing instructions for Snow's apprehension. The FBI had already done so, but not surprisingly, nothing had turned up. From Snow's history he could just as easily be in Mexico as he could in the United States. In fact, for him, crossing the border was probably easier than moving around the country. Hence the request to Interpol to Red Card him.

Next was PAP. I was surprised to find their headquarters in Dallas. The company recently had been taken private by an investment team led by someone named L. Wolfson. Revenue was a little over six billion, income 1.2 billion. Just as Interpol agent Lillie Holland had said, their specialty was orphan drugs, antibiotics in the Macrolides family. In fact, there was nothing in either of the files that added anything of value from what we had learned from the briefing.

- - - - -

The laptop crashing to the floor woke me. The time was six-fifteen. I stumbled into the guest room and fell onto the bed.

A moment later, or so it seemed, Angella stood over me holding two mugs. There was no mistaking the smell of freshly-brewed coffee.

"I won't even ask how late you stayed up. But if you're planning on showering——and I suggest you do——you better get after it. We need to walk out of here in fifteen minutes."

"Tiny can cool his jets. He can entertain himself with an extra four or five pecan pancakes while he's waiting." I reached for the offered mug. "Smells good. Thanks. You take good care of me."

"I try, but don't always succeed." She bent and kissed my forehead. "I looked over the files and there's not much there. Jimmy, do you know who L. Wolfson is? I didn't have time to Google him——or her."

"She's known in the business world as the Wolf. A few years back I investigated a company she had invested in. That's what Lil meant by *my prior involvement*. Not a pretty picture. Went bankrupt. Money disappeared into thin air. People lost their pensions. Enron sort of thing. In the end, the trail was cold. The Wolf made a ton of money. All legal from what I remember of the investigation."

"I take it you were not pleased with the outcome. And now Wolfson's involved with PAP. Coincidence?"

"Investigators shouldn't have opinions——or biases," I said. "We should allow the facts to take us where they will. Or so says the teaching manual. But after witnessing the suffering she and her company caused people, it's tough not to...to unload on someone. Folks covered their tracks well. FBI chased accounts all around the world. Lots of smoke. No real proof. And so far no money!"

"Suppose Kagan, or whoever put us onto this, knew of your past involvement with Wolfson?"

"Had to. It's no coincidence that the Wolf is CEO of PAP and I've been tagged for this assignment. I think that reason is stronger than the fact we know Snow. Lots of people know Snow."

- - - - -

We walked into *Ted's* only fifteen minutes late. True to form, Tiny had in front of him a half-eaten giant stack of pecan pancakes. A plate of bacon sat off to the side, and if I wasn't mistaken, he'd already consumed a helping of sausage. At nearly seven feet, he stood almost a foot taller than I and carried perhaps another hundred pounds. But for a big man, he was actually pretty light on his feet. Despite everything, I was not unhappy he was our liaison. That is, so long as I remembered he worked for the CIA and that our interests were not always aligned. Angella does not feel the same about him as I do, believing he has put his responsibilities to the CIA above his duties to us.

"Have a tough night?" I said to the big guy when we sat down across from him. "Worked up an appetite, I see."

Tiny drained his coffee and dabbed at his lips with his napkin. "Matter of fact, I did. Order and I'll tell you about it."

Karen, the owner, refilled Tiny's cup and, looking in my direction, asked, "You need more time?"

"Nothing to think about," I replied. "Three with pecans and coffee.

"I'll take one, also with pecans," Angella said. "But add a side of bacon."

Karen nodded and continued her rounds with the coffee pot.

"So," Angella said, her jaw set tight, "tell us about your night."

Several bites later, Tiny said, "Yesterday, wasn't a good day on the island. You, of course, know about the dead guy on the beach."

"Came down with a parachute," I said. "The instructor disappeared. Angella tried to resuscitate him." The CIA doesn't usually get involved in local mishaps, so my antennae went up.

"Kagan doesn't believe it was a coincidence you two were there?"

"We were out walking on the beach like we do most mornings. Is Kagan thinking the dead guy is linked to us?"

"Maybe his death was timed to get you involved."

"Maybe it just happened at that time."

"Aren't you the guy who preaches that coincidences are rare?"

Tiny was trying to tell us something. It was time to stop yapping and listen. "So, get on with it."

"The deceased's prints set off major alarm bells. FBI, Interpol, the works. His name's Larson Pettit. Seems he's been known to expedite people——read my lips, terrorists——into and out of the country. Been Red Carded by Interpol. The rascal's wanted for murder in South America, among other places."

"Why'd the bells go off?"

"Circumstantial——at this point. But Mr. Pettit's last known job was as a deck hand on a local pilot boat. Don't ask how he was not printed, but he managed. Maybe he took the place of someone else,"Tiny shrugged. "Government can't plug all the leaks."

"Didn't know they had pilot boats down here," I said.

"A few. They're used primarily for moving the drilling platforms and freighters through the pass and up the Brownsville shipping channel."

"I know Amfels builds and repairs the platforms, but what do they do with the freighters?"

"I frankly don't know what all they do. But I do know that a yard up there dismantles and salvages large ships, including military ships."

I had noticed the huge scrap yards in that area but hadn't connected them to scrap from ships. I was tempted to ask a bunch of questions, but I've learned with Tiny it is always wise to hold comments until all the facts are on the table. Clearly, there was more to the story than we had been told. "So far, nothing rings my bells," I said. "You got more?"

"Pettit, a deck hand mind you, was asking about Macrolides. The day before he fell out of the sky he was in the Coastal Studies Lab, the one down the island a ways, asking about drugs in marine life."

"He was also, from what you said earlier, a drug runner, man of many trades."

"Most likely addicted as well,"Tiny replied just as our breakfast came. We all fell silent as we worked through the wonderful pecan pancakes. Then Angella wiped her lips, put down her coffee cup and said, "Macrolides are one of the drugs PAP manufactures. Is that what ties Pettit to Snow———and to us?"

"Still think it's a coincidence they———his killer———damned near dumped his dead body on your head?"

"Are you saying his death is related to PAP? Or to Snow?" I asked, knowing Tiny would duck the answer.

"I'm a fact gatherer," the big guy responded, "not an investigator. Separation of labor type of thing. I do what I do. You do what you do. You tell me."

"Not enough to go on," I said, stalling to think this through. "Any idea who drove the chute? Or the launch plane?"

"If you're thinking Snow was the other jumper, I doubt it. Perhaps he was flying the plane. But if so, he's not registered. But hey, when did that ever stop these guys? Kapish?"

"Do we know where they took off from?" Angella asked. "Airport? Farm?"

"The plane came down the Rio Grande River from the direction of McAllen. The Coast Guard first has it imaged a bit northwest of Brownsville on the U.S. side. After dropping the chute the plane turned west, apparently heading back up the Rio Grande. That's all we have."

"So much for deep surveillance." I added.

"It landed somewhere," Angella commented. "Planes usually do. It shouldn't be that hard to find out where."

Tiny shrugged. "Texas is big. Lots of places to put down and most of them not monitored. Small planes are always coming and going. Low level radar tracking is darn-near impossible." Tiny glanced around, lowered his voice even further and said, "I have it on good authority that a drone training session was underway and all attention was focused on monitoring them. Crop dusters had free rein."

"Any identification on the chute———or the harness? I thought all packers have markings." Angella pressed.

"Being worked on," Tiny answered, telegraphing a lack of faith that anything of value would turn up. "These folks are pros.

Could have been self-packed. Question remains, why was Pettit killed?"

"How do you know a bureaucrat?" I asked, signaling I was tired of the twenty-questions routine.

"Tired old joke," Tiny said. "Full of questions. No answers."

SIX

"First things first," I said to Angella when Tiny finally ate his fill and took his leave, ostensibly to head back to Washington. "We should call McNaughton and thank her. You cool with that?" I was referring to Angella's dislike of the woman. At first I had thought it stemmed from jealousy, but the more I'm around Angella the more I think it's two alpha females going at it. Angella hides it well, but given the right circumstances she's as tough as they come.

"You make the call, I'll tag along."

- - - - -

"Cowboy," came the over-the-top greeting. "How the hell are you?"

"Holding my own, thanks. And you?"

"As usual. How's Angella? Heard she's recovered nicely."

"She's with me now. I'll put you on speakerphone. Ask her directly."

"Angella," McNaughton said, "hear you've recovered nicely."

"I owe that to you. Thanks for setting up the hospital."

"Don't mention it. Glad you're okay."

"Are you the secret admirer?"

The directness of the question caused McNaughton to hesitate for an instant. Something I had rarely, if ever, seen. "You might say I am," she replied, not looking happy to be addressing this subject.

"In that case, thanks also for the gorgeous boots. You went to far too much trouble———and expense. But I love them."

"Thought you'd enjoy them."

"Mine fit like a glove," I said. "Thanks from me as well."

"What the hell you talking about Cowboy?"

"My boots. You didn't have to do it."

"We're not on the same page."

"They're not from you?"

"Now why in the hell would I buy you a present? Boots no less! Cowboy, your wires are crossed."

McNaughton sounded genuine, but with her it was hard to know.

"Someone's playing with me then. Tiny delivered them to me at Angella's party."

"What makes you think they're not from the big guy himself?"

"He disclaims it. Besides, they're way too expensive for him."

"Don't bet on either premise. Anyway, wear them in good health."

"Did you enjoy your time down here on the Island?" I asked, anxious to change the subject.

"Great little getaway you have going down there. Best kept secret in the country. R&R got cut short. It may have looked to you like Vlad failed because power was never really lost. But the communication snafu was enough to allow a missile through. The President was furious. And stars roll when the boss is angry. Three generals got busted. I can't comment further, but needless to say, the military is not happy."

"Does that affect you?"

"When POTUS is angry it affects everybody. I'm not on the payroll, so there's not much they can do to me. But it's best if I keep a low profile."

"You involv———"

"This is neither the time nor the place for discussion. Let's just say, I'm an interested observer." McNaughton paused for an instant and then said, "Gotta go. Keep in touch."

"What the hell was that about?" I asked Angella when the phone went dead. "Is she or isn't she running this op?"

"My money's on her. As always, these people are never straight with what they're up to."

"In all truth, I don't like the sound of this. On the surface, it seems that all we need to do is find Snow, wrap him up and drag him home. But it didn't work out so easy the last time."

"You heard. Counterfeit medication means big money," Angella said, nodding in agreement with my assessment. "Big money begets big players. Big players spawn big problems. We're at a disadvantage against a well-organized and well-equipped operation. Witness the problem Mexico is having curtailing the drug lords. You and I are unlikely to apprehend Snow if he's dug in with the big guys."

"Add to that the fact that counterfeiting medications may be illegal in this country, but who knows how other countries treat the subject. Especially, if they're skimming off the top."

"No wonder Mommy Long Legs is backing off. She'll quickly outrun her cover."

My cell rang. It was Tiny informing me he had set up a meeting with the Wolf. She was currently in New Orleans and just leaving for a reception in Dallas. According to Tiny, she consented to pick us up at Cameron County Airport and fly us up to Dallas with her. We were on our own getting back home.

I repeated the arrangements for Angella's benefit, and added, "The Wolf's plane is scheduled to land in exactly one hour and fifteen minutes."

"Any rules imposed?"

"No recordings. And anything she says is off-the-record. Background only."

"That means if she lies we can't prosecute."

"We'll have to nail her later should the need arise."

- - - - -

Cameron Country Airport is not far from South Padre Island as the pelican flies. But access is around the west end of an estuary feeding Laguna Madre and driving time from SPI approaches a half-hour. The airport services crop dusters, freight, some private planes, and the Border Patrol. The illegal alien detention center is not far away and the few roads in the vicinity sport warnings not to pick up hitch-hikers. Laguna Atascosa Wildlife Refuge is a mile away at the end of a dirt road leading away from the airport. Snow had once held Angella hostage in the Refuge.

Driving into the small airport parking lot is reminiscent of being at airports in developing countries. There are only a few hangers scattered about, two fuel storage tanks, and a large rectangular building that appears to house the terminal, but just as easily could be a warehouse or a repair facility. The tower consists of a glassed-in enclosure sitting atop the rectangular structure.

No human was visible. Perhaps there was someone in the tower, but the heavily tinted glass was impossible to see through. The Wolf wasn't due to land for another fifteen minutes, so we remained in the car.

Nothing came or went while we waited. Not a plane. Not a car. Not even a jackrabbit.

Angella nudged my arm and pointed through the fence toward the western sky. At first I saw nothing. But then a speck appeared, visible only because of sun reflection. The speck grew wings and those wings lined up perfectly with the surprisingly long runway. Instead of landing, the jet screamed overhead, made a wide lazy circle and gently lowered onto the runway. A moment later the plane rolled to a smooth stop directly in front of the rectangular building.

Angella and I trotted toward the front of the building, found the front door, continued across the sparse interior, and came out through a door to the tarmac. We arrived at the plane just as the folding steps of the magnificent *Gulfstream* G450 touched the ground. Protocol demanded that we wait at the base of the stairs for an invitation to board.

A man in the uniform of the TSA came up behind us and said, "You two, come with me. I need to run you through the scanner before I can allow you out here."

I hadn't seen a scanner————or any type of inspection equipment————in the terminal. I reached for my TSA credentials, as did Angella. Thinking we were going for weapons caused him to recoil and reach for his radio.

"Homeland Security," I said. "We're here on business."

That made him relax enough to read our shields. Then he said, "This makes it easier, but we still must pat you down. You carrying?"

"We are."

"Let me see your creds again."

He studied both IDs for a long moment, as if something would instruct him as to what to do. He then snapped pictures of us as well as the IDs and said, "I'll just forward these on to headquarters. You might want to come inside, this usually takes a while."

Before he could step back, his cell sounded. He listened in silence for a long moment before responding with several, "Yes sirs!" The cell snapped closed. "I don't know who the hell you two are, but you've been cleared. Never seen it done this fast."

We were halfway up the stairs before he could finish his thought.

Angella stopped just short of the cabin door and turned back to me. "This reminds me of———"

"How we ended up in the Mexican jungle." I had been thinking the same thing. "But this time," I said, "we heard it directly from Tiny. Last time it was by text."

"So he———they———fixed up their act. Fooled me once..." Angella turned and started back down the steps. "No need to push forward, Jimmy. We can sort this out in the terminal."

Angella had a point. The last time we boarded a plane without knowing who was on it nearly cost us our lives. I turned and followed her down the ladder.

SEVEN

My feet hit the tarmac just as a husky female voice called down to us from above. "I have a schedule to maintain! Get on up here and get yourselves aboard." The voice belonged to a slightly over-weight woman wearing khaki slacks with a white uniform shirt sporting four gold bars on each shoulder. Her eyes were concealed behind wrap-around silvered sunglasses.

"And who might you be?" I called up to her.

"I'm the captain. I assume you are Redstone and Martinez. We were diverted down here to fetch you. Not my idea of running things. But here we are. If you want to come aboard then make it snappy. If you don't, then don't."

"Who else is aboard?" I asked, stalling.

"Chairman Wolfson is flying alone. Time is precious. Are you joining us or not? I frankly don't care either way."

I nodded toward Angella and reluctantly she turned back to the plane.

The captain, a woman I put to be in her late fifties, examined our official IDs before allowing either of us to pass.

I took that as a positive sign.

Satisfied, she said, "Sit over there. Chairman Wolfson will join you in a moment. We're slotted to land in Dallas at four-twenty. I intend to keep that slot."

I checked my watch. It was two-fifty. This puppy could move, having a cruising speed in the range of point eight mach, nearly six-hundred miles per hour. Road distance to Dallas, five hundred fifty miles.

The interior of the plane was tastefully decorated in shades of tan and brown, with soft leather seats screaming elegance. There was a group of four seats, two facing forward and two facing rear-ward. A desk separated the quad from another row having two seats that looked as if they could be reclined into beds. Two indi-vidual seats rounded out the cabin. I didn't see a bar or a serving area, but assumed they were cleverly hidden from sight.

A pudgy woman emerged from a small door near the rear of the cabin. She wore baggy gray sweats and a Dallas Mavericks sweatshirt with the number 41 across the back. Heavy-framed glasses masked her dark brown, almost black eyes. Her hair was cut tight and hugged her round face. She reminded me of the center from my high school football team. Short, compact and all business.

"I suppose I must welcome you aboard," she said without a trace of a smile. "My attorney tells me to cooperate with the government, so I cooperate. If it was my way, I'd tell you to...to go pound sand. I'm Lotte Wolfson. Call me Wolf."

"I'm Jimmy Redstone," I said, extending my hand in greeting. "Call me Jimmy. And this is my partner, Angella Martinez. We do appreciate you taking the time to talk with us."

She shook my hand and her iron grasp sent pain up my right arm. She then took Angella's hand, but did not grasp it so hard. "Meter's running, fire away," she said sitting in a rear facing seat and motioning for us to sit opposite her. "What am I being investigated for this time?"

Deciding to jump right in, I said, "An employee of PAP disappeared yesterday. We're just———"

"Why the hell are you asking me about a PAP employee? I'm the Chairman of the Board. I don't deal in personnel matters. Call Human Resources! Or better yet, call the head of Security. You're wasting my time, the both of you. I'd throw you the hell off the plane, but that would mess up the Captain's schedule. Lord knows, that won't play well."

The plane began moving, and Angella and I quickly fastened our seat belts. We taxied to the far end of the field, turned and immediately began racing down the runway. A moment later land fell away. We were airborne and a captive of the Wolf.

I decided to back up and to restart at the beginning. "How long have you...I mean your company...owned a portion of PAP?"

"A bit over six months. Six months and ten days to be exact."

"How large of an investment did you make?"

"By that I assume you mean Wolfson Investments?"

"Whoever owns the shares, yes."

"I assume you are familiar with federal regulations. All this is public record. Why are you wasting my time and yours on what you can find on-line?"

"Background."

"I call bullshit! Get on with why you two are sitting on my private plane. We didn't divert to lower God's country to answer stupid questions!"

"As a matter of curiosity, where did you just come from?" I didn't like the sound of my own question, so I rephrased it. "What city were you just in?"

"What the hell difference does that make?" she barked. Then, without waiting for an answer, she added, "If you must know, we came out of Biloxi, visiting a PAP facility. Actually, I holed up there for a few days. I had a bad stomach virus to be perfectly honest. I spent two nights in the hospital. They released me this morning."

"I take it from your earlier answer you have no knowledge of employees of PAP. Where they work, what they do? Would you say that's an accurate statement?"

"I told you. I don't manage day to day. I do know many of the employees. But I don't hire or fire them."

"Were you just visiting a PAP facility?"

"It's part of my duties as Chairman and part time CEO. I make certain things are what they are supposed to be. Too many stories abound of empty warehouses, barren manufacturing facilities, money disappearing into someone's pockets. That won't happen on my watch. I can assure you of that."

"Was everything okay at the facility?"

"That's none of your F'n business!"

"Whatever happened to cooperating?" I replied, refusing to be bullied by Wolfson.

"There are limits. Get on with it."

"What drugs does PAP manufacture?"

"Check the bloody records! Regulations up the wazoo! Can't do shit without you folks making the company fill out forms, get permissions, run tests. Drives the costs out of sight! Then you turn around and say our prices are too high. We can't breathe without someone logging something into a database."

I was trying to figure out if she was always this way, or whether something I did or said set her off. The possibility also existed that this was all an act to keep us away from the real questions.

"Are you invested in any other pharmaceutical companies?" I asked, keeping my voice calm, determined not to take the bait.

"Are you asking about PAP, or Wolfson Investments?"

"For starters, PAP."

"If it's not in the database then PAP's investments are none of your business. As for Wolfson Investments, that's beyond the scope of our discussions."

"Do I assume by your answer your cooperation has ended?"

"You may assume anything you like. You ask, I answer."

"Why did you select PAP? I mean for an investment."

Without hesitation, Wolfson replied, "Good return potential. That's why we make all our investments."

"What was the size of the investment?"

"Public record. Look it up. Why do you care?"

This lady could run for Congress. Never answer anything, or if you do, answer it with a question. "If it's all public record, why not just tell us?"

"Do your homework next time! You're wasting my time, Redstone. Time is money. Maybe not for the Feds, but it most certainly is for us working stiffs."

I had enough. I leaned as close to her as I could and lowered my voice. "The next time we talk Ms. Wolfson it will be in a federal building under subpoena. And I promise you when that happens you'll wish you had cooperated with us today."

"Don't threaten me, Redstone! I've been threatened by tougher people than you."

"Wanna bet?" I replied, instantly regretting my outburst. She had won this round.

Angella leaned forward in her seat. "It's obvious you two aren't ever going to be best friends. You're right, Ms. Wolfson, we should have studied your investments before we got on board. But, truth is, time didn't allow for it. Please help us out here. A person of great interest to us——and to me personally——disappeared. A guy by the name of Snow. He was recently hired by PAP to do logistics. Director of Logistics, to be exact. From my understanding, logistics is the movement of material from one place to another. PAP deals in prescription medications moving from place to place. Snow's only qualification, as far as we can determine, is moving illegal street drugs from Mexico to the states."

Wolfson's eyes narrowed. "Are you telling me we hired a criminal?"

"We are."

The Wolf closed her eyes. Lines formed across her forehead where her skin bunched up. A moment went by in this manner. Then she focused on Angella. "We vet everyone we hire at that level. It's not possible. That job is entirely too sensitive, and… and…critical to our future, to put a known criminal in command."

"Would you care to elaborate on that statement?" Angella asked.

"Which part? The vetting or the critical nature of the assignment?"

"Both, if you would."

"The vetting is handled by our security folks. I will follow up and get you the information. But for international work, we are pretty careful. Something went wrong, terribly wrong."

I could see her making a mental note to follow up, and trusted that she would.

"The sensitivity is clear. We manufacture pharmaceuticals in several countries and each off-shore site is carefully monitored to be certain the manufacturing process remains pure and that all finished product is accounted for."

"What does logistics have to do with the process?" Angella pressed, still keeping her voice low and non-judgmental. Like good friends talking.

"Critical. We need to move the finished product from the manufacturing site to the U. S. in secure ships. And we must do it to a really tight time schedule. Seems easy, but there are no FedExs or UPSs at sea. Without strict control, stuff gets lost. That's just the nature of the beast. We can't afford to have drugs lost———or tampered with."

"Mind talking about your investment in PAP? How it came about?" I asked, hoping to play off the relationship Angella had built.

Wolfson fell quiet. I couldn't determine if she was stonewalling———or thinking through the implications. Her face gave away nothing.

Angella wisely remained silent, waiting for the Wolf to speak.

Hard lines formed around Wolfson's thin lips. Then the lines softened perceptively. "The investment," she began, her tone less strident, "in PAP was, I admit, somewhat unusual for us. Our base expertise is shopping centers, strip malls, that type of thing. Over the years we've expanded, out of necessity, to retail. It began almost by accident when we invested in a department store, an anchor tenant, to keep them from going bust and taking the whole mall down. We really did it to protect our basic investment and ended up making a nice return when Walmart bought out our interest. That experience gave us some comfort in the retail space. Out of self-preservation we did that several more times. One of our investments was a regional pharmacy chain. Perhaps you recall the SOS pharmacies up in the Panhandle?"

"Embezzlement. Officer fraud," I answered. SOS was the company I had been assigned to investigate. Employees lost their jobs and some folks lost their pensions. The former president of SOS is now a longtime resident of Dalhart Prison. On suicide watch the last I heard. That case was a difficult one with money moving from account to account around the world. There was smoke around the CFO, but in the end, nothing stuck. That was all before the Wolf came on the scene.

"Bought it cheap. Turned it around. We did rather well. That got us interested in pharma."

"Was PAP in financial trouble when you invested?" Angella asked.

"What makes you ask such a question?" Wolfson snapped her head in Angella's direction, as if to bat the question away.

"The other investments you commented on were under financial stress," Angella replied. "It's only logical———"

"I see where you're coming from, Ms. Martinez. No. PAP is, and was, doing well."

"So why the investment?"

Again Wolfson fell silent. But this time it was clear she was working out the right answer. "Opportunistic is all I can say."

"Not sure I know———" The Wolf cut me off.

"Redstone, I'm not going to share our investment strategy with you. But let me say this. It wasn't my idea. The opportunity was presented to us by a business advisor. It made sense when we ran the numbers. Management was solid. Product line was expanding. PAP has a good business plan and good leadership." We expect to run a nice profit on it."

"The advisor's name?"

"GP Manhyme. He goes by GP."

"What's Manhyme's connection to PAP?"

"Silent."

Before I could say anything, she added, "By silent, I mean GP prefers to not make investments in his own name. He...he's an investor in Wolfson Investments. And in many other companies."

"Is there any reason for him to remain silent?"

"You'll have to ask him."

"Any guess?"

"Foreign born. Lebanese. He says it raises unnecessary questions. Personally, I think he prefers to remain out of the spotlight."

"Is it safe for us to assume the investment was based on...on private information?"

"Not in the sense you are thinking. This was a private negotiated deal. Everything's legal and proper. The lawyers saw to that." Wolfson checked her watch. "We land in fifteen minutes. You folks mind giving me some private time to get ready? I'm delivering the after-dinner talk this evening. You two can———"

"Is PAP on financial schedule?" I pressed. "Is the company performing as you expected?"

Ignoring my question, she said, "Time's up. You two can move forward, kick back, and have a drink. The bar is inside the lower right desk drawer. Don't say I didn't give you anything." Wolfson produced a laptop and promptly lost herself in it.

"One final question," I said from the aisle. "Does the name William Dermitt mean anything to you? Ever heard that name mentioned in any context?" Snow's given name is William Dermitt.

Without looking away from her keyboard, Wolfson replied, "Never heard that name in my life. Now leave me be. I have work to do."

Angella and I went forward to the row with two seats, skipping the bar. A few minutes later the jet began its descent. The green lights framing the Bank of America tower in downtown Dallas came into view off to the left. Ahead, I could see the landing lights for Love Field. We were scheduled to land at Addison, farther north, but I could not see any trace of the Addison runways. Several minutes later we banked to the right and when we straightened out the plane was over seemingly endless rows of houses and small buildings. I still could not see an airport.

Then the wheels hit solid ground. The jet stopped in front of a private hanger and the front door opened, its steps folding outward. I walked back to say goodbye to our hostess.

The Wolf was nowhere to be found.

EIGHT

"**W**e can catch a cab over to Love Field and a *Southwest* flight home, or, if you prefer, we can spend the night in Dallas and fly home in the morning." I was hoping Angella would opt for staying over. "Catch a nice dinner and———"

"How about an early dinner and a flight back tonight?" Angella countered.

"Last flight's about nine, if I recall." I have learned not to push Angella. "It's four-twenty and we can be downtown by five. That allows us to have time for something nice and still make the last fight."

"I'll follow your lead. Dallas is your domain, not mine. I'll get Tiny working on some things concerning the Wolf that bother me. She's a lot of bluster, but something's missing."

"Good thought. We can read about her and her investments on the way down to SPI after dinner."

I booked our flights home while Angella was on the phone to Tiny. I reserved a table at *Stephan Pyles'* new restaurant. I was assured we would be out in time to make our flight. Pyles was known for his Southwestern cooking and is a legend in and around Dallas. I last ate at his *Star Canyon* restaurant many years ago.

"Tiny's about to land at Andrews," Angella said, dropping her phone in her bag. "Said the preliminary autopsy report on the 'chute death indicates a puncture wound to the heart. Thin instrument, round. More like an ice pick than a knife."

"What about the tox report?" I asked. "Any clarification on the drugs?"

"He confirmed high levels consistent with addiction. Nothing further."

We fell silent, preferring not to speak while in the back seat of the taxi. I entered notes of our interview with Wolfson, such as it was, in my iPhone. I finished, encoded and filed them. I then sent Tiny a text giving him the file index code. I had come to enjoy an SPI website called *southpadretv.tv* and I brought the site up to kill the remaining time until we arrived at *Pyles*. I read a brief story written by Steve Hathcock, a local SPI businessman and author, about messages found on beaches in bottles. We were almost downtown when I noticed a headline reading: SHARKS CAUGHT IN FISH NET.

I was still reading when the taxi pulled to a stop on Ross Avenue in front of the restaurant.

A few minutes later Angella asked, "So, what's so interesting that you haven't said a word in fifteen minutes?"

"Maybe nothing. Maybe something. The Coast Guard found a large number of sharks caught in a fishing net right off Boca Chico beach where you were rescued. They think the net was abandoned by a Mexican boat illegally fishing in U.S. waters."

"Sharks? Illegal fishing?"

"I'm not following."

"Didn't Tiny tell us the dead guy Pettit visited the Coastal Studies Lab asking about medications found in marine life?"

"I recall that he did. Go on."

"The article I was reading said the number of sharks was unusually high. There's speculation they were sick. Also, dolphins have been found with respiratory problems. A few died while folks were taking care of them."

"And just where is this taking us?"

"Premature to speculate. For now, just filing away facts. Let's just enjoy our dinner and deal with all this later."

"Bet you can't do that," Angella teased, holding her wine glass up. "At least not until you've had a few more glasses of this. Good choice of restaurants by the way." She placed her hand over mine, smiled and said, "I love you."

"Love you as well. That's what makes this hard. The last time———"

"Jimmy. Listen to me. We're either in or we're out. There's no half-way. If you want to retire, I support it. In fact, I encourage you to get out. But if not, then, well…well, we must do this right."

What prompted her comment I didn't know. But instead of following up, I touched her glass with mine and said, "Nice work with the Wolf. I couldn't work her. She gave you everything you asked." My comment triggered a thought. "That happened once before with a female target. My partner, a female, got a confession out of the woman while all I managed to get was stonewalled."

"You going somewhere with this?"

"The suspect had a preference for women."

"Is that important?"

"Not by itself it isn't. Her pilot was a woman. Just facts like any other facts. In the end, the important ones will line up showing us a picture."

"In the end it might just be that I'm a better interrogator than you."

"It might," I said. "It just might."

"And will that…interfere with our relationship?"

"Let's just enjoy our dinner," I replied, holding up my mostly empty wine glass. "We'll have plenty of time for serious discussions later."

NINE

My PAP TO DO list was rather short. It read: Check Wolf-son Investments. Net worth of Wolfson? Flight plan for Wolfson jet. Drugs in sharks? Who is GP Manhyme?

We landed in Harlingen and exchanged lists while the plane was taxiing to the terminal. Angella's list was essentially the same as mine, except hers contained two additional items, both of which were excellent. Follow up on all prior Wolfson investments. See if Bill Snow (W. Dermitt) has connections to Wolfson Investments.

"Go ahead," I said, "update the file and give Tiny a heads up. His folks can do most of this from their desks. Also, add a note for Tiny to list all locations of PAP."

A moment later Angella said, "Done. Isn't technology won-derful? As fast as we think of what we want, somebody digs into a database and up it pops."

"Trick is to think of it."

"Better trick," Angella countered, "is to populate the database correctly."

We walked over to the SPI shuttle counter and paid for two-one-way tickets for the fifty-minute ride to the island. The shuttle was scheduled to leave in fifteen minutes. "I'm calling Contentus," I said to Angella. "I just had a thought."

"As in your former Texas Ranger boss?"

"One in the same. See any problem in that?"

"Politics. You be the judge."

"Nice punt. Come, we can talk outside. Shuttle won't leave without us."

"Isn't eleven-thirty a bit late to call?"

"That guy never sleeps."

I touched his number in my Favorites list and one ring later he answered. "My, my. If it isn't Jimmy Redstone himself. Been reading a lot about you in the briefings from Homeland Security. I take it this is not a personal call."

"Other than to ask how you're doing? It's about a matter we're working on."

"I assume the *we* includes Angella?"

"It does. We're partners as you well know."

"In every sense of the word, from what I hear." He paused to let that sink in. "So what can I do for you?"

"Remember that SOS matter up in the Panhandle?"

"Messy financial tangle. Former president is over at Dalhart, not doing well I understand. Money was never recovered."

"I need access to my notes."

"I can't allow it. Sorry."

"It's important."

"You wouldn't call if it were otherwise. There's still a piece to that investigation that hasn't been put to bed yet. I can't give out open files. What else can I do for you?"

"I'll call you if I think of anything."

"Do that. Here's a name for you. Hildigo Francese. Look him up in the morning. He works at the UT Pan American Coastal Studies Lab on the island."

"And what———"The line was dead.

"What did he say?" Angella asked when I put my phone away. "Are you getting your notes?"

"I'm guessing yes, but not certain. He gave us the name of Francese, Hildigo Francese. He works at the Costal Studies Lab and suggested we visit him in the morning."

"That's in Isla Blanca County Park. Isn't that where Pettit was asking about the sick———or dead———sharks?"

"Texas Rangers are always informed of murders, especially suspicious ones like Pettit. But how in the world did Contentus know our investigation of Wolfson overlapped the Pettit matter?"

"Didn't you once tell me your boss knew everything about you?"

"He did when I worked for him. But I don't work for him now."

"You sure about that?"

- - - - -

Hildigo Francese turned out to be younger than I had expected. No older than thirty and possibly even in his mid-twenties. A pang of what I can only call jealousy momentarily cursed through my mind. He was slight of build, with a full red beard that tended to curl at the ends to match his curly red hair. The sharks swimming in large tanks along the walls were larger than he was. Francese didn't stand a chance should he be unlucky enough to fall into the water with them.

"I take it you are an expert on sharks," I said, after we introduced ourselves.

"Hardly. There are over four hundred species, four hundred forty to be exact. Right now I'm interested in the Tiger shark, *Galeocerdo Cuvier*." He pointed to two sharks circling slowly beside me, their eyes never leaving my belt buckle. "These are rather small examples."

"I thought Tiger sharks were mostly in the Pacific," Angella said. I glanced at her and she added, "I remember that from my high school biology teacher. Don't recall much else."

"They can be found in the Gulf as well. They thrive in warm water."

"Is there something special about Tiger sharks that attract you?" I asked.

"Their eating habits. I'm studying their diet. It's widespread, similar to ours, in fact. They eat crustaceans, fish, birds, turtles, sea snakes, just to name a few varieties. And, in some instances, dolphins."

"Why is that interesting to you?" Angella was obviously into this, so I held my questions.

"I started into it mainly to learn about sharks for my Ph.D. thesis. I realized their diet and ours have similarities. Perhaps if I knew more about their diet, I could learn something useful for ours."

"So have you?" Angella asked, appearing genuinely interested. "Anything we should know and use for our diets? But, just so you understand, I don't intend to be eating dolphin any time soon."

"Nothing really, yet. But that's the nature of research. You spend a lifetime and sometimes all you have to show for it is a long black tunnel. Sometimes you get lucky. I plan to get lucky." He paused, studied Angella as I imagined he would study a fish species, and then he turned his attention to me. "I suppose you all are here for the same reasons those people from the State Police, correction, Texas Rangers, were here asking a million questions."

"Questions about what?"

"I filed a report pertaining to the drugs I found in the sharks. Let me back up first. About two weeks ago, a fishing net was found abandoned not far offshore. In the net were hundreds of sharks, and almost as many dolphins, all dead or dying. I was asked to examine them to see why so many died. Everyone assumed it was some form of marijuana they ingested. Usually, when that happens, the sharks get sick, but most survive, and the dolphins are essentially untouched by it. This time was different."

"So what did you find?"

"Ingested azithromycin."

"I'm not following," I said. "Why is that significant?"

"It's not typical to find drugs, other than occasionally marijuana, and possibly some coke, in the sea life. Never find man-made, or should I say prescription, drugs. Certainly not azithromycin or anything close to it."

"Any thought as to where the drugs came from?"

"That's what I'm trying to determine. My theory is that they were tossed or fell overboard by someone smuggling them into the country."

"Does the name Larson Pettit mean anything to you? Ever hear that name?"

"He came in here the morning before he...before he jumped out of that plane. No accounting for crazy things people do. He wanted to know if I knew anything about Macrolides——he pronounced it Microlights——in the water."

"What did he tell you he was? A scientist?"

"A deck hand, actually. He said he had reason to think drugs were going to be dropped in the bay."

"Did he tell you how he knew that?"

"He became all agitated when I asked. Told me it was none of my business. Said, if I knew what was good for me I'd stop asking questions and give him answers."

"So he threatened you?"

"Maybe not a threat, but he made me uncomfortable."

"What did you tell him?"

"I told him I thought the sharks ingested human medications."

"What was his response?"

"He said he had in his possession proof of who was responsible."

"Did he show the proof to you? Or tell you what it was?"

"I pushed him, but he got angry and told me to forget about him ever being here. If I kept my mouth shut he'd give me money. That's what he said. Make it worth my while. Said he intended to cash in big time. Go live on a beach and kick back, be able to buy all the blow he ever wanted. Then he got all excited and didn't make much more sense."

"Excited?" I repeated.

"Like talking faster than I could understand. I caught a few words. I understood *ship channel*. And *salvage*. Not much else. Oh, yah, he did say he wanted to see the area from the air. I didn't think he meant he was going to jump from a plane. I thought… he was going to find someone to fly him over the area. I told him I was interested in what he found." Francese paused before continuing, trying to decide what to say. "I'm not normally a pessimist, but I can say that it wouldn't take a lot more drugs in our waters before we'd go over the tipping point."

"Tipping point?" Angella asked. "What's that mean?"

"Easy. The drugs are threatening our sea life. There's a point of no return. In my opinion, we are almost there. If this continued we could lose all the sea life——forever."

"If what continued?" I asked.

"Like Pettit, I have reason to believe people are actually dropping human medications in the water. Probably to see what would happen. Perhaps to gauge the dispersion and perhaps the strength."

"To what end?"

Francese winched. His face contorted as if he had been bitten by something. "One's mind can dream up plenty of reasons—— none of them ending well. Listen, this stuff, the Macrolides, are attacking the marine phytoplankton, killing——"

"The what," Angella asked. "What are phyto——"

"Phytoplankton. They're single-celled algae. Believe it or not," Francese said, going into lecture mode, "they supply half the oxygen we breathe. Every other breath we take so to speak. The other half comes from endangered rain forests. Just imagine what would happen if we lost half our oxygen. And that's what these drugs are doing to us!"

"Getting back to Pettit. Did he say anything suggesting who the polluters are——or will be?"

"Nothing."

"Do you think we are at the tipping point?" Angella asked, circling back around. "Are you sure? I mean, are we talking a few hundred sharks. Or a few thousand?"

Francese looked away, his eyes focusing out over the dunes to the water gently rolling up onto the beach. "Look, I don't want to start something I can't...Oh, hell! What I mean is, I'm out of my element in this and I shouldn't say any more." He wrapped his arms around himself as if to fend off a sudden blast of cold air. But it was anything but chilly in the building.

Angella, playing off his body language said, "This is troubling you. As you know, we're from Homeland Security. We're the right people to talk to. It won't go any further than necessary."

Francese kept his eyes fixed on the water, his entire body now shaking.

Angella put a hand on his shoulder and in a calming, yet authoritative, voice, said, "If this is so serious then it's imperative you tell us what's troubling you. Our job is to investigate threats to the country."

The young man remained silent, but slowly brought his shaking under control. Without taking his eyes from the horizon, he said, "I'm afraid I could be making this worse than it really is. I've never...I'm new to this work and I really don't know what's expected. I don't want to lose my———"

"Nothing bad will happen to you," I said. "We'll keep what you say confidential."

"Promise I won't...get in trouble."

"Promise," I said, having no real ability to keep that promise. "I promise."

"I've never read about drugs like this anywhere, and especially not down here. The marine life, and I mean the phytoplankton as well as the fish and mammals, aren't capable of coping with what's out there. They'll die, that much I know for certain."

Angella processed what he had said quicker than I. "What makes you think the marine life can't cope? I mean, you seem so certain of their destruction."

"I can see it happening. Some of the drugs were resident in the dolphins. I put a tiny drop in with the plankton. They glow. The light went off the instant the drug hit the water." The young man wrapped his arms around his chest, stood for a moment and then, his shaking under control, continued, "Do you realize the economic impact? This whole area will be devastated! And not just the marine life."

"Devastated is a strong word," Angella said.

"I'm certain I'm right. More than certain."

"Why?" I asked.

"The drugs have been altered. That's why when we find a sick shark or dolphin, medications don't work. The altered drugs brought on the sickness and we have nothing to counteract the effect. I've tried several antidotes. Nothing works."

"Altered?" Angella said. "What's that mean?"

"Same basic formula as the real drug, but not exactly a perfect match. Spectral analysis is different."

"And the bottom line is?"

"Bottom line is the drugs I'm seeing are counterfeit in a way that even a small amount can cause widespread devastation. It won't stop with a few sharks or a small patch of water. The whole food chain will become contaminated. You asked how many sharks will die. It won't just be sharks. Every living organism, including humans, could be killed by this. If these altered drugs find their way into Laguna Madre, the bay could be…would be I predict… barren for hundreds, if not thousands of years. Take away that much oxygen and I doubt any mammal will survive. Take more drugs to do that in the Gulf, but because the fish migrate, it is not inconceivable that the entire Gulf of Mexico could become a dead sea——or worse."

"Say you are right," Angella prodded, "how long after contamination will that take? Weeks, months?"

"For the bay, weeks. For the Gulf, depends upon how much and where the drugs are placed. Hey, I know I sound like Chicken Little, but this will be worse than the sky falling."

He paused, turned to face us and added, "I know this sounds like I'm hysterical, and perhaps I am. Perhaps I'm overlooking something, but I think not. This is some bad stuff."

"How is the water right now? I assume you're testing it."

"That's the good news. The water is relatively okay——right now. Whatever was there is mostly gone. Or maybe…just maybe…sunlight killed the drugs. Don't know. Maybe they only dropped a small test amount."

When it became clear Francese had exhausted his knowledge——or perhaps he just didn't care to speak with us any longer——Angella spoke up. "We appreciate you speaking with us this morning. Here's my card. If anything further causes you concern——like the drug level going up——call or text me. We'll keep it private." Angella paused, and then added, "Is there anything else we should know?"

"Nothing I can think of." Francese turned to leave, but quickly turned back to us. "Almost forgot. In the morning pouch from Austin I found an envelope addressed to you, Agent Redstone. I'll get it."

Francese returned in less than a minute and handed me a large grey envelope. I didn't have to open it to know what was inside. My old boss had come through, as I had known he would.

TEN

We walked to my car in silence. Angella was lost in her own thoughts while I thumbed through the notes idly looking for something, but not knowing exactly what.

I drove out of the parking lot and headed north toward the exit of the park. I looked over at Angella, about to ask her what her take was, but the words never came out.

A man suddenly launched himself from the back floor, a knife in his right hand. Before I could react, he pressed the blade tight against Angella's throat.

The assailant, a dark-skinned man, mid-fifties, jet black hair, slicked straight back, nodded in my direction, as if to say, look forward and keep driving.

I did as I thought I had been instructed, then said, "You want me to drive or stop?"

One nod.

I asked, "Drive?"

Nod.

"I'll do as you say. Move that blade away from her neck. One bump and——"

"Shut your mouth!" came the heavily accented voice. "Lady, hands on the dash."

Angella did as instructed.

"Weapons," he barked, extending his left arm between the seats, palm open. "She dies if you do anything stupid! Be slow."

Using my left hand, I reached under my jacket and slowly extracted the Beretta. I had one eye on the road and one on Angella's neck. A red line had formed where the blade pressed against her skin. At any moment I expected to see blood running down her neck.

"Now your cell," he said, pointing my gun muzzle at my head.

When I complied, he said, "You also, lady. Gun first, then phone."

He eased the blade away from Angella's neck to allow her to move forward enough to free her service weapon.

When she held her Beretta up, he laid the knife on the back seat long enough to take the gun from her hand.

I followed his every movement in the rearview mirror. He looked away from me for an instant while he reached forward for Angella's gun. By the time I realized I had an opening, the knife was back against her neck.

My plan was to swerve and brake hard when he next reached forward for her cell. I was positive I could knock his gun away long enough to throw him off balance. But what if I knocked the muzzle in Angella's direction?

The decision was made for me when he yelled, "Toss your phone back here, Lady. Put both hands on the dash."

"You!" He was addressing me. "Obey speed limit! No trick! Go 'til I instruct you."

We drove out of the County park and continued north through town passing all the familiar stores. Past the police station and the City Hall and the new fire station. Then past *Paragraphs on Padre*, followed by *Ted's*. I glanced over at Angella and caught a glimpse of Teran walking down the steps from his *Island Fitness* gym. I visualized the hammocks swinging at *Pura Vida Cafe* and wished we could stop and have a leisurely smoothie.

A few blocks further on we passed the *Turtle Rescue* facility and then the *South Padre Island Convention Center*. Our captor seemed more intent on examining our cell phones than he was of us. The muzzle of my gun was close enough to my head to allow me to grab it. But with Angella so vulnerable to having her neck slashed, I decide to play it straight. Our best chance of breaking free was to mount a coordinated attack, but that was difficult to plan under the conditions.

A few miles further north the sand dunes rose up and bounded the roadway on either side. The Gulf was to our right and the Laguna Madre on our left. The road, I knew, ended about three miles further on. Beyond that there was only sand as far as the eye could see. About thirty-five miles of sand.

"Turn right!"

I followed our captor's command and drove off the roadway, through an opening in the dunes and onto a hard-packed sandy area that passed for a parking lot. Continuing onto the beach without a four-wheel drive was impossible. Our wheels would be spinning uselessly within seconds.

Just as the car moved onto the soft sand, our captor commanded, "Stop!"

Then he said, "Get out, both. Go north. Keys in car. Five minutes. No turn back. Go!"

- - - - -

"You okay?" I asked Angella as soon as we were on the sand heading toward the water. "Are you cut?"

"Feels like it, but don't stop to check now. I'll live."

Five minutes feels like an eternity when you're counting down. Somewhere about three minutes, I said, "This is enough time. Whatever he's doing, he's already done and gone. Let me see your neck."

There was a red welt-like line running diagonally across the front of her neck. The good news was I could see only two small spots of dried blood. "Mostly superficial," I said, relieved. "Let's head back."

"Jimmy," she said, "I was scared."

"If you weren't scared, you wouldn't be worth a darn. The real question is what you do when you're scared. Some people roll up, can't think straight."

"All I could think about was how to move the blade away from my throat. What happened to you out on the flats with Santiago is still so...so raw. At that time I wanted to put a bullet trough Santiago's brain but couldn't manage it."

"Listen to me. We're walking away from this encounter under our own power. That means we didn't make bad decisions. In the end, that's all that counts. Live to fight another day."

"I keep thinking that if the time came and I had to pull the trigger, could I do it? And kill someone? I don't think———"

"I have no doubt you'll do the right thing. Pulling the trigger is easier when it's your life or his———or your partner's."

"What if it's not me I'm protecting? What if it's... someone I don't even know? Then I have to choose between two lives. I'm not God."

"That badge you carry makes it your duty to protect the inno-cent. You shoot the perp. That's the rule of law. The world would be chaos otherwise. End of story."

"I only wish it were as simple as you make it sound."

"It is, my love. Just do it." I pulled her close and kissed her on the lips. I felt her body shutter. Adrenaline surges will do that——and worse.

ELEVEN

" **T**here you are!" exclaimed acting SPI Police Chief Lt. Jose Garcia when Angella and I came off the beach and into the parking lot where we had last seen our captor. Angella had been hesitant to get back earlier than he had proscribed, but I was confident he would be long gone. "Thought we'd lost you."

Before I could muster up a witty answer, two Cameron County SUV's with flashing red and blue lights, skidded to a stop not ten feet from us. Their doors flew open and almost immediately we were facing two shotguns.

Garcia held up his hand, as if to say, everything was under control.

But the uniformed men continued pointing their weapons at us. One called out, "We had a kidnapping report of federal officers."

"These are the officers," Garcia said, the beginnings of a smile spreading across his otherwise rustic face. "Put your weapons down."

The men looked at each other, shrugged, and laid their guns on the front seat of their vehicle, within easy reach. The one closest to me seemed disappointed that he couldn't use his weapon.

"How did you...who called it in?" I asked. I was confused as to how Garcia had arrived even before we reported the incident.

"You tell us, Redstone. You're the ones who got yourselves kidnapped. You tell us what happened."

I explained about being jumped in the parking lot in front of the Coastal Studies Lab and driving through town with a knife pressed against Angella's throat. I described the assailant and added, "He's unmistakable. He has a nasty scar, I assume from a knife fight, under his right eye."

I was angry with myself for not reading the signs. The car had been locked when we went in to the lab. It was unlocked when we came out. But my mind was focused on the report I had been handed and I wasn't processing the signs. My bad.

I have to hand it to the Acting Chief. He was pleasant, but thorough. He walked me through each aspect of what had transpired, recording every minute detail. When he was satisfied that he had it all right on the tape, he asked me to listen to the narrative. At the end he had me state my name, recite my HS ID number, add date of birth, and residence address. Then he asked me to verbally acknowledge that everything on the recording was accurate. It would all be reduced to writing and I would have to sign it. In this regard, I was being treated as though I had done something improper. The procedure was frustrating and my patience was wearing thin.

Angella was across the lot, presumably going through the same routine.

"Going to a lot a trouble for a simple carjacking," I said to Garcia. "What's up?"

"Now that your account is officially sealed, I'll give you mine. A professional courtesy type of thing if you will. Seems one of my officers saw you driving north through town a while ago, spotted a guy in the back seat he recognized from a fugitive warrant. He called it in. We put the warrant up on his in-car screen. He made the match. Chase on."

"So how———"

"Whoa. I'm getting there. The officer was driving north and spotted your car heading south. Only you're not driving. He turned around and gave chase. Suddenly the guy veered onto the sand, the wheels dug in and your car stopped. The perp jumped out and ran onto the beach heading south. Officer gave chase, but realized you might still be in the car, possibly wounded. He broke off, came back, found your weapons and phones, but no Redstone or Martinez." Garcia wiped his forehead, then continued, "Meanwhile we sealed the beach from the south and I came up here to seal it from the north."

"Did you find him? Who is he?"

"His name's Igletz Touchy. Known in the trade as Ig the Pig."

"Never heard of the guy."

"Nobody down here had until there was a break-in over at the Brownsville boat yard. Someone was on one of the boats looking for electronic equipment. The boat was waiting to be scrapped. Touchy's prints were lifted. FBI, at Interpol's request, posted his picture. Operates out of London, but believed to be Iranian based. Nasty background."

"I saw it in his eyes. The Pig was salivating to cut Angella's throat. My guess, he gets off torturing women."

"Your guess is right on. That's his sheet. Five we know about. Women are raped, breasts mutilated. Two were found tied upside down by their ankles, necks slit from ear to ear. As I said, he's one nasty operator."

"Psychopath."

"We don't have a work-up, but Interpol believes so. Question is: Why jump you two? He's not known to do men."

"I don't know why he's interested in us. Don't suppose it's random. Interpol, you say?"

"Is that important?"

"Everything is important at this stage." I didn't want to discuss our conversation with Holland and Plevin at this point. But it was hard to overlook the fact that we were working with London-based Interpol agents and then jumped by a thug who is well-known in London police circles. "Did you catch Ig?"

"I wouldn't be wasting my time talking to you if we had. He disappeared into thin air between here and Clayton's."

TWELVE

"What's going on down there?" Tiny demanded. "I leave you two alone for five minutes and———"

"First of all, it wasn't five minutes. It's been almost twenty-four hours since you were here. And second, how the hell do you know about the kidnapping?"

"Concede the first point. A little birdie told me the second. I've got some news for you. Flight plan has Wolfson's jet in Biloxi for three days. Before that in New York, Long Island, for two days. Backing up even further, the plane was in Denver, Dallas, Las Vegas, and San Jose. The only passenger we can say for certain who was on board on each landing was Wolfson herself."

"Did the plane remain at the airport while she was on the ground?"

"Apparently, she mostly stays on board when she's traveling. She now lives in Dallas. Has been there for three years. An area called Uptown."

I visualized the inside of her jet and realized the door in the rear of the plane must lead to a small cabin. "Nice life if you can get it."

"That woman made a lot of money in the past few years. Before that, she and her group did okay, but nothing spectacular. Mostly rentals in shopping malls."

"Those folks usually do well," I said.

"Not so much the low-end. Wolfson invested in second-rate strip malls. Usually bought them distressed, got them back on their feet and sold them. That works when the economy is working. Drive around and you'll see abandoned or run-down strips everywhere."

"So how——"

"Like she told you, she, I mean her investment group, invested in a department store, actually a dollar store with a huge space, in a strip mall that was dying. On the surface, it was a bad investment. But, as luck sometimes has it, Walmart bought out all the leases. Tore everything down and built a small-box store, mostly groceries, on the site. Wolfson Investments made over ten-million between the land and the leases."

"What do you have on SOS drugs?"

"Jimmy, that's what I love about working with you," Tiny replied, sarcasm in his voice. "You always have one more question than I'm prepared to answer. Talk to you soon."

- - - - -

"Wolfson's story, as far as it goes, checks out," I said to Angella after we finally broke free of the crime scene. Our weapons and my car had been impounded. There was little hope of getting either of them back anytime soon. Angella refused to discuss the kidnapping, so we were concentrating on HS business. "The Wolf was in Biloxi for three days, two of which she spent in The Regional Center being treated for a stomach ailment of unknown origin. Made her money, as she said, when Walmart bought her property."

"Got something for you as well," Angella said when I fell silent. "Recall in a past life when Tiny got himself from D.C. down here too fast and you questioned whether he had been here all along? Your thought was he had some advance information. When you questioned him he claimed he flew here on a T-38C Talon."

"That conversation took place at *Claytons,* if my memory serves me." Since that point, I have decided to trust the big guy. Angella, for many reasons, has not. "So, where are you———"

"He flew down again on a Talon. This time he was alone."

"You know this because———"

"I called a friend. More accurately, and in the interest of full disclosure, I called a friend of my former husband. A guy he went to school with. BBF type of thing. The guy's the manager of the Cameron County airport. I asked him about Tiny and what time he landed. He didn't know anything about Tiny. I suggested that possibly he came on a Talon. He confirmed for me that a Talon had recently landed. Turns out, he routinely videos small jet landings at the airport. Hobby sort of thing. I got the Talon on my cell, care to see?"

I watched the thirty-second video and saw nothing out of the ordinary. The camera had picked up the small distinctively shaped military jet trainer about a mile away and followed it as it smoothly touched down and then taxied to a stop just outside a hanger. The video cut off before the door opened. The only other plane visible was a private jet being refueled from a portable tank supported on a motorized handcart.

"Tiny handles that jet like he knows what he's doing," I said. "Assuming of course, Tiny actually flew the plane."

"Flew it himself, from what I was told," Angella replied. "The guy is a puzzle."

"Certainly is," I said, my mind processing something vague, not focusing on exactly what it was.

Angella's phone rang. I looked over her shoulder and saw a number I did not recognize.

"Oh, hello, Barrington," Angella said, glancing at her watch. "Isn't it late in London? It's almost one PM here." Angella touched the speakerphone button.

"It's four o'clock in Buenos Aires," our Interpol counterpart said. It's a beautiful fall day. But then again, all days down here are beautiful."

"You didn't call to give a weather forecast. Or a travel log. Is something on your mind?"

"My, my, Angella. A wee bit put out are we?"

"Oh, sorry. The morning's not going well. How are you? And why are you in Argentina?"

"Working the PAP pharma matter. A person using the given name of our target checked into an apartment day before yesterday. I'm following up on the lead."

"Is it the same person?"

"No visual contact as of this time. But passport photo matches. And the apartment seems to be what you term a safe house."

"What can we do to help?" I injected, being sure he knew I was listening in.

"Oh, good afternoon, Jimmy. Happy to have you join us. Is Angella still there? Can she hear me?"

"I'm here as well."

"Good. It's you I'm requesting to join me down here. There may be more going on than we know."

"I can't just leave. I'll require approval———"

"Bloody red-tape has been disposed of, actually. Wheels greased, I think is your saying. You are booked on a flight from...let me see...Brownsville to Houston, little layover and then onto Buenos Aires. You'll arrive early morning. Your flight leaves about five. Pack lightly, weather's comfortable down here."

"Is...is Lillie...that's her name isn't it?...there with you?"

"She's working this from headquarters. I'm working from the Argentine office. Jimmy, you will work it from the states."

"This is moving all too fast," Angella replied. "I have to check———"

"It's been cleared all the way up the bloody command. Kagan signed off five minutes ago. He asked me to invite you, actually. You can't very well refuse. I'll see you in the morning. For what it is worth, I very much look forward to working with you. Oh, and bring your bathing suit. The beaches are lovely and you have them mostly to yourself."

I was furious. My partner———and lover———was going off to work with some British guy who I knew nothing about. *Bring your bathing suit!* Indeed. I was pacing the room, making a mental list of reasons why Angella should not go.

Angella was in the bedroom, her suitcase out, packing. She hadn't missed a beat, as if she had known the call was coming——— and eager to comply. Overly eager, if you ask me.

"Jimmy," Angella called, "come in here and talk to me while I pack. You're pouting and I don't know why."

When I shuffled into the bedroom she said, "What's troubling you? You're acting like a teenager who didn't get his way."

When I didn't answer, she said, "Jealous? You're Jealous! That's what it is. All those frivolous reasons why I need to remain here boils down to a case of jealousy. Well, I'm flattered."

It wasn't just jealousy, but working without Angella just didn't sit well. And her being on assignment in a strange country without my backup was unsettling. "Sorry, it's just———"

"You've nothing to worry about. Barrington sounds like———"

Her response was cut off by my cell ringing. Tiny was on the line. "Just heard Angella's going south. Tell her it's okay to go without her weapon. Interpol will have one for her when she arrives. We'll need to clear it with Argentina, but that's routine. She'll have arrest privileges, but only for Americans. The Brit is coordinating internally for both of them. He'll meet Angella at Ministro Pistarini Airport. But keep in mind, he has no police authority."

Yea, he'll be there with a beach blanket and sandals. And one of those European Speedo thongs! "She's right here, you can tell her yourself." I handed the phone to Angella and retreated to the den to begin working on the PAP file. My mind was better off occupied than dwelling on what I couldn't change.

"Jimmy," Angella called from the doorway, before I could even sit down, "Tiny wants to brief you." She handed the cell back to me, kissed me on the cheek, and disappeared back into the bedroom.

"You investigated the embezzlement charges against SOS," Tiny began, "and did an admirable job putting the president of the company away. However, FBI believes the embezzlement went deeper even."

"I agree. But I couldn't find anything. Neither could the FBI."

"Wolfson, right after that, put up five million and arranged financing for fifteen. Three months later sold the company for over a hundred mil. Sounds too good to be true."

"Plenty of folks make money flipping businesses," I replied. "Are you onto something?"

"Let's just say, the only reason the buying price was so low was the massive transfer of assets out of the company. Timing was perfect for a takeover. Perhaps she knew what was about to happen."

"Insider information is rampant in these takeovers. Need more than suspicion."

"It is for people who specialize in turnarounds. Wolfson leases junk shopping centers. What the hell does she know about drugstores?"

"Are you suggesting———"

"FBI is asking. Now she's involved with PAP———and with Snow."

"Pettit, the guy killed on SPI, was asking about drug contaminated fish the day before he died. Macrolides specifically. PAP manufactures Macrolides." I thought for a moment, then said, "Also, that guy who jumped us was Middle Eastern. The guy who finances the Wolf is Lebanese. Have your crew put two and two together for me please."

"I'll see what I can get. Anything else?"

"Set something up with the PAP president. We won't get the time of day from Wolfson. Not yet anyway."

"Use Lillie Holland as well. Interpol is exceptional at tracing money through Europe. The PAP deal has a European, or at least a Middle East, flavor. A fresh look in that direction may turn up something."

I hung up with Tiny just as someone rapped on the door. Whoever it was lacked patience, because before I could get there he——or she——banged again. This time the knock count increased to four.

THIRTEEN

"Lt. Malone," I said pulling the door open, "what brings you here?" Malone was the acting co-chief of the SPI police force. She was also their chief investigator. The woman was solidly built and had a face that proclaimed no nonsense.

"I brought your weapons back. We lifted a good set of prints." She handed me an evidence bag. "Match to Igletz Touchy. You run in good company. He's wanted on two continents for murder and various other activities."

"Thanks for the speedy service," I said, hoping Malone would go away and leave me alone. Instead, she walked past me into the living room.

"Nice crib, Redstone. Angella here?"

"As a matter of fact, she is. She's a bit busy at the moment."

"I wanted to get your weapons back to the both of you. The way I see it, guns are for shooting bad guys. You can't do your job without your weapon. Don't quote me."

She was referring to Badman Tex, the guy I was accused of shooting in cold blood. Nobody is willing to leave that alone.

Malone didn't make a move to leave. I thought about making a smart remark about her joining Angella and I for afternoon tea and crumpets. Thinking is okay. Saying is not.

"You seem troubled Lieutenant. Something I did——or said?"

She shifted her weight, as if settling in for a siege. "I found an investigative file in your car. Looks like an old investigation of a company called SOS. Mind telling me what's going down?" She looked me directly in the eye, as if to say, *you lie and I'll have your butt*. "The full story. That file should not be in your possession. You're no longer employed by the great state of Texas."

"I told the Chief. Told you. Nothing to add."

"Ig the Pig was after something," she persisted. "He didn't hold Angella at knife point to steal your car. You're not reviewing old Ranger files to pass the time of day. Give it up, Redstone."

"Nothing more to add. You have any theories?"

"Thought you might have one or two. Look, I have a dead guy with a hole through his heart on my hands. I'm running my ass off and coming up dry. You got something, be nice and help me out. Get my drift?"

"I've got nothing that makes any sense, I can assure you."

"Try me."

"Actually, I have nothing."

"You and Angella were the lucky ones who found Pettit. Coincidence?"

"We just happened to be taking a morning walk. Dead guy falls out of the sky. In this case it is a coincidence."

"Pettit was talking to Francese, the guy at the Coastal Studies Lab, about sharks being full of drugs. You were talking to

Francese about sharks and drugs. You're abducted immediately after that. One and one? I'd say a clear linkage. Play nice, I may be able to help you along the line. Goodness knows you may need it."

"It usually adds up to two. But not always, as I've learned the hard way. I simply don't know much more than that."

"You're investigating Pettit's murder for Homeland Security? Is that correct?"

"Absolutely not. That's against the law, unless, of course, it's terrorism related. You have reason to think that's the case?"

Malone looked at me, much as I had looked at countless suspects, her eyes proclaiming she knew more than she was saying.

"Redstone, to be blunt, you're not known for always remaining on the right side of the line. Certainly, you're not known as a team guy."

"Sometimes the line gets fuzzy."

"Better get a new pair of glasses."

"Is that all, Lieutenant?"

"I suppose it will have to be. But I for one don't enjoy being bull-shitted. And you're in that zone now. Better keep your nose clean, get my drift?"

"Wipe it every chance I get. Can't help what just floats my way."

"Just keep your nose on your side and all will work out just fine. You hear anything we should know, you be certain to call me."

"Without a doubt," I replied.

FOURTEEN

Angella was off to the airport. In the mood I was in she didn't want me driving her. Reluctantly I agreed, silently acknowledging she was right. I was in a funk, behaving badly, and unable to take corrective action.

In an effort to settle my agitation, I grabbed the SOS file and slowly the whole sordid mess began to reform. In my prior investigation I concentrated on following the funds once the various SOS properties were sold. In each situation, the money never found its way back to the company, but was, instead, held in a trust account releasable only by signed order of the president of SOS. In each case, the president released the funds, which were never to be seen again. That is why he is in prison.

I hadn't remembered a company named Wolfson Investments being involved, but neither had I been aware of Loretta Wolfson. I checked my notes to see if I had remembered correctly. I had. No mention of Wolfson in any interview or in any of the thousands of files I had indexed. But she had told us she was involved. Tiny said it all checked out.

But I now saw what could be a pattern. The companies who had been involved were all named after Texas cities. Dallas Land Trust, Waco Specialty Acquisition, Temple First Realty, Austin Highway Investments, all of which are located north to south along the Interstate thirty-five corridor. I hadn't keyed on that before. But, in my own defense, I wasn't concentrating on the buyers, just on the money flow belonging to the sellers.

Based on this, I now knew for a certainty that the SOS embezzlement was well planned and went far beyond Raymond Prinz, SOS's then president.

I fired up the computer and searched for Dallas Land Trust. Found nothing.

I tried Waco Specialty Acquisition.

Same result. In fact, I found nothing relating to any of the buying companies. I tried in every way I could and found nothing. They were classic shells. Formed for a single purpose and then disbanded.

I sent a message to Tiny. I didn't want to use up what little stroke I still had with the Texas Secretary of State's office. Tiny's folks, particularly the FBI, could obtain in minutes what I'd have to bargain for and then perhaps wait weeks, or at least days, to obtain.

I again went back to the file and traced the sales as best I could. In each case, SOS bought the property from a company for a substantial amount, often in the fifty to one-hundred million dollar range. These were not insubstantial investments, all class A income producing properties.

In each case, a bank loaned only twenty-five percent of the funds. The properties were all liquidated within a year of purchase, the loans repaid, which made the banks happy.

But an interesting fact is that in each case the sales price was about half the purchase price. In all, three hundred million dollars was lost in real estate investments. And ninety million was lost in the trust fraud that I had investigated.

I did find another interesting fact. According to an article in the *San Antonio Express-News*, an investment company calling themselves San Antonio Partners, made an investment in SOS when SOS was in deep financial difficulty. The reporter quoted the managing director of San Antonio Partners, one Loretta Wolfson, as being optimistic about saving SOS from bankruptcy.

I ran San Antonio Partners through the Secretary of State on-line database and found Wolfson Investments as the managing partner. So the Wolf had not lied. She had been involved in SOS financing.

A follow up article pointed out that SOS indeed had made a spectacular comeback, and within six months was throwing off nice profits. San Antonio Partners then sold its interest to a group headed by GP Manhyme. That was the guy who wanted to maintain a low profile.

I made a note to have Tiny find out how SOS turned it around so fast? Who actually ran the company after President Prinz? Who was Manhyme? The Wolf had mentioned Manhyme. Manhyme had been the person who suggested that Wolfson invest in PAP. How very convenient. But not so far out of the ordinary. People deal with whom they trust and Wolfson had made a killing on SOS when Manhyme bought it. There was no reason not to follow his suggestion. The linkage proved nothing.

But it was all too tidy.

And where did all that money from SOS really go? Europe? Tiny was ahead of me on this. He had already suggested the Lebanese connection and I hadn't really put it all together. Initially,

I had thought the embezzlement was ninety million. But it was more like three hundred ninety million. But what did that all have to do with PAP?

I thought about PAP for a while, but the link between the company and counterfeit drugs———not to mention the dead guy on the beach and dead sharks———was tenuous at best.

My cell sounded. I recognized the British voice immediately as belonging to Lillie Holland, the Interpol agent. "As possibly you know," she began, without wasting a moment, "I've been requested by Director Kagan to take another view into possible money laundering involving SOS. The chap believes the missing funds are tied to drug counterfeiting and to some previous investigation you handled."

"I'm working on that file now," I replied, "so your timing is perfect. What do you have?"

"Tell you over dinner?"

"I have no reason to be in London. I have no travel———"

"Wasn't considering London? How does dinner at *Café Kranzler* sound? I'm under the impression it's rather quiet there. We can have a pleasant conversation without being disturbed."

She had me off balance. *Café Kranzler* was less than a mile from my condo, assuming we were both thinking of the same restaurant. "On the Island? South Padre?" I asked, revealing how off-balance I was.

"Arrived an hour ago. I'm famished."

"Are you serious?" I replied, not comfortable with where this was going. First, Angella is shipped off to South America with some playboy-type Interpol agent with instructions to bring her bathing suit. No sooner does she leave town than his boss arrives from across the Atlantic to have dinner with me. "You've flown all this way to give me information about bank accounts that easily could be provided securely in many other ways." Talk about the Feds wasting money. "Isn't that a bit…a bit extreme?"

"My dear chap, the question presented is whether or not you are available for dinner. Interpol's travel budget is not your concern. I'd rather not dine alone, but I will if you persist in your unflattering protestations."

"What time suits you?" I asked, growing increasingly more uncomfortable the more she spoke.

"Is there anything wrong with now?"

I checked my watch, thinking it was not later than five. In fact, it was just past seven-thirty. "Where should I pick you up?"

"Thank you for the generous offer, but I prefer to meet you at the restaurant."

- - - - -

I changed into fresh jeans and one of my few island shirts with a collar. I felt over-dressed.

A text arrived from Tiny as I was leaving my condo. EXPECT VISIT FROM LILLIE HOLLAND. A welcome message, even if it was a bit late.

I walked into *Café Kranzler*, my apprehension reduced based on Tiny's message. Four tables were occupied, two with families and one with a couple holding hands. I could only make out the top of a head at the fourth, the high-back of the opposing booth blocking my view.

"Jimmy. Over here."

The head moved sideways and stood, revealing the very plain face of a woman in her mid-fifties. The woman I had seen not long ago on my TV screen in the middle of the night. She stood, and I took in the slender body of someone who has obviously not over indulged herself. She looked frail, not the image of someone I would have identified as an Interpol agent, let alone a former MI Nine operative. From my memory, MI Nine handled British covert operations as well as POW escape. She just didn't look the type. But, I reminded myself not for the first time, if you look the type you wouldn't fool anyone.

"Come join me," Lillie said, extending her hand in greeting.

Two drinks were set out, one in front of her and one across the table, leaving me with the impression someone was off in the restroom and would return at any moment. It also confirmed my suspicion that this woman had been here longer than the ten minutes it had taken me from the time of her call.

I studied her face to assure myself she was the same person I had spoken with on the videoconference.

"Satisfied I'm genuine," she said, after observing me look at her longer than normal. "Sit, my dear man." She waved her arm in the direction of the second drink. Your Skinny Bones is waiting. I dare say you are even more attractive in person than in the dossier. And even more delightful."

A neat way of demonstrating she had studied me and my background. But anyone could have done that. Her voice, as well as her image, was that of the woman I had spoken with on the conference call. "You caught me by surprise," I said, sipping my drink. "Mind telling me why you flew across the Atlantic to deliver financial information. In my world such a gesture is... shall we say...extreme."

"My, my, Jimmy, aren't we feisty. We're working together, so meeting face to face isn't as uncommon as you are implying. It is my distinct understanding that you enjoy being...shall we characterize it as... close...with your partners."

I let the vague reference to my relationship with Angella slide. "I thought Interpol only worked databases, coordinating, not actual field work."

"Please understand my dear man you're doing the field work. I'm merely observing. All according to protocol and coordinated by Director Kagan."

"And Tiny?"

"Ah, yes, my old friend Tiny." Her eyes closed for a moment, as if recalling a forgotten memory. "Knew him in another life."

I couldn't determine if *another life* meant her other life or Tiny's. "Let's order, or have you taken care of that task as well?"

"Don't be a beast. We'll be spending a lot of time together. I have found it is best if we learn to play well with each other under such circumstances." She winked. "Get my meaning?"

Ignoring her obvious seductive tone, I replied, "I take it you haven't ordered."

"Heavens no, dear man. A drink maybe, but not a chap's dinner. A lady wouldn't dare." This time there could be no mistaking her intentions.

FIFTEEN

I picked up the menu, studied it longer than necessary, then waived to Susan, the owner, to take our orders.

That accomplished, I said, "So what is the big news you came all this way to deliver? I'm all ears."

"What a quaint expression. Such a hurry. Savor the moment, Agent Redstone. Savor the moment. Let's have a pleasant dinner and then we can adjourn to my room for a nip or two. Kick back, relax, talk. Get to know each other. This promises to be a long investigation."

My cell signaled a text. I studied the message, puzzled to say the least. The sender was British Airways and the message was a confirmation of a flight change. BA0195, non-stop from Heathrow to Houston Intercontinental had been rebooked until tomorrow. Passenger name: L. Holland.

I shoved the phone back into my pocket and looked up to see Lillie studying me. "I just received notification that your flight from London was delayed until tomorrow. Care to explain?"

"Let me see that," she said, extending her hand for my phone. I turned it so she could read the text.

"Typical cock-up. I put you on the notification list in the event my flight was delayed. I changed flights, forgot about the notification, my muddle. Can't rely too much on technology. I'm obviously here, so no need to fret."

She was obviously across the table, no denying that. In fact, she was right; we've all been victims of technology getting it wrong. "There's no denying you're here. Technology does sometimes cause difficulties. What were you saying?"

"I was about to ask about you. Tell me about yourself."

"It's all in my file," I said, always uncomfortable talking about what I do. "Everything there is to know about me."

"It's never all in the file. And in any case, that's business. What do you do for fun?"

I don't golf and I don't boat. Talking about Angella didn't seem appropriate. So instead, I just replied, "Catching wise guys takes up my time. What about you?"

"When I'm not *catching wise guys* as you say, my biggest delight is listening to music, going to concerts, hopefully in the company of a handsome man." She winked. "Get what I mean?" She reached across the table and patted my hand, allowing her fingers to linger.

I knew exactly what she meant and my discomfort rose, not because I had any thoughts of sleeping with this woman, but if she was coming on so overtly, I was concerned about the relationship her partner wanted with Angella. And I always thought the British were reserved. Angella was right. I was indeed jealous. Nothing I could do about it at this point, so I turned my attention to dinner, which was excellent, as it always is at *Kranzlers*. Lillie steadfastly refused to discuss business, except to ask at one point,

"So tell me, how is your investigation into the finances of SOS going?"

"Early stages, just gathering facts," I replied, taking a page from her book and not telling her in detail what I was working on.

"I understand you have obtained notes from a prior investigation," she pressed. "Do you see a linkage between the SOS situation and PAP? Any names pop up that we can follow?"

As far as I was aware, only four people knew about the notes. Contentus, Angella, Tiny, and myself. Unless my former boss told someone at Homeland Security or the FBI, then Interpol would have no way to know about the notes. I doubted he had done so. Contentus tells nobody about anything. Angella wouldn't have told anyone. I thought of her talking to playboy, but she wouldn't even see him until the morning. Tiny and his FBI-CIA buddies I couldn't vouch for. "At this point," I replied, evading a direct answer, "unless I misunderstand the Interpol protocol, any investigation I do other than what directly pertains to the missing person is an internal matter and off-limits to Interpol. Please correct me if I misunderstood the protocol."

I must have hit a nerve. Lillie backed off. "I have no intention or desire to violate the protocol in any aspect, my dear chap. Please excuse me if I have overstepped my limits. I thought…I thought we were getting along famously. Similar to you, I'm a naturally curious person. Occupational hazard, so to speak."

"Goes with the territory," I replied, settling back in my chair as if content with her answer. In fact, I was studying her movements. Everything about her seemed orchestrated, calculated. Her questions struck me as following a pattern. I was also curious why she needed to know the names of anyone I was investigating. I had given Tiny the name of GP Manhyme for Interpol to follow up on. Surely by now Lillie would have that name. So then why press me for names?

Lillie filed the silence. "Tell me, Jimmy," she began, "when you investigate a company do you, for example, focus on one player, or do you look at a broad spectrum? In my line of work, I am quite focused. Finding one person, tracing a hidden account, that sort of thing. I am curious how you work."

Before I could answer, the door to the small restaurant swung open. A man I recognized as a doctor at *Origins*, the local rehab center, came through the door followed by a group of three men and two women. It didn't take ten seconds, before the second of the two women broke off and headed directly to my table.

"So nice to see you, Jimmy," she beamed, her arms outstretched for a hug even before I could fully stand.

She embraced me, pulling me against her chest in what would have been a romantic moment if it had been anyone other than Joy Malcom. With her lips pressed against my ear, she whispered, as best as Joy can whisper, "Your choice of women is going distinctly downhill. If you have dumped Angella, or vice versa, give me a call. I'm in my last week at rehab." She released me. Pulling back, she laughed and said, "We're on a field trip. Teaching us all how to go out and enjoy ourselves without…without the vices we picked up along the way."

"Nice to see you, Joy. You're looking well." I turned to face Lillie, who now had her head turned away from us. "And this is Lillie. Lillie Holland, visiting from London. Lillie, this is Joy Malcom, a…a friend."

Lillie stood, held up her hand in greeting.

"Oh," Joy exclaimed, "I know you! You're the woman who came looking for that poor man who died jumping from a plane?"

"I'm afraid you have me confused with someone else. I just arrived in town."

"Oh, dear! Jimmy, every time I see you————" Joy broke off, studied Lillie a moment, then said, "You came into the woman's facility by mistake. I know it was you————or you have an identical sister. Twin maybe?"

"Sorry. You are mistaken," Lillie replied, her eyes becoming hostile.

"Joy," the doctor said, coming across the restaurant to retrieve her, "you need to join the rest of us. This is not————" He was looking directly at me, recognition in his face from our last, rather unpleasant, encounter. "Oh, it's you," he said, his look turning even more sour. "Please allow Ms. Malcom to rejoin our group."

"Doctor Sanchez," I said, "I was just saying hello to Joy. She's looking well. Joy, go enjoy your...outing."

"She is...doing well, I am happy to say," Sanchez said. "Come along, Joy."

"Coming," Joy said. "Nice to see you again, Jimmy. Please come visit. I like it when you visit."

"I'll do that. Keep up the good work."

Joy gave me a quick peck on the cheek, as if staking out her territory, before rejoining the already seated group across the restaurant.

"And what was that about?" Lillie asked when they had gone. "That woman seems, well, to be straight-up, a bit tiddly. Know her well?"

"Well, enough, I suppose. So tell me, if that wasn't you at the rehab center then who do you suppose it was?"

"Not anything I would know," she replied, draining her wine glass. "That woman's a wee bit off the edge for my taste."

"Maybe so, but she's not prone to making up stories."

"Mistaken identity, then. Rehab does that to people."

"So exactly when did you———"

Lillie pushed her chair back, stood, and announced, "I've got myself a bit bladdered, I have. Excuse me, I must spend a penny." On wobbling legs she made her way to the ladies' room.

When she returned, I took my turn. Upon coming back to the table, I found cups of coffee set out at our respective places and a crème brulee in the center, apparently positioned for sharing. More of Lillie's idea of togetherness. Bonding.

"Come on, Jimmy Redstone, loosen up. The night is young. If we can't eat together, then how can we work together?"

I wanted to say, *eating and working are two distinct activities.* But instead, I held up my coffee cup and said, "Here's to a flourishing business relationship."

"Cheers," Lillie responded, her right eye again closing in a wink.

We finished dessert; I paid the tab over protests by Lillie that she was on an expense account. I followed her out of the restaurant. Without invitation, Lillie opened the passenger door to my rental car and climbed in. Obviously, she was looking to me to drive her back to her apartment.

Suddenly, I was tired. The feeling came on faster than I had ever felt it come on before. I had to lean against the car to keep my legs from folding out from under me. I made it to the driver's door, but struggled with the knob.

Finally the door opened and I slipped inside. I closed my eyes to let the wave of exhaustion pass, but my head didn't clear.

"What seems to be the problem Jimmy? You appear right knackered."

"Right knackered?" I repeated, not understanding what the hell she was trying to say.

"Tired. Too tired to drive, by appearances."

I fumbled with the key, but couldn't find the slot to insert it into.

"You're not doing well at the task at hand," Lillie volunteered. "Allow me to drive."

"I'll drive," I insisted. "Give me a moment to catch my wind."

We sat there for what seemed like five minutes. I was getting worse, not better.

"Shall I ring up the emergency number? You don't look well."

"Take me home," I said, dropping the keys on the console beside me. I opened the door and staggered to the back seat.

Lillie came around and sat behind the wheel. I closed my eyes, but remembered to remind her to drive on the right side of the road.

"I'm okay. You just take it quiet. You'll require your strength to walk to the elevator. I certainly can't carry you."

I sat back, trying to give directions. But she once again instructed me to save my energy. Lillie seemed to know the way. We drove north ten blocks and then before I could say anything, we turned left toward the bay. She was headed directly for my building without a single instruction from me. Even in my altered state I knew that was wrong.

And how had she known about the elevator?

Lillie parked in the garage reserved for tenants and helped me out of the car. My legs were spongy, but did not collapse. My suspicions resurfaced when I realized I hadn't told her where to park———or even where I lived.

I planted my feet, intending to resist. My left arm started to move toward my weapon, but Lillie's arm was around me blocking the motion. She was holding me from falling and at the same time restraining my arms from forward motion. I resisted as best I could, but my muscles wouldn't cooperate.

From somewhere in the distance I heard Angella's voice talking to me. She was saying something's wrong. Warning me to be careful. "I'm on the bridge———"

Just as suddenly as the voice came to me it was gone. I looked around and saw nothing.

"Come along, Jimmy," Lillie's voice now said, "Up to your flat." Her strong arms propelled me forward. Arriving at the elevator, Lillie released my right arm allowing me to enter my pass code.

A moment later the elevator opened and we went up.

Lillie held up my keys and with visual difficulty I pointed to the door key.

"Nice premises you have here," Lillie said when the door closed behind us. "Comfortable. I think we have engaged in enough foreplay. I suggest we proceed directly to the sack."

Without answering, I stumbled toward the bedroom. The last thing I remember before falling into my bed was Lillie saying, "Thanks for the lovely dinner. Sorry to dine and dash. We'll do it again sometime soon. Pleasant dreams, Agent Redstone."

SIXTEEN

I opened my eyes. Not because I wanted to, but because some-one had their hands on the back of my shoulders and was shaking me. In the distance a familiar female voice called my name.

Lillie?

But the cadence was wrong, as was the accent. A heavy flavor of South Texas had replaced the English brogue.

My vision was blurry, but the voice reminded me of Angella.

It was Angella.

But then again, I had heard Angella's voice in the garage and it wasn't real then. Was it real now?

The room went dark again.

Then the shaking began anew. This time I made out two voices. One again sounded like Angella's, the other even more South Texas but also familiar.

I made out khaki covered legs. Lillie had been wearing a skirt. Angella had been in jeans when she left for the airport.

The shaking continued.

Forcing my eyes open, I was certain I saw the concerned face of Angella above me. Another female face was next to hers. I concentrated on the other face. Weather beaten harsh skin. Commanding expression. No nonsense type of commanding.

The face of Lt. Carrie Malone.

"Nice to have you back with us, Agent Redstone," the voice belonging to Malone said. "Can you sit up?"

She backed away, allowing Angella to help me roll onto my side. Gingerly, under Angella's control, I sat up and slowly swung my legs to the floor. I tried to stand and fell backward onto the bed. I tried again, and this time, with Angella's hand on my back to steady me, I managed to get to my feet and remain upright. My legs were spongy and when I tried to take a step, my knees gave out.

"Perhaps you should sit, Agent Redstone. Seems you were drugged. Get your bearings before you try to walk."

It was, indeed, Lt. Malone, and her eyes were focused on me in a concerned way, much like a parent realizing a child is in trouble.

"What time is it?" I asked, the words coming out in an exaggerated mumble. "Better yet, what day is it?"

"Six in the morning. We let you sleep it off as long as practical. Medics left two hours ago. Your vitals are stable. I didn't think you'd want to spend another night in the hospital."

"Angella!" I blinked several times to be sure I wasn't hallucinating. "What are you doing here? You're supposed to———"

"Long story. Short version, things didn't add up. It started when I tried to call you from the airport. You didn't answer."

"You never called. I don't———"

"I got to thinking. Why was I going all the way to Argentina when the United States, as well as Interpol, has agents stationed down there? I called Tiny and he also didn't answer his phone. I sent him a text and his reply made me agitated. That's what really set me off."

"What did he say?" I asked, my mind suddenly clearing.

"Not so much what, but his language was wrong. Text said, 'Don't piss up the operation. Get on the aeroplane.' Airplane was spelled A-E-R-O. I was certain that text did not come from Tiny. You know the old saying, fool me once, it's on you. Fool me twice, it's on me. I've seen that movie. I was not getting on that plane until I spoke to him——or you——live."

Angella was referring to the time a text message ostensibly from Tiny put us on a plane to a Mexican jungle where we were held captive. "Smart move," I said. "By any chance did you call me when you were coming across the causeway?"

"I did. I left a message."

That was the voice I had heard down in the parking garage. "I heard the message, but I believe from a device in Lillie's purse. So what's going on here? Where the hell's Lillie?"

"You tell me," Angella said. "You're the guy who had a fancy dinner with London Lil the instant I leave town. At *Kranzler's* no less. You certainly didn't waste much time." Her smile said she was faking jealousy, but I wasn't positive it was all an act.

"Who's London Lil?" Malone asked, her pencil ready to copy down my answer.

"A colleague. Based in London."

"I didn't realize Homeland Security had people in London."

"Interpol, actually."

"Interpol? Full name?"

"Lillie Holland. Age, mid-fifties. About five-one, five-two. Short, mousy-brown hair. Oversized glasses."

Malone pulled out her phone, dialed a number and walked out to the living room.

I searched the bed and the floor for my phone and found nothing but a pair of Angella's socks that she must have dropped when she hastily packed.

Malone came back into the room. "You two need to find better colleagues to run with. Nobody with that name, or who fits that description, has checked in or out of any hotel on this island."

"Not surprised," I said. "Not surprised at all."

Angella shot me a quizzical look, but remained silent. She was biding her time, knowing her turn to quiz me would come.

"Anything else missing?" Malone asked. "You've been duped——as well as drugged."

"I'll look and let you know."

"How about looking while I'm here? Makes it easier."

I knew what I'd find missing and I couldn't share the information with Malone. This attack was not isolated from our kidnapping. I knew it, and Malone knew it as well.

"In the last two days you've been kidnapped and drugged. It's time to go on the record with what you're into?"

"I would if I knew."

"Somehow, Redstone, I doubt you would even then."

"Lieutenant, we work for Homeland Security. We're on assignment. Yes, Larson Pettit is somehow involved. I'm not at liberty to say anything further. I'm sorry. But I do appreciate your concern for me. I truly do."

"I get the message, Redstone. I'll get out. But please, please, take care."

I resisted saying, *It's not care I need, but luck*. But the truth was I didn't have to say it. It was written on Malone's face. From her perspective, there was a high likelihood the next time she saw me I'd be a candidate for a body bag.

SEVENTEEN

As soon as the door closed I picked up the apartment phone to call Tiny, only to find the wire cut. I tried the bedroom phone, same results.

I looked around for my car keys and they were missing as well. I ran to the window hoping to catch Malone before she pulled away. No such luck. Her car was halfway down the block and I had no way to stop her.

My computer was in place and so was the hard drive. The data was encoded so that would not have helped anyone. But as I knew it would be, the file Contentus had given me was now gone.

"What time does *Paragraphs on Padre* open?" I asked Angella. I need to call Tiny from a phone that hasn't been compromised. Mine's gone, so I couldn't use it if I wanted to."

"Usually ten." She checked her watch. "Still have over three hours. You look awful and I could use some sleep as well."

It was almost noon when I next opened my eyes. Angella was in the shower and I joined her. By the time we arrived at

Paragraphs it was after one. Griff was working the store by himself and, accommodating man that he is, he gladly lent me his phone. I stepped outside and a moment later Tiny was on the line.

"Heard you went and got yourself high last night," Tiny said when he realized who was calling. "Malone called it in several hours ago. Don't bother with the details now. I assume because this is not your cell, it's gone."

"Correct."

"Then she knows we're onto her."

"What are you talking about?"

"You're lucky to be alive, my friend. That's one nasty———"

"Interpol! Lillie Holland works with us, not against us. What gives?"

"Not Interpol. Actually, not even Lillie Holland. You had dinner with an imposter. Her name is Sally Comings. Known in the trade as Shadowy Sal. She's one of the best, if not the best, in the business. Maybe the best who ever lived."

"Spitting image of Lillie," I said, "mannerisms and all. She does a great imitation. I tested her every way I know how. Usually, I'm not———"

"Surgery and makeup. She's an artist when it comes to impersonations. Even changes her eye color———and sex if need be. She's been doing Lillie for years and was a major problem until Interpol caught on. Kicked Lillie upstairs to a desk job. When Lillie works the field this is what happens. Kapish?"

"No, as a matter of fact I don't understand. She said she knew you———from another life."

"Accurate. Ole Sal and I have had a few run-ins over the years. She's a piece of work if ever there was one. Our files show she was captured months ago. Actually being held as a spy by Iran. Ironically, she was arrested under the name of Lillie Holland and couldn't prove she wasn't Lillie. At one point Iran attempted to trade her back to Britain, but the Brits wouldn't bite. That's why Lillie was allowed to work the field on this investigation. Interpol believes Shadowy Sal is locked up tight. She must have escaped——or been let out. Hey, never said we were perfect. That's why you earn the big bucks."

"But you texted me, telling me she was coming."

"I did nothing of the sort. But, in fact, Lil is coming over. Flight was delayed. She's due any moment, actually."

Despite the text message I had received while I was with the imposter, I actually now believed Tiny. Call me naive. "And while we're on the subject, why the hell aren't you returning my calls?"

"Nothing came in from you," the big man responded. "Want to see the logs? Your phone's now been cut from the network, but I doubt if Sal took it to use. She just took it to delay you from contacting us. Needless to say, Sal has vanished. We're on it, but don't hold out hope. She's a master at disguises. She must have a suitcase full of IDs. What did she get beside your phone?"

"The notes from my prior SOS investigation."

"What's in the notes they want?"

"Anyone's guess," I shrugged. "But she did ask me if I had focused in on anyone. My guess is that the person controlling the money for whatever's going down is the same person who embezzled the funds from SOS. They want to know if we're onto that person."

"Straight with me?"

"Straight."

"Is that why we're running Manhyme and those Texas companies?" Tiny asked.

"I think Manhyme is the key."

"I'll have a new phone delivered within an hour. Log on to the system and everything will be restored. Use the same number as before."

"While you're at it, send one along for Angella as well."

"Angella?"

"Long story. She's here. Never got on the plane to Buenos Aires."

"That's crazy. I got a text from her saying she landed forty minutes ago. How's that possible if she———"

"Our phones have been compromised. Must have done it when they snatched my car. They planned all along for us to get the phones back. The messages are being sent in Angella's name, even though they know she's not there. Does that concern you?"

"Everything concerns me. One of the reason's Holland's on her way over here is that her guy Plevin, after filing the report about Snow, disappeared."

"What the hell else is going on down there?" Another piece of information Tiny had withheld from me. Probably knowing I would have been on the first plane south if I had known earlier.

"That, my dear friend, exhausts my knowledge."

"You're knowledge is never exhausted. Give it to me straight."

"Not on an unsecure line. Log on to the system from your computer. You'll see the plan. New pass code for Lillie will also be there. It's a sequence."

"Does she have any more look-a-likes?"

"If we knew everything, Jimmy, there'd be no need for you." The phone went dead, as it always does when these guys don't want to answer any more questions.

EIGHTEEN

A ngella and I were back at the condo less than fifteen minutes
when the door buzzer went off. It was someone, sounding
exactly like Holland——or Shadowy Sal——downstairs. The
visitor asked to come up. I hadn't yet had time to fire up the
computer to obtain the pass code. "Hold a moment," I replied,
promptly trotting across the room to turn on the computer. I
explained the situation to Angella who took over the computer.

It took longer than I had expected, but finally Angella
retrieved what we had been looking for, a good picture of Lillie.
Her pass code turned out to be a sequence containing a fictitious
delayed flight number, four-sixty-two, the flight that Lillie supposedly had flown on. A flight of four-sixty-anything else meant
she had been compromised. My pass code was a simple, "Missed
that flight once or twice myself."

I went to the speaker and said, "Sorry to keep you waiting.
Are you still there?"

"I most certainly am here," came the reply.

"Sorry, for the delay. I had to put some clothes on."

"Thank the Lord. Now please kindly buzz me onto the lift."

A moment later a woman identical to the picture I held in my hand appeared outside my door. This woman also was an exact image of the woman who had drugged me.

I waved Angella into the bedroom and motioned for her to draw her gun. Cautiously, I opened the door and in Lillie swept, roller bag and all. She may have been a smidgen chunkier than the woman I had dinner with, but other than that they were identical.

Without saying anything in greeting, her first words were, "The loo please? Bladder's failing me."

A few moments later, Lillie Holland——or the woman presenting herself as Lillie Holland——came back into the living room, shoved out her hand and said, "How very nice to meet you in person. Heard you had a rather rough time of it."

"Not a good night, I can assure you. Nice to see you in person——for the second time," I said. Then added, "Have a nice flight?"

"Except for the delay of flight four-sixty-two, everything went well." She busied herself with her bag, not giving any indication she was waiting for a reply from me.

"Seems to be the norm these days," I replied, "missed that flight once or twice myself, as well."

Lillie looked up. "Mind walking a bit? I could use the fresh air."

"First, let me introduce you to Angella."

"Angella? She's in Argentina."

Angella stepped out of the bedroom, her Beretta out of sight. "Change of plans," she said. "Nice to meet you in the flesh."

"We were about to have a walk, stretch the muscles type of thing. Care to join us?"

"We're waiting for a delivery. I'll remain here if you don't mind. Jimmy can fill me in."

"Are you certain?"

"I'll remain here," Angella said uncharacteristically terse.

"We won't be long," I called to Angella. Turning to Holland, I asked, "Do you know about———"

Lillie's finger shot up and crossed her lips. Her head was shaking from side to side.

Outside, she remained quiet until we were two blocks south of my apartment building. We had walked to the end of a street and stepped down a slight embankment, the water from the bay just inches from our toes. A lone duck circled a few feet out, creating a ripple on the otherwise calm water.

Holland began, "This assignment has proven more danger-ous than we at first believed. Snow appears to be in league with a nasty group. My colleague, Barrington Plevin, has gone missing. He's a good agent, former Scotland Yard, knows how to take care of himself in the field. These folks are not to be underestimated."

"I found that out———the hard way."

"Please explain exactly what transpired."

I told Lillie about my encounter with Sally, adding as much detail as I recalled. When I finished, she echoed what Tiny had said. "I'm surprised she allowed you to live. Not her style. Close range stabbing is her specialty, usually accomplished with a com-mon device, such as a pencil or a pen. Her favorite is a nail file."

"I suppose, killing U.S. agents, Homeland Security, FBI, DEA, draws the type of attention these folks don't want, at least they don't want it right now. That's my take," I said, trying to remain on neutral ground with Lillie until I understood where this was going.

"Don't make the mistake of underestimating these cut-throats. If and when you, or I, become a threat to their operation, one or both of us will be found floating somewhere out there." Holland pointed toward the middle of the bay. "Make no mistake about that Mr. Redstone, no mistake at all."

"I received a text from British Airways saying your flight had been delayed. Was that real?"

"It was. It's my practice to add my partners onto the reservation so they are notified of arrival times, that sort of thing. Tiny is on the list as well."

"I thought it was a foul up. That woman is good. She should have been on the stage."

"She is. The world's her stage. She doesn't confine her acting to a theater though. She can imitate just about anyone. Had she been a legitimate actress, she would be rich and famous. She's that good."

"What about size? She's rather small."

"Expert with lifts and in at least one instance she used small stilts. She managed to talk her way into a bank vault posing as the six-foot manager. Make no mistake, she's talented——and ruthless."

"About the phone," I said. "How did she work that?" I thought I knew what had happened, but I wanted confirmation.

"One of her methods is to sabotage the target's phone. She downloads an app or something that lets her take control of incoming calls and messages. She can reroute any outgoing trans-mission."

"Apparently, she didn't think about blocking British Airways."

"She won't make that mistake again. You can be certain of that."

I thought about my calls to Tiny and his denial of receiving them. It now all made sense. My guess had been right. The kidnapper downloaded the nefarious application onto our phones when he took my car. But he had forgotten to take the Contentus file when he was forced to abandon the car quicker than expected.

Back to business. "Do you know a man named Pavel Torres?" I asked. "In Argentina?"

"Heard the name," Lillie replied. "A long time ago. Though I can't recall much about him."

"According to the file Tiny sent, Torres has been asked to look after Angella. Is he with Interpol?"

"Not to my knowledge." She retrieved her cell, typed in data and then said, "We'll know in a jiffy."

"Someone sent a false message about Angella's arrival. Her aborting the flight screwed up their timing."

"Or, my dear sir, that's what they want us to believe."

A fresh southerly breeze came up, causing the bay to churn ever so slightly. We sat on a stone bench, silence between us, allowing the facts, as we knew them, to gel. The silence was broken when Lillie, out of the blue, commented, "Am I right in thinking you have a special relationship with Angella?"

"She's my partner," I responded, off-guard and not knowing where this was going. I don't do well when I'm not in control, and it's been a while since I had any semblance of control.

"You need not pretend with me," Lillie said, sounding more like my grandmother than a colleague. "I agree, some would disapprove of sexual involvement with a partner. My view differs from the conventional. If it doesn't color your actions, then I find a sexual connection a healthy thing indeed. Doing what comes naturally doesn't seem to be such a bad concept. I'm sure you agree."

Lillie and I had to work together and I didn't understand where she was coming from or, for that matter, where she intended to go. It was time to redirect the conversation. "You said earlier you enjoyed being around the water. Do you spend much time on the water? Do you have a favorite activity?"

"Yes, but in an earlier life. After my injury, balance is not what it had been, I'm afraid."

"Injury?"

"In the Sudan. Landmine went off just behind the jeep in which I was riding. Defective sensor or something, otherwise I'd be dead. I lost my hearing for a long while but got it back enough to hear human speech. Mostly in the thousand cycle range. I don't hear much below that and nothing above two thousand. Music, my early passion, is out. Also, knocked my balance to hell. And Bob's your uncle."

"My uncle?"

"A saying. I suppose you'd say, *and there you have it*."

"Sorry about your injury."

"Goes with the territory, as you Americans are wont to say. Just lucky to be alive."

I held up my damaged right hand and said, "I know what you mean."

Lillie changed the direction of the conversation by asking, "The name Manhyme, the one you sent to us. Tell me more about him."

"Involved with a company Wolfson invested in. Company called SOS. If I understood Wolfson correctly, he was the one who suggested she become involved with PAP."

"Go on."

"About three hundred ninety million disappeared from SOS. The president of SOS is serving time in prison. We couldn't trace the money to others then. But now I believe Manhyme is the key to where it went."

"You're spot on. We know of this guy Manhyme, but via several aliases. For a while he limited his…shall we call them investments…to the Middle East. Mostly Lebanon. Mostly arms. He's had major dealings with Iran for the past five years. He was actually licensed by your government at one time." Lillie stopped talking and looked out over the water, but not before her jaw clenched ever so perceptively.

I waited for her to continue, but when she remained silent, I injected myself. "Hit a nerve?"

She slowly swung back to face me. "Not so much a nerve, old chap, but rather a thread. My nemesis, Sally Comings, has——actually still is as you now well know——making a career of espionage by posing as me. She's done untold damage. But, and here is where it gets murky. Manhyme is her half-brother. His money has funded——and most likely still funds——her operations."

"You already knew they were related. Something new just came to you. I can see it."

"Heavens, you're astute, Agent Redstone. Astute, indeed. Not many people have been able to read me over the years."

"I'll bet it took willpower to swallow the end of that sentence."

"Meaning just what might I inquire?"

"Astute, indeed. *For a Yank*," I said, smiling to lessen the impact.

"My, my. Such sensitivities. I've worked with you chaps most of my career and I have nothing but admiration." She paused, a twinkle formed in her eye. "Well, mostly, I should say."

"I trust you'll let me in on your new revelation," I pressed.

"You're not easily distracted, are you?"

"If that's what you're trying to do, I'll wait you out."

"No need. The man who...jumped you here————"

"Ig the Pig."

"Igletz Touchy. He and Sally are brother and sister. This is a Middle East operation all the way. Good chance it's Iran. And when brother and sister work together they are most effective, I'll say that much. This will get a lot more...shall we say...exciting...before it resolves." Holland again studied the water for a long moment. Without looking away, her voice barely audible, she said, "And make no mistake about it, Sally's worse than her brother. They are both smart, as well as ruthless. And, might I add, they make very few mistakes."

"Where does Manhyme fit into the picture?"

"As I said, he's the money guy. Much of what he does can be traced back to Iran in one-way or another. He lurks in the shadows. No criminal record. In fact, it wasn't until recently we even had the connection between the three of them. His background is in banking and corporate financing. Until recently his hands seemed clean and he was welcome in the highest circles."

"So what do you have on him now?"

"We've located several accounts in and out of four countries. Amounts total roughly to what went missing. Without getting into the nitty-gritty of it, Manhyme is associated with it all through various companies————and of course, various names. We now trace these folks using facial software and iris scans, so it's getting much harder for them to avoid detection."

"Any of those companies by chance named after Texas cities?"

Holland closed her eyes, as if in thought. Then she said, "I do believe you are on to something. All, in one way or another,

are controlled by a company called Route Thirty-Five Rollover.
I understand there is a highway thirty-five running north-south
through Texas."

"Bingo! Money came from SOS."

"The prime reason why I'm here is because of activity in those
accounts in recent weeks. Money's gone through three accounts
in two Swiss banks. It's in the Grand Caymans now, with instructions to move it to the Channel Islands. Unless I miss my guess,
it's coming either to the States or to Buenos Aries."

"Why Buenos Aries?"

"Sometimes, as you well know, you ride with your hunches.
Snow's most likely there. Snow is a drug runner, now dressed up
as an expeditor for PAP. You have a wonderful saying. You can put
lipstick on a monkey, but he's still a monkey."

"Pig. It's lipstick on a pig."

"Monkey. Pig. Ox. It's all the same. He's running illegal
drugs."

"PAP's into legal medications, not the hard stuff."

"Wish it were only so," Holland said, correcting me. Unless
I'm cockeyed, PAP's involved with counterfeit medications. Big
business. Profits through the roof. To do it on a large scale a lot
of money, to the tune of about two-hundred-fifty million Euros,
must be injected into the system. That's over three hundred million U.S."

"Matches the amount we're missing."

"Precisely. And what troubles me is that we are following the
money all too easily. It's as if they wanted us to follow it."

"Could they be daring us in some way?"

"Seems so. But for what?" Holland again studied the ebb and
flow of the water. "Are you aware that Larson Pettit was a deck
hand on a tug?"

"I am," I answered, surprised at the question.

"Tug's records show they moved a war ship up to Brownsville for demolition. That was just before Pettit quit his job and went into hiding."

"I'm not connecting the dots." Perhaps it was the drugs still in my system, but I was not following where this was going. "In hiding? Was that why he was in the rehab facility on the island? *Origins?*"

"Exactly."

Holland studied the water for another long period. Long enough for me to wonder if she was watching something out there or just thinking. "You appear troubled," I finally said. "Care to bring me in on the thought process?"

"Oh, sorry. Just put another piece together. Don't yet know what it means."

"And that is?"

"That war ship, and I know this from documents I read about a year ago, had been leased to the Israeli government. U.S. Navy had no further use for it and lent it out for training. The records show it was decommissioned. But in actual fact, the Israel navy trained on it. Now it's being scrapped."

"And Pettit was on the ship while it was being docked and made ready for scrapping. Is that what's troubling you?"

"Not only Pettit, but Touchy as well. That's how we got a lead on him. Break in at the shipyard. His prints were lifted."

NINETEEN

"I must admit it all does seem linked," I reluctantly conceded.

"Bet your jewels it's linked. The Pig breaks into a ship, the same ship a now dead guy was on. The dead guy, as one of his last acts on earth, asks about marine life poisoning by Macrolides. PAP manufactures Macrolides and your guy Snow, a known murderer and drug runner, hires onto PAP. He then surfaces in Argentina."

"Add to that Sally drugging me to get the SOS file and Pettit damn near falling on our heads. And why such a public murder in the air over the island during daylight? Whatever happened to a slit throat in a dark alley in the middle of the night?"

"Sally is a showgirl at heart. She's miserable because her antics are not on public display. She is much like John Wilkes Booth who killed your President and wanted everyone to know about it. He was angry when he wasn't held up as a hero. That said, maybe...just maybe...they required a public demonstration. For what purpose, I certainly don't know."

If Shadowy Sal murdered Pettit, then I indeed was lucky to be alive.

Obviously, Holland had the same thought. "Comings allowed you to live for a reason. I'm thinking it has to do with Angella being in Argentina."

"What's the connection?"

"You dead would mean Angella coming home. They must feel comfortable with her being down there."

I was now very much concerned for Angella. Even though she was home, it never bodes well when a law enforcement person is targeted. "If you're right that Pettit's killing was set up the way it was so that we would get involved, then someone has been tracking Angella and me."

"You two walk the beach every day? At the same time?"

Actually, we do. It's part of our daily routine. "Probably, within a few minutes on any given day."

Lillie smiled. "That sort of explains the parachute. They could have done it lots of ways. But given Sally's propensity for the dramatic, and her apparent desire to embed you two into it, it fits."

"Any thoughts as to why?"

"Perhaps you know something——or have something—— they want."

"Can't imagine what it would be." Now it was my turn to study the water. Nothing came to me, so I asked, "Next steps?"

"We need to play this with the knowledge that they want Angella in Argentina. So, let's not disappoint them. We'll send Angella down. She knows they want her. We can play with that."

I translated Holland's comment to mean we were bait being fed to the sharks. Knowledge only works in your favor when you use it wisely. I also couldn't get it out of my mind that Snow was in Argentina. The last thing I wanted was Angella going down there without me. "I suppose you have a plan worked out," I said, trying to appear cooperative while throwing barriers up as fast as I could think of them. "Good people assigned to cover her. Will the locals be in agreement and supportive of the operation?"

Holland looked away, again studied the water as if she wished she was out there. I gave her all the time she required, all the while realizing that agents who have worked in the field as long as she had didn't need this much time to think, they have the scenarios worked out before they begin the conversation. Something definitely was troubling her.

Finally she said, almost by way of apology, "Protection does present a problem, to tell the truth. We have reason to believe our local agents have been compromised. We'll need help from the U. S."

"Sounds to me like you need help from the Argentine government, not from American Homeland Security. This is a formula for disaster, if you ask me."

"Not really an option, now is it? We have PAP, a U. S. company, manufacturing drugs in Argentina, with an indication they might be doctored, pardon the pun. We also have about a half-billion dollars financing something that is potentially devastating. We can't very well ignore the signs because we're scared of a little action."

"That all begs the question. Going in blind is never a good option. And it seems that is what is on the table." Angella and I as bait again leaped to mind.

"Up to now, it's been logistical, not tactical. We're moving into a new phase."

"Mind elaborating?"

Again, Holland looked out over the water. When she finally spoke, her voice was conspiratorially low. "What I'm about to tell you is classified. I know you're cleared. But I've not been given the go-ahead by Interpol to share this with anyone outside Interpol."

"Go ahead."

"Keep it private?"

"Yes."

"Our communications with Interpol agents in Argentina often find their way into the wrong hands. Money laundering and drug movement, to name a few vices, are rampant. Every time we close in on a source the investigation is diverted. An account is suddenly closed, an informant disappears, often found with his neck slashed a few days later. That sort of behavior." She paused, as if to signify that the secret stuff was about to be shared. Her voiced lowered even further, "We have turned a few of their folks and now know that the corruption is near the top——if not at the top. That means nothing and nobody can be trusted."

"And you want Angella——and I——operating in that mess?"

"We know from our sources that they, whoever *they* are, are aware of Angella's presence, or supposed presence, in Argentina. We also know they want her alive——at least for a while. That works in her favor."

"Only until it doesn't! With no protection, she's vulnerable to whatever their whims are at any particular moment."

Ignoring my comment, Holland continued. "They are into mutant pharma. We know that from the work that kid, Hildigo Francese, the one from the Coastal Studies Lab, did. Your government has leaked information making it seem that the sharks ingested drugs dumped by Mexican illegals. In point of fact, the drugs were mutants brought north from Buenos Aires by a highly trained group of people. We, I mean the U. S. Coast Guard work-ing a task force with your ATF, were following the vessel carrying the mutant drugs. Shortly before the ship was to be boarded by the Coast Guard, an order came down from the ship's bridge to flush the cargo. That was no coincidence. Someone high up sent a signal. Our sources tell us that there was less than a kilo put into the water. You know about the devastation that kilo caused. Imagine what would happen if an entire cargo hold were to be dumped. We can't take a chance on it happening."

Holland again went silent, but I sensed she wasn't finished.

"Now that we know Sally and her deadly brother are involved, we know that factions in the Middle East, possibly Lebanon or Iran, most likely are also involved."

While Lillie was talking, a thought began to gel deep in the background. I could feel it, but couldn't bring it front and center.

Holland added, as if to highlight how important our mission was, "And let's not overlook my missing partner. We need to get down there and bring him out. He's a good man."

Why, I wondered, wasn't the British government, or Interpol itself, working that issue? I was about to confirm my suspicions that Angella was really supposed to be protecting Playboy Plevin, but I stopped short when I realized that at the mention of her partner, Holland's chin quivered for the briefest of moments.

Agents, especially ones as highly trained and experienced as Lillie Holland, know how to hide their real emotions, even from someone such as myself who has spent a lifetime reading people. What they project is what they want us to take away. My take away: Lillie and Barrington spend their quiet time together. And she wanted me to know it, but didn't desire to discuss it. This in spite of the fact she had not hesitated to voice her opinion on Angella's and my relationship.

"Frankly, Jimmy, I don't have faith in Interpol getting him out of there——not alive anyway. Too much money is involved. The U. S. can pull it off. The Argentine authorities may not like your country, not many do, but they respect the fact that America protects its own. Two eyes for an eye type of thing. They'll not overtly harm Angella. Your government will extract too high a price."

"You're speaking of the official Argentine government. But the Pig and his sister are mercenaries, in it for the money. They'll slash her throat without thinking twice." The thought of it made me shudder.

TWENTY

Holland's phone rang.

She handed her cell to me with a puzzled looked.

"Care to explain how you managed to get yourself drugged?" Contentus began the instant I said hello.

I mouthed to Holland that it was Miller Contentus, my former boss at the Texas Rangers. She didn't know—or pretended not to know——what I was talking about. To Contentus, I replied, "Impersonator dumped something in my coffee. I came back from the head to find coffee on the table. I drank it with dessert. Easy as that. My bad."

"I suppose she took the file. You didn't report it gone to Lt. Malone, but she had to be after something more than your phone."

"It's good to know your power of reasoning is as keen as ever," I quipped. Contentus didn't get to the top of the Texas Rangers being slow-witted. Neither did he get there by booking crap from people like me. But I no longer worked for him, so I had some latitude——but, as Angella had reminded me, probably not as much as I thought I had. "I think they were after the file when they dumped us on the beach."

"Any idea what's in there they're after?"

"Best guess. A name. They want to know if we've stumbled onto someone sensitive to them. Most likely a guy by the name of Manhyme. Any chance of sending me———"

"You kidding me?" Contentus shot back, even before I could finish my request. "Against regulations. Chain of evidence type of thing. You know better than to ask." He was speaking so loud that Holland could hear his every word.

"Just thought I'd try."

"Retrace your steps. Start with Coastal Studies, but wait until morning." The line went dead.

"Is that chap always abrupt?" Lillie asked when the phone went dead. "Man could have, how do you say it, cut you some slack." She began dialing her cell phone. "I'll request the file through the FBI."

"Don't bother. He was covering his ass. We'll have the file in the morning."

"You know that for certain?" she said, terminating the connection.

"His typical response is a 'no', with no explanation. When he gives a reason, even a bogus one like chain of evidence, he's covering his butt. Playing to the crowd, so to speak. He's been doing it that way for as long as I've known him. The replacement will be at the Coastal Studies Lab in the morning."

While I was speaking with Contentus, my elusive thought began to form more cogently. The problem was my mind was groggy. Not now, but at the time in question. We, Shadowy Sal and I, were in the garage waiting for the elevator. I recall hearing Angella's voice leaving a message on my cell telling me she was on the causeway. That's why Sal cut her time with me in the apartment. She had only minutes to find the file and get out before Angella would arrive.

My mind had been replaying what Angella had said, concentrating on getting the wording right. Something was wrong, but until now I had not been able to place what it was. I had been listening to an intercepted cell phone message, but I only heard Angella's voice and not my own answering message. It was as if I had been listening to the speech side of the conversation and not to what she heard.

I borrowed Holland's phone and called Angella. She confirmed that she indeed had left the message only after hearing my message instructing her to do so. "You certain it was my answering message? My voice."

"Certain. Why?"

"I heard your message when I was drugged, just before getting on the elevator. But I didn't hear my message being played to you."

"Are you certain a redirected call would have both messages?"

I thought about that possibility before responding. "Not positive of anything," I admitted. "Perhaps not. How would it only have one side?"

"That technology is beyond me. Sorry. Did Contentus get to you? I gave him Lillie's phone number. Your replacement phone just arrived and I downloaded your info from the main server. You're good to go."

Next I called Tiny to tie up another loose end. "So why did you lie about the boots?" I asked, confronting him directly. "McNaughton says mine didn't come from her."

"And you believe her?"

"No reason not to. Are you denying they came from you?"

"Better take it up with Mommy Long Legs. They didn't come from me."

"This is wasting time. You have any further information on Wolfson or Manhyme?"

"Everything. And nothing. All trails go cold. The guy has no past, if you believe the records, yet he's into every phase of the SOS deal and a hell of a lot of other deals. All seem to lose money, go into bankruptcy or get sold. Interpol has a long history of him under other names. Still working it."

So far, what he just told me correlates with what Holland had said. "So what's *everything* mean?"

"In every deal, there are a series of buys and sells, same pattern as the SOS transaction. All the companies involved are named after cities in the state where the target company is located. And all the companies are gone right after the transaction. Except... except one of the deals was in Nevada. It involved a casino. They had to provide background checks. There are prints on file——and detailed information. I'll be back to you when I get the results."

"I need that info by morning."

"Not where you're going."

The director has authorized you and Angella to work the Argentina piece. Others will tackle the files up here. You're leaving tomorrow."

"What about Lillie?"

"She's going with you."

"That's not what I meant. The fingerprint I sent. Is she confirmed?"

"Don't trust anyone, do you?"

"I trusted Lillie——Sally——and I got drugged——almost killed——for my efforts." I had obtained a print from a water glass Lillie, the second Lillie, had used in my condo. I wanted foolproof confirmation of who she is.

"Not easy to match. Her prints are blocked. I had to call in a favor. The bottom line is it's a perfect match."

"You positive?"

"As positive as you can be in this business. Look, everything we do is subject to government control. If they want to doctor fingerprints, DNA, voiceprints, iris scans, they can do it. We live——and literally die——on their databases. Kapish?"

"Any leads on Slippery Sal?" I asked, not following Tiny down the rat hole he was leading me into.

"Gone. Woman evaporated. Found the nail file she used on Pettit. His blood's on it. No prints though. Sally is most definitely the killer. But I suppose you knew that."

"Found where?"

"In the trash can outside your condo. Police speculate she threw it there after leaving you."

I had been thinking about the nail file ever since I learned of her propensity for killing with such objects. The chilling realization I had come to was that she had been taunting me when I had returned from the men's room at Kranzler's.

She had been filing her nails.

TWENTY-ONE

An hour later, after briefing Angella back in our condo, a thought struck me and I called Tiny to set up interviews with the folks over at the Brownsville docks. I wanted to know more about what had gone down over there. The information in the file that Tiny had provided was skimpy at best.

After going around with Tiny on getting this done, I lost my patience. "Tiny," I said, my voice rising along with my anger, "stop with the hard time on this, and get it done! We don't have much time before our flight leaves and I want to interview those folks before we take off. Kapish?"

"Believe me, I'm not the hold up. You hit a sensitive spot, perhaps jurisdictional, I don't know. What I do know is the powers that be said no. Spelled, H-E-L-L N-O!"

"Let me put it so the *powers that be* understand where I'm coming from. Angella and I won't be on that plane to Buenos Aires unless and until we interview the Brownsville Harbormaster as well as the security folks who intercepted Igletz Touchy.

I've read the FBI reports and, frankly, there are areas…I'll be polite…that are still…fuzzy."

"You draw a line in the sand; you throw your career away. Not a smart move. Kapish?"

"The government's asking me to lay my life on the line; I need to know the facts first hand. The only real linkage we have is that the Pig was caught breaking into a decommissioned military vessel at the scrap yard. The only link to PAP is that Pettit was also on that boat. Hell, lots of other people were on the same boat. That proves nothing!"

"Pettit was asking about medicated fish. Pettit was also killed, most likely, by the Pig's sister. The link is tight. Get your ass on that plane south and stop trying to second guess the brass!"

"I need to hear it firsthand."

"You've read the interview summaries. Nothing more there. Get over it."

"Then why the hold up?"

"Jurisdictional feud."

"Get them lined up. I'm leaving for Brownsville now. We pass the docks on our way to the airport. I'll do it cold if need be."

"Not advisable,"Tiny said, the line going dead.

- - - - - -

The closer our car came to the Port of Brownsville the angrier I became. I had no intention of being turned away at the gate by some overweight jackass employed by the shipyard to keep the riffraff out. I was determined to interview at least the Harbormaster and I wouldn't take no for an answer.

I wasn't focused on what Angella was saying, but out of the corner of my eye I took note that she was pointing off to my left to several oil platforms, positioned in the Brownsville ship channel. From what I had been told, the huge platforms were being constructed in sections by workers at the sprawling Keppel Amphels facility. Random flashes of bright light were visible amid the multi-story structures. Two freighters were tied up, one in front of the other, waiting to be reduced to scrap parts. One was fully intact while the bridge of the other had already been cut down.

"Jimmy! Pay attention! You've just blown past the entrance!" Angella admonished.

"What? It's still up ahead."

"I don't think so. I was out here a few years ago and as I recall you go in through the gate back there."

"I thought the entrance was closer to Brownsville. Big sign up ahead says Port of Brownsville. Turn is off to the right."

"I don't know where that goes, but I do know that you can get to the scrap yard through the entrance you just raced past. The ship reclamation docks are just beyond Amphels." She pointed off to the left and sure enough the hulk of a massive military vessel was now visible, its paint peeling. Part of its upper bridge works missing.

I made a quick U-turn and headed back east.

"Give him a chance," Angella cautioned. "I know you expect a hard time getting in, but give him a chance to show his colors."

"What are you talking about?" I barked. "Give who a chance?"

"The guard. The way you're behaving he'd be within his rights to arrest you the moment you bark at him. Just show him our credentials and if he asks what you're here for simply say you're here to inspect the docks. Be best if you stow that scowl as well."

"I'm not scowling!"

"Try smiling."

A large truck was blocking the entrance side of the guard shack. A tall, lanky guy, no more than twenty years old waived our car around to the left of the small brick building. He approached the passenger window and leaned down, waiting for Angella to open the window. Either he owned the sharpest razor in the world, or the kid had no facial hair.

Angella did exactly as she had instructed me to do; only her smile was genuine. "Homeland Security," she announced. "Here to inspect the docks." She thrust her shield into his face and motioned to me to hold mine up for him to see as well.

The young man blinked a few times, then stood and turned, obviously seeking guidance. He nodded in the direction of his partner who was busy arguing with the truck driver. A line of cars trying to leave the grounds was beginning to form ahead of me.

After about a minute of being ignored by his partner, the rosy-cheeked guard turned back to Angella, shrugged his shoulders, and waived us into the yard.

"Now where?" I asked, refusing to acknowledge the ease with which she had pulled that off.

"Make your way toward the military ship. I assume that's the Yellowstone over there. There only seems to be one. The other is merchant marine. The people we want shouldn't be far off."

This was Angella's day——or so it seemed. No sooner had we stepped out of the car, but a dark-complexioned man in his sixties, with gray hair and the trace of a mustache, approached. "I'm Ceceros Olivia, Superintendant of the yard. I understand you're here to inspect the docks. Wasn't informed you were coming. But, hey, that's a typical government operation. Most certainly you are welcome, provided, of course, your credentials are in order." The smile belied an underlying seriousness.

Olivia took his time reading, then rereading, our shields, even going so far as to match the numbers against the printed documentation. He reminded me of a baseball manager who stomps around on the mound with an errant pitcher, giving the reliever a few more minutes to warm-up. Was this guy stalling until reinforcements arrived?

Nothing in his manner suggested he was doing anything other than satisfying himself——or satisfying some government regulation——that all was in order. I didn't see anybody coming, but as I well know, they can fall out of the sky——or suddenly appear from under the water——if need be. My fists clenched in anticipation of trouble.

"You say you're here to inspect the docks," Olivia said, handing us our credentials. "What exactly are you inspecting?"

Angella must have sensed my renewed agitation. Without waiting for me to respond, she said, "We understand there was a break-in some time back. An unauthorized person on board the Yellowstone." She nodded in the direction of the destroyer tender tied next to us. "Can you tell us what happened?"

"Is that what this is about? Should have known. Poke the nest and the bees start streaming. Been no end of government types coming around since that guy was found on board AD-41." Seeing my puzzled look, he added, "Yellowstone. Commissioned in 1975. In commission only a short while. We had a sister ship, AD-44, the Shenandoah, in here some years back. See that pile over there? That's what's come off forty-one so far. All under contract to the Navy."

"So," I said, "who poked the nest?"

"Some foreign type. Middle-East if you ask me. Pulled a knife and would have cut Santos's throat if security hadn't happened along."

"Santos? Is that the guy who found him?" I knew that much from the reports, but wanted Olivia's take on the situation.

"He's one of the best cutters working in the yard. Listen, I'm not the person to talk to about what happened. I was up in my office," he said, indicating a modest cinder-block structure about 100 yards away. "Didn't see anything. All I know is what I've been told."

"Who should we talk with then?" Angella asked, smiling her most pleasant smile.

"Best talk with the two men involved. Santos and Grainger."

"Is Grainger the security guy?" I asked. The name Grainger had not appeared in any of the reports.

"Happens to be on duty today. Come with me and I'll call him over."

"What about the guy Santos?"

"Doesn't work for me. Don't know if he's working today. I suspect he is. Guy needs the money desperately. Works as much overtime as he can get. Has eight kids to support, along with a sick mother. He's also helping his brother out."

"Let's try Santos first." When possible, I prefer my interviews to follow the chronological order of the events.

"If he's here that should not be a problem." We had reached the block building and Olivia took us inside and showed us to a small room just inside the front door. "Wait here, I'll see what I can rustle up. No promises."

"Pleasant man," Angella commented when the door closed. "Put your fears to rest."

"Wonder who all interviewed these folks," I said. "We know about the FBI. I also believe there was a Navy report. Internal security type of thing. But Santos's allusion to swarming bees tells me there were more than two groups."

It took about twenty minutes and I was about to go find Superintendent Olivia when the door opened and a stooped-shouldered, weather-beaten old man shuffled into the room. "I'm Santos. You want me?"

We introduced ourselves and asked him to have a seat.

"Stand. Get back to work. On break. Minutes count."

"This won't take long. Is Santos your first or last name?"

"Santos is all."

Our talk with him was unofficial, so it wasn't worth wasting time getting the name correct. "Okay, Santos, tell us about the man you found on forty-one."

"Told them already. I was looking at work we had to do. Inventory, you call it. In radio room. Electronics. I was coming out. The man came in."

"Describe the man."

"Dark hair. Slick. *Significa hombre.*"

"What happened?"

"Nothing then. I was down the deck when he came after me. Grabbed me on the shoulder."

Santos then swiveled his head quickly, as if to tell us that the man, the Pig, from his description and from what he had told earlier investigators, had grabbed him and spun him around. That fact was not in any of the reports. "He spun you around?"

"*Si.* Knife." Santos ran his finger across his neck. There was no mistaken the universal gesture. The Pig had threatened to cut his throat. "Yelling about a radio."

"A radio? He wanted a radio?"

"Missing. He said I had it."

"Did you have a radio?"

"Never!" Santos checked his watch, then took a step toward the door.

"Was a radio missing?"

"*Sí*. Missing when I came."

"Go on."

"Angry. Cut my throat. Security stopped him."

"Is that Grainger?"

"*Sí señor*. Saved my life." He again checked his watch. "Señor, please. Have little ones to support. Sick mother. Back to work?"

"One last question. Did the man you see have a scar on his face? Under his eye?"

"*Sí señor. Significa hombre.*"

"You can go. Thank you for coming."

The door closed behind Santos when I thought of a question. I caught up to him just outside the building. "Santos," I called, "one more quick question."

The old man turned to face me, unspoken annoyance radiating from him.

"Do you have any idea where the radio went?"

"*Sí señor*. Deckhand took it."

"What deckhand?"

"No name I know. Saw picture on TV. Dead."

"The deckhand is dead?"

"*Sí señor*. Dead. Jump from plane. Dead."

"The deckhand who took the radio is the man who died on South Padre Island in the parachute?"

"*Sí señor.*"

"That will be all, Santos."

"*Gracias*," Angella added.

"So it seems Touchy was looking for a radio that Pettit had already taken," Angella said.

"What the hell kind of radio would Pettit steal?"

"Obviously one Larson Pettit thought was important," Angella responded.

"Reports just say radio. Nothing specific."

"Reports also say nothing about Pettit having it."

Reports are either withholding information or...or no one thought to ask Santos where the radio was.

"My money's on withholding," Angella said, "Goes with the territory.

"Certainly, Santos doesn't know either. I'll bet Grainger doesn't know any more about the radio than he does."

Indeed, our interview with Nevelle Grainger was a waste of time. He happened to be walking the deck when he came upon Igletz Touchy holding a knife to Santos' throat. Pulled his weapon and the Pig ran down the steps to the next deck and then jumped over the side into the ship channel. He was gone before help arrived. The Pig's prints were found on the railing.

TWENTY-TWO

Once again Angella and I were on a military flight, this time non-stop from Brownsville to Ezeiza International Airport, Argentina. We were alone in our section, separated from the other passengers by a locked door. I assumed those in the other compartment were military and perhaps diplomatic folks. The idea, as I understood it, was to insert us in the country with no one being the wiser. I wasn't thrilled about the plan because that would effectively make us fugitives unable to call upon the locals for help. Of course, that arrangement also allows our bosses to disavow any knowledge of our activities.

Protocol———or some such bureaucratic double-speak——— prevents the military from transporting Interpol agents. So, while Lillie Holland's commercial flight from Brownsville took off within fifteen minutes of ours, the wait time in Houston for the connecting flight delayed her arrival until mid-morning tomorrow, almost ten hours after we were on the ground.

Our flight was top notch. We were offered a wonderful steak dinner together with all the wine we cared to consume. I then took a nap.

"Time to put on your seat belts, folks," the cabin steward announced, his manner much more formal than called for. Whether or not he knew our names, I didn't know. The bulkhead clock, showing local time, now read midnight. It was indeed dark below us.

I don't suppose it is a coincidence that military flights, even unmarked ones such as ours, land when the airport is all but closed. We were instructed to remain in our cabin until the other passengers deplaned. When all was clear an escort would come for us we were told. They were taking every precaution to keep our identities private. Again, plausible deniability was working to our disadvantage.

Angella was just opening her eyes and I waited a few minutes to give her time to adjust to where she was.

She blew me a kiss.

I resisted the temptation to pull her close. Instead, I made do with a mouthed, *I love you*.

"So, big guy, what have you been up to?" she asked, realizing I had been awake for a while.

"A bit of sleep and some thinking. I mentally reviewed my SOS notes and I still can't imagine why they would go to so much trouble to lift them."

"Perhaps, Jimmy, if we knew who *they* were it would help."

"FBI is going to re-interview Raymond Prinz up in Dalhart, see if——"

"Refresh me on who Prinz is."

"Raymond Prinz was the President of SOS. The guy who transferred all that money out of the company. He's serving twenty years. I'm convinced he was duped. Manhyme is the guy who should be in prison. I make him for the brains. Wolfson's also most likely a dupe, but I can't be certain. The woman's a bit of a puzzle."

"Didn't you tell me you had nothing on Manhyme?"

"His lawyers have blocked meaningful conversation with him. Claims harassment. We have little to go on, and certainly not enough to arrest him. Interpol might now have enough to obtain a warrant, but I doubt it."

A flight attendant, a woman in her mid-fifties, I had not seen earlier came by. I guessed she had been working the other cabin. "I've been admiring your boots," she said to me. "Where did you get them?"

"Gift from a friend," I replied, stretching to retrieve them from the aisle. I only hoped my feet hadn't swollen to a point where they would be uncomfortable. Angella had wisely kept hers on her feet.

"Some friend! Hand tooled. My father was a boot maker. He's been gone a while now, but good leather craftsmanship is in my DNA. I love that hand scrolling. It took my father a lifetime to learn the craft. Both of you should wear them well, and in good health. Now let's get those seat backs and trays up and seat belts in place. East coast, Buenos Aires especially, is my favorite part of Argentina. Enjoy your time here. Just don't go wondering around to the bad parts."

"Such as?"

"Such as *Constitucion*. And *Avenida Colon*, particularly at night. Very poor areas. High crime as you might expect."

"Thanks," is all I could say. I had no doubt our time in Argentina was going to be anything but enjoyable.

- - - - -

I had been warned to be cautious of the cabs, so Tiny had ordered a private car to take us the fourteen miles into the heart of the city. But even with a private car, I was on guard. I had the driver circle around until I spotted *Avenida Corrientes*. I then asked him to drive us several blocks away before having him let us out. I didn't want him to know which hotel we were staying at. He was astute enough to know what we were doing and not happy about dropping us.

Under cross-examination, he finally assured us it was safe to walk. He then gratuitously added that it would be best if we allowed him to take us to, as he put it, our place for the night.

Declining his offer, we climbed out of the town car and walked in silence for several moments.

Angella said, "I suppose you're trying to insure no one knows where we're staying. But is this the best way?"

"That's the plan. First we walk over to where Snow was last seen. Thirty-one-thirty Corrientes Avenue to be exact. Then we find a hotel as close as possible. No advance planning. Just a random selection. That way, no one knows where we are and we can sleep with all four of our eyes closed."

"Lead the way. Thanks for the heads up about packing light. Dragging a heavy bag all over creation this time of night is not my idea of fun."

I had memorized the map of this area and Snow's apartment complex was not hard to find. Of course, we had no way of knowing if he was still there; if he was ever there; or if he was even in Argentina. But this was the best we had for now and Snow was the only real entry into this investigation——if indeed it was an entry at all.

The apartment was across the street from the massive *Abasto* shopping center, a low slung building housing a myriad of stores and shops. Midway down the block we passed *Hotel Abasto*. On the internet they called themselves the home of Tango. A dance floor in every room. I had never stayed in a hotel room with a dance floor and was curious what it looked like.

"Dance floor," Angella exclaimed. "How does that work?"

"Up for finding out? Or should we keep looking?"

"As good as the next, I suppose," Angella replied, not thrilled about the hotel.

So we pushed through the massive front door and entered a lobby that was mostly deserted. Behind the desk sat a lean clerk, his eyes closed, black ear buds in each ear, head gyrating like a bobble doll.

I tapped on the counter and he instantly jumped to his feet and plastered a massive smile on his bony face. *"Bienvenido al Hotel Abasto, el Señor y la Señora,"* he said, rubbing his eyes. *"¿Le gente prefiere una habitación?"*

"Sí, por favor. Algo agradable. Prohibido fumar," Angella said.

He studied his computer screen for the longest time. I didn't know if he had rooms, or if he didn't want us to register.

"Tengo una habitación en el décimo piso, lejos del ascensor. Voy a necesitar una tarjeta de crédito y su pasaporte."

Angella handed him the passports and a credit card from the identity package provided to us when we landed.

He made a pretense of studying our papers, then again said, *"Bienvenido al Hotel Abasto el Señor y la Señora. De Plata. El ascensor está a través del vestíbulo. Habitación treinta y cinco en el décimo piso. ¿Hay algo más que usted desea?"*

"No, eso será todo. Muchas gracias Senor," Angella responded.

"Por favor, disfrutar de su estancia con nosotros."

Riding up in the tiny elevator, I asked Angella, "What was all that about? Sounded like you gave him our life history."

"He just wished us a pleasant visit. Who dreams up these names? Mr. and Mrs. Silver? Jesse and Anna, no less."

"Keeping track of what name you are using at any given time must be a burden to real spooks."

"Tiny seems to do it just———"

I held up my finger, indicating we should pick this up in our room.

"Can't wait to see the room," Angella said, following my lead. "Maybe we can have private Tango lessons. You can buy me fishnet stockings if you're in the mood for buying presents."

"I saw the store in the lobby. They have a full range of dresses and outfits. Are you serious? Not my thing."

"We can make it your thing. We can learn together."

"You kidding me? You'll need a trigger finger faster than mine if you think I'll take dance lessons."

"No one has a faster———" Angella paused. "Sorry, didn't mean it that way." Red streaks formed on her neck. "I just meant I don't think I can ever pull the trigger on another human."

"They draw you down, you better shoot. Just picture yourself laying on a metal slab, buck naked, a hole through your forehead, a name tag tied to your big toe."

"You certainly have a way with words."

"Just trying to keep you———and me———alive. If you hesitate, one of us will be dead."

"Enough of this. This talk agitates me. You mentioning spooks on the elevator brought Tiny to mind. I expected to hear from him when we landed."

"Actually, I did when you were occupied at the desk. His guy Pavel Torres claims Snow hasn't left his room."

"Not likely," Angella responded, sounding cynical. "He's not one to sit. That man's got to keep moving."

"Torres is either in league with him," I said, "or Snow has another way out."

Angella surprised me by responding, "I'm betting on both, actually. What do we know of this guy Torres?"

"Won't bet against you. He's a friend of Tiny. Guessing CIA or equivalent. But Lillie Holland didn't know him. I thought Interpol knew everyone."

"That's what they'd like you to think. But they're no better than the rest of us. If it isn't in a database then they don't know it. Period."

"That woman gives me...well, I'm not comfortable around her. Let's just leave it at that." Angella's voice held a snippiness that I had not heard before. I chalked it up to lack of sleep.

"Either you're tired——or jealous."

"This is not jealousy! She's...well, off a bit. I can't put my finger on it, but she's off."

"She's concerned about her missing partner. From things she said, my take is they're lovers. When you had your...encounter with Snow, I was *off* as well."

"Don't remind me. I never want to see that man again—— or even hear his voice. I had nightmares about him for weeks. And here I am, hunting for him."

For my part, I wanted to find the snake. I owed him a bullet through his nether parts. But I kept that thought to myself. Changing the subject, I said, "Tiny also says they located where PAP is manufacturing azithromycin."

"How hard is that? They have to report all manufacturing activity and locations to the FDA for inspections and stuff like that. Let me see what his text said."

She took my cell, studied the message, then said, "The word manufacturing is in quotes. Suppose he's signaling he believes the

manufacturing location is where the legal drugs are being modified?"

"That scientist type we spoke with on the island. He said———"

"Hildigo Francese."

"Francese said the drugs were modified. So you're right, it
fits."

"That means they're hiding it from the FDA. Maybe that's
what Snow's mission is. Expediting the modification."

"Let's work it in the morning," I said. "It's nearly three. I'm
exhausted."

"Body time, one," Angella reminded me. "But who's keeping
track. I slept well on the flight. I'll work the file for a while."

"Good night," I called, slipping into the bathroom. "Pleasant
dreams."

TWENTY-THREE

You can be good or you can be lucky. Lucky trumps good. I awoke from a sound sleep with a sharp pain in my stomach. I tossed from side to side for a few moments before I was awake enough to realize the pain was real and not a dream.

I threw the covers off, thinking that if my body cooled down the pain would subside.

But it only grew worse.

Heart attack? Appendix?

Something I ate? Drank? Gas? The water I brushed my teeth with? Then I remembered I had been thirsty when I was preparing for bed, perhaps brought on by the dry air in the plane. Whatever the reason, I had consumed two glasses of water just before falling into bed.

Foolish. I know better.

I rolled over, preparing to get out of bed and go to the head. My hope was that the pain would pass and I would not require medical assistance. Diarrhea would be bad enough. How would going to the hospital work with me not actually being in the country? I wondered who Jesse Silver was, the person whose name I was now using. I hope he wasn't on the world's most wanted list. I am finding that the CIA, or whoever is controlling this mission, sometimes has a strange sense of humor.

My feet hit the floor and at the same time I heard the unmistakable click of the hall door latch opening. The door had a safety chain, but it would be no deterrent to a top professional. Nothing seemed to stop those folks.

I reached for my gun, which I always position on the bedside table on the right side of the bed. A habit I had formed as a young cop. My fingers closed on empty air. Belatedly, I remembered the drill. Our weapons were to be delivered in the morning. Military planes are not allowed to unload arms in the country. The exception was uniformed military personnel entering the country under specific invitation of Argentina. I certainly wasn't even close to that requirement.

I focused my hearing, but everything was now quiet.

Maybe I was dreaming? Hearing sounds that weren't, in fact, real? Possibly from another room? Another floor?

The muffled sound of what I took to be the chain being cut again captured my attention. I still could not be certain it was our room, but the odds were stacked against us.

The pain in my stomach caused me to double over. Gas passed. The pain eased a bit.

Angella was dead to the world in the other bed a step away. To awaken her without sound would require me to move close to her, making us easy targets. Even then it was doubtful I could get her fully awake without some verbal communication. Separation would be best.

The intruder———or intruders———had to negotiate past the entrance to the bathroom and across the wooden dance floor before coming into the bedroom area. Their eyes would be focused on the beds. I quickly placed two pillows under the sheet on my bed trying to make it look as though I was still tucked in. Not a good job, but in the dim light the intruder would see what he expected to see and would check it off as safe.

I moved as far from Angella as possible and flattened myself against the wall, breathing as slow and shallow as I could. The gas pain———or whatever it was———momentarily forgotten.

I waited.

And so did our night crawler.

There was no light from the hall, and no shadows, so I couldn't tell if the visitor was inside the room or in the hallway. I assumed in the room. If indeed it was our room being entered.

In the silence, Angella's breathing was rhythmic, breaking in and out of light snoring. I could clearly see her body rising and falling with every breath. The pillows stuffed under the sheets in the other bed were stone still———and silent.

A professional would know I was out of bed. So the question is, will he leave or continue with his plan? The plan could be a simple robbery. Grab a watch, a wallet, a passport, and be gone. This is one time I was hoping for a common thief.

But nothing valuable was visible. So if robbery was the motive, the thief would have already sized up the situation and been out of here. On the other hand, if the instructions were to eliminate us, the plan would only now be starting.

From my memory, even though the beds were in a separate alcove, they were visible from a few steps inside the doorway. So, if we were to be executed by gun at least two bullets would already have been fired. If noise was the concern, silencers would have been employed.

Close-in killing then became my focus. And in this situation it worked to our advantage——so far.

Shadowy Sal was a known close-in killer. If the intruder was Sally then she would have the killing weapon——most likely a thin bladed knife——in her right hand. That would be the hand closest to me when she cleared the wall barrier.

On the other hand, if this was Ig the Pig, most likely he was after Angella. He had held the knife in his left hand the last time, but that might have been for convenience in the car.

I heard nothing. And nothing was moving.

But then I smelled her. Faint, but real. That same distinctive scent I had first noticed back on the island over dinner at *Kranzler's*. One of the no-nos I had learned in Ranger training was absolutely no after-shave, or chemicals of any sort, were to ever be used. Ever! They linger on your skin, even after repeated washings. Our tracker dogs were trained to react to such scents.

Judging from Sally's scent, I estimated we were mere inches apart. I saw no shadow and felt no movement, but still I didn't dare move any part of me for fear of throwing my own shadow.

But if I could smell her, was the reciprocal true? I hadn't used anything other than soap on my body. But then I recalled the soap I had washed my face with had been the hotel's soap. And it had been scented.

My supposition is that the intruder knew where I was.

The only question now was who would move first? At any second I expected the knife to come around the corner and slash my left side. She knew my height and would go for my neck, or possibly my genitalia.

Even a false lunge on her part in the direction of my groin would provoke an involuntary cover-up movement on my part. That would expose my body to a lethal slice across the neck. I was in an untenable position.

Before I could act, she made her move. I heard her feet shuffle before I saw them. I moved to my right, away from the point of attack, ready to grab her arm when it came around the corner.

I let out a yell. My intention was to warn Angella. Sally might get one of us, but not both. At least not both by knife.

But her arm never appeared. Instead I heard footsteps running down the hall. I took a quick step around the corner and found the door to our room standing open. I ran into the hall in time to see a person of Sally's height disappear around the corner. By the time I arrived at the corner the door to the stairwell was closing. I had no intention of chasing anyone down ten flights of steps, particularly dressed only in my skivvies.

Then a horrible thought struck me. I had done the unthinkable! I had allowed the intruder to lure me from the room, leaving Angella unprotected. Talk about not having her back. I had abandoned my post, leaving her totally vulnerable. Had she done the same to me we would have had a serious discussion.

I raced back to the room, only to find the door closed. And locked!

No key. No cell. No pants. No weapon. Talk about being naked!

This was not a good start to our time in Argentina. I knocked on the door.

No answer.

I knocked louder.

Then I pounded.

Nothing moved within the room.

"Angella," I called, "open the door."

Still no movement.

"Angella. If you hear me, open the door." *Settle yourself, Jimmy,* I told myself. Hysterics won't solve anything. Never does. Perhaps, if Angella hadn't been nearly killed not so long ago this would be easier to manage.

Someone, most likely the Pig, was in there with her right now. His propensity for breast mutilation leaped to my mind and I pounded on the door even harder.

I was fighting what in others I would call a panic attack. In myself, I characterized it as coming to the aid of my partner——— and lover.

I took a deep breath.

And another.

I had to decide, and decide quickly, whether it would be faster to pick the lock or to push the door in.

I gathered my strength for one shoulder push. Then it came to me. In a stage whisper, I said into the wood, "Ted's pancakes are the best."

I had forgotten our agreed upon all-clear code. "Now open the damn door!"

Almost instantly the door opened. Angella, wearing jeans with a blue shirt hanging loose, stood with her feet firmly planted, her knees flexed. Her stance was right out of the textbook. She held a sharpened pencil in her right hand, point facing out, ready to plunge it into an assailant.

I harbored no doubt she'd put up a hell of a fight.

"Stand down," I said. "At least for now, danger's gone."

No sooner had I pulled the door closed behind me than she snapped, "Mind telling me what's going on? Why the hell are you running mostly naked in the common hall, screaming like you were at the high school prom?"

I gave her the short version, ending with, "I screwed up leaving you alone, the door wide open. I thought...I thought the Pig had come in and———"

"Calm down, Jimmy. I'm fine."

"Obviously, I'm not. I don't like to screw up like that."

"So, tell me, how the hell did your buddy Shadowy Sal——— or whoever———know we were here? We picked this place randomly."

"Maybe it's not so random. First of all, it's the closest hotel to where Snow is holing up."

"But they knew the room and everything. We're not here two hours and they have us tagged. Hell, not even Tiny can move so fast."

"Beats the hell out of me."

"You recognized her by fragrance. Impressive."

"I've been thinking. Sal's scent actually matches Holland. That's why she uses it."

"Honeysuckle. I smelled it in the condo after Lillie was there. I don't much care for it."

"So Sal matches Holland in scent, as well as dress. What the hell else matches?"

"It may have been Holland just now for all we know."

"May have been. But she doesn't land for another...let's see...five hours."

"So we think," Angella said, throwing a grimace. "So we think."

There was a knock at the door.

Both Angella and I jumped. I motioned for her to go into the bathroom. When Angella was ready, I called, "Who is it?"

"*Director de hotel. ¿Está todo bien? Se ha reportado el ruido.*"

"We are fine. Thanks," I replied. "The noise was from the hall. Not us." As best as I had understood him he was responding to a complaint of someone being noisy.

"Un caballero de nombre Tiny es en el vestíbulo. Le enviaré a la habitación?"

Angella whispered from behind me, "He says Tiny is in the lobby. Wants to know if he can send him up."

TWENTY-FOUR

"**H**ow the hell did you find us?" I barked when the door closed behind the big guy. Tiny arriving literally on the heels of Sally was, in my mind, not a coincidence. I knew by Angella's thin set lips she shared my concern.

"Whoa," the big guy said, his ever-present smile toning down a notch, "I thought I was in the company of southern hospitality. What brought on such agitation———and might I add———hostility?"

"We just had an unannounced visit from the Shadow," Angella replied. You're in the lobby as soon as she disappears down the stairs. How the hell should we greet you?"

"You can't seriously believe I'm in league with that scum. Frankly, I won't dignify that with a denial. What the hell happened?"

I repeated what I had just told Angella about my encounter with Shadowy Sal. Then I added, "So, how did you find us? Seems there must be a billboard announcing it."

"Easy, my dear Watson. You two, travel bags in hand, marched right past our stakeout of Snow. As if that weren't enough to identify you as newbie Americans, you were speaking about dance floors in English."

"Okay, so I wasn't trained in foreign operations. That only proves we shouldn't be here. Of the thousands of spooks you have working for the CIA we can hardly be the best choice to operate outside the country."

"Above my pay grade. Either you have powerful friends inside the agency——or perhaps you've made powerful enemies."

"I'm betting on enemies. Beginning with your friend, Director Kagan."

"Not my friend. He may be a lot of things, but he's not stupid. If this is his idea, there is good logic behind it. The bad guys wanted Angella down here, but not you. Suppose Sal was here to eliminate you from the equation. Isolate Angella."

The thought sent shivers down my spine. I glanced at Angella and noted her bemused expression hadn't changed. "So tell me how Sal found us. If she's not privy to your stakeout data how did she know the hotel——and the exact room number?"

"Got me on both counts. But I can tell you one thing," Tiny said, reaching into his bag and pulling out a red file, "you had a private conversation with Lillie Holland, the real Lillie Holland, when she arrived at your Condo, did you not?"

I visualized the two of us walking several blocks and then stopping at the end of a street overlooking the bay. I was certain no one could have been listening. "We did, down by the bay. So?"

"So, read this?" He thrust the file in my direction. "Then we can talk."

Every word of what we had said, both sides of the conversation, were neatly typed. It reminded me of a court transcript.

HOLLAND: This assignment has proven more dangerous than we at first believed. Snow appears to be in league with a nasty group. My colleague, Barrington Plevin, has gone missing. He's a good agent, former Scotland Yard, knows how to take care of himself in the field. These folks are not to be underestimated.

REDSTONE: I found that out——the hard way.

HOLLAND: Please explain exactly what transpired.

I didn't read it all, but enough to know we had been compromised. Skipping to the end, I read:

REDSTONE: You positive?

SILENCE:

REDSTONE: Any leads on Slippery Sal?

SILENCE:

REDSTONE: Found where?

"The silence," I said to Tiny, "is you talking on the phone when you told me about the nail file being found outside my condo."

Tiny responded, "That's what we surmised. Best we can figure, there was a recorder in close range to where you were. Picks up everything you're saying. Not more than four, five feet away."

"How do——"

"Lab geeks know all. No delay or whatever the technical term is. They insist it's a close plant."

"Unless the recorder was on Holland——or the spot she picked to talk to me was not as random as she made it seem—— there is no way our conversation could have been recorded."

"Don't fight the facts," Tiny said. "It definitely *was* recorded."

Angella had picked up the file, and characteristic of her, she read every word. Looking up, she said, "You two discussed our relationship. Is nothing sacred?"

"Not in this business it's not," Tiny responded, saving me from saying something stupid. "Assume everything you do and say is being observed."

"Thank you!" Angella sarcastically responded. "I knew you guys were observing us, but I wasn't aware the other side was as well. How do you live that way? It gives me the creeps."

"You do——or you get out. Nothing in the middle. Kapish?"

While the two of them were talking, I resurrected the thought I had had during that conversation with Holland. The thought about how it was I had heard Angella's voice leaving me a message, but had not heard my answering machine. "We're being recorded," I announced, finally realizing what was going on. "Right now, we're being recorded! This happened to us once before. That time Angella figured it was labels glued to our clothes. There was even one on my holster. A live recording explains how Sal knew our room number. Knew when we were sleeping. Knows everything we're saying and doing."

Both Angella and I immediately began searching for hidden microphones. Angella went into the bathroom to check her underwear. She had found labels ironed onto her bras the last lime.

"Nothing here, Jimmy," she called. "Your turn to look." But I had already stripped down to my skivvies and found nothing.

"Check your boots as well," Tiny admonished, his voice so low that I had to strain to hear him.

Both Angella and I had worn our new boots and I dutifully checked inside and out, first mine and then Angella's. Nothing turned up.

Tiny's cell gave a faint beep. He held it to his ear, then whispered, "Snow's on the move. Going south."

"What's that mean?" I asked, my voice barely louder than his. Angella leaned close to hear.

"Means they may be speeding up their plan. They didn't get the job done with you, so they're compressing the time. Go out, walk a few blocks and catch a cab. Be sure to take one that has not been following you. Change cabs twice. I'll keep you posted on where to go as info arrives."

"And pray tell, what are your plans, big guy?" I asked. I wanted him close, if for no other reason than to rule him out of the equation. "Be nice to have you with us. Especially if we can't have weapons."

"Forgot to tell you. There's been a snafu. Argentine government won't allow weapons. Says we need to use the locals."

"Okay," I snapped, my voice rising above a whisper, "for once let's do as they request. Let's use the locals. That would suit me just fine."

Angella nodded her agreement.

"Not if you value your life," Tiny said, his voice also rising. "They've been bought. That's exactly what the other side wants. A snitch assigned to you. Probably someone out there right now waiting for you to come out."

"And they won't follow us?"

"That, my dear friend, is my job. I go out first. Give me a minute and both of you follow me out. Turn left, go to the end of the block, cross the street into the market, walk half-way through, turn right and go straight to the side entrance. Once outside the market, cross the street and turn right again. At the end of the block turn anyway you want."

"Mind telling us where you got the transcript?"

"Interpol passed it along. Just one of many."

- - - - -

GO TOWARD SAN JUAN the message from Tiny read. We were in our third taxi and were now driving along the ship docks when the text arrived.

"Not good, *señor*." The beginnings of fright showed on the driver's otherwise pleasant face.

"Está bien." Angella replied. The fact she spoke Spanish seemed to calm him.

Ten minutes later, Tiny's next text read, CONTINUE TO CONSTITUCION. LOCATION TO FOLLOW.

I repeated the instructions to the driver who promptly slammed on the brakes. *"No es seguro para gringos. Por favor salga y tomar otro taxi."*

"He insists we get out and take another taxi. Says it's not safe for us——or even for him. He won't go another meter."

"Tell him there's a hundred dollars in it for him."

A heated exchange then ensued, resulting in the driver waving his arms and jumping out of the cab. He yanked open the back door and frantically motioned for us to get out.

"What's his problem?" I said, the taxi wheels spinning stones in our face as he pulled away. "The two of you were going at it like bitter enemies."

"Insulted we would think he'd sacrifice his family for so little money. He said he has a wife and four children. He also says gringos are not welcome there."

"Snow's going. We're following."

"Isn't that the area the flight attendant told us to stay away from?"

"I wouldn't know. And frankly, that's unimportant at the moment. There's nothing we can do about it."

Angella started to reply, but instead said, "Let's walk in the direction of that fueling station while we get a plan together."

Indeed, at the far end of the long block sat a one-story, cinderblock, bunker-looking building with what appeared to be a gas pump out front. We walked in that direction. Unsupervised children were darting back and forth, several of them focused on a soccer ball moving quickly from foot to foot. Even the youngest of them was infinitely better at controlling the ball than I had ever been.

The few adults we encountered as we neared the bunker had welcoming smiles and looked easy to approach. But not one of them asked if we were lost, or whether we required help. In fact, if I was to characterize their attitude toward us I would say, "studied unseeing". If anyone asked about gringos in the neighborhood, they would unhesitatingly claim they had seen nothing unusual.

Angella motioned for me to wait outside while she engaged a middle-aged attendant in conversation. Through the small window I could see their discussion was animated, with hand-gestures on both sides. To my eye it all seemed friendly enough, but whatever they were talking about caused agitation in the man. At one point Angella gave me a thumbs up, then turned back and continued her conversation.

A few minutes later she emerged saying, "We're in luck. His brother-in-law, Juan, lives a few blocks away and will drop us off on his way home from work. No promises about bringing us back."

"Take it," I said. "We don't need anybody hanging around there with us. No telling when we'll be ready to leave. The fact is we don't even know why we're going where we are and what we will find. Could be a big goose chase."

"Already accepted. Juan'll be by in a few minutes. His wife insists we join them for dinner. Home cooked *empanadas*. Smells great."

TWENTY-FIVE

A squat woman with features I associate with the Aztec culture appeared from a back-room. She identified herself as the wife of the man Angella had been speaking with. I was anxious to be on our way, but despite my protestations, she insisted we eat the *empanadas*.

I glanced around, looking in vain for anyone who could be the brother. Seeing no one of an age to drive us, I reluctantly followed the woman through the door-less entry to the cramped living area. Angella was right, the room smelled wonderful.

"Don't insult her," Angella said, "or we'll never get a ride." Even if I wanted to, there was no denying this forceful woman who obviously was accustomed to taking charge. She told us her name was Itzel. When I enquired, with Angella interpreting, as to the origin of the name, a large smile crossed her face. She replied, "Ancestors were from central Mexico. Itzel is a corrupted form of Ixchel, meaning Rainbow Lady, in Nahuati."

"Beautiful name, to match a beautiful woman," I replied. I don't know what Angella actually said to her, but the woman blushed and turned her head away from me.

Indeed, the raw beauty emanating from this woman, smiling broadly as we ate her home cooking, was overpowering. Even her husband, sitting off to the side, was infected with the mood. It was as if we had known each other a lifetime, yet neither of us could speak directly to the other.

I don't know about Angella, but I enjoyed perhaps the best meal I have ever eaten south of the border. Several times, Itzel tried to warn us not to go. She said to Angella, "Juan works the ship yard and even he's been robbed. Animals, all of them. Gives us all a bad name. Gringos especially they dislike."

Angella tried to calm her, but Itzel waved her off saying, in what little English she could muster, "Him know," she said, pointing in my direction, "not friend on dock." She looked Angella up and down as she would a goat she was about to purchase——or slaughter—— before saying, "You, treat like friend. You have use to them."

When Itzel realized I was not backing down, she called to someone out the window, who, it turned out, was the missing Juan. He came into the building looking sheepish.

Itzel spoke sharply to the missing Juan in rapid-fire Spanish.

"What did she say to Juan?" I asked Angella on the way to Juan's truck, a rusted Silverado with missing fenders, sporting dents and creases on every surface. If I had been told this truck had been a supply vehicle in the Falklands war, I would have believed it.

"She told Juan to take us now. He is to watch where he leaves us. She reminded him we are guests in their country. Albeit, not very smart guests."

We hadn't gone more than ten meters when more information from Tiny arrived. I read the address to Juan. He nodded, but said nothing. Soon we were passing one-story buildings, mostly wood, painted bright blues and greens, each with yellow or orange trim. At one time they might have been small businesses, perhaps grocery, clothing or hardware stores. Now the businesses were closed, but I sensed they were being used for dwellings, maybe housing the homeless.

After driving five more minutes we could see the ship channel ahead. From my research I knew the channel snaked its way south amid large flat warehouses, many of which were now abandoned. Docks, most with freighters tied to them, lined both sides of the channel. The closer we came to the warehouse area the sparser the structures became. Soon we entered what looked to be a buffer area with scrub weeds growing through the foundations of demolished homes. Angella leaned close and said, "Looks like a no-man's zone from a bad movie."

A block from the channel Juan stopped the car and said, *"Allí, el almacén en frente de ese buque."*

"He says the location you asked for is that building; he calls it a store, in front of that boat." She pointed in the direction of a large, flat-looking cargo ship. "He says to be careful."

The instant we stepped out, he gunned the engine and was gone, dust from the road quickly settling around us.

"A warehouse. Not a store. Place looks deserted. No cars in the lot behind the building." I wasn't particularly happy with the surroundings. We were easy targets out here. "Snow's around here somewhere," I said.

"At least you think that's who we've been following. After all, texts from Tiny are suspect in my mind."

"Good point," I acknowledged. Angella's doubt was justi-
fied. Whoever had tried to take us out earlier didn't suddenly
turn tail and run. Goal oriented people seldom stop short. And
Shadowy Sal was certainly goal oriented. It was only a matter
of time and opportunity, neither of which we had much control
over.

Angella was slightly behind me as we cautiously approached
the low-silhouetted building. I was studying the terrain for movement, shadows, anything to give us an edge. But nothing was
moving and nothing seemed out of place.

At the same time, the very nothingness was unsettling. No
cars were visible in any direction. Warehouses implied cargo.
Cargo implied trucks. But there weren't any trucks either. The
chirping of birds that had been prevalent back near the painted
buildings was now missing.

Only one dusty street separated us from the channel, where
the stench of seawater mixed with rotting garbage overwhelmed
the senses. The cargo ships were tied at odd angles, leaving only
an extremely narrow portion of navigable water. Judging from
their rusting hulls, many of these ships appeared to have been
abandoned, their responsible owners long gone.

Angella touched my hip. "Why do you suppose nothing is
growing in this block? Everything back there is so lush."

"Chemicals would be my guess. Toxic material imported and
stored here, some maybe even created here. Convenient to move
in and out. I'll bet the material has leached into the ground."

"And we're walking through this gunk! No wonder no one
else is out here." Angella studied her feet, then said, "I can almost
see my boots decaying."

"Look hard enough and you'll see anything you wish to see."

"I'm not——" Angelina stopped in mid sentence.

I looked to where her eyes were focused. She had detected movement off to our side.

Where they had come from I don't know, but dockhands had suddenly appeared pushing a dolly across the road in the direction of a freighter angled in among the other ships. The boat, even though in need of a thorough scrape and paint job, was one of the few that looked to be in active service. The others around it had found permanent graves. Wooden scaffolding, a rope hanging from a top post, was positioned on the dock at the ship's bow. The scaffolding swayed in the breeze, giving the impression that at any moment it was likely to topple into the brown water of the channel.

As we watched, one of the dockhands tied the dangling end of the rope around several pallets of material carried on the dolly. He then raised his right arm and the pallets were hauled upward, stopping just short of the top of the scaffolding and slightly above deck level. The pallets hung in mid-air, swaying with increasing vigor, looking as though at any moment they would come crashing down.

The pallets held several individual containers, each with markings, none of which I could make out clearly.

A man standing on the bow of the boat reached out a long stick and hooked the rope as it came into range. He then proceeded to swing the pallets toward him until they were positioned over the deck. He then signaled for the rope to be lowered.

When the pallets were safely on the deck, another deckhand untied the rope and threw it over the side and back down to the dock. The pallets from a second dolly were then similarly tied to the rope end and raised to the deck.

"There are markings on those containers, but I can't read them," I said to Angella. "I hope you can do better."

"I need to be closer. I wonder if this second batch is the same as the first."

I moved closer, expecting at any moment to find a knife at my throat——or a gun pointed at my heart. But the workers didn't seem to care that we were watching them. We inched closer to a point where I could smell their sweat. They still had no apparent concerns.

Angella whispered, "The markings on the containers read, *PanAm Pharma*. Can you see them?"

"I can make out the large PAP above the lettering, but nothing else."

Angella moved closer to the water, studied the containers for a long-moment, and then came back to where I was standing. "Azithromycin. Port of New Orleans. Ms Honey."

"The name of that tub of rust is Honey?" I said, pointing to the lettering on the ship's bow. "Boat's registered in Isle of Man."

Angella took out her cell phone and snapped several pictures, beginning with the cartons and then capturing the freighter and its surroundings. She then texted the pictures to Tiny.

Satisfied, Angella turned to me and instantly her eyes went wide with fear.

I spun around to see what had caused such a violent reaction in my partner and came face to face with William Dermitt, known to us as Bill Snow. He was standing directly behind me, his gun pointing at my head.

TWENTY-SIX

"So we meet again, Agent Redstone." Shifting his eyes momentarily in Angella's direction, Snow said, "Angella, my dear, so glad to see you looking well."

"No thanks to you," Angella spit back. Her eyes were angrier than I had ever seen.

"On the contrary, my dear. You're alive today because of my generosity."

The first rule when a gun is pointed at you is to keep the gunman talking. But this conversation was not the right one to be having. "May I remind you," I said, struggling for a non-controversial beginning point, "you gave me the wrong combination. But that's all in the past. We let you go. You're a free man. Don't blow it now."

"You call it free when my every move is being monitored. Every time I turn around a video camera is in my face. I can't get on an airplane without hours, sometimes days, of delay."

"You're alive aren't you? You managed to get down here, didn't you? Be thankful."

"Listen, Redstone, the way I figure it, we're even. But the truth is I don't give a rat's ass if we're even or not! I'll do what I have to do."

"And what is that?"

"I'm here to expedite a shipment of drugs. Legitimate drugs, I might add. And I uncovered———"

"If you'll put that gun down I'll be better able to concentrate on what your needs are. We might even be able to help."

"I put it down and you'll take me in. That's not going to happen."

"Taking you in is not my mission," I said. While I was speaking I noticed Angella slowly edging to his right, angling for his gun hand. Taking her lead, I began to ever so slightly move in the opposite direction. His eyes were concentrating on me, apparently discounting Angella as a threat. "My mission is to see what you're up to. Headquarters became worried when you...you dropped off their radar. We know you're working logistics for PAP. Just want to confirm you're now on the right side."

"See that," he said, his left arm motioning in the direction of the last of the pallets being moved onto the ship, "those drugs have been mixed with———" Snow lowered his voice. "I've said more than I should. I'll say nothing further."

His eyes told me he wanted to talk. My job was to encourage him. "I understand the FDA inspects all drugs during manufacture. In effect, by talking to me you're working with the Feds. So what's the problem?"

Snow glanced around. Lowered his voice even further and said, "This is bad, man. Real bad. PAP's main manufacturing facility is located up the channel about a quarter mile. That's where these containers were inspected——and electronically sealed. That way they know where the drugs are at all times. Done by timing I'm told. Any unscheduled stops and alarms go off back home."

"All on the up and up. Inspected and sealed. Nothing to worry about then," I said. "You're doing fine."

But Snow was agitated. I was troubled because he was a hardened drug runner with nerves of steel. Something big must have happened to upset him. "So what is troubling you?" I asked, sensing he wanted to talk.

"Look, I'm a drug runner. You know that. But this is much more than that and——" Snow looked around, satisfied himself no one was listening, then continued, "Frankly, I…I don't like what I saw."

"So what was it?" I asked.

"The medication was cut," he blurted, as often happens when a criminal thinks he is about to be blamed for something he considers worse than what he actually did. "They added some nasty stuff."

"Are you telling me you had no hand in that?"

"The cutting yes. I arranged for it. What the hell do I care about Medicare fraud? Old people lived long enough, if you ask me. They don't need no free government handouts. But that's not what they're planning. They're working with some really nasty dudes. They plan to——"

"What? What do they plan?"

"I'll cut a deal for what I know. Drop all charges against me. Give me my life back."

"Give us a preview."

"Foreign dudes. Going to kill everything. Going to hold—
—" I'll tell everything, you give me assurances my charges will
be dropped."

"Names. Of these foreign dudes."

"I couldn't get names. But one mean son-of-a-bitch looks
like he was in a knife fight. Slash down his right cheek. Hair
slicked back. Guy loves knives. He talks about cutting women."

"Put the gun down. I listen better when I'm not in the line
of fire. We can help you, but I need to talk with folks back home.
That'll take a few hours."

"I need the gun for show. Down here, eyes are everywhere.
They see me put the gun down, I'm good as dead. They get wind
I'm making a deal; they'll put a bullet through my head. Or
that Arab bastard'll slash my throat. I've seen him use the knife.
Man's vicious."

Angella's arm, the one about to strike Snow's gun, relaxed.

I said, "We need to know what they're doing? Give me something to negotiate with and I'll do my best."

"Biological attack on American soil. Starts with South Padre
Island and contaminates Laguna Madre as a demonstration of the
devastation the mutant drugs can cause. I'm not saying anything
more."

"You have more?" I coaxed. Guys like Snow need to talk. I
was giving him all the rope he required.

"You gotta give me something in return. All I'll say is, it's
big——and scares the hell out of me. I may be into drugs, but
not mass killing."

"Listen to me, Snow. I got one chance to get you a deal. One
chance. You give me what you got, maybe not all the fine points,
and I'll go to bat for you. Something will work out. Right now

the whole world is looking for you. It's only a matter of time until you're brought in. Dead or alive, they don't care which."

"I trust you, Redstone. I'll give you what I know, but in turn I want my freedom."

"I understand," I said. Adding, "I should be able to get it done." In fact, I had great doubt he'd ever be free. Not after causing the death of a Washington cop.

"Okay. They plan on delivering a deadly virus to New York City on a commercial airplane. The plane explodes when it lands. The disease can't be controlled because the drug that cures it is a mutant———of no effect. I overheard the Arab talking to some woman. They were talking about destroying New York as the very least that would happen. They have high hopes of wiping out the entire east coast if things go the right way." Snow waved the gun in my face. "That better be enough for———"

Snow's arm flew upward. His gun discharged, sending several rounds barely over my head.

Angella fell face down onto the filthy dock.

I had been concentrating on his eyes, trying to anticipate his intentions and certainly had not seen this coming. In fact, I had thought he was about to lower his weapon———not fire it.

I dove toward Angella, not knowing if she was still alive, but trying to protect her from further impact in the event she had survived the initial rounds.

Snow landed on my back. "What the hell!" I exclaimed, pushing him off. He put up no resistance.

"Stay down," Angella whispered.

I lay there several long seconds before she spoke, her voice still low and all business. "You okay, Jimmy? "Someone shot Snow. I can't spot the shooter."

"Not hit, if that's what you're asking." I rolled Snow over and examined him. "Got him at the base of the neck," I announced. "One hell of a shot."

"I didn't catch what he said about South Padre Island," Angella said. "But what they have planned for New York sounds———"

"What about Padre?" A familiar voice asked.

Startled, I looked up to find Tiny walking toward us from the direction of the channel. It never ceases to amaze me that a man of his height and girth could appear out of nowhere as he often did. "Is this your handiwork?" I asked, after climbing to my feet.

"Tiny bent and studied Snow for a moment. "Wish I could take credit for it. Neat hit. But not me."

I looked around. "Who then?"

"Redstone, you have to be the only person in the world who questions a gift horse. Snow was about to put a bullet in you."

"Not exactly accurate," Angella said, dusting off her jeans. "He was telling us———"

"About the *Honey* stopping here," I injected, purposefully over-speaking Angella. The less we told Tiny at this point the better. Someone had shot Snow and it most likely was not for our benefit.

"What did he tell you? What about SPI?"

"Didn't get a chance to finish," I responded. "Any idea who shot him?"

Tiny looked over my shoulder. "If I were a betting man, I'd put my money on the little guy behind you. The one holding the Glock pointed at your head."

TWENTY-SEVEN

Sure enough, standing beside the warehouse was a man, no larger than a boy, his arms hanging lose, his pistol three sizes too large for his frame.

Tiny motioned for him to come over. Had I been armed I would have drawn on him. Remembering the accuracy of his shot, I also would most likely now be lying beside Snow.

When the little man with the big gun was within ten feet of us, Tiny said, "Redstone, Martinez, meet Pavel Torres. Longtime friend. We go way back. He's the guy I asked to watch over Angella."

Torres reached behind him and shoved the gun into his pants. Then he extended his arm in my direction.

His grip was surprisingly firm for a man of his diminutive stature. I put him at under five feet, but muscular.

He bowed in the direction of Angella, but did not extend his hand.

He might have been the guy Tiny hired to watch over Angella, but he was also the guy who had sent me an e-mail announcing her safe arrival in Buenos Aires when, in fact, Angella never even boarded the plane in Houston. Proving once again Tiny was in league with some strange folks.

"You nail this guy?" I asked, knowing the answer, but wanting to see how up front he was.

"Might have."

"In this country you admit nothing," Tiny explained, "friend or foe."

"Can't say I'm sorry to see him leave this earth," Angella added, "trash as far as I'm concerned."

Based on what Snow had done to her, I couldn't fault her sentiment. But had Angella been in the position of pulling the trigger, I don't believe she would have shot to kill.

Tiny said to his friend. "Call it in, Pavel. Then get lost. I'll take it from here."

"That okay with you?" Tiny asked, turning in my direction.

"No problem with Torres leaving, if that's what you're asking. We need to have the warehouse searched." I wanted to know what they were cutting the drugs with. The contamination part had me concerned. My eye took in the wasted fields around the factory where nothing, not a blade of grass, not even a semblance of a weed, grew. Seagulls were perched on all the buildings except for the warehouse where the cartons had come from.

"Could be problematic," Tiny replied. "Entirely up to the *Policia Bonaeerense*. Unless we give the shooter to them they'll drag their feet. Truth is the *Comisario* assigned to this precinct is most likely in the building owner's pocket. He won't allow a search. Need to call in the Nationals. Takes political pull for that.

We can arrange it, but…but we'll have to give something up in exchange. I'll work it."

Torres pulled out the littlest cell phone I had ever seen, half the size of his tiny hand. He spoke a few fast Spanish sentences I doubt even Angella could translate. He then turned and sprinted across the street disappearing around the side of the building, careful not to go across the dead field.

"If you two want to leave, now's your chance."

The thought was tempting. Facing the police department of a foreign country, especially with assumed names, was not how I had planned my day.

Angella had a hand on my arm as if to say, "Leaving is not a good idea."

I turned to her thinking I'd persuade her it was best if we were not found with a dead body at our feet——and phony papers in our pockets.

But her grasp of my arm increased before I could mount my argument. Her look was one of raw terror.

An army of uniformed men had surrounded us and were closing in from every direction. They were dressed in black from head to toe and carried automatic weapons pointed directly at us.

I had been trained as an Army Ranger and this is how we appeared when we approached a stronghold. The recalled motto, "Shoot first, talk second," flashed in my brain and gave me chills. This had every indication of not ending well for us.

Then the realization hit: This operation had been mounted long before Torres called them.

My thought was interrupted by a husky female voice, barking in heavily accented English, "Hands over your heads! Step apart! Now!"

Several black-clad figures knelt down, their weapons pointed directly at us.

"The woman," the female voice screamed. "Flat on the ground!"

Angella immediately went to her knees and then lowered herself onto the filthy dock for the second time. She kept her head a few inches above ground level, doing her best to prevent the cinders from cutting into her skin.

"Head down! All the way down! Don't move! Now you," the voice commanded, her assault weapon pointing at me. "Turn around and get down! Keep your hands where I can see them!"

I also did as I was told. When I was down I could no longer see Angella or Tiny. There was no possibility of a coordinated escape effort; even assuming we were capable of mounting one.

"You, over there. Large man. Hands where I can see them. Sit!"

Why Tiny was allowed to sit and we had our faces pressed in the grit and filth of the dock I didn't understand. I filed that away for future analysis———assuming we had a future.

"Search them!" the woman directed.

Almost immediately, two men came and stood over me, one of them knelt and pressed his knee into my back. If I had thought of going anywhere, I couldn't now if I had tried.

The other man went through my pockets. Finding no weapon, he announced, "*Nada de que preocuparse.*"

From behind me I heard another man say, "*Nada.*"

"You," the woman said, "big one. What are those papers you are waving in my face?"

"Diplomatic," Tiny said. "Look at them."

"You two," the commander barked, "Stand."

When we did so, she said, "What are you doing in this neighborhood?"

How much could I safely say? In fact, who am I? Jimmy Redstone or…or Jesse Silver?

Tiny saved me by saying, "These folks are with U.S. Homeland Security. There was an understanding that U.S. drugs were being…being manufactured in this factory. They are investigating."

"And you? What are you doing here?"

"They called the embassy for a ride back to their hotel. I came to get them."

"Your papers say you are a military attaché. Not a chauffeur. You are telling me bull shit!"

"Double duty."

"Bull shit! I'm no fool. Did you shoot him?"

"I did not," Tiny said. "And neither did they."

"They have names?"

"Jesse Silver and Anna Silver."

"Why do I believe you are lying to me?"

"About the killing I am not. We have no weapons."

"I see that much. But you could have thrown them in the water. If you didn't shoot him, then who did?"

"Don't know."

"Who called us?"

"I don't know," Tiny said. "I demand that we be taken to the American Embassy."

"You, maybe. But these ones don't have immunity. I do not see their names on your papers."

"What is your name and rank," Tiny asked in a voice that sounded as if he was in charge.

"*Comisario Novia Muñoz*," the woman in command said, adding, "Chief of the warehouse district. Do you know who the dead man is?"

"William Dermitt. He's wanted by the U. S. for drug running——and murder. Interpol is looking for him as well. An Interpol agent came here a few days ago by invitation of your government. Name of Barrington Plevin."

She leaned her head close to an older man who was standing off to her right. They exchanged words before she turned back to us. "This is *Oficial Principal* Diego Varela. He will be conducting the investigation. Officer Varela informs me that Interpol has reported Señor Plevin missing under suspicious circumstances."

Diego Varela's slow movements and slumped shoulders, coupled with his withered yellow mustache and tired eyes gave away the fact that he had lead a hard life and was not enthusiastic about his assignment. His voice confirmed that assessment. "Please tell your embassy we will first examine the body and then we will release him to the U.S. government for transport back to his home."

"How long will that require?"Tiny asked.

"How long until it rains?" he responded. "Some things are in God's hands."

"Stand down," Comisario Muñoz announced to the soldiers guarding us. "Search the building. Do not touch anything. We are looking for the shooter, and nothing else."

Several of the men in black then broke away from the rest and trotted across the street in the direction of the warehouse.

"And the cargo ship as well," I added.

"That will not be possible, señor." Diego Varela injected, Perfuntura Naval Argentina has jurisdiction over the water." He glanced over my shoulder, a smile forming on his weathered face. He then said, "As they say in your country, it's too late, that ship has sailed!" His boss, the Comisario, joined him in a good laugh while flies pecked away at the corpse.

TWENTY-EIGHT

As is customary in most places around the world, they separated Angella, Tiny and I. Then each of us told our respective stories. I had the distinct impression Varela didn't much care what I said. He asked no probing questions, allowing me to tell what I wanted to tell. In his mind, this was a mere formality and he wasn't going to allow it to interfere with his otherwise leisurely day. After all, he was investigating a dead American found holding an unfired gun in a part of the city where American's aren't typically found——alive. The bullet hole through the dead guy apparently came from someone other than us since we had no weapons.

After a while an ambulance pulled up, two men in green and white jackets climbed out, looked over the body and then walked over to the channel. Leaning against one of the decaying hulls that overhang the quay, they had a leisurely smoke.

"They like the dead ones," Oficial Principal Varela commented. "No rush. This one," he said, pointing to where Snow lay, "is in no hurry to get anywhere. His time is forever. Cold is cold." He laughed, pleased with his own humor.

Suddenly there was a commotion from across the road as someone rushed from the warehouse and shouted for Varela to come over.

Varela said to me, "*Señor*, do not leave us. I will return." He turned and marched off toward the shouting man. His smile was an indication that his choice of words had been intentional. Most likely imitating McArthur without really knowing where the saying came from. This man seemed to have a fascination with things——or at least sayings——American.

It didn't take Varela long before he was back, now holding a cell phone positioned so I could see a picture he had apparently taken. "Know this *hombre*?"

It took me a moment before the image snapped home. I was looking at Barrington Plevin III, formerly of Scotland Yard and now with Interpol. "That's Plevin. Barrington Plevin. The Interpol agent I spoke about earlier."

"Barely alive, I will add." Varela motioned to the two orderlies, one clearly entertaining the other with a funny story. They were each working on their second cigarette. "*!Usted dos! Conseguir su perezosa asnos aquí! Ahora!*"

When the men ambled over to us, both still giddy from the story, Varela pointed to the warehouse and said something in Spanish. The men immediately turned serious, ran to the ambulance, jumped inside and raced it across the street. They then ran inside the warehouse, one of them carrying a stretcher.

Several minutes later they loaded the stretcher into the back of the ambulance. They then raced off, the ambulance siren wailing.

I said to Varela, "Pardon me, *Oficial Principal*, but may I please inspect the inside of that building. It is important for my investigation. I am looking for——"

"It is out of my control. I have been instructed to return you and the *señorita* to your hotel where you are to remain until dismissed."

"Who must I see to gain entrance? I need to see inside," I pressed.

"Provincial Minister of Security."

I was pressing Varela when Tiny walked over. "Leave it lie," he said. "I've already put in the request. It's working its way up. Apparently these guys have been instructed to deal only with the immediate killing. What goes on in this building is not their concern."

"By the time we obtain permission, anything of value for us will have vanished."

"Unfortunately Redstone, all governments don't share our priorities."

I wondered if any government did, but took Tiny's advice and let it lie. "Meanwhile, we're under house arrest, or so it seems."

"Be thankful it's not the prison. At least you have a dance floor. Practice your tango. It'll do you good. The hotel has a great pool. Bar tab's on Uncle."

"I suppose they're letting you walk away from this."

"Diplomatic immunity still works. Out of their control."

"And just how do you suggest we keep Shady Sal from slitting our throats?"

"I'll arrange twenty-four-seven coverage outside your door. That work for you? For the record, it's Shadowy Sal."

"For the record," I said when Varela's attention was momentarily diverted, "bring us two sharp knives, just in case."

"Oh, ye of little faith."

"And long memory. Bring the knives."

"Come along," Angella called to me, "we're going back to the hotel."

Tiny leaned close. "Here, take this."

He handed me what felt like a credit card. I glanced down, and sure enough, it was an AMEX card. "And what, pray tell, am I to do with Albert Marrow's credit card?"

"For one thing, you can pay your bar tab. For another," he leaned down so that his mouth was next to my ear, "don't run your finger along the edge. Sharper than a knife." Tiny then separated from me and within a few seconds was across the street talking to a security escort.

I turned my head for one last look at the freighter, now slowly making its way to the open Caribbean beyond the harbor. I was positive we'd be seeing a lot more of *Ms Honey*, now heading for the Port of New Orleans.

I captured a lasting mental image of the vessel. Superimposed on that image was a rat gnawing on Snow's right ear, his feces soaking through his pants.

TWENTY-NINE

"Let me get this straight," Angella said from across the room. She was in deep shadow having insisted we keep the heavy drapes closed. "That little guy Torres, Tiny's so-called investigator, happened to let go a shot just as Snow was giving us information to secure a deal for his freedom. Something had Snow spooked. Turns out it wasn't paranoia."

"Not a coincidence either in my mind," I said. "They knew he was about to give them up." Angella and I had been honing our thoughts for several hours and not likely to break new ground anytime soon.

"Gives me the shivers thinking about how the hell the shooter knew when to pull the trigger? Tiny being there———and knowing who the shooter was———really gets to me."

"Everything we know about Torres, and it isn't much, came from Tiny."

"For a guy who has our backs he seems to be a step slow. Showing up just after Shadowy Sal fails to kill one or both of us, is not…shall we say…particularly helpful."

"Look at it this way. We're alive, aren't we?" I felt obliged to defend Tiny, but truth was, I was questioning his behavior as well.

"Because of him, or despite him? That is the question," Angella said before falling silent for several minutes. I assumed she was walking through all the possibilities once again. "Still bothers me," she finally said, "the police didn't seem much interested. Searched the warehouse, the last place a shooter would hide. Didn't set any perimeters. Torres walked right past them and they never saw him."

"Alice in Wonderland effect. They see what they want to see."

"Speaking of police. They got there all too fast. And all too quiet. Wouldn't they have had to be there before us to have us surrounded as they did?"

"They could have come in by water. But truth is that would have taken more time than actually elapsed. I'm leaning with you. They were in place *before* the shooting."

"I saw nothing moving on that stinking channel. They had to have been positioned on one of the hulks. Could it be that they were there to catch us and the shooting confused their plans. We think Torres was the shooter. But maybe he wasn't."

"I don't know what to think," I said, "other than they didn't care a hoot about Snow. Left him rotting on the dock. He's not their problem apparently."

"They cared about Plevin though. Got him to a hospital fast."

"He's Interpol. Federal Police have jurisdiction in such matters and they're the equivalent of our FBI. I've heard some bad stories about them. Take no prisoners kind of thing. The locals don't mess around. See how fast *Comisario Muñoz* cleared out. Left *Oficial Principal* Varela to clean up the mess."

"From the looks of it," Angella said, finally slumping in a chair, "Varela's highest and best use is to clean up behind that woman. Hear anything more on Plevin?"

"Nothing yet." Just as I said it, a text arrived. I was hoping it was an update on Plevin's condition. Instead, it was from Tiny. I turned back to Angella. "Tiny says thumbs up on getting into the warehouse. We can ride along. Scheduled two hours from now."

"When did the text arrive?"

"Minute ago."

"I suppose we have time for lunch. Mind if we have something sent up?"

"Like minds. Any idea what you want?"

"Make it simple. A burger."

I ordered two burgers and two Buds.

I wanted to eat on the balcony overlooking the pool. Angella outvoted me. So we sat at the round table at the side of the small dance floor and enjoyed our picnic in the room, the drapes remained closed. The mood matched the room condition; gloomy.

Our conversation over lunch, steered by Angella, carefully avoided business-related discussions. She told me about growing up with her sister and her brothers and how important it was to be thought of as tough.

"Now, Mr. Jimmy Redstone, she said, washing the last of the burger down, it is due time you told me about your son Lester. All I know is that he's in his mid-thirties, lives in Alaska and mostly doesn't work."

"I thought we had agreed not to discuss stomach-wrenching topics when we ate?"

"Business-related. With you, all family matters would be off-limits if your definition was followed."

"Not much to tell you, really. Kid wants to live with nature. That's okay with me, if he could support himself. When I try to cut him off, his mother gets on the phone."

"Does he work at all?"

"Somewhat. He's what's called a freelance harvest fisherman. Hires himself out on the longliners."

"Longliners?"

"Fishing boats that use long lines with hand-baited hooks tied onto short runner lines. Think they call them snoods. He goes out for the halibut and black cod. Says he's pretty good, but it's hard work. The pay is actually surprising good."

"So?"

"So, you only get paid when you go out. Capitalism at work."

"I take it he doesn't sign on all that much. Is that what you're saying?"

"Not as much as he should."

"That's what gets to you, then."

"You might say that. He says it's just too cold. I tell him to come south, fish down here. He says he won't make any more money here working all year than he does up there working a few months. Kid's probably right."

"What's that look? Something troubling you?"

"Just that…nothing."

"It's not nothing. I know you all too well. Out with it."

"Halibut season, at least for him, begins about now."

"That means he'll be working. That's good news."

"That also means he's broke———unless he worked this winter. But, if he had, he would have called to tell me."

"I can understand him calling for money. He needs to call to get it. But if he's working, then not calling is…well to be expected."

"He'd call anyway. Just to show me he was working."

"So call him."

I hesitated. I looked up and saw Angella's eyes telling me to do what I knew I should do. I reluctantly picked up my cell and dialed his number. Talking with my son was always stressful. Our work ethics were a mismatch.

A message came on saying the line had been temporarily disconnected.

"That's what happens when you don't pay the bill," Angella gently reminded me.

"Something's wrong. He usually calls me when he's out of money. I take care of the boring bills it seems."

I tried again. Same result. I looked through my contact list, found what I wanted, and hit the send button.

"Who are you calling?"

"His mother. She always knows where he is."

A moment later her perpetually sad sounding voice came on the line. We spoke a few painful minutes while I listened to her never-ending string of complaints about what life has done to her.

"So," Angella said when I hung up, "what's the big drama?"

"About her or Les?"

"I could care less about her. Ex-any things; be it wives, husbands, boyfriends, anything; are bores. Tell me about your son."

"He actually worked this winter. That's the good news. The bad news is he was injured. Apparently, he's allergic to some medication they gave him. Got a settlement and, here's what's interesting."

"Can't wait to hear," Angella said.

"He's on his way down here."

"Argentina? How'd he———"

"Sorry. SPI. The settlement with the insurance company lined up a job on a fishing boat out of Port Isabel. Part of his rehab requires him to be in the sun. Six months minimum."

"How's he traveling? Flying?"

"Unless someone's paying, he's driving. Truth is the junker he drives couldn't make it that far. Hell, I'd be surprised if they allowed it in the country."

"Alaska *is* in the country."

"He's got to go through Canada. His car is unsafe standing still. Sorry. That's not nice."

"Maybe he broke down?"

"That's what his mother thought when I called. Or he was in an accident. Obviously, I haven't heard from him. I suppose he intends to surprise me."

The phone rang. I half-expected it to be my son. But the caller ID said TINY. "What can I do for you?" I answered, trying to keep the sarcasm from my voice and not doing a particularly good job. "You enjoying your day?"

Ignoring my comment, Tiny said, "Called to give you a couple updates. Some good, some bad."

"Good first. We could use good news."

"Plevin is in guarded condition. No major wounds. Dehydrated mostly. He's expected to make a full recovery."

"Next?"

"His partner and boss, Lillie Holland, was diverted back to London. They now have traced the SOS missing money and she's off to confirm they have it right. Said she looks forward to completing the mission with you on the phone."

She and Plevin had more than a working relationship. He's in the hospital. I would have thought she would have remained in country. There was more to this than Tiny was saying.

"Was that the good or the bad news?"

"You tell me. My bad news is the inspection of the warehouse is cancelled."

"Mind telling me why?" As if the reason mattered.

"Can't inspect what doesn't exist. Twenty minutes ago it blew apart. Only thing remaining is the concrete back wall. Everything else is vapor."

"Trace material," I pressed, "we need to see what chemicals they were using."

"This is Argentina, not New York. Ever hear of CSI—Argentina? I'm afraid that's a dead end."

"There's always trace!"

"Jimmy, State negotiated a deal with the locals. Your choice is to take a few days——they'll go along with a week——enjoy the sights, enjoy the beach, no investigations of any sort. Pure tourist. You can even travel into the countryside, if that's your desire. You two can practice the tango and come back home experts. Government will supply an official guide for traveling and even a dance instructor. Spare no expense."

My translation: police escort.

"Or you can get on a plane this afternoon and head home."

I didn't have to consult with Angella, who sat listening to my every word, the curtains pulled tightly closed behind her, to know what her choice would be. "What time's the flight?" I asked Tiny.

"Car is on the way. Knew you wouldn't stay. Military flight leaves when you arrive at the airport. Nothing is too good for you two."

The line went dead.

THIRTY

The first day back on our own island was spent cleaning house, stocking the refrigerator, changing the bed linens and washing windows. Domestic chores that kept our minds and bodies occupied without requiring strategic planning and analysis. If I were a psychologist, I would diagnose early-stage burnout, or whatever the technical term is. Along those lines, by tacit agreement, neither of us verbalized our assignment.

Our second day was spent filing reports, talking with Director Kagan and reading Tiny's report as well as other information that had been filtered from nameless operatives stationed in and around Buenos Aires and other parts of the world. I was, frankly, surprised at the quantity of the information that had been gathered. The satellite images of Snow being shot and the massive explosion that had pulverized a concrete warehouse were vivid. The taped conversations were detailed—and extensive. They even had positive confirmation that Shadowy Sal had, indeed, been in our room. No surprise, but what they didn't have is why.

They knew the PAP drugs had been cut, but did not know with what. And of course, they didn't know why? Speculation 1: PAP was trying to increase its profits. Speculation 2: A terrorist plot was underway.

The official Argentina incident report was short and to the point. INCIDENT: American found dead on *Constitucion* quay. COD: Bullet penetrating base of neck. DECEASED: William Dermitt: ADDRESS: Illegal Alien. Possibly American. No record of entering country. WITNESSES: None. SUSPECTS: None. DISPOSITION: Closed.

Tiny's take. "It's good Argentina did not investigate. That could have compromised our investigation. Say thanks."

"You saying you had a hand in them closing the file so quickly?"

"Let's just say I greased the skids. A few of the locals owed me."

"Everyone seems to owe you."

"Nature of the beast. Scratch the back principle at its best."

I wanted to ask him if he also facilitated the warehouse blowing up and Torres disappearing, but thought better of it. "Is the cargo ship watch in place?"

"It's been in place since before that tub left Argentine waters. Not only is it being tracked by satellite, but it's being imaged as well. Guy takes a wiz over the side, we'll know it. Nothing is coming on or off that crate we don't know about."

"ETA in New Orleans?"

"Two weeks from today."

"Any luck in tracking down ownership? From a report Holland filed, the money traced from SOS found its way to the Isle of Man. *Ms Honey* is registered in the Isle of Man, just as you told us. Seems to be an Israeli vessel. Money came through Israel, unreported to our government. Wolfson is a large Israeli supporter. You put the pieces together."

"What's your take?"

"How many times do I have to tell you, I'm a hunter/gatherer. Not a deducer/extrapolator."

"And I'm Peter Pan! What's the latest on how Snow got to Argentina?"

"Funny you should ask. Just came across my desk less than an hour ago. Private jet. Gulfstream G350 with US registration. Owned by F. Harrison Banks. Running it down now."

"So Tiny has a lead on the plane," Angella commented when she was certain I had hung up. "Wouldn't doubt if he flew it in himself."

That was yesterday.

Today Angella and I have Lillie Holland's files on the *Ms Honey*, which Angella has dubbed the Honey Pot, spread before us. The old tub changed official names five times. And changed countries of registration four times.

"Why the change of country?" Angella asked. "Doesn't that present some kind of trouble? I mean for tax and other legal issues."

"Flags of convenience. Some countries, Panama, Cyprus, Hong Kong, come to mind, protect the ship owner so they can't be sued for activities such as carrying weapons, or spilling oil. It's also known as false flags."

"Is that legal?"

"I'm not a maritime lawyer, I don't know. I just know it's done for some reason. Honey Pot is now flying the flag of the Isle of Man. Its previous name was Haifa under a Panama registration."

"Haifa? Sounds like Israel. That ties in with the Wolf——and PAP. Wasn't she speaking to a Jewish group?"

"She was."

"And PAP's drugs are on board."

"Before Haifa, the ship was known as *Willow Roost* and before that *Silent Motion*. Both out of Panama. Going back even further we have *Rosa Two*, registered in Hong Kong and *Ym West* out of Cyprus. Before that *Medicap* from Cyprus."

"A real United Nations," Angella commented. "Think we can trace the real ownership?"

"That's just it. If you believe the records, the ship's owner-ship changed each time."

"If you believed the records, you wouldn't have brought it up. What are you thinking?" Angella asked.

"I can understand name changes going back ten, twenty years. But all this has occurred in the last few years."

"Are you keying it to the SOS embezzlement?"

"I am. Now we need to find who the real owner is."

"Isn't that Lillie's job at Interpol? Trace the money——and the ownership. Hey, suppose the names mean anything? Like an acronym?"

"Take a letter from each and make something of it? Don't see it. Why do that? There are easier ways to send messages."

"It's worth calling the anagram idea to Tiny's attention. Let the FBI cryptology wonks burn grey matter over it. The Israel connection has my attention. Haifa. Wolfson. Is something going on there?" Angella's lips tightened, as they often did when she was working through a set of facts.

Instead of concentrating on naming clues, I worked on trying to uncover a pattern for the registration countries.

None came to mind. But I was intrigued with the fact that Interpol had traced the money embezzled from SOS to the Isle of Man. Wikipedia, my new best friend, says the Isle of Man, or Mann as it is also known, is a self-governing Crown Dependency of the United Kingdom, located in the Irish Sea between the islands of Great Britain and Ireland. This is an area known as the British Isles.

It was curious that all the transactions occurred within a two-year period. They must employ a full-time sign painter on the Honey Pot just to keep the name current.

"Curious," I said to Angella when she looked up from her computer, "that tub is ancient, but yet the registrations go back only about eighteen months."

"Who owned it before that?"

"File is blank. Commercial vessels, as I recall from an investigation years ago, have ID numbers, called International Maritime numbers. The numbers are permanently attached to their hulls. They're not supposed to ever change, even when ownership changes. But no one seems to inspect."

"Surely, Lillie Holland knows about the ID numbers."

"We'll see what she turns up——if anything. That woman troubles me."

"Speaking of turning up," Angella said, "been expecting your son. You worried?"

"Les runs on his own clock. Never could predict what he'd do. Smart kid, all things considered. But we're exact opposites. I tell you I'll be there at eleven, set your watch by it. He says eleven, be lucky he shows up in the same month. Kid has the attention span of a puppy. Could have driven as far as Montana and put on his skis. We may never see him this far south."

"You know, Jimmy, I've been thinking about what we're doing. And truth is I can't wrap my mind around what's going on. I mean, Snow went missing, so we gave chase. He's dead, so what are we doing?"

"DNA on Snow is positive," I replied, distracted by Angella's demeanor. Her hard-set eyes told me she had given a lot of thought to what she was saying. "I'm listening. Go on."

"Look, they have us reviewing old files on SOS and PAP. Why? Those are stale commercial transactions. And certainly not Homeland Security issues. That's FBI stuff."

Angella had a good point. But in defense, I countered, "Drugs may have been tampered with in Argentina by these same people," I reminded her.

"Can you say, DEA? This is not HS's ballgame. So why are we still working it?"

The old adage, *when all around you are in a panic and you're calm it just means you don't have all the facts,* played in my head. I repeated it for Angella.

"So, what facts are we missing?"

"For starters, what is the mystery substance that was mixed into the azithromycin? The warehouse was torched before we could investigate. And how did whatever it was get into Argentina in the first place? Actually, my biggest concern———concern's the wrong word, puzzlement———is why did they use a ship whose name has changed five times in eighteen months? The whole operation smells bad."

"Nothing in what you said comes under the umbrella of Homeland Security concerns," Angella again reminded me. "Well, possibly the drug cutting is."

"More like an FDA problem. I'd think FBI would be all over it."

"You can certainly call Tiny," Angella said, shrugging, "see what he says. I don't hold out much hope he'll shed any light on anything."

The subject of Tiny had been delicate since our return. We both harbored suspicions, but neither was willing to openly say anything of importance. Angella broke the silence. "Snow was taken out by Tiny's friend. Tiny has some explaining to do."

I got Tiny on the line and, as expected, he shed very little light on the subject. But he did say, "Director Kagan is working this with Interpol. He's still on-board with you two working it, putting the pieces together. Plevin remains in intensive care, but looking better. Holland's back at her desk and out of harm's way, so to speak. That impersonation episode has Interpol concerned."

"Any trace of ole Sal?" I asked. "Does anyone know how she got in and out of Argentina?"

Without hesitation, Tiny responded, "Probably same as Snow, but we don't yet know how they're tied though."

"There's a lot we don't know?" Angella commented, rolling her eyes. Her head was leaning against mine so she could hear Tiny directly.

"Nature of what we do," Tiny answered. "Bad guys spend every waking minute planning, training, running scams. It only takes once. It's a variation of crying wolf."

"Drag that by again?" Angella said. "Slow this time."

"If you cry wolf enough times," Tiny patiently explained, "no one believes you. So if you're planning a bad act then run a bunch of operations that appear suspicious, but, in fact, are harmless. Their thinking is our guard will be down when the real activity begins, regardless of how suspicious it appears."

"And they believe that will work?"

"Has in the past," I said, knowing full well Tiny would never admit to the truth of my statement. "We simply don't have the resources to react to every suspicious activity."

"Need to be smarter than the bad guys," Tiny said. "Along that line, CIA intercepted a communication that I want you to read.

Just put the transcript in the file. Read it, but don't comment or
discuss it between yourselves. Text me with your thoughts."

"What's the subject?"

"Pull up the file. It's all there."

"Now?"

"Now. And don't say a word."

THIRTY-ONE

Angella already had the file open by the time I walked to her computer.

SPEAKER 1 (Male): You saying you had a hand in them closing the file so quickly?

SPEAKER 1: Everyone seems to owe you one.

SPEAKER 1: Is the cargo ship watch in place?

SPEAKER 1: ETA in New Orleans?

SPEAKER 1: Any luck in tracking down ownership? From a report Holland filed, the money traced from SOS found its way to the Isle of Man. *Ms Honey* is registered in the Isle of Man, just as you told us. Seems to be an Israeli vessel. Money came through Israel, unreported to our government. Wolfson is a large Israeli supporter. You put the pieces together.

SPEAKER 1: And I'm Peter Pan! What's the latest on how Snow got to Argentina?

SPEAKER 2 (Female) So Tiny has a lead on the plane. Wouldn't doubt if he flew it in himself.

Angella started to respond and I held up my hand. I reached
for my cell phone and typed: ANGELLA & I. OUR CONDO.
YESTERDAY. SEARCHING NOW FOR MICS.

Response was immediate. CQ ADVANCE TECHNICAL
TEAM ARRIVING YOUR CONDO ELEVEN HUNDRED
HOURS. MAINTAIN SILENCE.

"That's in six minutes," I unnecessarily said to Angella, breaking the rule.

A resigned look on her face, Angella leaned close and whispered in my ear, "I'll go down and let them in. I suppose they'll
come in the front door."

Unless they land on the roof and come through the window. Wisely,
for once, I kept my thoughts to myself.

- - - - -

In fact, the team came in the front door, three of them, and
rode up in the elevator with Angella.

"They haven't said a word," Angella whispered when we were
alone. "All nods and hand signals."

"Keeps them alive," I whispered back. I felt like a teenager
sneaking around the house, afraid of being caught, but doing
nothing of any consequence.

While we were exchanging secrets, one of the team
approached, his headshakes telling us he did not approve of the
whispers. We moved apart.

A small device in his palm began to flash. He circled the
room, and as he did so the lights became brighter and dimmer as
he moved. An electronic version of *hot* and *cold,* one of my favorite childhood games.

After a complete tour of the room even a neophyte like me knew what the verdict was. When the device was close to me, all the lights strobed brilliantly. The further away it moved, the dimmer they became.

The team member motioned for me to empty my pockets and to place the contents on the dining room table. I did so and stepped back. A quick pass of the meter over the table told us immediately that we had not yet found the transmitter.

Moving back toward me, the lights again danced wildly. It didn't take long before we isolated the location.

The transmitter had been expertly sewn into my new boots——the boots Tiny had given me at Angella's birthday party. One of the team members quickly slipped a bag over the boots and sealed the top.

He then studied his meter and after a few seconds walked over to Angella. Sure enough, the meter went wild.

Angella's boots were then quarantined the same as mine had been.

Several minutes later the team pronounced us and our condo clean——provided the boots remained in the sealed bags. Within minutes the team was gone, never having spoken one word.

"This isn't the first time microphones have been planted on us," Angella announced, barely concealing her disgust, "but I can't help feeling violated."

Judging from the workmanship, we concluded the same workman crafted both sets of boots. The FBI would now inter-view the boot maker and everybody who had an opportunity to touch the boots since manufacture. I trusted they would also interrogate Tiny. I also guessed nothing would be found.

"This explains a lot," I said. "I heard your voice when you left a voice message but never heard my answering machine. That's because the communication was coming from your boot, not from your cell as everyone thought. I can kick myself for not figuring that out."

"More troubling to me," Angella said, "is that Snow was killed just as he was about to come over to our side. I'm thinking they were listening via the microphones in our boots."

"That little guy, what's his name, Pavel Torres, is mixed up in whatever this is. He was acting on instructions."

Angella said, "I'm not ruling out Tiny. I know you're not as down on him as I am, but still———"

"This doesn't add up. Why give us transcripts? He's being duped as well. Think about Buenos Aires and Hotel Abasto. Recall that Shadowy Sal knew exactly which room we were in. She heard, via the boots, the manager give us the room number. But Tiny only knew the hotel, not the room."

"He could have been faking," Angella replied, still pissed at being bugged. "He's a smart guy. He could have held back know-ing we'd find out about the bug sooner or later."

"Nothing we can do about it at this moment. It's in the FBI's capable hands."

"What was Tiny saying about Director Kagan a few minutes ago. Words of wisdom?"

"He's convinced there's more to it than a drug fraud."

"Like what?" Angella asked, suddenly alert.

"We wouldn't have jobs if they could figure that out them-selves."

"Why don't they just board the vessel and see for themselves?"

"The ship's in international waters, flying the flag of the Isle of Man. Isle of Man won't allow boarding without more proof of wrongdoing. Kagan says they are sovereign for this purpose and won't interfere."

"Surely, they can't just land in New Orleans without being inspected."

"They'll be boarded alright, but not until they're within the U.S. Territorial waters."

"You mean while they're at sea they're immune from boarding?"

"Not exactly. If we have good reason to believe a major crime has been committed we can board. Isle of Man doesn't believe medication fraud arises to that level. Apparently it's politically unwise to move in now. The ship is being monitored. Nothing snarky has occurred."

"While you were talking, a thought came to me," Angella said, her eyes alive with the excitement of adding a piece to the puzzle. "We flew to Dallas on a Gulfstream jet. Tiny said a Gulfstream jet may have taken Snow to Argentina. Shouldn't we run that to ground?"

"Strike you as too much of a coincidence both planes are identical?" I asked, thinking Angella just might be on to something.

"Planes are strictly controlled by the FAA and go by registration numbers. I think they're called a tail number. But, come to think about it more, Gulfstreams are popular and the FBI would know if the same plane had been used, especially considering it was an international flight. This is probably just a coincidence."

Following Angella's comment, I sent a text to Tiny asking him to forward any pictures they have of the Gulfstream in Argentina. I planned to compare them to the picture Angella obtained of Wolf's plane in Port Isabel.

I turned to Angella. "Ask your friend out at the airport to send along any pictures of any Gulfstream landings at the airport."

"You have something in mind?"

"Shadowy Sal is lurking somewhere in this. I was fooled once and that's enough for me. I don't want to meet up with that snake again if I can help it."

Angella laughed. "You afraid she'll pose as me?"

"She's not tall enough to pull it off. But truth is she's good enough."

Angella didn't appreciate my comment and I spent the next fifteen minutes settling her.

Then a break——of sorts——came. The picture of the jet Tiny sent matched perfectly with the picture of the jet we flew to Dallas on.

"Matches right down to the dirt streak inside the zero of the four-fifty on the tail," I said. "See that? You're onto something, partner!"

"Now that you point it out." But the tail numbers are differ... Bingo! Do you see what I see?"

"I never see what you see," I responded. "What?"

"Tail number on Wolfson's plane is N thirty-six AF. Registration on the jet in Argentina is N thirty-six AE!"

"Not following."

"Black tape under the F makes it an E. Instant change of ownership!"

Angella immediately relayed the information to Tiny. Within five minutes Tiny's return text read:

N-36AF ORIGINALLY A 1972 BEECHCRAFT OWNED BY F HARRISON BANKS

"Someone bought the old plane for its number. Wonder who and when?"

"And why," Angella added.

"So they can fly the jet around without having it tied back to PAP. Same plane, same pilot, different owner depending on the tail number, E or F."

"Surely there are easier ways to hide ownership than that."

"Perhaps, but this way the airport log shows the jet to be in New Orleans when in fact it's in Texas——or Argentina."

"As I said, we still don't know why."

"Get an address for this F Harrison Banks. Let's pay him a visit."

"Or her," Angella reminded me.

"Or her," I conceded. "Or her."

"Last known address," Angella said, reading Tiny's message, "was a ranch north of a place called Botines? Know it?"

"Over in Webb County. Just north of Laredo. Not much out there. I spent time at the court house there a few years back. Can't say as that was my most pleasant assignment, but not a bad place. Some great places to have barbeque. They do it right. Smoke their own beef."

"Sounds like you're fixin' for a road trip."

"Take us four, maybe five, hours driving. We could round up a flight, but we have time on our hands."

"Overnight?"

"Why not? Government sponsored travel. Pack a bag. We'll have a picnic along the way."

THIRTY-TWO

An hour later we were on the causeway heading west toward McAllen. From there we would continue west on highway eighty-three to Laredo, essentially following the Rio Grande River upstream. A divided highway until Roma. Easy driving and plenty of time to think.

Just beyond McAllen my cell sounded.

"Hi, Dad," came the voice of my son. Only he had a stuffy nose, a cold perhaps, and I could hardly make out what he was saying. "I'm on my way down to your parts."

"I heard," I responded. "Where are you?"

"Making my way. Slow going. Be there tomorrow, or the next day."

"Take your time. Be safe."

"Got me some work on a fishing boat. It'll be nice to be warm."

"Beats freezing, if you want my opinion."

"I hear you livin' with someone. Don't know how I feel 'bout that."

"Who'd you hear that from?" His mother had no real way to know.

"Mother told me."

"How'd she know?" I couldn't imagine who could have told her.

"Ask her, if you want to know."

"Where are you now?"

"Denver."

"That will take you longer than one day. No hurry, I'm on my way to Laredo. Staying overnight. Be back tomorrow."

"What's in Laredo?"

"I'm seeing a man about a plane."

"You buying a plane?"

"Not just yet. Investigating an old plane."

"Two days then."

"Drive carefully."

"I always do."

"So, he's on his way," Angella said. "I look forward to meeting him. From what I gather from your expression he asked about me. Right?"

"He did."

"I'll go over to Port Isabel, live in my place while he's here."

"Don't be silly."

"You sure?"

"I talk to him twice a year. It's not his say about my relation-ships."

"Relationships? Plural?" Do you have something you want to discuss?"

"Nothing at all. He's causing trouble and not even here yet."

"Looking forward to his visit?"

"Mixed. Maybe we can rebuild."

"There's always hope."

"From your lips. We'll see. I wonder what kind of job he got. He's pretty good around fishing boats and there certainly are plenty of them down here."

Angella frowned. "I never knew the locals to hire people from afar. They usually need to see them in person, watch them move around on a boat. Size them up. Many of those boats go out for weeks, sometimes months, at a time. They don't want to be caught out there with a spongy-kneed landlubber. Someone could get hurt———or worse."

- - - - -

We were twenty miles east of Zapata and passing through the town of Lopeno when I saw a sign for Falcon Reservoir. "We can have our picnic over by the reservoir. Pick up some sandwiches, a few beers. We'll make a nice day of it."

"Sounds good."

"The reservoir is fed from the Rio Grande and sits on the border. Big recreational area. My father brought me down here years ago. I even brought Les once." I had forgotten about those outings with my father. Just the two of us. We'd do a little fishing, but mostly talking. About what I don't recall, but we talked——— almost non-stop we talked. I could never get Les to talk with me. He'd go along, but the silence was maddening.

"Slow down," Angella said, breaking into my thoughts. "There's a *Stop N Go*." She pointed to a small building attached to a gas station. "You can fill up while I get lunch."

We found a secluded spot and settled in, the water calm, an occasional ripple caused by a passing fishing boat. We found a large Burr Oak, still laden with acorns, some a good two inches long. I brushed the ground free of the acorns and sat facing the water, my back leaning on the tree trunk.

Angella nestled in my lap, her hair just under my chin, the scent of her delicious. We sat quietly, savoring the time together, eating our lunch. I was thankful for what hadn't happened to either of us in Buenos Aires. I also began thinking of what life would bring if I resigned from Homeland Security. What would I do? What would Angella do?

I may have dozed, but whatever, I wasn't aware we had a visitor until he accidently——or purposely——stepped on a fallen branch about fifteen feet from where we sat. My eyes opened in time to see a short-barreled shotgun pointing directly at us. The gun's owner appeared to have come across the border, only there wasn't a boat at the water's edge and he wasn't wet. My conclusion: He had come by car. This was no simple holdup or he would have already taken what he wanted and split.

Angella's body stiffened when she realized what was about to happen. We both had our weapons, but drawing and aiming from our present position was not possible.

My second conclusion: He hadn't already shot us for a reason. Was it because other folks were within viewing or hearing distance? Was it because he had orders to do something else? Maybe he had been told to stage the killing to make it look like a robbery, or carjacking.

"You want my money?" I called to him. "Here." I slowly moved my right hand toward my pocket, which brought it closer to the Beretta.

"No, no," he shouted, the shotgun gesturing wildly, "*Mantenga las manos alejadas.*"

So he knew I had a gun. Conclusion three: My initial assessment had been spot on. And, unless we're extremely lucky, it was going to end poorly.

From Angella's grasp of my hand it was clear she also had read the signs. The three most critical actions now were to keep the shooter calm, gain separation between Angella and me, as we had done in Argentina, and create a diversion. In these situations time worked against the shooter. But unless he was trained, or a pure psychopath, he would take time to work up to pulling the trigger.

"*Estar!*"

Angella began to get up and I followed, but not before I ran my hand along the ground hoping to locate an acorn.

"*Para el agua!*"

Apparently he planned to shoot us in the water. Angella started toward the reservoir, moving to her left. I started walking in the direction of the water, but moved to my right. When we passed him we were each about four yards on either side. His eyes were darting between us as he slowly walked backward. The shotgun continued to move from me to Angella and back again.

I was willing Angella to do something to distract him. Stumble, make a noise, anything that would cause him to look her way, even for an instant. Once we were in the water, we'd have no chance.

But she didn't do anything, other than walk dutifully down the slope toward the water. The shooter had managed to move behind us making it easier for him to watch us both.

The water was less than ten yards away and time was running out. I tightened my grip on the acorn, intending to flip it sidearm at his head. I was certain the motion of me doing it would immediately draw fire and with a shotgun his aim didn't have to be particularly good.

My hope was that while he was concentrating on me, Angella could get a shot off. She was an expert target shooter and at the shooting range she practiced drawing and shooting all in a single motion. I had no doubt one shot from her would be lethal, but only if she could make the heavy transition from target practice to homicide. My plan was that his first shot would only wound me. But I've seen enough to know, man makes plans and God laughs.

I fell back to my Army Ranger training. Make the plan. Think through all the pieces in order of execution. Then countdown. Okay. On three.

One. His eyes were on me, watching my every movement. He seemed to know I was about to take some action. I relaxed my face and allowed my arms to swing free.

Two. He's watching Angella. His shotgun is pointed downward, resting against his right leg. That's the side closest to me, meaning he will twist toward me when he's ready to fire, turning slightly away from Angella. The fact that the gun is down means he's concerned about a passerby seeing him. Or the shotgun is a bluff.

Three. His eyes are back on me, but I realize that fact a fraction too late. My right arm is already moving with the count. His eyes lock on my hand, the muzzle of his shotgun moves upward.

Angella continued down toward the water, apparently not realizing what was about to happen. Suddenly, she lost her footing, perhaps slipping on an acorn, perhaps in the soft mud of the slope.

The shotgun was almost level with my head when I let loose of the acorn, snapping my wrist as hard as I could while aiming for the middle of his face.

A searing pain shot up my left arm, a residual from when a bullet had shattered my wrist bone. I reached for my Beretta with my left hand, not trusting my weakened right.

The acorn hit the target just under his neck, causing the shotgun to jerk upward slightly, discharging as it moved.

The load ripped a path through the tree foliage, dislodging several acorns.

My left-handed draw was too slow, giving the shooter plenty of time to re-aim and shoot. I finally got my weapon free, slipped off the safety, and started to bring it to bear on him. But I was too late. He had pumped a fresh load into the chamber and the lethal weapon was now pointing directly at Angella.

I could see the muscles in the shooter's arm tighten as he began to apply pressure to the trigger. He wasn't a professional, but I had no doubt he would pull the trigger. The distance to Angella was so small he could hardly avoid killing her, no matter how poor a shot he was.

The sound of the weapon firing again sounded through the trees. This time no acorns fell.

THIRTY-THREE

The shooter was on the ground writhing in pain, his left leg all but destroyed. It took me a full moment to piece together what had actually happened. And when I did I realized, not for the first time, that to survive in my business, luck or a higher power, had to have you in good stead.

Angella's fall had, in fact, been staged. She had drawn her weapon on the way down, just as she had practiced. She then shot him though his knee, shattering his leg.

Actually, as it turned out, the shooter had short-stroked the pump and the shell latch had not fully engaged the new shell. Remington eight-seventies are known for that problem. This dude hadn't bothered with the upgrade. We could have apprehended this loser without firing a shot.

"So tell me," I said to Angella while we waited for the locals to arrive, "why not take him out. A head shot. Something in the chest. Making him a cripple wouldn't have saved you if the shotgun hadn't jammed."

"Don't make me feel worse than I do, Jimmy. I've never shot anyone before. It's not as easy as it seems. I didn't want to...I didn't want to explain his death to the powers...or to myself, quite frankly."

"We both could be dead here in the mud," I replied, trying to be the teacher and failing miserably. "Rats are equal opportunity; they don't care if you're a good guy or what. They could be eating us as they did Snow."

"Unlike a rat, I care!" Angella set her chin hard, scrambled to her feet and started toward the car.

Adrenalin rushing through the blood stream causes different reactions in different people. For me, my mind becomes sharp and focused and processes faster, which has the effect of everything external appearing in slow motion. I have no idea how Angella's body reacts to the overwhelming stress of a shotgun about to be discharged. In the past, she has reacted extremely well under pressure, so I was surprised at her storming off.

Angella's jeans were wet with mud and debris. "Angella," I called. I was intending to tell her not to sit on my seats with filthy pants. Instead, I said, "Sorry. Please come back and work through this with me."

Angella continued to the car, opened the door, but didn't climb in. She hung there, seemingly undecided. Then she turned, and with the determined stride of someone who knows what she wants, came back down the slope to where I was still sitting.

"You're a junkie, you know that, don't you?" Angella stood over me like a mother does with a petulant son. "You are addicted to the rush. Flight or fight is the conventional thinking. Not for you. You never even considered anything but going after him."

"I didn't shoot him?" After he went down I could easily have put a round through his brain. "Give me credit."

"Thank God. He's going nowhere. And thank God he jammed it. My brother had one like that and the same thing happened when he got excited and moved too fast."

"My point, and take this as a teaching moment, is that if the gun hadn't jammed you'd be...point is...when a life is on the line, mine or yours, take the perp out. Don't even think about it. Do it."

She leaned down and kissed me on the cheek. "I'm sorry I let you down. God I feel awful."

Angella had turned white. Her hands were shaking violently.

"Here, sit. It's PNS overshooting. Parasympathetic nervous reaction. Counters the SNS, the sympathetic reaction."

"What the hell are you babbling about? I'm about to vomit and you're giving me a text book lecture."

"Not unexpected," I said. "Your body is trying to attain homeostasis."

"Stop with the technical talk!" Angella exclaimed, and promptly lost it in the dirt beside her.

Before I could comfort her, the EMS van rolled up. I pointed to where the shooter lay, less than a foot from where he had fallen. His first impulse had been to crawl away, but he had given up that hope when he realized he'd bleed out if Angella or I didn't come to his assistance.

I had tied his shirt around his leg just above the knee and gave him instructions to maintain pressure on the wound. Preserving crime scenes is what it's all about, so we had been careful where we tramped and what we touched.

The two guys coming down the slope, a stretcher suspended between them, had no such concerns. Frankly, I had no desire to take charge, the tranquilizing affect of PNS having overshot its mark.

"Stable, but critical," one of them said into a headset. "Lost a lot of blood. Compound fracture of left tibia. Patella shattered. Right ear lacerated. Have him on the dock in fifteen. Out."

Angella, who I thought had recovered, bent over and dry heaved.

"Are you the shooter?" A deep voice from above and behind me asked. I looked up to see a Texas State Police officer looking down at me, his right hand resting on his holster.

"Help me stand," I said. "Better yet, help her up." I nodded toward Angella who was again sitting upright, but looking pale, "We can discuss what happened someplace more comfortable. You might want to call the crime scene folks. This will take a while."

"Both of you don't move," he immediately responded in a voice that left no doubt he was accustomed to having things go his way. "Remain exactly where you are! Now, answer my question. Did you shoot him?"

"No," I answered truthfully, telling myself if he wants to play hard-ass it's okay by me. We'll do it his way.

"Your weapon," he said, pulling his own and pointing it at me, "where is it?"

"In my holster where it belongs."

"Bring it out slowly and lay it on the ground."

"I am a———"

"Just bring out your weapon, cut the chatter! And do it slowly if you want to keep your hand."

I did as he said, wondering how long it would take him to realize the real shooter still had her weapon and if she had been bent on mischief would have already taken off his know-it-all head.

This was shaping up to be a long afternoon and not of the kind I had envisioned.

"We are Homeland Security officers," Angella said, now standing beside the State Police officer. Obviously, he had not thought of her as a threat.

"You working with him?" the big guy responded, doubt beginning to creep into his voice. "Your credentials. Slowly."

Angella handed him hers, and even before I could reach for mine, he pointed his gun away.

"Okay, what the hell's going on? Is he illegal?"

"Don't know a damn thing about him. He pulled a shotgun on us. Discharged it in my direction. Angella shot him."

"Slow down. Hold it. I've got to call this in." He started toward his car, then turned back and said, "That your car?"

I nodded.

"You can wait there if you like. This might take a while."

THIRTY-FOUR

Lieutenant Miller Contentus, my former Texas Ranger boss, was pacing my room at the El Bandito motel on the outskirts of Laredo. I hadn't seen Angella for hours. I knew she was at the same motel, but we had been separated and not allowed to communicate. We were both now in the Mother-May-I mode with neither of us being permitted to leave our rooms without being granted permission.

The frown finally worked its way off Contentus' face. I took that to be a good sign. I wasn't certain he believed my story, but there was nothing I could do to control what he thought.

"Pray tell me once again Redstone, how throwing an acorn at a shooter with a shotgun was calculated to get you home alive."

We'd been over this several times, and each time I repeated the story it sounded sillier than before.

"You couldn't have drawn on him?"

"You think he'd be alive right now if I could have? As I told you, I was trying to divert his attention, let Angella do the heavy lifting."

"She claims you called her out for not putting a round through his brain."

"Teaching moment. She went for his leg. He still could have taken at least one of us out. We caught a break when the gun jammed."

"Any more thoughts on why he chose to shoot at Angella when you were making the threatening motion?"

"Like you said, he wasn't afraid of the acorn. Or just maybe he knew I couldn't draw with my right hand."

"I'm glad you're with Homeland Security. You're their problem now." Changing the subject, he said, "What I don't understand is why the hell a guy like Hernandez Ocha would even agree to attack you two? The only rap we have on him is a two-bit misdemeanor, betting at a cockfight."

"Told you all I know," I replied, not wanting to go over it yet again. "We drove out here to talk to the rancher who sold a seventy-two Beachcraft to someone. That someone is using the tail numbers on a jet plane involved in trans-border activity. That's harmless enough."

"What's harmless?"

"Me interviewing some old guy. Could have called, but truth is we're killing time until that cargo ship, Angella calls it the *Honey Pot*, enters U.S. waters. Then we can board and get to the bottom of what's going down."

"That's more than I need to know. From my perspective who knew you were coming out this way?"

"That's just it, no one."

"Someone had to. Ocha says he was hired to take Angella down."

"So, why didn't he? He could have put her down right away. He had the opportunity. No one was around."

"Says he wasn't prepared for *dispar a una mujer*. Says he wasn't paid enough to shoot a woman."

I wondered how much a woman was worth these days on the hit market. Contentus was not the person to ask. "Who *was* paying him?"

"Sixty-four dollar question. He claims he doesn't know. Whoever it is they better take to the road. Ocha lost his left leg. The man's lucky to be alive. He'll go after whoever called, sure as we're talking. Might take a while, but he'll do it. Guys like him never blame themselves. They'd be in another line of work if they did."

"It won't happen soon enough for my purposes. I mean on this investigation."

Contentus reached into his carry bag and produced a folder containing an interview summary. The person being interviewed was F. Harrison Banks, who just happened to be the person Angella and I had come out here to talk with.

The interview produced little, except that the purchaser paid two hundred fifty for a one hundred thirty-five thousand dollar plane. Stapled to the inside flap of the file was a picture.

"Is this the purchaser?" I asked Contentus. Standing on a grass field leaning up against an ancient airplane, was none other than the person who flew us to Dallas. Only the person in the picture appeared to be a man. The pilot we had met was a woman. Same build, same everything, except the clothes. "That's Wolfson's pilot," I said to Contentus. "Only thing, when he flew us he was a woman. The plot thickens, as they say."

"Recognize the person off to the right?"

"Shit! Now that you ask! I thought that was the farmer's wife. That's Shadowy Sal!" I exclaimed, caught completely off guard. "Hair is shorter than when she and I met, but that's her all right."

"FBI just confirmed a positive face print match."

"What do you make of her involved with buying the plane?" I asked.

"My business is what happens in Texas. To the extent this spills over to national security business, I won't speculate. You're on your own for that." He threw a salute. "You're free to go. I suggest you round up Angella and head home. She needs to unwind. If she worked for me, I'd ground her for a month. Give her time to come down."

THIRTY-FIVE

Angella was uncharacteristically silent on the ride home. "Penny for your thoughts," I finally said, as we approached Laguna Vista. We were now less than fifteen minutes from South Padre Island and home. I've always been comforted coming home to my own place after a road trip, especially one that didn't go according to plan. I was looking forward to some quality down time.

"You'd be wasting your money," Angella replied. Her voice sounded far away, flat.

"Hey, I'm a big spender. Up it to a quarter."

"Spend thrift."

"You still…shall we say…peeved at me?"

"Not at you so much."

"Who then?"

"Me. I screwed up. I had thought it through on the way to the water. I knew exactly what I was going to do, and that included putting a round through his brain. But when instinct took over, it was his knee I went for."

"I didn't say you screwed up. I just said————"

"You didn't have to. "Guillimo said it for you. About took my head off."

Guillimo was Johnny Guillimo, Texas Ranger, the man who took over my slot when I was transferred to Homeland Security. Nice guy. Hardnosed, by the book kind of guy. "So, what did he say?"

"Exactly what you were trying to say. Man draws on you; you put a hole between his eyes. Period."

Changing the sore subject, I asked, "You have a thought how they tracked us to the reservoir?"

"Thought they told you. Easy. GPS locator planted in your car under the back seat."

"They must have done it when they drove off with the car at the beach. I never thought to check!" But something was wrong. They had just used a stringer to come after us. A second rate hack who didn't want to be involved————not with a woman anyway. "I think this was put together in a hurry. Could it be they didn't want us interviewing the plane————Banks?"

"They had no way to know we were going there. Boots were sealed before we discussed anything about the road trip."

"Sure about that?"

"Pretty sure," Angella said, a tinge of uncertainty crossing her face. "Anyway they knew they wanted us stopped." She went silent again, lost in thought.

I let her have her space, knowing she'd talk when she gathered herself.

"Jimmy, this just proves what I said————or maybe didn't say, but was thinking————when we're on assignment everything we say or do is being monitored."

"By our side or theirs?"

"Both, if you ask me," she replied, echoing my sentiment entirely.

"Gives me the creeps. I told you this before, but going forward when we're on assignment we'll...we'll live our lives...as partners."

"What are———"

"Jimmy, don't make this harder than it is. Business partners. Separate bedrooms, that sort of thing."

"How separate?"

"Separate. 'Nuff said."

"Starting?"

"Started."

"Love me?"

"This is not about love. Well, that's not accurate. It is about love. I love you deeply. I want that part of our lives private. I'll be there for you when the time is right. I want you there for me as well. Let's just concentrate our energies on solving what it is we're paid to solve. The rest will work out fine."

"Are you aware Shadowy Sal was with the Wolf's pilot when that old Beachcraft was purchased?"

"How do you know that?"

I told Angella about the picture, then added, "They, whoever they are, are using the same aircraft to transport the Wolf as they are to move people———and whatever else———in and out of the country."

"Your conclusion?"

"PAP is in this up to their corporate gunnels."

"Into what?"

"That is the sixty-four dollar question," I said, repeating what Contentus had said to me earlier.

"Okay, correct me when I go wrong. A jet plane with different tail numbers is moving people around. A cargo ship with different countries of registration, and possibly different owners, is moving cargo around. In some cases the cargo is drugs from PAP. Cargo ship makes a stop along the channels of Buenos Aires. PAP hires a known illegal drug facilitator to be chief of logistics. Guy is killed when he seems to be ready to spill the beans. Drug shipment is due to land in New Orleans." She thought for a moment, and then said, "What have I forgotten?"

I mentally ticked off my list. "Someone, most likely, Shadowy Sal, killed a guy who was a deckhand on a boat, military boat, set for demolition." I thought for a moment, then added, "And someone kidnapped us on SPI and again this morning."

"What do you suppose we're doing that's causing them to be so focused on us?"

I ticked off the possibilities and came up short. "Only thing that makes sense is that we're closest to the Texas connection. PAP, SOS. Something to do with those transactions."

"Let's revisit the Wolf," Angella suggested. "Get her take on Snow now that he's gone. After all, he was her employee, whether she knew it or not. Answering our questions on that subject is no longer optional."

"Are you up for a quick trip to Dallas?"

"Only thing I'm up for is a nice dinner and home to bed, if you really want to know the truth."

"Sounds like a plan."

"How about Sea Ranch?" She checked her watch. "How about picking me up at nine?"

"Picking you up?"

"Turn left here," she announced, "you're dropping me at my house. Weren't you listening? I'm moving back to my own place for the duration. Besides, my sister is there and it'll be nice to kick back with her for a while."

"Is she joining us for dinner?" I said, barely concealing the sarcasm.

"I hadn't thought of it. But if she's available, that's not a half-bad idea. I'll text you if she's joining us. She can drive, save you crossing the bridge to pick me up."

I pulled up in front of Angella's house and spotted Jayme's car in the drive. Angella leaned over and kissed me on the cheek, thought better of it and moved her lips down to meet mine.

"Stop pouting," she said when she opened the door to leave. "It's only temporary. Nothing's changed. Your son will be more comfortable with me over here. Trust me on that."

I had forgotten about Les. I checked my messages. Apparently, his car had finally given up the ghost in Denver and he was on a Southwest Airlines flight through Houston to Harlingen. His plane was scheduled to land ten minutes ago. Too bad I hadn't known that sooner, I could have picked him up.

I jumped out of my car, hoping to catch Angella before she disappeared into her house. But the door was just closing behind her. I walked up the steps and knocked.

Jayme opened the door. "Well, hi there. Didn't you just drop her off? Separation get to you?"

"Where is she? We need to talk."

"Bathroom. Made a beeline. Want a drink. I was just fixing one for her. From the looks of you two," Jayme said, "I should double the whiskey."

"No thanks. Just ask her to call me as soon as she can."

Jayme threw a salute. "You got it, boss. Anything else?"

"Enough for now," I said, heading for the door before I said or did something I'd regret.

- - - - -

"Hi, Dad," the voice on my cell said shortly after I got back to the condo.

"Les?" Since I have only one son, it had to be Les on the line, but I could not discern that from his voice.

"Let's meet for dinner. I'm famished. Allergic to peanuts and that's all they had on the plane. I haven't eaten all day."

"Sounds good to me. We can go out as soon as you get here."

"Just to warn you. You know I got injured on a fishing boat up in the Bering. Well, I don't look all that good. Doctors claim it's an allergic reaction to the medication. That's why I can't eat peanuts. Face puffed up. Splotchy. Itchy all over."

"How about a visit to the hospital?" I suggested.

"Doctor says it'll pass. Take time to get through my body, but it's not harmful."

"You can stay here with me as long as you like."

"No, Dad. I'm staying on the boat where I work. Thanks anyway. I'm standing in front of the boat now and as soon as I hang up, I'm getting on board. That way, after dinner I can just come back here and crash."

Medication at work, I thought. It's not like him to plan that far ahead.

"Oh, and dad," he added, "I miss home cooking. How about something that doesn't taste commercial. Any home cooking kind of places down here?"

"*Gabriella's*. As a kid you liked Italian. This place is the best."

"Still do."

"Should I come for you now? Or do you need time to unpack? Where's the ship tied up?"

"Now works, if that's okay by you. But I'll meet you there. Easier for me to get there than try to tell you where I am. See you in a half-hour."

"As you wish. Gabriella's is on the island, not far from the bridge."

"I'm sure the cab will know where to go."

- - - - -

I was at Gabriella's early and refrained from having anything stronger than a lime in my water. I had discussed the visit with Angella at length and her advice was, and I quote, 'to cool my jets'.

She was right on. My mind was racing a mile a minute. I hadn't seen Lester for close to ten years and had only spoken to him a few times a year, usually when he needed money, or needed bailed out of some misadventure. I didn't know what to expect or how I would react. Sending money was almost easier than meeting him in person. I consoled myself with the thought that at least this time he was on his way to what seemed a decent paying job.

But his medical situation concerned me. Allergic reactions to medications and goodness knows what else are not a good thing. If he was true to form he would have downplayed the seriousness of the situation.

Gabriella's was unusually slow and it was easy to keep my eye on the front door. The few times it opened my heart raced, but for no good reason. Les was not among the folks who came in.

A half-hour passed and I checked for messages, half expecting one that cancelled dinner.

Exactly one hour after Les had said he would join me a person of his height came through the front door, pausing at the small *maître de* stand. The hostess pointed in my direction.

Tired. Sick. Injured. Looks horrible. Beat-up. In need of help. These were the thoughts that flashed through my mind as my son walked toward me. I stood.

"Lester?" I said tentatively.

"Hi, Dad," came the feeble reply. "I told you I wasn't reacting well to the medicine. Made me puffy is all. I'll be fine."

Indeed, his voice sounded stronger than he looked. I took his hand, and his grip was as it always had been, strong. I started to pull him toward me for a hug, but he held back.

"Let's hold off on the hugs. My chest is still sore from where the rope hit." We sat and he said, "Freak accident. No one's fault, really. We were hauling in one of the long lines. Catch was excellent, line was full. I was working the capstan and the line, metal inner braid and all, snapped. Came back at me like a bullet."

"Thought those boats had shields in place to prevent that."

"It did. Line sliced right through the Plexiglas. The bitter end just caught me. Good thing it wasn't more than that. Cut my chest. If the shield hadn't caught it, it would have cut me in half. I got stitched back together. Everything is okay now except for the medication. Doctors say a month, two at most, it'll go away. Sunlight is good for it apparently."

"I'd think you'd have unemployment compensation———something. Isn't that federally mandated?"

"This is it. Guy down here is a friend of the ship owner where I was hurt. He said to come down here, go out with them here. Get full Bering Straits pay on a Gulf of Mexico transport. Easy work. One-year guarantee. Chance to get ahead for once. You want me to pass it up?"

"Not if you're up to it. But you don't appear——"

"Just the medication. Little slow of foot, but even that's almost back. They know of my lifting restriction. Got me signed on as Chief Mate. I run the operation. No heavy work. Just lots of coordination."

"Fishing? Shrimp?"

"Supply transport. We leave in the morning. Deliveries to vessels and platforms. Think of it as a floating Walmart."

"Supply ship. Most of that is based on the north coast. New Orleans. Biloxi."

"Heading that way. Hey, let's eat, I'm starved."

THIRTY-SIX

Over dinner I asked Les the name of the boat he was hurt on and he replied, "Drop it, Dad. I settled with them. It's behind me."

"But it's not right. There could be long-term…let's just say the injury could be worse than——"

"Drop it, will you! Allow me to live my life my way. You want to know why I don't call or visit more often…this is a good example. You let nothing alone. You analyze everything every way from Thursday. At least Mom stays out of my business!"

"Sorry, Son. Just trying to help." In fact, I wasn't sorry. I was doing what I thought a father should do; understand his son. But clearly it wasn't working. It had never worked.

"I'm doing just fine on my own. Give me space. I'd thought you'd be happy to know I'm working, got a good gig going. Even working here in Texas near you. You should be happy for me. But no, you have to trample over that as well."

Needless to say, the remainder of the dinner conversation was strained, as it always seemed to be. Why I thought our relationship would improve after such a long time is beyond me. All the normal father/son topics had long ago passed us by. I hesitantly asked about his life in the wilderness and he described his cabin and the unrelenting cold that not even a roaring fire could eliminate.

I couldn't pin him down as to romantic interests, but had the feeling there was, or had been, someone important in his life. The swelling in his face made it hard for him to converse, so much of dinner was spent in silence.

Walking out of the restaurant, I said, "Hope you enjoyed the spaghetti. They make it fresh to order. Don't know how they get it all done."

"I very much enjoyed it, I did. Thanks for dinner."

"Where can I take you? I'll drop you at the boat."

"I'd planned to take a taxi."

"That's not necessary. Where is this boat of yours docked?"

"Over in Port Isabel. Taxi is fine."

"Get in. No trouble at all."

He hesitated, then said, "Okay. I don't know the street, but I do know the way. Across the bridge and turn left."

I did as he instructed and after making a few wrong turns, we pulled into a Texaco filling station sitting back from the mostly residential street. Behind the station was a channel and steps led down to a wooden dock running along the edge of the water. Shadows of trawlers could be seen further up the dock.

"What the boat's name?" I asked as he climbed from the car.

"*Miss Rosie*. But it's anything but. My cabin is okay. I share it with two others. Both older. But the boat's a dump. We're scheduled to be out a month. Up north that's normal, but down here in the heat...so I won't see you until I get back."

"I understand. Hope you feel better soon. If not, be sure to———"

"Dad! I'm a big boy now, remember."

I remembered all right. A grown up who hadn't changed since he graduated high school———or possibly grade school.

"God be with you," I said into the wind as I watched him slowly walk up the boarding ramp and onto *Miss Rosie*. No sooner had he gained the deck but a black German Sheppard appeared from some hidden recess and sat at his feet, tail wagging excitedly. Les bent to pet the animal.

Nothing about this visit felt right. It was hard to make myself believe this stranger was my flesh and blood. As far back as I can remember my son had no use for dogs. I made a mental note to call my ex and get her take on it all. But that thought was even more distressing than this visit.

I called Angella thinking I could catch her and Jayme over at the *Sea Ranch* and have a drink with them to wash away the overhanging gloom. That's one of the best places on the island to do it.

"What is it, Jimmy?" a groggy voice asked. "What's so important you have to call in the middle of the night?"

"It's not even eleven, for God's sake. What's going on? Where are you?"

"In bed, where the hell else?"

"What happened to your night out at the *Sea Ranch*?"

"Jayme voted for a night in. Had pizza delivered and downed a few beers. So much for girls' night. Jayme nodded off before I did."

"Sorry to wake you. See you in the morning? How about *Ted's* at nine?"

"Nine it is. Love you."

"Love you. Someone's calling. See you at nine."

- - - - -

"This is Jimmy," I said into the phone as soon as Angella's call terminated. I tried to catch the calling number but it had come up unknown.

"This is Lotte Wolfson," the new voice said. "Trust this is not too late to call. I suppose a guy in your profession works all hours."

"Not too late at all," I replied, wondering what the Wolf wanted with me at this hour———or any hour.

"Can't say anything now. Can we meet in the morning?"

"I'm on the island. South Padre. You're in———"

"Dallas. I'll be on the island by nine-thirty at the latest. Coming in Southwest."

"In the morning? Southwest?"

"Of course in the morning. Enough said."

"Meet us at *Ted's*. Come hungry. Best pecan pancakes in the world."

"Us?"

"My partner, Angella, and I."

"If that's the only way. The fewer ears the better."

"After we eat we can find a quiet place."

"It's important that we speak. I love *Ted's*. Order for me."

THIRTY-SEVEN

I walked into *Ted's* at five minutes to nine and took a table in the back corner. I held my fingers up to indicate we'd have three for breakfast.

Angella had not yet arrived. On a whim, I checked the SWA schedule from Dallas and saw that the earliest plane was scheduled to land at eight-thirty. That meant the earliest the Wolf could arrive on the island was nine-thirty, just as she had said. At least that matched up. But again I reminded myself, professionals always get those things right. A good example of the Darwin principal at work.

I leaned back, sipped hot coffee and tried to wrap my brain around what Wolfson wanted from me. I came up blank. Well, not exactly blank because I ended up with a long list of questions for her.

At nine-twenty, I called Angella to see what was holding her up. It was so unlike her to be late and not call or text.

"Sorry, Jimmy," she said. "My friend from the Cameron County Airport called. He sent a video and I had to wait to get it. It wouldn't open. I'm on the bridge. Tell you about the video when I see you."

The front door opened and in walked Loretta Wolfson, dressed in jeans, boots up past her calves, and a blue starched blouse. As fixed up as she tried to be, she was still dumpy looking. Her arm was outstretched in greeting.

A far cry from the last time we had visited with her on her plane.

"You're looking well-rested," she said. "Where's your side kick? Glad you decided to do this one-on-one."

"Sorry to disappoint you. She's running late. Be here in a moment. I just ordered." I waved for coffee and Karen immediately filled the Wolf's mug. I motioned for her to fill Angella's as well.

Angella walked through the door even before Karen had finished pouring. Wolfson's back was to the door, and so she didn't see the look of surprise——followed by panic——that flashed across Angella's face. If I hadn't known her better, I would have thought she was about to draw on our guest.

"Angella," I said standing, "you know Ms Wolfson. She's come down to visit with us."

The Wolf reached out her hand in greeting. Angella studied her carefully and then walked around behind her so that she could sit with her back to the wall to my left.

"Pancakes will be here in a moment," I said, breaking what seemed to be an awkward silence. "I assume you're going with the pecans."

"Is there anything else?" Angella replied, her face still registering distress. "Lotte, that's what you go by, right? When did you arrive? I didn't know you were on the Island."

"Came down this morning," Wolfson responded, keeping her face neutral.

"May I ask how?" Angella pressed, taking the lead.

It was out of character for Angella to be firing questions from the hip, but I knew to allow her the lead.

"Southwest. From Dallas."

"Into Harlingen?"

"Where else?"

The pancakes arrived and Angella turned her attention to her breakfast. I said to the Wolf, "You seem to know your way around the island. Been here often?"

"I'm a real-estate developer. This run with PanAmerican is new to me. Before that I traveled all over the southwest looking for properties. Shopping centers, strip malls mostly. As a girl my family had a place here. I have friends who live here now. I watched this island grow up. I noticed you now have a great looking bookstore just a block from here."

"*Paragraphs on Padre*," I said, instantly recalling how Griff and Joni were able to obtain books I needed on satellites to help us solve a major problem. "So," I said, lowering my voice, "what was it you wanted to speak with us about?"

Angella, who had barely touched her pancakes, now sat back, her eyes never leaving the Wolf.

"You asked about that guy Snow we hired. You do know he was killed in Argentina? Right?"

"We are aware of his death," I replied, not going into more detail.

"What you don't know is that he called me that morning. Told me we had to talk. He had information for me."

"Did he say what information?"

"We were going to discuss that in person." She looked away and I had the distinct impression she was fighting back tears. "But unfortunately some hoodlum shot him in a bad part of town."

"Your processing facility is in that part of town, if I recall."

"God no! Much further up the channel in a good area. No one will tell me what Snow was doing down there."

"When we last spoke, you disclaimed all knowledge of Snow. You now want to change your story?"

The Wolf fell silent, studied her cup for a while, swallowed hard, then said, "Last time I didn't know how much…shit…I'd stepped in. I thought we had a small problem in Argentina and didn't want it becoming…well, a federal case. Get what I mean? But now, it seems the problem, well it's about to consume me. Truth is I hired Snow to report back to me what was going on with our deliveries. A report I saw made me think PAP is being manipulated. I have the sense documents are being withheld from me. I may be Chairman, but actions are taking place I never authorized, but bear my signature. But truth is I can't put my finger on anything concrete."

Angella leaned forward. "Can you provide examples of what's bothering you?"

"The thing that caught my attention initially was that ordering information always follows a pattern. Suddenly, about three months ago, the pattern changed. Orders for certain drugs in the Macrolides family, Azithromycin in particular, jumped. There is no reason for that drug to increase in sales so dramatically." The Wolf looked away again, her eyes hazed over for an instant before she said, "And I got a call from a guy named Pettit. Said he had important information for me. Wanted to meet in person."

"Did you meet with him?"

"Actually, I never spoke to him, he left a cryptic message. I never got the chance to speak with him in person before he———" Lotte looked away again, absently sipping her coffee before again taking a breath. "I'm sure you know this already, but he was killed. Right here on the island, I might add."

"Technically," I said, "over the island. But close enough."

"He left a second message confirming our appointment. According to him I was scheduled to pick him up at a small airport about fifty miles from here. From what I read in the paper, the meeting time was around the time he was killed. But the truth is I never had such an appointment. As I said, I was in the hospital."

We knew Wolfson had been in the hospital, so that much of her story checked out. "Did this guy Pettit say anything more?"

"Something to do about communications and drug mutants. I don't know what he was talking about, but I'm concerned about our product being compromised. We keep tight controls, from manufacture to delivery. I believe someone has compromised———or is about to compromise———the supply chain."

"Isn't that something you should have reported to the FDA?" I asked, making my voice as user-friendly as possible, considering the circumstances.

"Look, I'm really new to the pharmaceutical game. Perhaps I screwed up. But the last thing I want is the Feds climbing over us. From my limited dealings, your sister agencies are a nightmare to deal with. As you might imagine."

"That's no excuse but let's move on. Would any of your supply vessels stop at the location where Snow was shot?"

"God no! Their stops are tightly controlled———and timed. That's what puzzles me about Snow being where he was."

"What exactly do you believe is happening?"

"This is probably not a good place to discuss sensitive matters. You had suggested we go someplace private. How about your condo?"

"Instead, how about the beach?" Angella suggested, "We can talk down by the water. That's as safe as anywhere."

"If you say so."

In the parking lot, Wolfson started to climb into the back seat of my car and Angella said, "You sit up front. I'll ride in back."

"Wolfson shot her a *just what's got your tights in a wad* look, but did as she had been instructed.

I drove a few blocks north, passed *Clayton's,* and turned in at the next beach access point. We all got out and walked single file through the dune opening, Angella bringing up the rear. At water's edge, we turned north and walked about a quarter mile. The only people around were two locals racing homemade go-carts propelled by sails. It was easy to see how they could gain speed going downwind——north in this wind——but how they planned to come back south is a mystery to me. When they tried to turn it was clear it was a puzzle to them as well since they kept tipping over.

I had been watching these two yahoos while Wolfson continued walking, lost in her own thoughts. I hurried to catch up and when I did she stopped and reached into her handbag.

Immediately, Angella had her Beretta out and focused on the Wolf's chest. "Take your hand out of the bag," Angella demanded, "and do it slowly. Drop the bag and move away."

"Angella!" I shouted, "What——"

"She's an imposter, Jimmy. We're being duped again! This is not Wolfson!" She then instructed the Wolfson look-alike to lie face down on the hard packed sand, much as we had been forced to do in Argentina.

Angella made sense. That's how Pettit was killed. Lured to the airplane by a Wolfson look-alike and stabbed by Shadowy Sal. But there were any number of missing pieces. As a precaution, I drew my weapon as well. "Keep your hands where I can see them. Angella, kick the bag away."

"What the hell...what are you...what's got into you two? What imposter? I'm Loretta Wolfson. I called you last night. Have you two gone crazy?"

I nodded to Angella, who then moved in close to the Wolf and patted her down. When Angella finished, I said, "Roll over slowly and sit up. Don't get to your feet."

When the Wolf did as I instructed, I said to Angella, "Mind bringing me up to speed here?"

Without taking her eyes from the Wolf, Angella retrieved her cell phone, and one-handed scrolled down her screen, then handed the phone to me. "May have to shield it from the light, but that video I told you about, the one from my friend over at Cameron County airport. Look at it."

It took me several passes, but finally I was able to see what was troubling Angella. The PAP jet we had flown on was landing at the county airport. The time stamp at the top showed yesterday. The time was eighteen hundred and twenty-seven minutes. At fifty-seven minutes past the hour the stairs folded down and a minute later Shadowy Sal emerged. Based on the video, if the woman sitting at my feet was anyone other than Shadowy Sal I'll eat my old boots.

"So we meet again, Sally Comings." I said to our captive. "Don't know what your game is, but you're at the end of the line. You are under arrest. Anything you say can and will be used against you."

"I don't know what the hell you're talking about!" the Wolf screamed, "I'm Loretta Wolfson. Who the hell is Sally Comings?"

"Great actress, that's who!" Angella said, stepping back a few feet, but keeping her weapon poised to shoot.

"I don't know what the hell you're saying. I'm Loretta Wolfson!" she repeated, again reaching for her purse.

This time Angella kicked it into the surf. "Don't move an inch further," Angella commanded. "Put your arms behind you!"

"I was just getting my ID. It's in my wallet. Get it before the water destroys everything!"

"Fooled me once," I said. "That's once too many. It won't take much for me to put a hole through your head! You'd better listen and listen well."

The Wolf reluctantly put her hands behind her. But it was clear from the burning intensity in her eyes that her business with us was not finished.

"And just what do you intend on doing with me, Agent Redstone?"

"I suggest you just remain quiet," Angella snapped, "until we confirm your identity."

I holstered the Beretta and opened my cell phone, intending to turn on the fingerprint app. At that same time a black Sheppard, much like the one I had seen on *Miss Rosie,* came racing across the dunes and directly for Angella.

I reached for my gun, but again because of my hand injury I was too slow. The dog continued directly for Angella. But instead of leaping for Angella's throat, the dog stopped at her legs, tail wagging wildly.

Angella glanced down, I assume to make certain the dog was not going to take a chunk out of a leg. Taking advantage of the distraction, our prisoner jumped to her feet and began running toward the dunes.

Angella leveled her Beretta at the fleeing prisoner and in accordance with existing protocol, yelled, "Stop, or I'll shoot!"

THIRTY-EIGHT

The German Shepherd caught up to our captive before we did. The two of them got tangled and the Shadow lost her footing in the sand halfway up the ten-foot mound.

An attractive slender woman carrying a leash appeared on top of the dune. "Hydra what are you doing?" she yelled, addressing the dog. Assessing the situation, the woman turned to Shadowy Sal and said, "Sorry! She's just looking for a friend. She didn't bite you did she?" Sudden panic crossed the woman's face. "She never bites. Are you okay?" The woman then saw Angella running in their direction, the gun in her hand. "Don't shoot Hydra!" the woman pleaded. "She's harmless! She's a good dog. She loves to make new friends. Oh my God, don't shoot her!"

"Call that dog away," I shouted. "Get that leash on and get her away!"

The woman ran to her dog, slipped a loop over her snoot and yanked the dog toward her. When the dog was secured, I said, "Now get back off the dunes and away from here as fast as you can go. Comings, you don't move!"

The woman and her dog quickly disappeared over the dune in the direction she had come. Comings lay still on the sand. "Don't move," I instructed, "if you know what's good for you. Hold still while I print you. A sudden move and Angella will put a hole through you!" To myself, I added, "at a location of her choice."

I pressed Shadowy Sal's fingertips firmly against the glass of my phone. I then hit the send button.

Normally these checks take minutes, sometimes hours, to run. I used the high-priority button and this time the answer was back in less than twenty seconds.

"Okay, you can stand up now, Ms. Wolfson," I said to our prisoner. To Angella, I added, "She's not the Shadow."

"Positive?"

"As positive as these things ever are. Check her purse for weapons."

Angella trotted back across the beach and soon confirmed there was no weapon, including nail files, in the now all but destroyed handbag. I holstered my weapon.

"What the hell's this about?" Wolfson demanded, struggling to regain her composure. "I come down here to ask for help and you all but shoot me on the beach."

I held the cell phone out to her. "Tell me what you see."

"My plane rolling to a stop. But that's not me coming down the ramp. Who the hell is it? My build, walks like me, but not me! The time shows last night. Only I was in Dallas then!"

"Can you confirm that?"

"Will you take the word of two thousand people? I gave the *reason-to-give* talk at the Jewish Federation kick-off dinner. We raised over a million dollars."

Tiny called. "Understand you just processed the Wolf's fingerprints. What's up?"

He listened to what I had to say, then said, "Wait on the line. This should take but a minute."

It didn't even take that long.

"The plane's still at the airport,"Tiny reported. "Wolfson did deliver a talk in Dallas last night. Hold another minute, maybe two."

This time it took him five minutes before he announced, "We have her on video at Dallas Love, coming through security at thirty-five minutes past five this morning. She passed out of security in Harlingen ten minutes after the plane landed at twenty past eight. Limo was waiting for her. Driver claims he dropped her at *Ted's* about nine twenty-five. Unless the imposter gave that talk in Dallas, you have the real Wolfson woman with you."

Another dead end.

"That's all for now," I told Tiny, then added, "one other thing, Tiny. Personal, if you will. And private. My son, Les, was injured on a fishing boat operating in the Bering Straits. Says he settled with them, but he looks horrible. If I recall right, even if there's a settlement, they have to log the incident. Can you get me the record? It may come in handy if he doesn't heal properly. He's had some sort of major allergic reaction."

"They settle all the time. And often don't file incident reports. But there are ways to find out what went down. I'll see what I can do."

"Owe you one."

"Everyone owes me one. That's how I get my work done."

While I was on the phone with Tiny, Angella had led Lotte back down to the water. I joined them. "Checks out fine. But running like that could have cost you your life."

"I panicked. Sorry."

There was no use berating her, so I said, "When we last met, you were coming from New Orleans. You had been sick. Is that right?"

"Food poisoning. I spent the night in the hospital."

"Did you miss any important meetings? Perhaps they were cancelled." I was playing off something Tiny had said about Sally impersonating Wolfson at the talk."

"Matter of fact, we had to cancel an executive meeting."

"Do me a favor. Contact someone you trust on the committee and see if the meeting actually occurred. You can do so by pretending to have misplaced your notes and are looking for clarification. Or, frankly, do it any way you wish."

"You really think...you think———"

"Not thinking. Just checking."

The Wolf walked a few feet down the beach, used her cell phone and talked animatedly to someone for several minutes.

Her face told the story. The meeting had occurred.

"They had the meeting and discussed the logistics for the drug shipment. Apparently, I had approved the cargo ship stopping at that warehouse. The one I never heard about. That means———"

"That means your company, PanAm Pharma, has been hijacked by some very dangerous people."

"My God! I have to get back, fix the pro———"

"If they find out you know you're then no longer of any use to them. That could be dangerous for you."

"What did I get myself into?" she exclaimed. "I'm a business woman, not a criminal! What do you suggest I do?"

"Play their game. Say nothing. They've manipulated your movements for a while. Unless we tip them off, they need to be able to impersonate you, so you should be safe. Something big is coming. We must find out what it is."

"What should I do?"

"We'll bring in a top FBI team. Wire you, wire your plane. Give you twenty-four-seven coverage. It's dangerous, but we'll have your back."

"The way you put it, it's more dangerous if I do nothing."

"Pardon this question, but we need to get on that plane with a technical expert. We need to know about the pilot, any friends you bring about, everything."

"I understand."

"You ever...ever bring *friends* back to the plane?"

"Is that question a polite way of asking if I sleep around?"

"There is no polite way to ask that. You don't have to *sleep around*, as you say, to have friends spend the night."

"From time to time, I have someone stay on board with me. But, if you must know, my preference is not men."

"Let me show you a picture. Tell me what you see."

I brought up a copy of the picture Contentus had handed me of the buyer of the plane in South Texas. I purposely held my hand over Shadowy Sal.

"Oh, my God! That's my pilot! Only...only she's dressed in men's clothes!"

"Is your pilot male or female?"

"Most definitely female."

I didn't have to probe any deeper to know why Wolfson was so certain. The FBI would give us all the answers we required. Her DNA and her prints were all over the plane. In a few hours we'd know more about the woman than even her own mother.

I uncovered the image of Shadowy Sal. "Recognize that woman?"

"My God! That's the woman coming off my airplane!"

"Now let's get you back to Dallas," I said, "or wherever you are supposed to be, and we'll begin from there."

"And do what?"

"Keep with your normal routine. The FBI will intercept you when they are ready. Something you said a moment ago triggered a thought. You said, at the meeting you missed, they discussed allowing the ship to stop at the warehouse. Why's that important? I mean, you don't control the boat, so who cares where it stops?"

"It's complicated and highly technical. But pharmaceuticals for use in the U. S. must be manufactured and transported under strict controls. We manufacture certain Macrolides in Argentina for several reasons. One is that a main ingredient is grown there and freshness is paramount. Second, it's a way for our government to help their economy——in exchange for them reducing the illegal drug growth. Our big concern is that once the product leaves the plant it is subject to tampering."

"It's hard to stop tampering on the high seas," I said.

"Yes——and no," Wolfson answered. "Yes and no. Every container we ship is sealed with tamper proof seals. Also, every container has a GPS tag embedded in it. The route and speed of the ship, and a dozen other variables, are all programmed into a computer. The computer then downloads that information to each GPS tag. If any tag at any time is out of position, then we are alerted."

"Sounds complicated," Angella injected.

"Electronics and databases. Once the tags are in place the rest is easy. For example, if a container stopped someplace where it was not scheduled to stop, the GPS tag would tell us it was out of position. If a container was to be removed from the ship, we'd have a log."

"But the cargo ship could modify its travel plan, break down, any number of factors could go wrong."

"Yes, and then we'd know it and have to provide shore side security, or if a new route was to be programmed then we'd have to be sure the new route was cleared with U. S. Customs. It's elaborate, but it works."

"Until it doesn't," I said.

"If someone was to get his or her hands on the product what could they do?" Angella asked.

"Most likely cut it. That way they'd take, say a container for every ten containers on board. That would be a ten percent cut for us and a major windfall profit for them."

"Wouldn't you know it?"

"Not if the log sheets all tally. If the GPS tags don't show a problem, there's no need to recheck."

"Who makes the final determination about final checking?"

"It's costly and time-consuming to do it. When a ship arrives, I am given all of the paperwork, electronic mostly. I review it all and then decide to intervene or leave it alone. Believe me, there are a lot of cross-checks that must be right before I allow a product into the main-stream pharma channel."

"So that really allows for an imposter, does it not?"

"Only if she knew my pass codes. It's pretty foolproof."

"Nothing's foolproof," Angella injected. "Trust me, nothing's foolproof."

"You think my life is…is in danger?"

"Not so long as they don't know you know. You're their ticket to something. Frankly, we don't yet know what that something is."

"Will you ever? I mean, before it's too late?"

"I certainly hope so. No guarantees in this business though."

"I hope so as well."

"You better get yourself back to Dallas before your keepers figure out where you went. The FBI will be in touch."

"How will I know it's them?"

"Use the pass code Snow in honor of your fallen employee."

THIRTY-NINE

"Score one for the FBI," Tiny said an hour later. "You know that guy Hernandez Ocha that Angella shot by the Rio Grande. Turns out, he's singing like Tweety Pie."

"What's that two-bit weasel got to sing about———other than cock fights? The FBI planning to raid the fights? Maybe hold a press conference holding up a bunch of half-dead cocks. Your tax money at work type of thing!"

"I'll ignore your sarcasm, Redstone. But one of these days you'll go too———"

The line went silent, so silent I thought he had hung up as he usually does when he doesn't want to answer a question. "You still there?" I finally asked.

"Taking a few deep breaths. You know, you're not the easiest guy in the world to work with. You think you're the smartest guy in the room. Well, let me break it to you, Redstone, you're not indispensible. None of us are, if you want the truth."

I didn't need a lecture from Tiny at this point. My suspicions of him were still too recent, too raw, to allow a proper perspective and I knew if I got started I'd say things that would be better off not said, at least for now.

The phone was again silent. Tiny was waiting for a response from me. That meant he did have information to impart. Most likely important information or he would have cut out by now. "Okay, sorry, give me what you have," I said, my tone reconciliatory, or at least as reconciliatory as I knew how to make it.

"Ocha doesn't want to lose his security clearance. But he doesn't have a clue it's too late for that. Hold a federal agent at gunpoint, it's automatic. He'll never get another clearance. Claims he's being blackmailed by, of all people, Igletz Touchy."

"The Pig! Security clearance? What———"

"You know, the Pig's prints were found on the military vessel, the *Yellowstone*, over at the Brownsville salvage dock. Your interview with Santos noted Touchy had something to do with a missing radio. Well, get this. Ocha holds a secure communications clearance. Would you believe it? The man's a genius with radios! Ocha was also on the *Yellowstone*."

"That's not listed in the reports," I said.

"No need to list him. His prints were found there, but he had clearance. In short, he belonged on the boat."

"Continue," I said, knowing Tiny had only given me a partial story.

"According to Ocha, the Pig was looking for an authentication memory chip from one of the ship's radios."

"What the hell's an auth———"

"The authentication chip is used to verify that a particular transmission came from a particular boat———and that it was authorized. The chip the Pig was looking for authenticates not only a ship, but a country."

"Country?"

"Israel, to be specific. The *Yellowstone* was lent to Israel for several years after it was decommissioned. Apparently, one of the authentication chips went missing. Ocha knows for a fact it was in the *Yellowstone* when the boat came into Brownsville. Then it went missing."

"It went missing before or after the Pig went aboard?"

"Before."

"Does that snake have any idea who took it?"

"Should make you guess, but I'll————"

"Pettit!" I said, not waiting for Tiny's twenty-question routine. "Larson Pettit took it!"

"Indeed. Good show, Redstone. I knew there was a reason the President likes you."

"Any more for me?"

"Doesn't seem like you need much."

This time the line did, indeed, go dead.

I repeated the conversation for Angella, and then added, "Pettit found more than just the authentication chip. That alone would not have sent him to the marine biology lab though."

"Are you thinking something was on the chip? Some communication maybe?"

"Bingo! Someone recorded a message————must have been a terrifying message————and was going to send the message using the Israel authentication chip. That ties in with Wolfson."

"Ties in tighter with Sally Comings. She's the one who killed the poor guy."

"So we're looking for a chip," I said. "Confirm with Tiny that such a chip would be small. Get the exact size. But I bet it's one of those that can fit in a camera memory slot."

Angella got busy on her cell and while she was busy I replayed my Kranzler's encounter with Shadowy Sal.

"Ange," I called while she was still on the phone, "be back in about an hour. I'm going over to talk with Joy Malcom. Something she said back at Kranzler's has me interested."

Origins, where Joy Malcom had been confined for drug treatment, said they had no one registered under that name. A little gentle persuasion and they admitted that she had been released a few days earlier. I drove the few blocks to her apartment overlooking the Gulf of Mexico, took the elevator to her floor and rang the bell.

"Oh, Jimmy," Joy exclaimed when the door opened, "what a nice surprise! Come on in and make yourself comfortable. I'd offer you a drink but...but you know I can't have anything of that nature in the place. Cold water? Maybe a little lime?"

"Nothing thanks. You're looking well."

"Don't just stand there, give me a great big hug. I'm out now and feeling, well, you know, lonely."

The hug was involuntary. Joy pulled me close———way too close———and held on long after she should have let go.

When she finally let up, she said, "So you're not with Angella any more. Dating around? I must say, you can do better than that woman you were with." She did a teen-aged girl twirl, her shoulders back, chest out. "How's that for someone my age? Hey, I'm doing nothing for dinner tonight. I'll buy. You can be my date. I'd love to go out with you."

"You have your facts confused," I said. "That was...was a business relationship. I'm still with Angella."

Her shoulders fell and a childish pout formed on her face. "Oh, you've just broken my heart, Jimmy Redstone, you have. What can a girl do? You and I, we are perfect for each other."

I know I shouldn't ask, but I said, "How do you figure?"

"I love crime stuff. Murders and everything. And you are always around when someone gets killed. I can help you find the murderers. I'm good at solving mysteries. And I know everyone on this island———well, almost everyone."

"I'll bet you do, Joy. I'll just bet you do."

"So, if you didn't come to ask me for a date, just why did you come?"

"About that woman...my business associate. You said she was at *Origins* looking for Larson Pettit."

"Oh, the man who was killed in the parachute. See, that's what I said, you're always around when someone is killed."

"Are you sure it was her? The same woman?"

"One in the same."

"Did you know Larson?"

"He worked in the shipyard. I think with the tow service, but I'm not sure. We hung out together. Drinks, some...other stuff."

"Do drugs together?"

"Now, Jimmy, I'm not admitting anything. But we did hang out together. That's all I'm saying."

"Did you and he talk at *Origins?*"

"You do know the men and women are separate? Women are at Hannah's House."

"Yes."

"But we do have some classes together sometimes. Just after he came in we had a class and he hugged me. Only he never had hugged me before. This time he whispered something about his dog."

"What about his dog?"

"I only caught his name. He said other stuff, but I didn't hear it."

"You only heard the dog's name?"

"Snider. Or Slider. Something like that. He was saying something about drugs but poor guy was talking so fast I couldn't understand him."

"Where is the dog?"

"I reckon at the dog shelter. Poor dog. What will he do without Larson?"

"Maybe you should go adopt him," I said. "Assuming he's at the shelter."

"You think I can take care of a dog? I never had one. Is it much work?"

About the same as a husband, is what I wanted to say. "Might do you good," I said instead.

"I'll think about it. Any chance of dinner tonight? Just you and me? We won't call it a date. Just two friends out to dinner. I'd like that."

"Afraid not. I promised Angella."

"Then you better get out of here before she starts thinking we're…you just better go now."

"Take care of yourself, Joy."

"Don't be a stranger, Jimmy Redstone. Just don't be a stranger, you hear." She blew me a kiss.

- - - - -

At least ten small dogs, each barking at a different pitch, met me at the door of the *Island Dog Wash*. I didn't know if they wanted let out, or were just happy to see a new face———or in their case, smell a new smell. I hoped smelling my shoes was all they had in mind.

Cats were calling from cages that seemed to be open, yet none of them ventured out into the room. Dogs were sleeping on sofas and chairs as far back as I could see. A woman had a dog tied onto a table and was rinsing suds from his back.

I walked toward her and said, "Hi. I'm Jimmy Redstone and I have a question about a dog."

"You came to the right place. What's the question?"

"You have——or had——a dog in here name of Snider? Or Slider?"

"Oh, you mean Slider. Right over there." She pointed to a small white beagle with brown splashes, sleeping on a table, his paws over his ears as if that would keep the noise out. "He's up for adoption."

"Why is that?"

"Are you from around here?"

"I am."

"Then you heard 'bout the guy who got himself killed in a parachute accident. That's his dog."

"How long's he been here?"

"A few weeks now. Came in a few days before Larson, Mr. Pettit, got killed."

"Did he bring the dog in here often?"

"Just when he'd be on a boat a long time. The dog would stay with us for a week, sometimes two, at a time. Good dog. It's a shame about Mr. Pettit. Nice man."

"Would Slider make a good home for...a woman who never had a dog? A woman who...needs...a companion?"

"Slider would be perfect. All he'd need is a new collar? Has all his shots, everything."

"What's wrong with———"

"See, he has no collar. Someone stole it a few days ago. Fact is, day after poor Larson died."

"What happened?"

"Someone broke in. We were out to supper. We only left the animals an hour. Someone came in and took Slider."

"He's still here. I don't———"

"They took him, took his collar off and left him somewhere." She looked over at the sleeping dog, then added, "Poor baby, found his way back. He was in the doorway the next morning, paws bleeding and hair mangy. He hadn't eaten. He was hungry. He's okay now. All fixed up."

I went over to where Slider was sleeping and touched the dog behind his ears. He immediately woke up and once his big eyes were open I knew he was the perfect dog for Joy Malcom.

"How much will it cost to adopt him? He's not for me, but for a friend. A woman friend."

"Slider will make a nice present. He's a loving dog. Never any trouble. Never. Easy temper."

"How much?"

"We are a non-profit shelter. You make a donation. His unpaid costs are around two hundred dollars."

I paid them three-hundred and was planning to take Slider over to Joy when I thought better of it. I decided to call her and tell her to come pick up the dog. There was less chance for an entanglement doing it that way.

FORTY

"The Wolf becomes the prey," Angella said when I arrived back at the condo. "Under it all, I'm beginning to believe Lotte's a decent person. Far cry from our first encounter."

"We're her ticket to staying alive. So now she's turned on the charm."

"Someone, and I suppose it's Manhyme, is using her. For what it's not clear."

"I agree," I said, coming around to Angella's position. "Everything she's told us squares with what we know."

I dialed Lillie Holland thinking I would tell her about the impersonation of Wolfson by her nemesis, Shadowy Sal.

"Just the person I was thinking about," Lillie said, more upbeat than I had remembered her. "Some good news for a change. Plevin's out of hospital and making his way home. He appears to be well on his way to recovery."

"Any update from him on what he found in Argentina? Especially in that warehouse?"

"Let's do this on a secure connection," Lillie immediately responded. "I'm in possession of videos you should see."

"I'll have Tiny set it up. This may take a while."

"All I have is time. What precipitated your call? Forgot to inquire, I did."

I started to tell her about Sal impersonating the Wolf, but thought better of it. If she was worried about the connection being compromised, then I should be concerned as well. "Let's hold this until we're secure. Tell you what. Angella and I will head down to the Coast Guard station. If you'll talk to Tiny——or Kagan——and have them set up a military connection that will be the best——and quickest."

"Capital idea, Redstone. After all, it is your Air Force's data we will be viewing. How long will it take for you to be there?"

"Give us fifteen minutes."

"Perfect. By the way, an old friend of mine——and yours I'm told——will join us on the viewing."

I hesitated to ask, but Angella did it for me by exclaiming, "And just who will that be?"

"Oh, hello Angella," Holland said, "I didn't know you were listening in." Holland sounded miffed. Frankly, she was right. Protocol requires that I inform her upfront of Angella's presence.

"Let's keep that as my little surprise to you. Fair play and all that," Holland jabbed. "Besides, anticipation adds spice to life. See you in fifteen."

- - - - -

The world map was displayed on the drop-down screen when we walked into the conference room at Coast Guard Station South Padre Island. "Cowboy! You're looking well. And you also

Angella, none the worse for wear I see. Can't say that much for Mr. Ocha. Personally, I would have aimed higher."

The screen flickered and Lillie's face suddenly appeared beside that of Cindy McNaughton's. "Oh, sorry," Holland said, her British accent pronounced in contrast to the general's clipped New England drawl. "I meant to be on line sooner. Jimmy, Angella, I understand you know General McNaughton."

Knowing her was not the issue. Knowing why she was on the call was.

"The General will join us for this," Holland said, yielding no other information as to why Cindy was present. "Please note the green balloons," Holland began the briefing with no further introduction. "They represent the *Ms Honey* from the moment the PAP cargo was placed on board until present. Let's follow its progress."

The symbol of a hand appeared in the South Caribbean Sea and made its way toward Argentina, finally coming to stop at a dock on the *Rio la Matanza*. The map had expanded to show the river weaving its way south through various Buenos Aires neighborhoods.

"I'll now expand the balloon and see what we have."

Immediately, several boxes appeared, each with columns of information I could not decipher.

"Each box represents a sealed container," Holland continued, all business now, "loaded from the PAP ground facility in Buenos Aires. The information tells us what the material is, when it was manufactured, who inspected it during manufacture, who packed it, who supervised the packing, who inspected the sealing, all the way down to where on the ship the container was placed."

I recalled something Snow had said shortly before he was killed. "Is this what is meant by electronically sealing the cargo?"

"Affirmative. Each container has its own transponder, giving us, among other things, precise GPS coordinates of its location along with the time at any location. Shorthand version is that not one container has deviated from the planned route of the ship and not one container has had its seal broken." Holland paused, as if waiting for a response.

"Something is troubling you," I asked. "So what is it?" For now, I thought it wise to keep to myself the fact that the database timetable had been altered by Shadowy Sal impersonating the Wolf.

"The ship is steaming faster than it ever has in the past." McNaughton had taken over. "We've compared the last twenty tracks for this vessel and this track is five knots faster. Meaning that, when the *Honey* enters the Gulf of Mexico it will be about ten hours ahead of its expected schedule."

"Won't that cause the tracking devices to signal a problem?" Angella asked. "I thought they were set to the ship's course and speed."

McNaughton was quick to reply. "They are. That's precisely the problem. They haven't come up as being out of schedule."

"Meaning," I said, "someone knew ahead of time the *Honey* would be making better time than it normally does."

"Precisely, Agent Redstone. Precisely."

"The Wolf imposter most likely," Angella replied. "She must have changed the database posing as the Wo———Wolfson.

Silence on the line for a moment and then Holland said, "Obviously, you two have information I don't have about the security tracking. Care to share?"

I told her about the impersonation of Loretta Wolfson by Comings and that Comings approved a time schedule change while Wolfson was sick in the hospital.

When I finished, Holland said, "It's easy to leave a hospital for several hours. All you require is someone to lie for you. Or better yet, bribe someone. I very much doubt if, in fact, we have a real imposter. I agree the time schedule was changed, but I am not yet ready to lay this all at the feet of Comings. All too convenient for my blood."

"The FBI is working it as we speak," McNaughton said. "For now our assumption is that Wolfson has been co-opted and didn't know it until Redstone and Angella pointed it out to her. We'll know more after she's interviewed later in the day. My question is, is Sally good enough to pull off such an impersonation?"

Holland immediately answered, "More than talented enough. She's a first class actress and could have made it in Hollywood without doubt. She does men as well as women. Pulls it off like nobody I've ever seen. If you're spot on about her being impersonated, then Wolfson was targeted from the start. And, I might add, this operation is well-planned———as well as well financed."

"Following that logic then, we should be focused on GP Manhyme, the friend who put Wolfson onto PAP in the first instance," I said.

"He's the chap who laundered the money," Holland added. "Traced it through the Bank of Israel to Man."

"Lil," McNaughton interrupted, "what significance do you place on the decrease in transit time for the *Honey*? From my experience, ships don't change steaming speeds easily."

"Assuming the worst," Holland said, "the ship will spend an extra day in the Gulf of Mexico that is unaccounted for." The screen went blank momentarily and when it came back live, the faces of McNaughton and Holland had been replaced with a large graph showing several days along the bottom and line arcs of various colors stretching from left to right.

"On the screen I've positioned a time progression of vessels in and around the Gulf taken from your Air Force satellites. I hasten to point out that all friendly military assets have been electronically removed, as have been all vessels that cannot possibly intercept the *Honey*."

Now I understood why McNaughton was on the connection. As a former Marine General, logistics and military operations come second nature. "Was anything else removed from the graph?" I asked, suspecting the powers that be never share all information.

"Not that I know," Holland replied, tentatively.

"In the interest of full disclosure," McNaughton began, her tone that of one who is about to fess up after being caught with her hand in the cookie jar, "all vessels known to be…shall we say… safe, have been removed as well. For example, drilling platforms and their supply ships are not there."

I didn't like the sound of that, but from painful past experience I knew not to challenge Lucinda McNaughton unless I had the facts to support myself. "Any chance of obtaining a list of the names and any other info we have on each of the blips…vessels… on this chart?"

"What type of information are you referring to, Agent Redstone?" Holland asked, seemingly peeved I would question her presentation.

"Like their destinations, their ownership, flag country, cargo, military, that type of thing."

"I'll add it to the file," Holland answered, using her official British efficiency voice. "Most of the vessels are fishing boats and supply boats and are of no concern to us."

"Seems to me," I pressed, not trusting that all the information would be forthcoming, "we have eliminated a ton of vessels in an operation that we have not yet quantized. Is that smart?" I was actually thinking military ships. Not one had been shown. And Holland most likely wouldn't even have that information.

"Smart or not, it is what it is, Cowboy," McNaughton chastised. "Work with the hand you have. Move on."

FORTY-ONE

"I know she may have saved my life, but that doesn't mean I have to like her." Angella had been fussing over McNaughton's attitude with no sign of letting up. "Is there any sense in withholding from us information on any of the ships out there? The line was secure. We're cleared for top security. Can't imagine hiding it from Holland."

"Just their way. They give you only what they think you need. Compartmentalize."

"You'd think after September eleventh they would have learned."

"They have. I can't imagine how bad it must have been before that," I replied, doing what McNaughton told us to do and trying to focus on the hand we had been dealt. Trouble was there were still too many cards in the hole. "Have you been able to bring up the ship log from the file?"

"I have it. I'm looking for the connection to the projector so we can blow it up."

No sooner had the shipping information in the Gulf of Mexico come up on the screen but in walked Captain Ernest Boyle,
the head man for Coast Guard operations from Corpus to the
Mexican border.

"Heard you were prowling about, Redstone. Sorry I couldn't
join you sooner. And you also, Ms. Martinez. I haven't seen you
since your evacuation. You're looking well, all things considered."

All things considered meant removing an explosive device
from her buttocks. Boyle brought out the worst in me. I likened
it to the primal instinct of pending danger all animals have to one
extent or another. They may not know the precise danger, but
they know to take action. I couldn't control my emotion, but in a
civilized society I was expected to control my response. Smiling
as best I could, I said, "You're looking fit yourself, Captain."

"I work hard to keep it this way. Plenty of clean sea air and
light on the rum. Works wonders."

I didn't know if he was trying to send me a message, but I
wasn't buying in. The two of us had almost come to blows several
times in the past and with my damaged right hand this was not a
good time to get into it with him.

"What I don't understand, Redstone, was why the device
implanted in Angella didn't go off sooner. Mind explaining it to
me?"

"A shield material was over it. So long as the shield covered
the detonator, the device was safe. Simple but effective."

"Some things don't have to be complicated to work. Hey,
what's up there on the screen? Looks like our chart overlays but
minus some assets."

Here's where the rubber meets the road. We were in a
Coast Guard facility, using Coast Guard equipment. Boyle was
the Coast Guard person in charge. But I had no way to know if

he was authorized to see this or not. I found it strange that he showed up after Holland and McNaughton signed off. Angella was studying me, obviously wondering what I was going to do or say. Making my decision, I said, "You're quite right, Commander, these overlays show vessels in the Gulf."

"Obviously, not all of them," he replied. "Why the sub-set?"

Now we were into our mission and I was not prepared to go beyond what he could easily find out on his own. I was borrow-ing a page from McNaughton. "Captain," I began, forcing a larger than normal smile, "we are tracking a cargo ship. This one over here." I pointed the laser pointer to an orange box at the entrance to the Gulf between Cancun and Cuba.

"And why is that vessel so damn important that you and Mar-tinez came here to use a secure connection to see charts that any Internet savvy guru can download?"

"That, my dear Captain, is, as they say, the twenty-four dollar question."

"And what information is contained in those little boxes next to each vessel."

"Cargo and destination descriptions."

"And just why do you require such information? I don't have access to that data."

I leaned forward and wrote the name McNaughton on a piece of paper and added her phone number. "You know this woman, Captain. She holds all the answers. Call her and get whatever you require. Right now, Angella and I would like to finish our review and then get out of your hair."

The man turned redder than I had ever seen him. At first I thought I would have to put my right hand to the test. But Boyle backed off. "If you ever fall off the dock, Redstone, don't bother calling the Coast Guard for help. We're busy." With that, he turned and stormed out of the room.

"What was that about?" Angella asked when the door closed.

"Put it behind us. Man gets the sea equivalent of ants in his pants when anything involves water and he's not in the loop. If he was supposed to have been briefed, he would have been here."

"Cut him a break. He may have just arrived. Just 'cause you dislike him is no———"

"His helicopter is parked outside. I noticed it on the way in. He knew we were here, yet he only showed his face when McNaughton got off the line. He's being kept out of the operation for a purpose. Maybe the powers that be don't want the military involved."

"Coast Guard is not military———strictly speaking. Part of Homeland Security."

"Hybrid, actually. I still think of them as military. I'll bet McNaughton does as well."

I turned to the chart and said, "Let's move on. Read off the ship names. I'll jot them down. If I understand right, all these boats could possibly intersect the *Honey*. Do I have that right?"

"That's what I understand as well."

The fourth name on the list was the *Rosie*. "Hold it for a moment. The *Rosie*? When will it intersect the *Honey*? My son's on the *Rosie*."

"Reminds me of one of those dreaded word problems," Angella replied with no trace of a smile. "If a ship is going ten knots west, how long will it take to intersect a ship going twenty knots north if the Captain is eating a fish sandwich? Never could work those things."

"You're lucky I didn't ask the eye color of the Captain?"

"What are you babbling about?"

"Never mind. Part of an old joke. Remind me to tell you some time."

Angella scribbled a bunch of numbers onto a pad, did some additions and subtractions and then entered two numbers on her phone calculator. She tapped a button and triumphantly exclaimed, "In twenty-two and one-half hours, more or less, they will meet if both remain on course, and at their current speeds."

"How long until the Captain finishes his sandwich?"

"Will you stop! This is difficult enough."

"Now that you proved you can do it, please calculate the intersecting time for the other boats on this chart."

"Are you kidding? There's at least twenty of them."

"You needn't factor in any sandwiches. Assume the captain's are sleeping."

"Funny, funny." Angella bent over her paper.

I studied the chart a bit longer and then said, "Hold it. Put down your pencil."

"Did I flunk or something?"

"You aced it, actually. Convert the intersection time for the *Rosie* into actual time."

Angella dutifully added twenty-two and one-half hours onto the time shown at the top of the box labeled *Rosie* and announced, "Nine fifteen PM tomorrow."

"Add one for EST and five more for Zulu. That gives us zero-three-hundred fifteen."

"If you say so."

"Not just me," I said. "Look at the bottom set of numbers on the *Rosie* box."

"Three-hundred-fifteen. Someone already made the calculation."

"All the boxes have numbers," I said.

"You're right, Jimmy. Hey, look at this? Two intersect the *Honey* almost at the same time."

"The *Rosie* and something named *Irisl Bijar*."

I brought up my phone browser and searched on *Irisl*. A moment later I said to Angella, "According to Wikipedia, *Irisl* stands for Iranian Republic of Iran Shipping Lines Group and owns over a hundred cargo ships and controls close to two-hundred. It's the largest fleet in the Middle East. And I quote, 'However since American sanctions over Iran's support for various groups and nuclear program have begun to hinder *Irisl* operations, the organization has renamed its ships under shell companies in order to continue trading in banned goods.'"

"Iranian and Israeli vessels on intercepting trajectories," Angella said, her lips pulling tightly together. "This should be interesting indeed."

FORTY-TWO

"What I don't follow," Tiny said, "is why an Iranian ship would be rendezvousing with an Israeli ship. The two don't speak on land. I can't believe the sea is any different."

"The *Rosie* is also still on track but not the *Irisl*, which had slowed several hours ago. Not a coincidence my son is on board the *Rosie,* but why?"

We were in our apartment in the midst of a briefing prompted by Tiny calling us with the news that a Coast Guard helicopter from SPI was out over the Gulf following the path of the *Rosie*.

"Boyle putting two and two together," Angella said. "Is there a military aspect to this? Could any of these ships be carrying missiles? Lethal weapons?"

"No way for us to know," I replied, "but nothing in the report shows it. The *Bijar* is a small twenty-thousand ton dry cargo freighter carrying bulk rice."

"But it turned west, southwest hours ago. Heading directly for SPI."

"It now appears," Tiny said, "of the nine ships that could have intersected the *Honey*, six of them have either changed speed or altered course. Of the three still on course to intersect, we have the *Rosie*," Tiny said, mentally ticking off the facts as I had laid them out, "and two Japanese fishing boats."

Angella studied her computer intently before looking up. "The Japanese are headed home according to the CIA logs. But, my question is, shouldn't they be heading south toward the channel? Last we saw, they were going due east."

"Under treaty with Mexico, they can't come within one hundred miles of the Cancun coast. They should have already turned and we'll see their new track on the next satellite pass if they are, in fact, heading out of the Gulf. We'll know within the hour. As an aside, the CIA raised one of the crew on short-wave. Unofficially, I hasten to add. Conversation confirms both Japanese ships are heading to Panama. The crew is looking forward to leave and picking up a new ship in a week. That comports with our official ship log from the Pacific."

"Is there anything the CIA doesn't track?"

"I'm not aware of anything," Tiny said, a trace of pride in his voice. "If it all doesn't match up, all hell breaks loose. Hold it a moment." Tiny went off line. When he returned he said, "New data is in. The Japanese trawlers did, in fact, turn south. But the *Honey* turned west. Apparently she did so just after the last satellite pass. And sped up again. That tub must be hauling ass because it's made significant progress into the Gulf. Now at twenty-three point eight-four north and eighty-seven point nine west."

"What about *Rosie*?"

"Seems to have slowed. Hanging around twenty-five point eight north, ninety-four west."

"And the *Bijar*?"

"Northeast of *Honey*."

"Coordinates?" Angella said, "I'm plotting all this."

"Twenty-three point two north, eighty-eight point one west."

"So," Angella said after studying the Gulf of Mexico and her pointers, "we should expect the *Bijar* to turn south if there is to be a meeting."

"Right on," Tiny replied. "We're estimating the rendezvous to occur, if at all, at twenty-five point eight north and ninety-one point nine west."

"Enough of that you guys," I said. "Translate."

"All three will come together, again if nothing changes, in about two-hundred fifty nautical miles."

"Time?" I asked.

"Assuming twenty knots," Angella said, seemingly enjoying her math problems, "about twelve to thirteen hours." She flashed a smile in my direction, "And the Captain's eyes are green, case you're wondering."

"The *Honey* has been averaging over thirty knots for the past few days," Tiny reminded us.

"Okay, then between eight and thirteen hours. Isn't the *Honey* scheduled to dock in New Orleans?" Angella asked.

"Affirmative," I replied.

"It is," Tiny confirmed.

"Well, the ship is now west of New Orleans. She doesn't seem to be headed in the right direction."

"Eventually she will have to get there," I said, "but seems she's taking a detour."

"As you said, your son is on the *Rosie,* Jimmy," Tiny commented. "I agree, that's not a coincidence. To add to the confusion, I can't find any record of his injury up in Alaska."

"He said it was settled. Paid him off with a job on the *Rosie*."

"I can't find any financial connection between the *Rosie* and any fishing boat in Alaska," Tiny pressed. "Nothing comes up. We ran it every which way."

Thinking of the *Rosie* reminded me of the Coast Guard helicopter going in that direction. I asked Tiny about it.

"Recalled. McNaughton spoke to her friend Jamison. Short version, Captain Boyle is back on the hard. I'm told he's fuming."

"Jamison! How'd he get involved?" Retired General Maxwell Jamison is the President's go-to military man when it comes to terrorism and international relations. "I thought this was domestic. Maybe global with Interpol, but not terrorism."

"It was until three hours ago," Tiny said, a hint of more to follow in his voice.

Angella bit. "Are you going to level with us? Or are we back to twenty questions?"

"Now, now, Martinez, there's no call for sarcasm. Play nice."

"Not sarcastic as much as…well letting you know I'm bristling for not being fully briefed."

"Understand something, both of you. At any given time there is more going on in the world than what you're concerned with. People are dying. Good people trying to protect what we believe in. Operations have priorities and frankly, this may come as a shock to you, your operations are not always on the top of the list. Also," Tiny said, settling into his lecture mode, "it is vitally necessary to filter what we receive and categorize it so that we can deal with it intelligently. This, by necessity, takes time."

"Enough with the schooling," I said, "What's changed?"

"Still out of focus, but here is what we have. The CIA began picking up snippets of conversation about an Israel sponsored terrorist operation being mounted against the United States."

"Israel against the U.S.? That's nonsense and you know it!"

"Hold on, Redstone, let me give you what we have. Attributed initially to unidentified Arab Brotherhood operatives, Israel was going to launch a biological attack on the U.S. by contaminating our water. The CIA dismissed the chatter at first as either wishful thinking or diversion tactics."

I studied Tiny, and then asked, "What changed?"

"The vessel tasked to perform the mission is none other than the *Honey*, under commission to PAP. Then an Interpol agent found the missing link to the chain of title of the *Honey*. Latest intel on ownership is Asdod Shipping. Israel all the way."

"Has that been confirmed?" Angella inquired.

"Not in any official manner, no," Tiny replied. "But sometimes appearances are reality. BBC, an hour ago, received a copy of the title documents showing the *Honey* as being formerly named *Haifa*. Wire services have picked that up, and both the British government as well as our State Department, are frantically trying to play it down."

"Any success?" Angella followed up.

"Yes and no. Yes, in the sense it is not already on the news. But no, if you think it will remain silent. The fact that the *Honey* is now off course and heading west toward South Texas is not going to help matters."

"But," I added, "the only thing we know about the *Honey* is that it is carrying pharmaceuticals under close transit control."

"Not exactly accurate," Tiny was quick to point out. "We also know the *Honey* made an unscheduled stop along the south channel after those pharmaceuticals were loaded. We know that something was loaded aboard from a warehouse and that shortly thereafter the warehouse blew apart."

"Speculation."

"International incidents are always sparked by speculation. What is the White House supposed to say?"

"No comment, I would think," I said, visualizing three ships steaming toward a common point in the Gulf of Mexico. One from Israel, one from Iran and one from Port Isabel. The Mid-East conflict brought to the Gulf of Mexico. "We know of no wrong doing by anyone," I said to Tiny, actually trying to convince myself.

"Until fifteen minutes ago," Tiny said. "I just received an update. You two better get yourselves back to the CG station as fast as your wheels will take you."

"What's this about?"

"Video just released to the media lines it up for us."

"Lines what up?" Tiny is the master at spoon-feeding and was now at his best.

"You'll have to see for yourself. But in light of the video, the State Department has demanded an in-person explanation from the Israeli Ambassador."

"So what's on this video?"

"Not just what, but who made it."

"So who already?"

"None other than your friend Loretta Wolfson announcing that PanAm Pharma hired an Israeli owned cargo ship to transport highly controlled medication to the United States. En route, so she claims, the captain of the ship opened the sealed cargo and delivered a part of it to another ship."

"That's not true. There has been no such meeting at sea! Not yet anyway."

"The world doesn't know what we know. But hear me out on this. The transmission was encoded using the Israeli code and bore the unique identity of Israel."

"They used the stolen chip!" I said, thinking back to the missing dog collar and the death of Larson Pettit by Shadowy Sal's hand over our heads at SPI.

"Indeed they did. Israel cancelled that chip months ago. Every intelligence service in the world knows not to trust anything transmitted using that chip. But," the big guy paused, letting what he just said register, "countries, and there are more than you can imagine, ignore the facts when it's convenient to do so."

"What is the U. S. doing?"

"Playing it low key. Informing governments that the code chip has been decertified and that any message using that chip is phony. In the interest of not escalating the problem further, a decision has been made, for better or worse, to keep our military and Coast Guard away. We don't want to be seen as helping either side in any way."

"You want us to view the video. What's there you haven't told us?"

"Keep in mind, from our satellite reports, the boats have not yet come together. Yet the video clearly shows the transfer."

I didn't relish going back to the Coast Guard Station. That would mean interacting with Captain Boyle once again and I didn't need another encounter. "What's so important that we have to see it ourselves? And don't say a picture is worth——"

"Your son is clearly seen climbing from the *Honey* to the *Rosie* with a carton of the supposedly lethal material."

"Les?"

"Without a doubt."

"And what does Les do with the material aboard the *Rosie?*"

"For starters, he dumps some or all of it overboard."

FORTY-THREE

"But we know from the tracking———as well as the actual video———the *Rosie* and the *Honey* never came closer than two-hundred fifty nautical miles of each other, at least before that video was released," Angella said as we raced down Padre Boulevard toward the Coast Guard station.

We were following a police escort arranged for by Tiny, which seemed a bit excessive given that there were so few cars on the road and we were only going four miles.

One step inside the station and Captain Boyle appeared. "So here we go again, Redstone. I should kick you the hell out of here. My job's to keep the waters in the western Gulf free of mischief and you go and have me called off the hunt!"

"I had nothing to do with that, I assure you, Captain."

"Not the way I see it! Your son dumped highly toxic material into the Gulf. You're protecting him! You know what that'll do to fishing? The economy of the entire southwest will be compromised!"

"Is that now confirmed? The toxic dump, I mean." I wanted this conversation to remain based on facts, not speculation.

"Not officially, but it's happening fast. We intercepted trawler traffic. Sharks are coming up lethargic, dazed, about two hundred miles out. Unless we do something…my hands are tied on this…fishing will all but be destroyed. They won't even allow the Game and Wildlife wardens out."

"I assure you, I don't know any more than you do. I was told to come here to view video. That's all I know."

"Brief me afterward." He abruptly turned and disappeared around a corner.

"Wonder why they're not including Boyle?" Angella asked. "I would think they'd want him in the loop."

"Maybe it's us who are out of the loop. He seems well informed. Actually, knows more than we do."

"That remains to be seen."

We walked into the now familiar conference room and immediately McNaughton's voice filled the room. "What the hell took you two so long? Time's critical here. There's a report circulating that fish are already dying. The video Tiny told you about has gone viral. It's just a matter of time until CNN or BBC broadcasts it. The Israeli ambassador has categorically denied all knowledge. He even denied the *Honey* is an Israeli vessel."

"Play the original video, would you. The one showing my son moving between ships."

A moment later the room dimmed and the view from a low flying airplane came on showing a calm body of water below. Into the frame appeared a small, in comparison to the openness of the water, supply boat. It appeared to be the same one Les was on. A moment later the camera showed a view of the bow and the name *Rosie* bobbed into view.

McNaughton then said, "The lat-lon coordinates indicate this video was captured ten miles off the coast of SPI. But, we have reason to believe the coordinates have been doctored."

My son then appeared on deck, the black dog at his heels. Two other seamen also came into view, but their faces were not captured.

"Is that Les?" Angella said. "I recognize him from your pictures, but he seems to have gained some bulk."

"Medication. He looked horrible when I saw him a few days ago." I said to McNaughton, "That does appear to be my son. He was hurt on a long lines fishing boat up in the Bering Sea and had a bad reaction to the medication."

"Looks to be moving okay," McNaughton replied.

Another, much larger, ship came into view and the *Rosie* was now pulling alongside. Ropes were tossed down from the new boat and the two seamen pulled the *Rosie* tight against the larger hull. A ladder was then dropped and Les scrambled up the side, the dog waiting on deck of the *Rosie*.

"Is that supposed to be the *Honey*?" I asked.

"It is, Cowboy. In a few frames you'll see the name. There it is. *Honey*. Clear as day."

"Jimmy," Angella said, fumbling with her phone. Something's wrong." She continued working her phone while I watched Les take several packages from the *Honey* and pass them down the ladder to one of the deckhands. He then took a carton, slid his legs through the railing and proceeded down the ladder with the package.

The camera then pulled back, prominently displaying the name *Honey* as the larger ship moved away. The video ended with Les pouring the contents of the carton over the side of the *Rosie*.

"Here it is!" exclaimed Angella. "I thought I'd lost it." She turned her phone to me. "See that?"

I did. The ship with the name H*oney* tied up between two rusting freighters in Buenos Aires. Snow had died on the dock in front of this very same ship.

"The same———"

"Not so fast, Jimmy," Angella cautioned me. "Not so fast. Two things. On the one we saw in Argentina that railing was bent. I remember saying to myself that it was useless to stop anyone from falling overboard. It's not bent now."

"Could have fixed it at sea. And second?"

"Second, the script is wrong. See here, *Honey* is all initial caps. If we go back in the video, the name *Honey* has a large H and ONEY are in small letters."

The video was backed up and that portion again came onto the screen. Angella was right. Different lettering.

"Sharp eyes," McNaughton said. "None of our geeks picked that up. They noticed the railing and thought maybe it had been repaired. But they certainly didn't repaint the name. Now let me play another video. This one of Wolfson announcing the transfer of the medications."

Sure enough, there was the Wolf, standing at a podium delivering an address to a group of people. Behind her was the typical blue background with the name of the sponsoring organization repeatedly printed on it at various angles. In this case the printing said Jewish International Alliance. I could not determine if it was the Wolf herself or Shadowy Sal.

Before I could say anything, McNaughton said, "This is a doctored video. There is no organization called Jewish International Alliance. The podium says *Hilton Midtown*. From the table arrangements and food on the table they believe the original video was shot during a *Friends of Persia* rally two weeks ago. The hotel believes this particular video was made during a rehearsal several hours before the actual dinner. The audience was photo shopped in afterward."

"Clever. And well planned," I said. "How does Israel, or any country, refute this *hard* evidence? We have Iran blowing up Israeli diplomats. They claim it is retaliation for Israel killing its nuclear scientists. Israel denies it. Iran denies it. People believe whom-ever they want to believe."

"If fish begin dying, Israel will come under intense pressure. The UN will pass a resolution. The U.S. will be forced to veto yet another sanction."

"So tell me, why is the *Irisl Bijar*, an Iranian owned ship, about to rendezvous with the *Honey* and presumably with the *Rosie?*"

"Never said we knew everything, Cowboy. You and Angella have work to do."

"Why not just board the *Honey* and find out what really is going on?" Angella asked.

"Now how would that play out, my dear? The world is watching Israel dump toxins in our water. The U.S. raids the vessel and does what? We already know the story is phony. So we raid the boat and just say, 'Nothing's here. See, here are the medications untouched.' No one will believe us. Most likely they'll claim we're in league."

"Bring in a neutral observer. A scientist who is believable."

"It used to work that way. Afraid now even the scientists have agendas. It'll appear as a cover-up I'm afraid."

"What exactly is our mission going forward from this point?" I asked McNaughton, desiring clarification.

"Simple. Defuse the situation. Keep the U.S. out of sight at all costs."

"And if there is a massive fish kill?"

"Be sure someone other than the U. S. takes the fall."

"And just who should that someone be?"

"Whoever is the most convenient. Personally, since Iran is already on the world's sanction list, I wouldn't mind piling it on. But if the stuff truly came in on an Israeli owned ship, you can let the chips fall where they fall."

"You know from the facts it wasn't Israel. Wolfson's been compromised!"

"Says you."

"Whoa! You just got finished saying the video of her announcement was staged."

"Ever hear of double-think? In the battle for public opinion——particularly on the Internet——it is not uncommon to make it appear manipulated. Then, when we go public and denounce it as a phony, they produce evidence that it was real. The claim is that we doctored it. People who hate us just use it as further proof of how bad we really are. Rallies their base type of thing."

"Since when does our government walk away from a friend when we know for a fact the friend is not the source of the trouble?"

"I know of no such fact!"

I thought the line had gone dead, which is McNaughton's way when she is finished, but she added, "Oh, and Cowboy, word from the Commander In Chief, keep the military the hell out of this. You need transport, use commercial."

FORTY-FOUR

"I thought the General was your good buddy," Angella said, smiling at me as if to emphasize that only she, Angella, had my back.

"That buzzing sound you heard, that was the saw," I said. "We're out on a limb and they're hacking away."

"The only question remaining is how long do we have before the limb is completely severed?"

"It's not how soon. It's how high we'll be when the limb separates."

"I don't suppose this will be a soft landing either." Angella studied her computer screen a moment and then added, "The buzz just got louder." She turned the screen to face me.

ISRAEL AMBASADOR
CALLED TO STATE DEPARTMENT
TO EXPLAIN TAMPERED DRUGS

Earlier today, Loretta Wolfson, President of PanAm Pharma, reported that potentially lethal medications being transported by an Israeli owned cargo ship from Buenos Aires to New Orleans rendezvoused with a supply boat from Port Isabel, Texas and the Captain of the Israeli ship handed the medications to a ship hand from the supply ship.

The Israeli owned ship is called the *HONEY* and carries the flag of the Isle of Man for convenience. According to Ms. Wolfson, the medication is manufactured under strict controls in Argentina and shipped to the United States for sale, mostly for use by Medicare recipients. When mixed with a certain chemical, the medication becomes highly toxic to marine life, especially to sharks and dolphins.

The Coast Guard has confirmed the presence of the HONEY within the Gulf of Mexico and has also confirmed that the supply vessel ROSIE is known to be in the vicinity of the HONEY.

Reached for further comment, Captain Ernest Boyle, the Commander of Coast Guard Station South Padre Island, refused to elaborate, except to say that his station is monitoring vessel movement and will take whatever action is necessary as the situation develops. Captain Boyle has denied that the HONEY and the ROSIE have been within fifty miles of each other.

Captain Boyle's statement, however, does not comport with a video recently released showing the two vessels, the *HONEY* and the ROSIE, tied together in the Gulf of Mexico. The video calls into question involvement by the United States in illegal drug activities. Also called into question is the involvement of the U.S. Military in covering for Israel.

This comes on the heels of Israel being accused by Iran of killing several of Iran's top nuclear advisors.

Ms. Wolfson is a known contributor to Jewish causes and was a motivational speaker at a Jewish fundraising dinner recently held in Dallas.

When I finished reading the article, Angella turned the computer back in her direction. A moment later it was again turned toward me.

HOMELAND SECURITY
INVOLVED WITH TOXIC MEDICATION DUMP

Despite denials by the U.S. State Department, it is now clear that Homeland Security has been meeting with PanAm Pharma President Loretta Wolfson and with Interpol Agent Lillie Holland for weeks, all pertaining to drugs transported on the *HONEY*.

Reliable sources indicate that Homeland Security agent Jimmy Redstone, seen recently (below photo) having a candlelight dinner with Interpol Agent Holland at an upscale South Padre Island restaurant, traveled to Buenos Aires to oversee shipment of the medication.

The second picture below shows Redstone and his partner Angella Martinez, standing on the dock with the *HONEY* behind them.

The *HONEY* was making an unscheduled stop during transit of the South Channel in Buenos Aires. The Argentine government maintains that neither Redstone nor Martinez were ever legally present in their country and are anxious to talk with both of them about the incident.

The third picture shows Redstone having dinner with his son, a deckhand on the supply ship ROSIE. The ROSIE is said to be dumping toxic drugs in the Gulf of Mexico. It is believed the toxic drugs come from the HONEY, the same ship Redstone and Martinez are seen with in Argentina.

Continued requests to the Coast Guard and to the Military command go unanswered. However, marine biologists have confirmed the toxic deaths of several sharks and dolphins in the Gulf of Mexico.

"How did they get all this stuff? The pictures, the video, everything?"

"Professionals. I never saw a camera, or anyone who could have taken the pictures, did you?"

"On the dock in Argentina, Tiny was there. So was that small guy. Torres. Pavel Torres. The guy we have down for dispatching Snow. Assuming, of course, it wasn't Tiny. But I don't recall anyone taking pictures."

"No wonder McNaughton packed her tent and ran," I said. "In another few hours we may not even exist——I mean in their database. Plausible deniability. Like the gun-running episode with Mexico. Claim executive privilege and stonewall."

"Jimmy Redstone? Angella Martinez? Don't recall anyone with those names working for us. I'll check and get back to you on that," Angella said, in her perfect imitation of the President's Press Secretary.

"Oh, shit!" I exclaimed. "Our names in Buenos Aires. Jesse and Anna Silver could be Jewish. Close enough. Our side knew about the Jewish connection before we even got involved. They knew about the missing radio code chip and about Wolfson's involvement——at least in the money laundering. I was puzzled how Interpol could trace a ship back through several names and not get all the way back."

Angella nodded and added, her voice sounding remarkably like McNaughton's, "*Oh, and Cowboy, keep the military out of this. You need transport, use commercial*."

"Don't rub it in. We're hanging out there and you're right, the saw blade *is* getting louder. But one thing I know, doing nothing won't help us. Let's get out to the *Honey* and see what's really going on. We'll start from there."

"Any thoughts? That's a long way to swim."

"You got a friend at the airport. Call him."

"What should I tell him?"

"We need a ride about five hundred miles off-shore, more or less. We may want to board a cargo ship. Don't say much more than that."

"It's the more or less that worries me. Not a lot of refueling places out there."

"We're going out and back, right?"

"At least the plane is. See what he can do for us."

"Kayak is what he'll say. Make it a double, we'll take turns."

"Let me know what he says. Tiny's on the line, I'll take it in the bedroom."

- - - - -

"Suppose you heard the news," Tiny said the instant I hit the ACCEPT button. "State Department is all over us. We've been working furiously to remain clear of the latest Israel/Iran feud and now we're the bad guys brokering the deal. The Wolf broke this thing wide open with that video."

"We went over all this. You know it's doctored. That's an imposter. Shadowy Sal made that video sure as I'm talking to you."

"Don't be too certain. Wolfson went missing. FBI met her in the Love Field parking garage. Agents said she was coopera- tive, gave them background information, set up meeting loca- tions. They put her under twenty-four-seven surveillance. She met with them twice more."

"Sounds encouraging," I said, knowing more was to come and that I wouldn't like what I was about to hear.

"It was all good until she missed the next appointment. The log shows she left her hotel and drove to Addison Field. Boarded her private jet. Flight plan was for New Orleans, actually Shreve- port Regional. This was not planned, so by the time the local office got someone out there, the plane had landed and was in a private hanger. No sign of the Wolf. No video of her exiting the hanger."

"Anyone check the flight plan?"

"That's just it. It's gone."

"Jet planes don't just disappear," I reminded Tiny.

"This one did. No flight plan. No authorized take off. We checked the computer logs. Even checked the tower hand logs. That plane never took off."

"So, your conclusion is that Wolfson's a plant?" I said.

"The tape was made that day," Tiny answered.

"I actually doubt the tape was made when you think it was made," I said. "But even so, it wasn't made by her."

"What makes you so certain?" Tiny asked his interest clearly peaked.

"I just know. Instead of treating her as a felon you should be hunting her as a kidnap victim. She could lead you to who's

behind this mess. I'd begin with finding G.P. Manhyme and working from there."

"We've concluded there is no such person. Fictitious name."

"So much for using records and databases for your research.
You guys need shoe leather on the dirt."

"You have something to say," Tiny snapped, his humor gone.
"Say it."

I had a lot to say and most of it would get me fired——or
worse. But I did have a lead for him. "Jet planes don't vanish.
Look up tail number N-36AE in the FAA database. I'm willing to
bet a plane with that tail number took off from Shreveport at the
appropriate time. You'll find the plane. Can't vouch for finding
the Wolf. I've got to go now. Angella is signaling. Unless I miss
my guess, she just copped us a ride."

"Word of advice, Redstone. McNaughton's no longer running interference for you. The bad guys are not your only enemies. Kapish?"

FORTY-FIVE

Angella was on the phone smiling broadly, almost mischievously, when I rejoined her in the living room. She was enjoying a private joke and I hoped it was not at my expense.

"Mind sharing?" I said when Angella held up her right thumb. She said a few more words into the phone and then hung up.

"Remember my connection with the Cameron County airfield is through a friend of my former husband?"

I nodded.

"I told him what we were looking for and he's the one who suggested it. I would never have thought of it on my own."

"Suggested what?" She was turning into Tiny, spoon-feeding information in bite-sized portions.

"Ever hear of a guy who goes by the name of Spider Freeman?"

"Don't say as I recall the name."

"Local color. Hey, I didn't mean that as a slur. Freeman is black——and old. No one knows for sure his exact age, but he flew in Korea. And in Vietnam."

"Eighty, at least. Does he still have a valid ticket?"

"Fussy, fussy."

"It would be nice to know this wasn't a one way trip."

"Actually, it's our only choice. And as it so happens, I met Spider several years back. Several, as in fifteen or so. I was doing volunteer work at Harlingen General when a ten-year old was brought in. Took a round in the neck when a drug bust went bad. Freeman was working in the emergency room then. He shows up wearing a Hawaiian shirt, short pants and white shoes. Wore glasses bigger than his head with tufts of white hair sprouting above the glasses. Beard trimmed close and whiter than the hair on his head. Looks like Colonial Sanders."

"What's this got to do with flying us five hundred miles off-shore?"

"Patience is a virtue. I learned it from you."

"Cut to——"

"The name Spider comes from him being all arms and legs. Small man. Goes only about five-four. And that's on a good day. But it's all energy. Ever hear of the Black Aces?"

"Legends. Usually fly support, non-combat missions. Rescue, fighter escort, enforcement of embargoes."

"You got it. Spider was a trainer. He flew every type of plane out there. Including seaplanes."

"Don't tell me we're going out on——"

"He founded an organization he calls Heavenly Angels. It's really a group for kids in trouble. Encourages them to help others. His idea is that if they become passionate for something they won't have time for drugs. Over a thousand kids have gone on to one of the military academies because of him. He refurbished an old seaplane and flies the senior cadets out on search and rescue missions."

"Were does he get funding?"

"He's a doctor. Pumps all his money into it. He travels Texas and a few other states with air shows showing off the plane and asking for support. The man is a legend. I caught him just in time. In the morning he's scheduled to fly to San Antonio to participate in a fly-over. Plane's being cleaned and fueled as we speak. It has a range of about two-thousand miles. That translates into about twelve to fifteen hours."

"How do you know so much about him?"

Angella looked down before she answered. "He saved one of my brothers."

The smile had transformed into deep sadness. I was momentarily confused by the tear in the corner of her eye. Then it came to me. "That's the brother who died a few years ago. Isn't it?"

She nodded and turned to face the window.

"And you don't hold it against this Spider character?"

"On the contrary. I'm thankful to Doc Freeman. Better in Iraq than crossing the Rio Grande River as a mule. My brother loved flying and died doing the only thing that ever mattered to him. My parents remember him as the hero he was. Not as another drug addicted low-life."

"So, when do we get to meet this Spider?"

"Can you say, *Laguna Bob's?*"

"Eighty, and at the bar?"

"Looks ninety. Moves like fifty."

"I only care what he thinks like."

"Try twenty-five. Still thinks and behaves as if he were in Cambodia. He talks like he just fell off a hay wagon. Don't let that fool you. The man, at least if you believe his stories, has several purple-hearts and goodness knows what else. He's credited with saving the lives of dozens of men and doesn't weigh a hundred pounds wet."

- - - - -

Angella didn't have to point out Freeman. He was exactly as she had described, only more animated than she had let on. Indeed, with his beard trimmed to a point, he was a caricature, in miniature, of Colonel Sanders. His arms were flying in every direction as the crowd around him laughed and shouted as he told an old war story.

"Bet they heard that tale, whatever it is he's telling, a million times," Angella commented. "But he's a good ol' boy and every person here wants a piece of him. He's saved more kids in this valley from ruin than any other single person and that's not counting all the lives he's saved over at the hospital before he retired. I bet his drinking buddies are mostly related to someone whose life's been touched by him."

I edged closer and heard him say "...hell, with waiting on the Huey's for dinner. We were so far behind the enemy lines in the mountains above Lung Thmey, would have taken them all night to reach us anyway. Hadn't a lick for twenty hours. Heaved a grenade into the headwaters of the Tonlé Sap, that mud hole posing as a river, and low and behold manna from heaven. All the fish we could eat. Had us a good ol' fashion Texas bar-bee-q. Only usin' fish 'stead of pig! Fried 'em right up."

"How was it?" one of the regulars, a guy wearing shorts and an ancient leather cowboy hat, called. "Could you eat the fish after you blew them to bits?"

"The concussion killed some; others flew right out of the water onto dry land, or what passed for dry land. If you spit out the shrapnel, it tasted better than what my old pappa hung up to smoke. Like near the fried chick'n my momma made."

"Didn't the noise give away your position?" the same guy asked.

"Too hungry to give a care. Noise rose up the enemy, sure. Those was hiding by the river got blown up. They was beyond caring. Others ran. Huey got 'um. All in all, a good day's work."

Several of the crowd held up beer bottles in tribute. The man in the hat yelled, "Next round's on me."

Freeman yelled back. "Not so fast. This here round is for the kids. Put your money in the kitty for the Angels. We'll skip a round."

"Hell," the old cowboy said, "one round for the kids, and one for us. Anyone else want to pony up for the kids? Cost you a round." Three hands went up.

Freeman looked up, saw Angella and said, "Excuse me boys, I see a lovely damsel in distress." He slid through the crowd and threw his bony arms around Angella. "Good to see you looking well, young lady. Rumor has it you got into some trouble down on Brazos Beach." He looked up at me. "You part of the problem, Son, or you working on the solution?"

I reached out my hand. "Jimmy Redstone, Texas…Homeland Security. Working on the solution———most of the time."

"Call me Spider, everyone else does. So you're part of the problem. Better take better care of this young woman." He turned back to Angella, "How's the family? Father? Mother? Hey, I thought I saw Jayme a few days back."

"She's over at my house, chilling out. I'll tell her you said hello."

"I'm here most nights. She can come by and tell me hello herself. Lovely girl. Needs to find herself a good man. Hear you want to catch a ride."

I glanced around to be sure no one was listening. It was hard to determine. "Let's step outside, if you don't mind."

At the end of the dock that stretches into Laguna Madre, Spider said, "Back in the saddle again. Nothing gets the blood going like flying missions over enemy territory."

"I wouldn't characterize taking us out over the Gulf as being in enemy territory."

"But they are enemy vessels, are they not?"

"I wouldn't say an Israeli cargo ship is an enemy."

"Told one of them was Iranian."

"Possibly. And one is a supply boat from Port Isabel."

"Which one? I know several seamen on those boats."

"*Miss Rosie*," I replied. "Know anyone on that one?"

"Sure as hell do! Radio operator is a kid came through our Angel program. At fourteen he damn near passed from an overdose. Got him in time. Joined the Angels. Now he's full-time employed. Fact is he's one of the guys who recruit kids into the program. To look at him, you'd think he'd cut your throat soon as talk to you. But underneath the facade, he loves these kids. Need more like him. Tell me about the mission from your view, Redstone."

"We need to go out to the *Honey* and see what's aboard. We also need to board the *Rosie* and do the same."

"You know where the vessels are? I mean exact coordinates. Gulf's a big place. Don't want to wonder around out there in no-man's land."

"Right now, about five hundred miles. I'll update the coordinates before we takeoff."

"We'll be flying the Catalina. Got a four thousand kilometer range. Cruise at two-eighty. The one I'm flying has some extra tank capacity. We'll top her up. You're in luck. Gulf is relatively calm with no harsh weather predicted. We can land and take off, providin' the waves remain under two feet. Taking off's the problem. Land her in anything."

"What's the chance of getting out there at first light?"

"Near hundred percent, you tell me where they are. Distance controls take off time."

I called Tiny. "Got us a ride. Non-military. Check that. Former Air Force trainer. We're going out on a Catalina, borrowed from an air show. What's the latest coordinates of all three?" I waited while he went off to do what Tiny does. When he came back, I said, "Better yet, text me. Don't want to get a number wrong and fly off into the sunrise never to be seen again."

"You screw this up," Tiny quipped, "and flying off the ends of the earth will be the least of your problems. McNaughton's already taking the heat."

"What'd she do wrong?"

"Media's bombarding the President for not backing Israel. Others are yelling he's precipitating a war with Iran by siding with Israel, allowing them safe passage. As if we could stop them in international waters. He's tasked Madam General with resolving this without a diplomatic mess."

Spider tapped my arm. He had received my forwarded text and had punched the numbers into his cell. I looked up, and he yelled, "Like we did it in Nam, got to adjust for time changes. Only over there it was going west, getting earlier. Here we're going east, it's getting later. We're going a bit south, so need to factor that in as well."

"Bottom line?" I said, not bothering with the fine print.

"Wheels up at exactly one-fifteen. Mission briefing is zero forty-five hours. Bring your own wet clothes. Lightweight neoprene will do the trick. Don't forget foot covering. You might be in the water a while." Without waiting to see if I, or Angella, had questions he turned and made his way across the sand and back into *Laguna Bob's*.

I returned my attention to Tiny, but not before I heard Spider shout, "Okay, boys. Line 'em up tall. Night's young. Who's with me?"

"Who the hell you talking to?" Tiny asked when I came back on the line. "Can hardly hear with the wind noise, but he sounds pumped."

"Pilot."

"You got a kid?"

"That kid is eighty."

"Don't know what the hell you're doing down there Redstone and I don't want to know. But you best not screw this up."

"You said that before. What's going on that I don't know?"

"Presidential feces is racing downhill. Everyone's scrambling to get out of range."

I was about as far downhill as one could get. And I could do nothing about the range.

FORTY-SIX

"Closed the place down," Spider said when Angella and I walked onto the tarmac two hours later. I had caught about an hour's worth of sleep and Angella, of all things, washed her hair.

"Just like old times in Nam," Spider called when he saw us coming through the gate. Nothing like alcohol to settle the nerves, clear the mind, get ready for battle."

"Is that what you told your patients?" I asked, not understanding how a medical doctor could ever believe alcohol consumption cleared the mind. "Or the Angel kids?"

"Cadets. Not discussin' these times. Talkin' 'bout combat times. Going to war, not knowing if you're coming back. Bad business, you not ready. Alcohol was my friend. Friend of everyone I flew with. Not say'n it's good. Say'n it was. Let you do things you didn't know you could. Ever jump out of a plane?"

"Army Rangers in another life," I replied.

"Tell me you didn't have a friend." He turned to face Angella. "And you, Miss Ange, I know you never did jump from anything higher than ten feet. I'm packing parachutes, but don't reckon we'll use them. They'll open automatically if you don't pull the cord."

"Never worn one," Angella said, "wouldn't know how to put it on."

"I've taken the liberty of asking Cadet Lopez to join us tonight. She's in need of off-shore hours for graduation. Your request is indeed timely. She'll show you what to do."

I started to protest, but his resolve told me I'd be wasting my breath. So I stopped short of actually voicing my concern.

At that moment, a compact, overweight girl, I guessed to be eighteen, or close to it, came out from behind the fuselage, a flashlight in one hand and a logbook in the other. "Jimmy Redstone, Angella Martinez," Doc Freeman said, "please meet Senior Cadet Leader Katrine Lopez."

Katrine slipped the logbook under her arm and reached out a hand. "Pleased to meet you," she said, her eyes averted and her grip weak.

This was not looking good.

Katrine, in a barely audible voice, said, "Everything checks out okay. The chutes are inside." She then scrambled into the plane.

Doc Freeman called to her. "Katrine. Remember what you've been instructed about taking command. Look up when you speak. And talk so people can hear you."

I noted only three chutes on the bench that passed for seats. "Where's the fourth?"

"This here's my baby, Doc replied. Been with her since she was commissioned. Been good to me. She goes, I go. Deal I have with the ol' lady. No time to change that now."

Angella's eyes set hard. "Doc Freeman, I can't allow this on account of me. Pack a parachute or I'm not———"

"Listen young woman. At my age lots of things are lurking round the corner. Cancer, strokes, heart. Hell, slip and fall do you in. If I worried 'bout any of those I'd have no fun. A piece of cake to what I've been through. Now let Katrine help you strap on the chute and let's get moving. We're nearing our window."

Angella looked pleadingly in my direction, but said nothing further.

I reached for the chute, but instead of slipping it on I threw it on the floor at my feet. "I suppose you want me in the second seat. Can't fly this, but I can handle the radios if need be."

"If you don't mind. Out over the water, Katrine can switch. Actually, don't need help. Been flying this ol' lady so long can do it in my sleep."

"Or drunk," I was tempted to say, but swallowed my thoughts as I climbed up under the wing of the massive seagoing airplane. The overhead wing was painted bright yellow and a blue ring circled the nose in front of the cockpit. It would be hard to miss this baby.

Angella followed my lead and stepped up to the door opening to the rear seats. The seats behind the cockpit were nothing more than benches bolted to the fuselage struts along each side with chest belts secured to the frame. Both benches stopped short of the back and in their place were several life raft bags positioned on top of massive rope coils.

The Spider saw me studying the accommodations and said, "Training the kids. They need to know how to get down and up those ropes. We launch the rafts and then practice. Do it in the bay mostly."

"I remember those days all too well," I said. "It's harder than it appears. At least for me it was."

"When they master getting themselves out of the raft and into old Betsy then they need to do it carrying someone else. Only a few of them ever master that." The Spider glanced at his watch, and then said, "Close the door. It's about time to take our leave of terra firma. Strap yourself in back there young lady, we're on a mission."

The dials came alive and Doc Freeman spent the next ten minutes setting numbers into various instruments. Then the left propeller began to turn, followed quickly by the right. He then spoke some words into his headset, much of which I did not understand.

One final check of the instruments and the big plane began lumbering toward the main runway area, amber lights leading the way. I could see several runways ahead of us, each outlined with green lights. Everything else was pitch dark.

"Wind is ten knots out of the southeast," Freeman said, now all business. "Allows us to use the long east/west runway. The field is not manned at this time, so we'll use the UNICOM frequency, which down here is one-two-two-point-eight. You can set it in that radio, if you would be so kind."

A moment later while we sat at the west end of the runway, our engines turning softly, a controller from some unknown location responded to Doc's request for takeoff instructions.

A moment later I heard, "N-thirty-seven-H-A, Catalina, cleared for takeoff on runway zero-nine-zero. Military traffic eleven o'clock, twenty thousand. You're cleared to ten thousand. Maintain heading after takeoff. Continue on frequency one-two-two-point-eight until advised otherwise."

"Catalina. Ten thousand on heading ninety. Aye, aye, tower."

"God be with you, Doc."

"That was one of the boys graduated few years back. Workin' Harlingen. Doing double duty tonight monitoring UNICOM. They take great care of me."

The plane held its ground as the engines revved to speed. When Doc was satisfied all was in working order, and nothing had shaken loose, he let off the brakes and we began rolling into the darkness, slowly at first with the propellers screaming. Then ever so gradually the lumbering plane gained pull on the air as its momentum continually increased.

The white lights demarking the end of the runway raced toward us and I was certain we would not lift off before they were under the wheels.

But I should not have doubted the old man. The wheels actually cleared by more than twenty feet. The terrain was flat for another five thousand feet, but at the end of my vision I could see trees rising far higher than we were. Our trajectory did not appear to be steep enough to clear the trees.

Suddenly, the landing lights went off and all was in darkness below us. The trees were no longer visible.

"Son, I'm in charge of flying. Park service is in charge of trimming. They get a little behind from time to time. Can't be helped."

We were out over the Laguna Madre and I could see the lights of the causeway and of the few high-rise buildings on South Padre Island off to the south. Then we were over the island and an instant later out over the Gulf of Mexico.

My headset came alive. "Catalina. Cleared to twenty thousand. Do you have a preferred heading?"

"One-twenty should do it," Doc replied. "Is that available?"

"Roger, Doc. Nothing out there tonight. The lanes are yours. Maintain twenty thousand. How far you plan on going?"

"Give or take six hundred."

"Roger. Nice night for a drive."

"Thank you for your help. Catalina, out."

"Chatty bunch tonight," I said to Spider, who had sat back, obviously allowing the plane to fly itself. He appeared as comfortable in the cockpit as I feel driving my car on a deserted highway. I suppose after sixty-some years doing it second nature would have taken over.

"As I said, many of the controllers and even the pilots in the Valley have at one time or another been involved with the Angels, as cadets themselves or as instructors and mentors. Right today, we have three-hundred-twenty cadets in the program." He paused, a broad smile spreading across his face. "I suppose there's no time like the present to hit you up for a contribution. Go ahead, dig deep. Every penny goes to the kids."

"Would a hundred be the proper response?"

"Thousand would feel a lot better. You know how much fuel this thing burns training those kids?"

"Settle for five and some in-kind service. I'll give you eight hours a month hands-on time with the cadets."

"I know a good deal when I hear one. You're on. Now go change seats with Katrine. She needs time driving this bird. Catch a few winks if you want. I'll call you when we're on station. Be another two hours and fifty minutes."

I twisted backward to see how Angella was taking the bouncing ride and should not have been surprised to find her with her cell phone pressed against a small porthole.

When I joined her, she said, "What is it exactly we're supposed to find out here?"

"I've been thinking the same thing. Sounded like a better idea last night. I suppose we'll land and see if they'll allow us on board."

"You can't be serious. That ship is not a common carrier, stopping along the way to pick up passengers, especially not ones that arrive by seaplane."

"I hear you. If they won't let us aboard, we'll do the next best thing."

"That is?"

"Take pictures. See if we can determine who and what's on board."

"We know an Israeli captain did not give tainted drugs to the *Rosie*. From all indications, the two boats never really came together."

"That's what we determined from the videos," I said, "but still...I'm concerned. I want to know if it's really an Israeli owned ship."

"Interpol never did run the chain all the way home."

"Be good if we could get the ship number, see what it ties to."

"Can't they fudge the number?" Angella asked, always the practical one.

"Don't know. Suppose so. But to what? It needs to key to something in the books somewhere."

We fell silent for a while and I might have dozed off. When I looked up, Doc Freeman was standing above me. "Thought I'd stretch, take a pee break. Old knees aren't what they used to be. Lock up on me from time to time. Never know when that will occur. Back also. Lower spine mostly. Can go for a stout one, but will have to settle for a quick nip." He produced a flask of what I assumed was not water, and proceeded to take several swallows. "Fix me right up."

The unmistakable smell of bourbon filled the cabin. Since I couldn't do anything about it, there was no sense saying anything. I know from conversations I've had over the years that a few of the old timers mixed alcohol and war. But we weren't at war, and several lives were at stake beside his own.

"Don't look so disapproving young man. Got this mission well under control. Katrine is doing just fine. Target is dead ahead. They're closer than the initial coordinates and much further north. We're actually approaching from the southeast. Over flew them a ways. Had to drop low, barely five thousand feet, to spot the ship. Caught them on radar. I thought you might like to raise them on either VHF or short wave. See if you can board, if that remains your desire. Gulf is a bit more boisterous than I had hoped, but Katrine will take her down if need be. She's flying first chair and I plan to have her finish the mission. She's much sharper than she seems. Being raised by her father, mother's spending time for welfare fraud. Getting extra money to feed the family doesn't seem like something she should be doing time for. But, I don't make the laws. Kid got herself addicted on her brother's stuff. Been clean for fifteen months now. One of our best. Angella, if you can spend time with her it would be good. She wants to be a cop."

"God help her is all I can say," Angella quipped.

"Self-help's all she's got. Better make the most of it. Under it, she's tough."

"Doc," Katrine yelled back, "better come quick. There's a man calling for us on UNICOM. He sounds foreign."

FORTY-SEVEN

Katrine was in the left set and Doc slid in beside her on the right. He flipped the loudspeakers on so that we could hear the conversation.

Indeed, the voice was foreign. Middle Eastern English. Couldn't determine if Israel or a neighbor. The voice was saying, "Airplane approaching from the southeast. Altitude five thousand feet, coordinates twenty-six-dot-one north and ninety-four-dot-seven west. Identify yourself and state your intentions."

Doc reached for the microphone. "This is Catalina, November-three-seven-hotel-alpha. Please identify yourself and your location."

The response back was immediate. "What is your purpose?"

"Flying," the Spider responded. "Who are you? Where are you?"

"A boat of the high sea. Go away."

"Repeat. Identity and location?"

"Go away from this area."

"We are in international waters. Will maintain course. Iden-tify yourself."

"Turn around. Go back where came from."

I leaned forward before doc could respond and said to him, "Pass me the mike." When he did, I keyed it and said, "This is Catalina, November-three-seven-hotel-alpha. I am calling the motor ship *Honey*. *Honey* please respond."

Silence.

I repeated the request several times, but received no further communication. I then said to Doc, "Let's try the short wave."

He leaned forward, turned on a radio, adjusted a dial, then said, "Go ahead, it's on."

I again repeated the request several times, but still received no response.

Doc said, "Take her down to three thousand. Go!"

"Two boats down there," Angella announced. "One at four o'clock and the other at one. Just enough light to see them."

"That's correct," Doc responded. "About three miles north. Don't know which of those was calling us, but one certainly was. Continue on this course."

Angella, watching through her cell phone view finder, exclaimed, "Jimmy, people are going over the side of the boat at one o'clock. Here look!"

I grabbed a pair of binoculars from the bulkhead and held them to the porthole. Although sunrise was still a half-hour away, there was just enough light to see forms of people, pre-sumably the ship's crew, going down ropes and ladders into the relatively warm water of the Gulf of Mexico. Judging from the number of people going into the water, a major evacuation was underway.

I got on the radio and tried to call the *Honey* several times on the short wave radio and then switched to UNICOM, where we had heard them————or someone————before. No answer.

Then, without warning, the water in the vicinity of the *Honey* burst into flames. A few seconds later the noise of an explosion reached our ears, followed almost immediately by the Catalina being rocked from side to side so violently that I had to grab the fuselage for support.

Doc immediately reached for the control yoke, but Katrine had it under control.

A second explosion followed almost immediately after the first and the *Honey* listed to port, her stern settling low in the water.

"Fly a four mile circle around the vessel on fire," Doc instructed Katrine. He switched frequencies on the radio, listened a while and then said to us, "It's not being reported by either vessel." He then keyed his mike and said, "Mayday, mayday, mayday. This is airplane Catalina, November-three-seven-hotel-alpha reporting mayday."

The loudspeaker cracked, "Coast Guard South Padre Island to the vessel calling mayday. Identify yourself."

"This is airplane Catalina, November-three-seven-hotel-alpha calling mayday."

"Coast Guard South Padre Island to the vessel calling, what is the nature of the mayday?"

"Cargo vessel has exploded. Crew is in the water. From our information the vessel appears to be the *Ms Honey*." Doc went on to calmly provide the exact coordinates of the vessel, the sea conditions, his position and altitude. As a rough count he told them there appeared to be between twenty and thirty people in the water. "Another vessel is approaching from the east. They have searchlights on the water. Lifeboats are visible just outside the flame area."

"Coast Guard South Padre Island to the vessel calling, please identify all souls aboard your vessel."

"We are an aircraft, Catalina sea plane to be exact with four people aboard."

"Coast Guard South Padre Island to the vessel calling, names of the four souls please."

"Doc Freeman, pilot. Katrine Lopez, co-pilot. Jimmy Redstone, passenger. Angella Martinez, passenger."

"Coast Guard South Padre Island to the vessel calling please be sure all souls aboard your vessel are wearing floatation devices."

"Catalina aircraft to the Coast Guard nerd on the microphone, we are an airplane flying three-thousand feet above the Gulf of Mexico. We don't need no stinking life vests!"

"Coast Guard South Padre Island to the vessel calling," the voice was now one that Angella and I could both easily recognize, "put Redstone on."

"Redstone, here," I said into the outstretched mike, "what can I do for you Captain?"

"For starters, you can watch your mouth! Second, be advised we have dispatched assets. ETA, ninety minutes. The vessel on fire is, in fact, the *Honey*. The *Bijar* is in the vicinity."

"Correction, Captain. The *Bijar* is rescuing crew in the life boats."

"I don't recognize the name Katrine Lopez. Please elaborate."

"One of Doc's senior Cadets."

"Of all the…Be sure she does not take control of the plane. I want Doc at the controls. Understood?"

"Unfortunately, I'm not in charge of the airplane. That's Doc's call."

"Put him on!"

"Catalina airplane November-three-seven-hotel-alpha. Doc Freeman here." The Spider's grin was large enough to swallow his own head.

"Listen to me you old...just listen to me! You're not dealing with some cadet-training mission a mile offshore. It's an inter-national...just you maintain command of your vessel and do not, I repeat, do not, allow Cadet Lopez to fly that plane. That is a direct order. Acknowledge."

"Catalina airplane November-three-seven-hotel-alpha to Coast Guard Station South Padre Island. Static on the line broke up your communication. Catalina off channel sixteen." Freeman looked back at me. "He's Coast Guard. Deals with boats! Who the hell does he think he is giving directions to an airplane?"

"The Coast Guard does have authority over anything approaching our shores," I reminded Spider. "When you set down, you'll be a boat as well."

"We're out here in the middle of the friggn' Gulf. Boat sink-ing below us. People in the water. We're trained for sea rescue. What the hell's wrong with———"

The UNICOM frequency went live. "Catalina, November-three-seven-hotel-alpha, this is Gulf Sector Air Control."

"Gulf Sector Air control, this is Catalina, November-three-seven-hotel-alpha. How may I oblige?"

"You are cleared to ten thousand feet on a heading of two-seven-zero."

Two-seven-zero, or due west, was the bearing home.

"Negative. Remaining on scene until all survivors are out of the water and accounted for."

"Catalina. Not required. Coast Guard Station South Padre Island has dispatched two rescue helicopters and a transport vessel. Navy has assets in the area. They are coordinating."

"We are on scene and will remain until I am satisfied everyone is safe."

"Negative that. Military has closed the airspace over———"

"Imagine that," Doc exclaimed, "two radios going on the fritz at the same time. Katrine, take us down to one thousand feet and circle the burning ship. Remain outside the fire area. There may be turbulence so keep a heavy hand on the controls."

The right wing dipped and the nose fell as we circled back toward the smoldering wreckage. Five minutes later Angella exclaimed, "Jimmy, if I saw what I think I just saw, there's trouble down there."

"More than an explosion and fire?"

"Let me rerun the video. Give me a mom...Oh, yes. Here it is. Look!"

Angella held the phone screen up so that I could see. She had clearly captured several men being thrown over the side of a life raft before it sped off in the direction of the *Bijar*.

I pressed my face against the porthole and within a minute it was clear that all of the rafts were now being unloaded at the Bijar. Clearly several, perhaps as many as ten, crew remained behind in the water.

"Fly a larger circle," Doc commanded Katrine, "you're too close to the smoke. Take her up to three thousand and hold."

Katrine pulled the engine power levers toward her and gently raised the nose. She was remaining calm even in the face of the turmoil below her. I was proud of the young woman and promised myself I'd double my commitment to the *Heavenly* Angels.

Angella again called my attention to what was going on below us. "They've hauled all the life rafts on board the *Bijar*. If I'm not mistaken, I see the water disturbance where they're turning and applying power. They appear to be moving away."

The binoculars confirmed what Angella was saying. The *Bijar* was clearly steaming away. Judging from the turbulence, they were in a hurry. I didn't know if they were running from something or to something, but the result was the same. There were several *Honey* crew in the water and not a lifeboat anywhere on the horizon.

Doc Freeman saw the same thing. "Take her back down to a thousand feet. Remain out of the smoke area."

Katrine followed instructions and within a few minutes we were circling over the water.

"You do recall how to land in this chop, do you not?"

"I pick the place I want to land, position the plane downwind and then turn back into the wind and come down slowly."

"In this chop, keep the nose up. Don't want the pontoons to bury under a wave. When you're on the water go a little heavier on the back elevators. That helps keep the nose up and us from flipping right the hell over."

"I practiced in the surf. I'm okay," came the confident response of the eighteen-year old.

"Be happy for it. Now get your speed right. Bring speed down. Keep glide angle where you have it. Jimmy, Angella, now it's time for life jackets and belts. This might be a bit...rough."

In fact, it was one of the better landings I have experienced, given that the landing surface was moving up and down about two feet every few seconds.

"There they are. Looks like eight. Can't take them all. Not enough fuel remaining for the load. Two, maybe three, at most."

We taxied several feet toward the crew and Doc said, "Cut the
starboard engine and keep the nose into the wind as best you can.
Those men will have to move fast." He turned toward us, "Jimmy,
drag two of the life rafts forward. When we stop, Angella will
open the starboard door and you push the rear ends out one at a
time. Secure the front and Angella can remove the strap. Give it
a quick pull, it'll release. For God sake, don't release it in here."

I slid first one and then the other life raft between the benches
and positioned them just inside the door.

"Stop here," Doc commanded. "Open the door."

Angella fought the heavy door open and when she did so a
large wave caught her full in the face and knocked her back.

I shoved the first raft forward and reached for the strap.
Angella, still spitting water, beat me to it and ripped it free. The
boat began to expand and I shoved it completely out into the rest-
less sea. It began to float away.

"Leave it go," Doc ordered. "The crew in the water will
recover it. Let the second out."

A moment later two rafts were floating downwind in the
direction of the crew.

"Close the door. Cut down on the water intake."

We did and it took several minutes before the people in the
water secured the rafts and began pulling themselves up over the
gunnels. Several men required assistance, but within five minutes
I counted five people in one boat and three in the other.

The Catalina had been blown about five hundred feet down
wind before someone in the five-boat picked up the headphone-
set that each boat apparently had.

"Seaplane, what are your instructions?" came the voice from
the raft.

"Tell them to put on the headphones in the other raft," Doc said. "Is anyone injured?"

"Two are dead. Gone. One is dead in this boat." Silence for a moment, then the spokesman said, "Other boat reports all alive, but Captain was shot in the shoulder and leg. Looks bad. He lost a lot of blood."

"Any other injuries?" Doc asked.

"One in this boat. Bad burns. Everyone else is stable."

"Put the injured man from your boat into the other boat. We'll bring them both aboard the plane. Coast Guard is on the way. Hour max. You'll be okay. Just stay clear of the burning wreckage."

We watched from a distance as the two rafts slowly came together. Then one man, wrapped in what appeared to be towels or ripped shirts, was carefully lifted from one to the other.

"Move clear of the pick-up raft," Doc said into the mike. "We are coming for those two." To Katrine, he said, "Taxi over toward them. Can you manage with the port engine alone?"

"Affirmative, but unstable."

"Take it slow."

Katrine did a good job maneuvering the seaplane, which was now so unstable in the waves that I was close to losing it. Only by focusing on the horizon was I able to keep my stomach contents where they belonged.

When the fuselage finally was positioned beside the raft, Doc said, "Open the door." Into the microphone he said, "Lift one of the injured up." To us he yelled, "Jimmy and Angella, reach down and get your arms around his waist and pull him in."

An easy task on solid flat land. Near impossible when the plane and raft were moving to different drummers.

It took nearly ten minutes to wrestle the burned man into the plane. From his appearance, it didn't seem likely he'd survive the trip to the hospital.

Then we turned our attention to the Captain, who still had fire in his eyes but no use of the right side of his body. Just as we were about to pull him into the plane, my right wrist, the one that had nearly been lost to a gunman's bullet, gave out and the Captain fell back into the raft.

Doc Freeman threw his headphone off and climbed over the seat to be by the door. He hung halfway out and yelled, "Try it again. On three, heave. One! Two! Three! Heave!"

The Captain, a man who weighed two-seventy if he weighed an ounce, started up toward us. Angella had him under his injured right arm and Doc, hanging out as far as he possibly could, wrapped his arms around his waist.

Slowly, the man rose from the raft. First his head appeared, then his midsection. Then...then just his head.

He was slipping back and pulling Doc with him. Doc's body was slowly sliding across the fuselage and his torso was now hanging far out of the seaplane. I dove across the plane and caught Doc's legs. I wrapped my arms around him and pulled as hard as I could.

A breaking wave caught the plane's nose and it seemed both the Captain and the good doctor would be lost over the side. But, and I'm only guessing as to what happened, the raft then lifted even further than the plane and all three of them, the Captain, Spider and Angella, found themselves sprawled on the fuselage floor between the benches.

Angella recovered herself and pulled the door closed. Then she said, "Get him stretched out, Jimmy. Put him beside the other one."

I helped her move the Captain and saw the silent scream of pain in his eyes. For the moment there was nothing I could do so I returned my attention to the cockpit, expecting to see Katrine and the Doc preparing to take us off.

But Doc Freeman's seat was empty.

He was still lying where he had landed. I ran to him, getting there the same time as Angella.

"He hit his head," I said, "judging from the angle of his neck."

"Maybe so, but he's had a heart attack as well," Angella announced. "He can't catch his breath and he's blue around the mouth. Jimmy, this doesn't look good. Doc Freeman, can you hear me?"

"He's trying to talk, Angella. Get closer."

"Can you hear me?" Angella repeated, this time with her ear only inches from his mouth.

"He says he's not feeling well. Chest hurts. Thought I was sitting on him." She turned back to Freeman. "Take it easy. We'll get you to the hospital soon."

"What's that you said?" Angella again put her ear almost against his mouth. Then she said, "Okay. Now just relax. We'll get you home safely."

The look on Angella's face when she stood told a thousand unpleasant stories. I just didn't know which one was the most pressing.

It didn't take long to find out.

Angella, her voice remaining calm as it always does in crises, said, "Doc wants you to know we may not have enough fuel to get home."

FORTY-EIGHT

"I'm keeping her right here on the water where the Coast Guard can find us," Katrine insisted. "We can't make it back and I don't want to kill Doc by crashing!"

We had been going around for a few minutes and Katrine, who was now the only person who could fly the plane, was not backing down.

"He'll die anyway if we don't get him to a hospital," I argued. "The Coast Guard has other priorities." I wasn't going to discuss the drugs on board the *Honey*, or for that matter, any of the other compounding problems, not the least of which, we were not supposed to be where we were.

"Use the oxygen," Katrine commanded. "That's what it's there for." She had taken heed of Doc's instructions and was talking in a firm command voice. She was certainly also looking us directly in the eyes.

"Angella has it on him, but he's still not breathing well."

"The Coast Guard can give us fuel," Katrine said.

"They don't carry aviation fuel. They're boat people." Actually, that's not entirely true, but Katrine didn't have to know otherwise.

"Where are they?" our young pilot asked, the traces of panic creeping into her otherwise steady voice. "Coast Guard should be here by now! They don't answer the radio!"

"We can't reach them now that we're on the water. Line of sight works well when we're a mile up. Down here, lucky to get a mile with the antenna height of this plane."

"I'm waiting. Not enough to get home."

"Listen to me Katrine. I've flown planes long before you were born. This plane lands on water. If you run out of fuel, just land. Call them on the way down. They'll come get us. We'll be closer to shore, mostly home."

"I never landed this in the water without power. I know it's tricky because I won't be able to keep the pontoons up properly. We'll roll."

"Won't have to. We'll land in the water just before you run out. That's the best way to save Doc. Fastest."

Katrine thought about that for a long minute. She glanced back to where Doc was lying, an oxygen mask covering his face. His breathing had improved marginally, but he could no longer speak. Angella had whispered to me that he might have had a stroke, as well. The right side of his body seemed cold.

"Doc told me you were a pilot," Katrine said to me, doubt creeping into her voice. "When was that?"

"I was just a bit older than you are now," I replied, not wanting to go into all of my training. "That was in another life."

"If I fly her home, will you sit up front and help me. You can calculate the fuel reserve. I can't do the math and fly."

"That I can do," I replied, thankful she had come around. I mentally went over the steps of calculating fuel reserve the way I had been taught, long before all the modern gadgets. You start with how much fuel you have at a given time and then a measured time later you take another fuel reading. By subtracting one from the other you know how much fuel you actually burned. That allows you to then calculate the burn rate, assuming it's constant, which it never really is. Knowing the burn rate you can determine when you will run out. "When you get airborne we'll take the first reading," I said, anxious to be out of the water before the rescue planes arrived. I didn't want to give up access to *Honey's* captain, who seemed to be dazed, but otherwise okay.

"Wind's coming up," Katrine said, "Gulf's getting choppier. That's why I'm going. Could get thrown over if the waves get any steeper."

In fact, Katrine had been struggling to coax the big machine to remain upright despite taking several breaking waves over the nose. Her demeanor and determination made the kid a natural.

Once the decision was made, Katrine lost no time applying power and carefully lifting the huge cumbersome machine free of the water. Passing through three thousand feet she reached for the radio control. "Gulf Control, this is Catalina, November-three-seven-hotel-alpha, requesting permission up to ten thousand feet, heading two-seventy."

"Roger, Catalina. Radio working again? Permission to ten-thousand. Maintain heading two-seven-zero. Be advised of traffic at one o'clock at thirteen thousand feet."

"Roger control. Traffic at thirteen thousand, my one o'clock. No visual contact as of yet."

"Catalina, you headed home?"

"Affirmative, control. Maintaining ten-thousand feet."

"Catalina. Put Doc on."

I nodded to Katrine and clicked my microphone. "This is Jimmy Redstone, passenger. Unfortunately, Doc is incapacitated. He had what appears to be a heart attack. Perhaps a stroke as well. We also have two wounded on board." I proceeded to give the condition of the two men. I then added, "Captain has a concern about fuel reserves. We're monitoring to see if we can make it or if we have to take her down."

"Catalina, you are cleared for emergency priority to Harlingen. Keep us informed on the fuel situation and any change in the status of your passengers. Standing by to assist. We will clear the air space."

"Catalina," a new voice broke in, "this is Coast Guard Corpus. We have dispatched an evacuation helicopter. Should intersect within twenty minutes. Copter will escort you."

"Thank you, Coast Guard Corpus. We'll be keeping an eye peeled." The last thing I wanted was the Coast Guard escorting us. Explosions at sea are one thing. The Laws of the Sea requires assistance to be rendered. That is outside my control. However, my very explicit instructions were to not involve the military, including the Coast Guard, in my activities. My only hope was that Lucinda McNaughton would find a way to turn the helicopter around.

I walked back to check on Angella and our injured passengers. The large medicine supply kit lay open and the ripped bloody shirt that had been wrapped around the burn victim had been replaced by sterile gauze. The Captain's bleeding had been staunched and the man seemed to be resting comfortably. At least the pain in his eyes had diminished. There was no change in the Spider, except that his breathing seemed to be shallower.

"Fuel calculation," I said to Katrine when I returned to the cockpit, "is not good." "The way I see it is you have between forty minutes to an hour."

"That's way better than I thought. Given an hour, we make it to base with some left over. Forty minutes is iffy."

"I'll run a new calculation thirty minutes from now and then we'll decide what's best."

Twenty minutes later, Katrine announced, "Coast Guard copter is behind us. If we go down, they'll be right there hauling us out."

"That's good to know," I responded, still not wanting the Coast Guard involved. But truth be told, their presence was reassuring.

I again went to the back of the plane, this time to give Angella the latest on our situation. Her comment was, "For goodness sakes, Jimmy, if there's any doubt don't fly over land and people. Put her down in the water and let Captain Boyle earn his keep."

"Hell, speaking of Boyle, I forgot something. See you on the other side."

I went forward and immediately called Boyle.

"You still in the air," he said. "I thought you were calling because you crashed landed that thing. Got nine lives, you do."

"I need you to quarantine the *Rosie*. Drugs on board could kill marine——"

"Cool your jets, Redstone. There's nothing on the *Rosie* that doesn't belong there."

"How the hell do you know without testing?"

"DEA and ATF intercepted the boat a mile offshore, if you must know. Clean as the day it was launched, figuratively speaking of course."

"My son, has————"

"Found no evidence of your son either. Anything else you want? We're busy."

"You seem to have it all under control," I said, the sarcasm stronger than called for.

"You are to report to me the instant you're down, you understand. There is a lot…a lot to discuss about————"

I snapped the radio off.

"South Padre Island five minutes ahead," Katrine called. "Eighteen minutes to the Port Isabel field. Twenty, max. Can't make Harlingen. I'm down at a thousand feet."

My fuel calculations told me that we had, at most, seven minutes. I checked the fuel gauges. It wasn't hard. The red needles on both main gauges were across the empty line. The needle of the auxiliary gauge was halfway across the black empty stripe.

"Best estimate, five minutes of flying, no more," I said.

"Helicopter's not there any more. Left four minutes ago. Been thinking what we can do. What would you say if I landed in the surf and drove her onto the beach? I can do it."

"Can you drive it all the way to the beach or do you need help? Perhaps a boat standing by? That surf is rough."

"Rather do it alone," came the surprisingly steely voice. All traces of panic gone now. "Don't want anyone getting into the prop."

"Ever do it before?"

"Doc showed us an old film of him doing it once. Caught a wave and rode it in. Out in the Pacific somewhere."

"Pick a place, if you can, where there's close street access. Minutes count if we're to save the Doc. Up by the Tiki will work." I studied the fast approaching beach. The waves looked to be less than two feet high, but were packed tightly together.

"We'll have the wind on our beam," Katrine said. "I'll line up with the waves. Take us north a little. Main thing is not to flip."

I pointed slightly to our right to a location just south of Clayton's. "That's perfect. No one's in the water." I turned back to Angella. "Better strap on tight. Call SPI Chief Garcia and tell him we'll require several ambulances. We don't need Boyle taking charge of this."

Katrine, instead of putting the plane in the surf, passed directly over the beach and came in low over Laguna Madre. She was attempting to reach Cameron County Airport, just beyond the bay.

The needle of the auxiliary tank was clearly resting against the empty stop. Why the engine continued I didn't know.

Then it sputtered.

Katrine immediately banked to the left. The big plane's nose dropped, but at the same instant the engines roared back to life. It was enough to propel the plane back out over the Gulf. We were now only several feet above the wave tops and the color of the water below us showed four distinct sandbars. The plane had continued to turn and was now heading back toward the beach. Judging from the angle of the nose, we were going to touchdown on the fourth bar.

I braced for the impact.

But Katrine managed to pass over the fourth bar, and then over the third.

The engines gave one final gasp and then went silent. All we had going for us was the plane's ability to glide, but we were too low to achieve any distance.

"Caught an updraft off the water," Katrine announced, not giving any indication that she was concerned——or even knew——the plane would flip if the surf broke over a pontoon. "Birds use the uplift for fishing," she said, "so can we!"

At the very last moment before the plane hit the water, Katrine managed to force the nose up. Landing a seaplane on a river or lake is one thing. The runway stretches forever. Approaching a beach is a far different situation. The white sand was rushing at us faster than my mind could process.

The plane, helped along by the surging surf, and with the wind behind us, raced across the breaking water, the pontoons suddenly coming into contact with dry sand. The tail flew upward as the nose dug in.

A wave washed ashore bringing with it enough water to lift the pontoon just enough to settle the tail and keep the plane from cart wheeling. The good news was that we were upright and moving across the beach. The bad news, old Betsy was not showing signs of slowing. Ahead, the concrete wall of the Tiki was quickly approaching.

Then, as if the hand of Superman had grabbed hold of the tail, the concrete stopped racing toward us as the nose fell into the sand.

No one in the plane moved.

I turned to Katrine. "Give me five, woman! Give me five! Nice work! You're a natural born pilot!"

Angella raced forward and threw her arms around the young girl. "I second what he just said. If you ever, ever need a reference for anything, I'm your person."

Sirens could be heard in the background and it would be only a matter of moments until the ambulances would be here for our wounded.

The grin suddenly vanished from Katrine's face. She said, "Am I going to be in trouble with the man for flying? They'll never let me fly again!"

"Absolutely not," I said, not certain I knew what actually would happen, but I knew that I would protect her at all cost.

"Or for landing on this beach?"

"No. No. You're just fine," I insisted.

"You sure? I don't have any good luck with white people! Doc was my...my friend. The only friend I really ever had. Will he live?"

"I hope so," I replied, "I really hope so."

"What will they do to me?" The entire time she had been flying her eyes had held excitement, a sense that she could control the situation. Now all I saw was deep fear.

"They'll ask you a million questions. Just answer them honestly. You did nothing wrong. You saved lives. Just remember that. You saved lives."

No sooner than I said those words than a larger than life jet ski flew across the surf and came to rest on the sand just behind the Catalina. Two other slightly smaller jet skis came up on either side.

Climbing from the first vehicle, his face red with anger was none other than United States Coast Guard Captain Ernest Boyle himself.

FORTY-NINE

The first words out of Boyle's mouth were, "You're coming with me, Redstone. Get on the ski!" He motioned for Angella to go with one of the other men.

"What ever happened to, *glad you're alive,* or better yet, *thanks for rescuing those folks from the water?*" I said in reply.

"Get your sorry ass on here! You're wasting precious time."

"We've got work to do here, Captain. We're not going anywhere with you."

"You're under arrest," Boyle shouted, taking a step forward to restrain me.

I backed away, clenching my fists in preparation for decking him if he so much as took another step in my direction.

Angella intervened. "Charges? What are the charges?"

"Piracy, for starters! Entering the country illegally for another! Are you coming peacefully, or must I———"

I took a step toward him, and Angella had the presence to grab my arm. She said to Boyle, "Are you for real? You're Coast Guard not Border Patrol."

"I have the same power of arrest you do, Redstone. We both report to the Department of Homeland Security. Piracy is most certainly a felony. I repeat, you're under——-"

"First of all," I said, "we never left the United States. Second of all, I don't have the bloodiest idea of what piracy you are talking about. And, most importantly, our feet are on solid sand. In fact, sand above the high water line. You have no jurisdiction on land, so knock it off. You're making a fool of yourself."

The two uniformed men with him set their feet as if they were preparing to draw on us at the slightest provocation. I lowered my voice and softened my tone. "We have three very sick men on board. One is a citizen, the other two I am not certain of. All three of them are in urgent need of medical attention. Are you prepared to offer them medical help?"

"I most certainly do have authority to arrest you, wherever you are. Frankly, I'm not at all interested——"

Before Boyle had the chance to dig himself in deeper, a South Padre Island patrol car screamed onto the beach, followed close behind by two ambulances and a fire truck. First responders poured out of the vehicles and raced to the plane.

Police Lt. Carrie Malone came directly to where we were standing. "Redstone, why am I not surprised to find you involved with a crash-landed plane on the beach? Hey, isn't this ol' Doc Freeman's plane? The one he trains...oh, good morning, Captain Boyle, didn't recognize you at first. How'd you get here? Oh, are those yours?" She asked pointing to the jet skis now bobbing in the surf.

"These two," he said, nodding toward me and Angella, "are———"

Boyle's words were drowned out by the screaming engines of a medivac helicopter landing less than twenty-five yards south of where the seaplane had come to rest. Before Boyle could repeat what was on his mind, one of the first responder medics called down from the plane, "Got three males in need of medical evacuation. Old guy needs to be transported pronto. Oh," he said, spotting the helicopter, "we're in business. We'll evac the old guy first. The other two are stable."

"Not so fast there," Boyle called, "Two of those men are illegal aliens. The others are———"

"Is that what you're doing here, Captain?" Malone said. "These prisoners or something?" She stuck her head inside the plane and then added, "The old guy goes by Spider. Ol' Doc Freeman. He's certainly not an illegal. I don't know anything 'bout the other two."

"Illegal," Boyle replied.

"Border Patrol's been notified," Malone called. "These folks aren't going anywhere any time soon from what I can see. One caught a few rounds. The other appears to be badly burnt. Time enough to process them at the hospital."

"These two," Boyle said, again nodding toward Angella and me, "are coming with me."

"On those?" Malone said, indicating the jet skis. "Since when are you patrolling in those? I'd like our department to have some." Then she added, "They would be great for watching fireworks."

"Are you mocking me?" Boyle said, taking a step in Malone's direction. "I'm on official business!"

"In case you didn't realize it, Captain, so am I. Only I'm driving a police car. It's the one with the flashing red and blue lights with the word POLICE on the door. And you're here on what appears to be rented water mopeds. Mind explaining what's going on?"

"Not your business what I drive or what mission I'm on! Our job is to patrol the waters, prevent unauthorized intrusions. Piracies on the high seas. These two are my———"

"I hate to break it to you, Captain, but you're on sand. Water's the blue stuff behind you."

If Boyle could possibly hate anyone more than he hated me it would now be Lt. Malone. His hand inched down toward his weapon. The motion did not go unnoticed by Malone.

"In case you're thinking of drawing your piece, forget it. You're military. You have authority out there," she said, waving her arm toward the Gulf. "But right now, as I see it, you're in the town of South Padre Island where I represent the law. Unless of course, martial law has been declared."

Boyle's face turned even deeper red. He looked as if he was about to jump up and down. "I'll have you know Coast Guard has Title Fourteen arrest authority and these two have…have entered the country…illegally…among other things. I'm taking them with me."

"If you're referring to Homeland Security Agents Redstone and Martinez, I have good reason to believe they are both United States citizens and to my knowledge have never left the country. Isn't that right Agents Redstone and Martinez?"

"Correct," I said. "We took a ride with Doc and Cadet Lopez on a training flight, that's all."

"Hey," Malone said, "with Doc out, who landed that thing?"

"Cadet Lopez," I said, nodding toward the eighteen year old, now sitting off by herself. "Fuel was iffy to make the air field. She didn't want to chance it. Brought it down on the beach."

Boyle started toward Lopez and Lt. Malone snapped, "Hold on a moment, Captain. Let me get to the bottom of this. We'll work something out with these two."

Boyle took another step toward us. Stopped. Did a military about face and retreated to the water's edge.

"You, Lopez," Malone called over to Katrine who had her head down, her fingers idly drawing and erasing lines in the sand. "You deserve a medal for landing this beast without so much as a dented wing or broken wheel. Didn't even throw sand in anyone's eyes far as I can see." Malone walked over to where the girl sat, touched her forehead and then motioned for one of the fire rescue team to come over.

A woman, about Angella's age, walked forward. Malone, in a quiet voice said to her, "This child's been through a lot. She's scared and may be going into shock. Treat her gently. She's a hero." Malone then turned to me. "What the hell's got into Boyle? The Coast Guard doesn't patrol in those toys. He wants your hide. Care to tell me what it is?"

"We flew a mission for Homeland Security. Doc was flying. Lopez was co-pilot. We wanted to ascertain exactly who was in charge of a cargo ship that had toxic medications on board. We have reason to believe the drugs have fallen into the wrong hands."

"Did you get the information you went for?"

"Couldn't. The ship blew apart before we could make contact."

"Is that how he got burned?" Malone said, nodding in the direction of the man being carried off the plane on a stretcher.

"And the other one, the boat Captain, was shot in the water by someone from the rescue boat," I added.

"The rescue boat shot him!"

"Seems there was an Iranian registered ship tagging along. It came over, picked up several crew, pushed others out of the life rafts and then shot the Captain."

"Where does Boyle fit into this?"

"Not certain. He didn't want the girl flying. Gave Doc strict instructions. Some air command, maybe Coast Guard for all I know, refused to allow us to land in the water to pick up survivors. Refusing to render assistance is against all maritime law if my understanding is correct."

"But you landed anyway?"

"Doc did. Radio went out."

"Does Boyle know you have the ship captain?"

"I believe he knows. We reported it to air control."

"The man's got a bolt loose, if you ask me."

"He got here almost as soon as we landed. A rescue helicopter had been assigned to follow us home. It disappeared a few miles out. They must have anticipated we'd have to land on the beach. Angella debriefed the Captain on the flight home. That's what he wants, our debriefing. We may be caught in a major jurisdictional dispute."

"My guess," Malone said, for what it's worth, "is that Boyle was told to bring you back to CG station. For some reason they don't want you mixing with us civilians. Their patrol boats can't land on the beach so they used the jets. Actually, we've noticed they've been using them lately for chasing drugs coming ashore."

"That explains the *how*," I replied, "but not the *why*. Surely he doesn't really believe he can arrest us."

"You're overlooking a key fact, Redstone," Malone said, glancing toward the surf where Boyle and his men were standing, their eyes fixed on her, their hands resting on their weapon holsters. "You're now Homeland Security."

"Your point, Lieutenant?"

"You're the property of the U.S. government."

FIFTY

I had been ignoring the vibration in my pocket long enough. I knew it had to be either Tiny or McNaughton. Frankly, I preferred Tiny, but if I was having trouble with the Coast Guard, the General would be the one to work it out. Captain Boyle had even less love for McNaughton than he had for me.

"Don't you people ever answer the tele?" the British voice of Lillie Holland said by way of greeting. "Gracious me, such manners."

"Sorry. I've been a bit busy. What can I do for Interpol this fine day?"

"I should say you have been busy. I should say you have. It's on all the networks. Of course, I doubt very much if their version is accurate, but there you are none the less." She paused, then added, "I assume you were in that hideous sea plane. Right out of the Great War it was."

"What are you referring to?" I wondered how she could have known we crash landed the plane on the beach. I glanced around to see if cameras had been set up, but noted that they were just arriving. Their trucks were not allowed on the beach, so cables were being run in every direction. A wind-swept reporter, black mike in hand, was bent over Katrine.

"The recon pictures of the seaplane flying over the *Honey*. I understand you were a passenger in that craft. Video clearly shows the plane passing over the *Honey* and immediately thereafter the ship exploded. You've created quite the controversy, I must say. What, with the flag of the United States emblazoned on the top of each wing, you did it up royal. Several governments have demanded a statement from your President. Syria has called for sanctions."

I had been unaware of the flags painted on the wing tops and the image of it in my mind sent a chill down my spine. "I suppose," I managed to respond, "it makes no difference that we did nothing other than observe."

"Not exactly all you did, Mr. Redstone. You landed next to the burning ship and deployed life rafts. Then you took off, leaving behind two boats of survivors. I'm surprised you've not been arrested. You very much violated maritime protocol."

This was one of those times that the wisest thing I could do was stop talking. But there were so many unanswered questions. Not the least of which was where was my son in all this? Certainly he was being manipulated, just as I have been. I saw no way this was going to end well for him————or for me. "So," I said to Holland, "what's your take on all this?"

"Officially, you and your government are international villains. You can be hunted down and tried for piracy. If anyone died, murder will be the charge."

"Unofficially?"

"You've been framed by experts who've been planning for a long time to discredit the United States. You and Angella are a means to their end. Convenient foils."

"Your thoughts as to the source?"

"My money's on Iran———or some group working on their behalf. Hours ago, twenty-five million dollars was transferred into Manhyme's personal Swiss bank account."

"From?"

"From Iran. As far as we can determine, there are no restrictions. The money's his. I assume, for a job well-done."

Lt. Malone's hand was on my arm. "I've been instructed to get you two off the beach and into protective custody." She once again glanced toward Boyle and his crew. "Let's go. Hang up your phone."

I started to ask Holland what the end game was in her mind, but before I could get the words out, Malone grabbed the phone, turned it off, and shoved it in her pocket.

"Come, quickly," she snapped. "The good Captain has called for reinforcements. I don't need a fight with the military. This could get real ugly real fast. Get moving."

I glanced at Angella who nodded in the direction of Katrine. "What about the girl?" I asked Malone. "We can't just leave her."

"She's okay. Medics have her under control. She's one tough kid. I don't want the press talking to her so we're putting her into protective custody. Not your worry right now."

We turned south onto Padre boulevard just as a Coast Guard van, blue lights flashing, slowed to make the turn onto the beach access street. I recognized the driver as the sentry who was always so polite when he ushered us to the conference room at Coast Guard headquarters. I wasn't sure if he, in turn, recognized us. But I was certain he held his assault rifle at the ready.

Malone was studying her rearview mirror to be sure we weren't being chased. "Where are you taking us?" I asked, trying to piece together the authority the Coast Guard had over civilians———and over local police departments. But, as Malone had pointed out, it was a moot point. I belonged to the government.

"Frankly, I don't know where you two are going. And from the way this is heating up, I don't want to know. I'll be dropping you off across the bridge. You'll be picked up there by some friendlies. Or at least I assume they're friendlies."

"Friendly to whom?"

"To be determined."

"Hints?"

"I have no way to know. I have enough trouble handling my business, I don't need to handle yours as well."

The ride through town and across the causeway took less than ten minutes going the speed we were going. Our lights and siren were on. I assumed this was so not because we needed them, but just so that anyone asking where we had been taken would know it was off island.

"Out!" Malone commanded, when we reached the *Pirate's Landing* parking lot at the base of the causeway bridge. "Walk toward the water. You'll be met. I don't want to know who picks you up."

We did as we were told and walked toward the pier, Port Isabel's famous landmark lighthouse towering over our heads. I was contemplating ducking down an alley and getting lost. I told Angella my thought and she immediately said, "Forget it, Jimmy. You heard what Malone said about ownership. They'll have you in irons——or worse——if you break ranks. Let it play."

I didn't have time to argue before a car slowed beside us. The driver's window rolled down a crack and a familiar voice said, "Need a lift?"

The voice belonged to perhaps the only person in the world I'd trust at this point, my former Texas Ranger boss, Lt. Miller Contentus.

When I just stood there looking, unable to form a decent question, he barked, "Get in already. Judging from what's been going on, we're most likely being taped."

I climbed in back and motioned for Angella to sit up front with Contentus. She didn't know him all that well and I wanted her to be able to study him while we were driving. That way we could compare notes later. Tiny, or McNaughton, or whoever was leading this mission, must have anticipated I'd bolt, given half a chance. That's why they sent Contentus. That was good news——and bad. The bad part was that this was proof they knew they owned me, now and forever.

We headed west on Highway 100 and drove for twelve minutes, Contentus saying nothing. I knew that anything I said, could—— and would——be used against me. For what, I didn't know.

Suddenly, he made a U-turn and drove back east several minutes. His cell sounded and he held it to his ear not saying anything.

A moment later he braked and turned right onto a small dirt road, more in the nature of a donkey path. We were heading south across unplanted marshy fields. I half expected alligators to appear along the road, a further reminder of my superior's total control.

Then it hit me where we were going. Rumors had been circulating for over a year that a super-secret underground bunker that had been constructed in this area during the cold-war, had been reopened——or never actually closed. My guess was that the facility was being used by Border Patrol for secret training—— and detention. The location had been dubbed Camp South, but I didn't know anyone who admitted seeing the facility in person.

If indeed Camp South existed, then it would be a hardened facility equipped with the latest electronic equipment, and perhaps also having its own landing field. In times of national emergencies, the President, or members of Congress, could be housed here.

I studied the terrain, but could see nothing but tall grass and sand.

Suddenly, grapefruit trees filled in on either side of the road. Soon we were deep in what appeared to be a working orchard. Only I wouldn't have been surprised to learn the fruit was as fake as some of the information we had been given.

A quarter of a mile further along, the roadway slopped downward. A sharp curve to the right and we drove into a concrete-reinforced tunnel, lights high on the wall leading the way. About a hundred yards further along four metal pilings rising from the concrete floor prevented our passage. Contentus rolled to a stop.

Four pilings rose from the ground behind him. We were not going forward or backward.

A Marine guard appeared from a small door in the side of the tunnel. Contentus held out his credentials and motioned for us to do the same. When the guard was satisfied, the metal pilings in front of us retracted into the ground and we drove forward.

As we drove, the tunnel gradually widened until we were within what appeared to be a massive cave, its walls also lined with reinforced concrete. A second set of pilings blocked our way.

Massive doors I hadn't noticed on the way in slid closed behind us. For all practical purposes, we were now captive in what appeared to be an impenetrable underground bunker.

Then Contentus spoke. "You two get out here. They will scan you and take your weapons for safekeeping. I won't be staying, so I get to keep mine."

"What's going on? Chauffeur is not your highest and best calling."

"They put out a code ninety-nine on you both. Weapons were authorized. I told them I'd bring you here. It was the only way I knew to keep you both alive." He started to turn the car around, stopped and rolled down his window. "For what it's worth, I almost forgot. Here's a picture of the person who had the transmitters sewn into your boots. Hope it helps. Cheers."

Four people in uniforms of the Secret Service, two men and two women, came through a door and walked directly toward us. "Mr. Redstone, please step this way," one of the men said, walking off to my right. Angella was led to the other side of the room.

The search of my person was efficient and thorough——and performed courteously. I was scanned for electronic surveillance equipment and pronounced clean.

A moment later Angella was also pronounced good to go. We were each given gun safes to put our weapons in and each safe was locked individually and the key handed to us. This was one impressive operation.

We were ushered onto an elevator. Instead of going up, it went down.

I unfolded the paper Contentus had given me and there, staring back at us was Loretta Wolfson, the Wolf herself.

FIFTY-ONE

I have no way of knowing how far down we went. But it seemed a long way. I quipped to Angella, "I feel it getting warmer by the second."

"Get used to it."

"Are you trying to tell me something about my ultimate destiny?"

"If the shoe——"

The elevator stopped moving. The door slid open and if my greatest fear was of an eternity being spent with people you never really wanted to deal with again, then my worst nightmare had just come true.

"Well, Cowboy, what the hell took you so long in getting here?" Lucinda McNaughton said. "We've been waiting." She swept her arm around the room." I suppose you know everyone here."

Everyone was Tiny, FBI Deputy Director Chris Kagan, and a guy I hadn't known was involved with this mission, Special Agent Sylvan Jacobs. Jacobs, based in San Antonio, headed the Southwestern area for the FBI.

"While we're dealing in surprises," I said, looking around, "is there anyone else here who plans to jump out of a wall, or better yet, a cake?"

"If you're asking is the President here? The answer is no—— at least not that we know anyway," McNaughton replied. "Neither is your new best-buddy Captain Boyle."

As always, wherever McNaughton was there was certain to be a well-stocked buffet table. This was no exception. She said, "You two must be starved. Help yourself." She winked in the direction of Tiny. "Goodness knows, he has."

In fact, I was hungry and helped myself to an over-stuffed ham sandwich. Halfway through my sandwich, Kagan said, "I see Miller gave you the picture. Help us. Is that the Wolfson woman or are we looking at Sally Comings?"

"Can't tell," I said. "Ange, what's your take?"

"Same. Sally's too good at makeup to know for certain."

Kagan looked back at me. "What's your gut, Redstone?"

"Shadowy Sal. I believe Wolfson's been had."

"Anyone wish to say otherwise?" Kagan asked. Looking around, he said, "Seeing none, I think we'll conclude Comings is behind the surveillance."

"Our take," Jacobs began, "is that this has been a carefully orchestrated operation from the beginning. The most dangerous kind. So far, almost perfect. In fact, if Angella hadn't cut the Argentine trip short and foiled Coming's timing, we might not have a clue even now."

Kagan interrupted, "Walk us back a bit. How would Comings know to plant the transmitters on Redstone and Martinez? I mean, how would she know I'd select those two for this mission?"

"Snow," McNaughton replied. "Someone knew Snow was on the run. That someone also knew there was animosity between

Snow and Redstone. Also, and I think this may be the most important fact, Redstone investigated the SOS business a while ago. He
testified in open court. SOS tied us into PAP———and that put
Wolfson in our sights. Just what they wanted. They needed for
us to focus on Wolfson."

"Am I to understand that Snow was used to bait me?" Kagan
pressed.

"Getting us to Buenos Aires was the easy part," Jacobs said.
"But doing so with the right guy meant they had to use bait that
would cause us to send the right person. Angella knows, or knew,
Snow better than anyone. So she was logical. Thus, plant a transmitter on her and keep tabs. Angella knowing Snow. Jimmy
investigating SOS. Killing Pettit over their heads. They all but
guaranteed you'd pick the Redstone/Martinez team."

"But once they established the link to Wolfson, Jimmy———
and even Angella———became expendable," Kagan said.

"Sally tried to eliminate them in Argentina."

"But why Wolfson?" I asked, "she seems to be———"

"Ties it to Israel," Jacobson responded. "Use PAPs drugs, the
ship she hired under the Israel flag, show the world pictures of her
supporting Israel and the Israel ship dumping toxic drugs into the
Gulf. Agendas take over. That's why they enticed Jimmy's son,
Lester, down here."

"I'm not following that part," I said.

"You are aware of the video showing your son moving drugs,
tampered drugs, off the *Honey*, are you not?"

"Yes," I reluctantly admitted, even though I had pushed it out
of my mind.

"That, together with your picture on the dock in Argentina in
front of drug pallets being lifted onto the *Honey*, ties the U. S. to
the drugs and to Israel. The State Department cannot plausibly

deny our involvement. Our picture, your picture to be exact, is all over this mess. Add to it that you were in the plane that appears to have attacked the *Honey* and———"

"We're not sequestered miles underground simply to discuss who planted a transmitter in my boot. So———"

"So," McNaughton said, "you're right. We're here because of what's coming next. Or at least, what could come next. Tiny, the floor's yours."

The big man stood, walked to the side of the room and touched a button. A screen made its way down the wall, and a moment later an aerial view of what appeared to be the Gulf of Mexico came alive. This was similar to the view that Captain Boyle had shown us several times. However, there was only one ship and, judging from the coordinates at the bottom of the screen, it was steaming west.

"That's the ship…that's the one that picked up some of the crew from the *Honey*. I believe its name is *Bijar*."

"It's on its way here," McNaughton injected, rolling her eyes. "The World press is standing by to give it a hero's welcome."

"You have to be kidding!" I exclaimed. "They shot the Captain of the *Honey* and threw about ten crew off the life-rafts."

"Tell us about that," Kagan pressed me. "I understand you refused to take survivors with you. Picked up some, but left others."

"Doc Freeman said the plane had limited capacity."

Kagan had no intention of backing down. "That plane definitely has enough capacity for all the survivors."

"Capacity is based on fuel load. We were low on fuel. Perhaps that is why he said we couldn't get more people home. How do I know?"

"I understand old Doc Freeman may not make it," Kagan said, showing no emotion at the news.

"Shame," I said. "Nice guy. Vietnam Ace. Loves his cadets."

"Not an Ace, Redstone. Not even a doctor. But one hell of a good pilot. And his work here in Texas for the kids is the best in the country. For the record, he's not eighty, or whatever age he told you. He's eighty-seven. Go on."

I told them what had happened, ending with that sorry episode on the beach with Captain Boyle.

"That might have been my fault," McNaughton said. "As you might know, Boyle and I have, shall we say, not been seeing eye to eye recently. That's led to some harsh words——on both sides. When I learned your plane was short of fuel, I didn't anticipate it making it all the way to the beach. I instructed Boyle to meet the plane wherever it might come down and transport you and Angella to CG headquarters immediately. No passing GO type of thing. We didn't want you interviewed by the press, or even by the locals, until you were debriefed. Our plan was to deny any government official was even on the plane. Boyle started with the *what ifs*. What if it landed too far out? What if it landed and flipped? What if it landed among the fishing fleet? What if it landed on the beach? I suggested his bars were at stake if he didn't shut up and do as he was told. When he protested the water might be too shallow for his patrol boats I jokingly told him to use one of the confiscated toys they're forever taking from drug runners. Went a bit overboard. Passive, aggressive. Happens."

A rare apology from McNaughton, if, in fact it was an apology. May have just been a statement of fact. I let it drop.

"You say the *Honey* exploded beneath you when you were off to the side and not directly over it?"

"I wasn't flying, but that's my recall."

"Satellite pictures show you directly over the *Honey* when the first flash occurred. Is that possible?"

"Angella was taking pictures and may have video."

Angella brought the video up on her cell phone. Tiny handed her a cord. She snapped it into the base of her phone and the images she had captured replaced those we had been watching of the *Bijar*.

The *Honey* was almost below the seaplane. The lens had actually captured part of the fuselage as well as part of the *Bijar*. The video segment was short, but as luck would have it, the explosion on the *Honey* occurred just after our plane passed directly overhead.

"Play that again," Director Kagan said. "Better yet, send that file to me so that we can run it through our equipment. I want it in slow motion."

It took a few minutes to transfer the video and to queue it up on the house equipment. When it came up, it had time stamps across the side and latitude/longitude numbers were superimposed on each ship.

"I didn't realize there was so much information contained in the raw video," Angella said. "I should never have turned it off."

"That could be problematic young lady," Kagan responded, as dour as ever.

The motion had been slowed down and just as the flash was first seen, Tiny said, "Freeze!"

Then he said, "Back up a few frames."

"There! See it?"

"See what," I asked. The scene was an instant before the first flash of the explosion and all looked fine with the *Honey*. No one was visible on deck. Nothing unusual. "Looks okay to me."

"Now back up a frame." Pause. "Another." Pause. "Another." Pause. "One more." Pause. "There stop!" Tiny picked up a laser pointer and focused it on the deck.

"Nothing's there," I said, puzzled as to what it was we were supposed to be seeing.

"Precisely. Now advance a frame. Keep watching this area. See the line appear? Here."

"Advance another frame. The line becomes what appears to be a small basketball. More like a softball. See it?"

Now that Tiny pointed it out, it was clear that an object had come into the picture. An object slightly larger than a softball.

"I see it," Kagan said, his shrug silently adding, "so what?"

"Advance another," Tiny said.

Same ball.

"Advance two."

Same ball.

"One more."

Then we all understood what Tiny had seen. How he had seen it is beyond me, but he had. The softball was gone, replaced by a bright light.

"Step through several more," Tiny commanded.

As the frames progressed it was clear that the bright light that had replaced the softball was, in fact, the first stages of the explosion that destroyed the *Honey*.

"Where did the ball, shall we say bomb, come from?" Kagan asked. "Suppose it could have been dropped from the plane."

"That's precisely what the international community, especially Iran, is claiming," McNaughton said. "State's very much concerned."

"Does the video yield a clue?"

"Play it backward and let's see,"Tiny said.

It took a moment and then the explosion, in all its vivid color, burst on the screen, only to be sucked into a ball, which in turn moved off to the left and disappeared.

"Stop here,"Tiny said. "Blow this frame up." Pause. "Larger." Pause. "Larger." Pause. "That's enough. Hold it."

"What are you seeing?" I asked Tiny, again not following what had captured his attention. It was obvious he had done this many more times than I had.

"That blur," he said, focusing the red laser dot on a grayish smudge, "could be the bomb captured in mid-flight."

Kagan remarked, "Or it could be just what it appears to be, a smudge."

Tiny, undaunted, said, "Now go back another frame and blow it up to the same size."

The process was repeated for about twenty-five frames. Tiny then said, "Maybe the tech folks can do this electronically, but visual alone won't confirm what I'm thinking."

"And that is?" McNaughton bit.

"The *Bijar* propelled a bomb onto the *Honey*. Angella's video didn't start early enough to have captured the launching, but something seems to be moving between frames. Maybe a heat sensitive satellite image will *see* the actual launch. We now can calculate the exact time of the launch, if indeed a missile was fired, so if we have footage it should be retrievable."

Kagan moved to the side of the room and spoke into his cell. Actually, I was surprised to find that our phones worked this far below ground, but then I recalled they had special relay antennas set up to facilitate communication. I reminded myself, what was relayed could also be intercepted and recorded.

Back at the table, Kagan said, "It could take a few hours, but if they have it we'll get it. Satellite data collected over the water is fed to the Coast Guard for analysis. Don't imagine our friend Captain Boyle will be in a hurry to sign off on our getting it though."

McNaughton reached for her phone.

"Hold it, Cindy. Let's give Boyle a chance to play straight before you pin his ears back."

McNaughton flipped her phone closed. "I say we go on the assumption the *Bijar* sank the *Honey*. Why?"

That was the precise question I had been wrestling with since we had first seen the bomb. I said, "Follow me for a moment. *Honey* had medication. It may——or may not——have been tampered with. Or cut as someone suggested. But we did see a video of medications being removed from the Honey and loaded onto the *Rosie*."

"By your son, no less, Redstone." Kagan reminded me. "By your very own son."

"By my son. Correct. But we also know a few other facts. First, my son is not now on the *Rosie*. Second, the *Rosie* is clean. Third, those drugs were not transferred from the *Honey*. At least not from the *Honey* that was sunk."

"You're reaching, Jimmy." Jacobs said. "That video is pretty clear. I watched it several times. The drugs came from the *Honey*. The same ship you were seen supervising the loading in Argentina."

"Queue up that video," I said. "Tiny may be good at spotting bombs, but Angella also has sharp eyes and spots things as well."

Jacobs found the video on his iPad, connected the device to the same cable Angella used earlier and the troubling video we had seen yesterday was big as life in front of us.

Angella flipped open her cell. "If you have another cable, I can put this up there. Or you can look."

She placed the cell in the middle of the table and the group all leaned forward. Kagan said, "And just what are we looking at young lady."

"This picture was taken on the dock in Buenos Aires. That's the *Honey* angled in at the dock. Those pallets are PAP's medications that are being reloaded."

"So it is. What then?" Kagan said, patience not his highest virtue.

"Note the name on the ship," Angella replied, keeping her voice pleasant, a slight smile on her face. The first I had seen in hours.

"Noted," Kagan said.

"Note the type face, or whatever it's called. The name's in bold caps."

"Okay."

"Now look at the name on the ship in the video."

It was Tiny who spoke the obvious. "Video shows the name painted in lower case. Let's go back to the video from Angella's cell just before she blew."

When Angella's video came up, the name *Honey* was seen in bold caps, just as it had been back at the dock in Argentina.

"Point well made," Kagan acknowledged. "We're being duped. Okay, Redstone, continue."

"The *Bijar* is owned and operated by Iran. Am I correct?"

"Assume so," Kagan said.

"*Bijar* is on its way to Port Isabel? Correct?"

"Assume so. Continue."

"Iran is under sanctions. That means, I assume, that under normal conditions it would not be allowed to enter the United States."

"Continue."

"All this drama is a prelude to something Iran wants to pull off. Something requiring a ship under their control access to a harbor in the States."

"Wild leap, Redstone," Kagan said. "Off base now."

"With all due respect, Sir," Jacobs said to his boss, "Jimmy may be onto something. We all know Iran is about to detonate an atomic weapon. We also know Israel is a threat to prevent it. Did so in the past and they will do so again. That's why Israel is being blamed for the medications on the *Honey*. A diversion. This has nothing to do with the *Honey*———or with PAP———or with Israel." He paused, took a deep breath and said what everyone in the room was thinking. "This has everything in the world to do with Iran and its nuclear ambitions. And with the fact that an Iranian cargo vessel, carrying an unknown but supposedly highly toxic cargo, is, at this very moment, steaming directly, and with our blessing, toward South Padre Island."

FIFTY-TWO

"You're onto something, Redstone," an electronic voice boomed. At the same time, a screen I hadn't noticed at the side of the room came alive. The image coming into focus was that of several men in different color military uniforms sitting around a table in a room almost identical to the one we were in. The voice belonged to the only person in the room not wearing a uniform. "The drugs were transferred, if a transfer actually did occur which is doubtful at best, from a vessel other than the *Honey*."

Retired General Maxwell Jamison was speaking. The President calls in Jamison whenever the country goes on red alert. Jamison's longtime lover, Cindy McNaughton, herself a retired Marine General, was sitting opposite me. Seems the President used them as a team. "Jimmy Redstone, Angella Martinez, I want you to meet the Joint Chiefs of Staff. Chairman, General Milton Harris, Army; Admiral Wilkens, Navy; General Bolloester,

Marine Commandant; General Dixon, Air Force; and General Hayden, National Guard."

Introductions made, I said, "I suppose you've been listening to our little session. Are we on track or spinning wheels?"

"I'd say, on track," General Harris said. "Max has been saying some nice things about you and Agent Martinez and I personally wish to thank you. We have a mess on our hands for certain. I don't mind telling you, the Israeli's are chomping to take the Iran nuclear site out. Problem is it's hardened and not practical to go in."

"What do you folks believe is Iran's end game?" I asked, perhaps overstepping my bounds.

"We're of a mixed mind. Some of us think the *Bijar*, is carrying a nuclear weapon. Perhaps not one capable of being delivered by missile, but one capable of being detonated."

"The other view?" I asked.

"Something to do with the medications. Why else introduce all that medical tampering baloney?"

"I suppose you've considered stopping the *Bijar*, boarding it, finding out what it has aboard."

"To that end, Admiral Wilkens has a Navy SEAL contingent ready to go. But the problem is, if they detonate we're in even deeper trouble. We could, however, sink the ship. Recover the nuke from the sea before the saltwater corrodes it. That operational plan, of course, has its drawbacks, particularly the loss of life that would entail if we inadvertently set it off."

A thought struck me and with it a knot formed in my stomach. Without thinking it through, I said, "Angella help me. What was that marine biologist's name? The one with the UT Coastal Studies Lab?"

"Hildigo something," she replied, but couldn't immediately recall his last name. "Hildigo Francese. Is that who you mean?"

"Him. Remember he told us about the dead sharks. And claimed that guy Pettit was talking about tampered medications and contaminated fish."

"And dead plankton."

"Where you going with this, Redstone?" Jamison barked. "Dead fish. We got a nuclear disaster looming and you're talking about———"

"The *Bijar* is not far away. If it has nuclear weapons as you say, there's not much you can do about it. And frankly, why in the hell would they set off a nuke down here? They'd be steaming for New York, Washington, Boston. Put it on a private airplane, anything but not South Padre Island, for goodness sakes. But if they have mutilated the medication, the PAP Macrolides, into something that destroys marine life. Then———"

"Stop right there, Redstone. If marine life was gone, Iran, or whoever is behind this, would be gone as well. We all breathe the same oxygen. It would all be compromised. Some things are possible in theory, but can never be used because of assured mutual destruction."

"What would Iran care about mass destruction at this stage? If they could do it, they would. Let us clean up the mess as we always do."

Jamison said nothing, but waved his hand slightly. I took that as my signal to continue. "The *Bijar* comes into the Western Gulf of Mexico, or even into Laguna Madre, one of the world's richest marine environments. They now have the whole world watching, believing Israel is about to turn on the United States. That's a fight people would pay to see. A little bit of the toxin, enough to kill everything within a contained radius, is discharged into the water. They're open about it so you can verify that the dead marine life came from their dump. But they do it in such a way that you are powerless to stop them. The threat, of course, is that they will release more toxins if we don't give them what they want."

I stopped talking. These were smart men. I didn't have to elaborate on the devastation a toxic drug discharge would cause. Or that the U. S. would soon be held hostage to what the world believes to be an Israeli ship.

"To what end?" General Harris asked.

"To the end that the U.S. Government lifts the sanctions———or pledges not to support Israel if and when Israel attacks them. Lots of things we can give Iran to prevent further dumping. We might even be persuaded to support their having a nuclear weapon. In short, classic hardball blackmail."

I again stopped talking.

No one in either forum said anything.

A minute of silence in this context is an eternity. I finally said, "I take it I hit a nerve."

"Whether you did or not is not the question," General Jamison said. "The question on the table is what do you suggest we do about it———assuming you are correct in your assessment."

"As someone said earlier, blowing them out of the water makes it worse, not better. If we assume I'm right about the drugs and their intentions, then my suggestion is to board the vessel, find the material and either confiscate it or render it useless."

"We have no authority to board the *Irisl Bijar*," Navy Admiral Wilkens snapped. "That will be considered an act of piracy———or at least an act of aggression."

I wanted to point out that as long as we play by the rules they'll win. But that thought was better held close. The Joint

Chiefs didn't require a lecture from me on the rules of engage-
ment. "Even in our waters?" I asked.

"The President doesn't want to get into a dispute of territorial limits. And we don't want them to come close enough to
provoke a dispute. We want this contained as far from our shores
as possible. The United Nations is even calling for an assurance of
safe passage. The President doesn't have many options."

"Who the hell cares———"

"We'll be back to you, Redstone," General Harris said. "Stand
by."

The screen went dead.

"Are they still able to hear us?" I asked.

"They are," McNaughton said. "They always are."

FIFTY-THREE

While we waited, Angella checked on Doc Freeman and was told he was in intensive care, but expected to survive. That was indeed good news.

I called Hildigo Francese and he confirmed what I had been thinking. There were no new reports of sick fish in the Gulf of Mexico. In fact, the Gulf seemed particularly clean. To me that meant the video showing my son throwing toxic material overboard had been made up——and most likely even put on tape at an earlier time. That conclusion meant that Lester was actually down here for a period of time before calling me. That was troubling in its own way.

I wondered how much they were paying him to do what he was doing. I was certain he had been duped——or drugged—— and not aware of what he had gotten himself into.

The real breakthrough came with the interrogation of the *Honey* Captain. The interrogation Angella had begun on the plane, but had been unable to complete. The shot to his arm had shattered his radius, but he was lucky in that the bullet to his leg hit only soft tissue. The most important fact was that he knew the actual international maritime number of the hull.

By cross-checking against international records, the FBI determined that the *Honey* was originally named the *Iran Asal*. The captain, a man named Hormoz Asgari, had been educated in the United States and spoke near perfect English. He claimed he was set up. He saw the missile coming from the *Bijar* and was shot to prevent him from testifying as to what actually happened. Shortly before the bombing, they had been boarded and several pallets of PAP medications had been removed from the ship. He called it pirating in the Gulf of Mexico. He also said that the crew members who were saved by the *Bijar* were traitors. They had helped in the capture of the medications.

"That supports your theory, Cowboy," McNaughton said. "Nice piece of work you two."

Kagan, who had been off to the side talking to someone on his cell called across the room, "I second that, Redstone, Martinez. A bit unorthodox for me, but if it works then I can't say too much."

I turned to Jacobs. "Lost in all this is that slime Sally Comings, AKA Shadowy Sal. Any word on her?"

"Nothing reliable. We have reports of her being in London. Then in Cleveland. Also in Paris. Latest sighting shows she's in New Orleans as of several days ago. We know from your report she was in Buenos Aires, trying to take you out. But no one actually saw her come or go."

"Could there possibly be more than one? Just thinking."

"Anything's possible," Kagan injected, "but we doubt it. She knows how to move around and must have a persona she uses that we don't know about. Probably flies commercial under that name, whatever it is. Old Sal put a damper on Lillie Holland's career.

At one time, Holland was one of the best operatives Interpol had. When she got co-opted by Comings she became a liability in the field——as you found out."

"How positive are you that they are, in fact two different people? I mean Comings and Holland?" This was a wild hair, but one that had been nagging at me for a while.

"You're off the reservation, Redstone. A mile off. Holland's been known to Interpol for decades. She was a POW negotiator before that. You have reason to think otherwise?"

"A natural distrust perhaps. I had dinner with the imposter and she's a hell of an actress. Nailed Holland perfectly. Holland has an eye tick. Comings copied it perfectly."

"I can tell you Interpol has bio-metric pass codes on Holland that I understand can't be faked. An imposter couldn't have taken over."

"Databases can be tampered with," I replied. "But...let's assume Holland *is* the real agent. Let us also assume she created 'ole Sal herself!"

"Interesting thought, Redstone. Interesting indeed. A turned agent operating in the open. Not bad. I'll check it out."

Jacobs moved close. "So, what else is troubling you? It's written all over you."

I told Jacobs about my conversations with Holland and how she seemed to know exactly what I was saying and doing. After giving him some specifics, including Holland knowing what was discussed on the beach at South Padre Island shortly after the discussion took place, I said, "So, how did she know all that? And in some cases she knew within a few minutes. Did you brief her or what?"

"I'll check the briefing reports and the file access logs," Jacobs replied, his eyes narrowed in concern. Unexplained facts troubled him. In that regard, we were both very much alike. "To my knowledge, only specifically authorized people have had access to the video of you on the beach. I can't imagine we'd be sharing this with Interpol."

Jacobs went off to check the computer and I had a chance to talk to Angella in private.

"You holding up okay, Jimmy?" she asked the moment we were alone. "I'm worried about you."

"Funny, I was about to ask you the same thing."

"I don't have a son mixed up in whatever this is. That can't be very comforting. I'm sure you've picked up on the fact that he must have been down here long before he contacted you."

"That upsets me, certainly. But I just know he's doing whatever it is against his will. Has to be."

"You had dinner with him. You didn't say anything about him seeming duped."

"He was suffering with allergy. Mostly out of it, I'd say."

"Out of it, from what little you've said about him, is his typical state. Hey, I'm sorry. This is painful for you, I know. I'm really sorry for saying what I just said. No call for it."

"He's troubling——on many levels."

"Sorry. I know you hurt."

Changing the subject, I said, "What do you think the Joint Chiefs are drumming up? I didn't expect them to take so long." The more I concentrated on business, the easier this was going to be for me.

"Whatever it is, it's taking them a while."

"Must be complicated," I said, thankful Angella had backed off Les. "I remember exercises years ago. Had to have a role for each branch or the operation didn't come off. If airplanes were called for, they had to use both Air Force and Navy, that sort of thing. Hope they still don't work that way."

"My father is fond of saying if you asked a man with a hammer to fix a problem you could bet a hammer would be involved in the solution."

"We just asked a bunch of men with war ships, planes, troops, and rockets to fix a problem. Are you suggesting their solution will involve one or more of the above?"

"I'm suggesting some sort of physical destruction is being considered. Probably debating exactly how far they can go." Angella cocked her head. "Just saying."

FIFTY-FOUR

"Listen up, folks," Jamison said, when he finally came back on line. "We have a lot to accomplish and little time to do it. I see we're missing Cindy and Kagan. For this part of the briefing they're as useless as...never mind...we'll go on without them. In exactly, one hour and ten minutes the *Bijar* will become disabled. Not important how, just know it will happen. *Bijar* will try to reestablish power, but won't be able to do so. At the time this occurs, they will still be outside our clear territorial control but will be in a tenuous position. They'll be forced to ask for a new generator. We'll comply, but will insist on sending our own workman aboard to install it."

"Will they allow that?" I asked.

"Hold your questions, if you will. Time is not on our side. This is an operation; not a debate. Treat it as such, Redstone."

"Yes Sir," I snapped.

"Redstone and Martinez will board with the engineers. You will be searched, so leave your weapons where they are. Your mission is to find the drugs and render them useless."

Momentarily forgetting my admonition to remain silent, I started to ask how we were to do that. But I was saved from another tongue-lashing by a distraction when McNaughton rejoined us.

"You will find the drugs using a combination of devices. One of them cutting edge and one as old as they come. I'll explain in a moment. When you board the vessel, you will find knives already positioned for you, as well as small explosives to open doors or safes. You will have twenty-five minutes total. A diversion will occur to occupy the crew, but you can expect the medication to be guarded in some manner. Did I see McNaughton rejoin us a moment ago? Anything to report on the machinery?"

"It's on its way to Port Isabel," McNaughton answered, her tone crisp and to the point. "Everything will be in place in forty-five minutes."

"Good," Jamison replied, "Captain Boyle is being briefed as we speak. I'll bring up the operational screen and you can follow the activity. What you are about to see is coming live from a camera positioned a few minutes ago on the deck of the *Bijar*."

Instantly, the view of Jamison and the other Generals was replaced by a dog's eye view of the deck of a cargo ship. "Audio has been positioned as well," Jamison's voice informed us, "but there's no need to mix that in just yet." Jamison went silent for several long seconds, then he said, "In exactly seven minutes and ten seconds two SEALs will board and position knives and small explosive packages for your use. You'll be able to see exactly where each is positioned."

The sound went off again, this time for several minutes. The screen showed the empty deck of the *Bijar* with an occasional deckhand crossing directly below the camera.

Then Jamison's voice again cut into the room. "Minute and a half to go. We'll start the briefing on how you are to find and dispose of the drugs. Redstone, we have every reason to believe your son, Lester, is on board. His dog is trained to bark and warn him when anyone gets close to the drugs. You'll each board with a dog whistle tuned to a frequency that causes distress in that breed of dog. Their natural instinct when in distress is to run to what they've been trained to guard. Following?"

"Following," I responded. I was not sure where this was going, but I was feeling as if Angella and I were being hung out.

"You'll also have with you...let's hold it here, it's show time."

A countdown clock appeared on the screen showing four. Then three. Two. One. Then plus one. Plus two. Plus three.

A shadow moved across the screen off to the right of the camera. The camera rotated and the grey clad body of a SEAL could be seen bent over and placing a small package under a coil of rope.

"That kit contains a knife and an explosive," Jamison said. "Note its location below the fan-room sign on the starboard side. Same thing is occurring on the port side. Mirror image locations."

In fact, I couldn't read the words on the sign, but a picture of a fan served the same purpose.

The SEAL, moving with a fluid motion I knew I could never achieve, repeated the placement, only this time the package was placed inside a bulkhead tool drawer next to a hatchway leading below decks.

The SEAL was then gone as quickly as he——or she——
had appeared. My assumption was over the side, but I couldn't
be certain.

The image of the deserted deck returned to the screen along
with Jamison's voice. "As you see, the knives and explosives are
in place. You should have no trouble locating them. Now back
to finding the drugs. The dog will lead the way once you blow
the whistle. You will be issued a hand-held mass-spectrometer
already set to what we are looking for. When you find the target
drugs, the spectrometer will be used to determine how to neutralize them. We've already calculated the possibilities. You'll
have with you in your work kits numbered packets. The spectrometer will tell you which number to use and how much to
mix."

"Question?" I asked tentatively.

"Go."

"What if the machine comes up blank?"

"Then we got this all wrong and we're on to plan B."

"What's plan B?"

"We'll be sure to let you know when we hatch it."

The room fell silent as Jamison clicked off. But the live video
feed from the ship's deck captured my son walking out of the
hatchway, the dog walking a step behind him taking the opportunity to relieve himself directly into the camera lens.

"At least give them credit for a semblance of a plan," Jacobs
said, when I rolled my eyes. Could have been a rocket launch
countdown. Blow the ship to yesteryear. Then deny it ever
existed. Been done before, be done again."

"For your information, Cowboy, that is Plan B," McNaughton said. "If you can't find tampered drugs, or you can't for any
reason neutralize them, they'll sink the ship right where it is.

Explaining a second explosion is much easier than dealing with a nuke going off——especially in our territory. You clear on that?"

"Clear as can be," I responded. There was nothing I could do to change their decision, except concentrate on finding the contaminated cargo and rendering it harmless. "I assume they won't wait for us or the crew to leave the ship before they blow it to hell?"

"I'm not privy to the exact operational aspects, but for your planning purposes expect that to be true, yes."

"Why do I feel Angella and I are getting set up? Civilians going aboard disguised as Coast Guard, armed with a dog whistle."

"And a knife, Redstone. Don't forget the knife."

"Why not have us make a tape confessing that Angella and I were the two behind all this. And then on camera we shoot ourselves."

"You better hope they didn't hear you. They may change Plan B to accommodate you."

"I'll powder my nose."

Ignoring my comment, McNaughton said, "I've arranged for you to be trained with the spectrometer and the packets. They'll do that at Coast Guard headquarters. Helicopter will pick you two up in six minutes. There's just enough time to get you there, get you trained and have you board the supply ship taking the new generator and other parts out to the *Bijar*. Get something to eat if you wish. Plan for a long night."

"*Bijar* has reported engine trouble," a voice I did not recognize said over the speaker system. "Refusing help." Latitude and longitude coordinates were being relayed, along with a ton of other detailed information that I did not understand.

Jacobs said, "Time to go. Good luck, both of you. I know you won't believe this, but I honestly wish I was going with you."

"Thanks for the support, Sylvan. Appreciate it."

"Know one thing," Jacobs said, his voice barely audible, "I'll have your backs."

Jacobs' comment felt better than the current promise we had from Tiny.

"Cowboy!" McNaughton said coming into the room. "They need you two on the flight deck, pronto."

"We're on our way," I said. "Just saying goodbye."

"Angella," McNaughton said, rushing toward her, arms open for a hug. "Take care of yourself. We need you back here in one piece. You also Cowboy, for what it's worth. You also."

FIFTY-FIVE

In the end, Captain Boyle balked at allowing Angella and I to dress in Coast Guard uniforms and pled his case to Jamison. The compromise was that we'd each be issued jeans and blue work shirts. The spectrometer turned out to be simple to use; just place the pointed end in the substance and wait ten seconds. It was programmed to do the rest. If there was no antidote for the medication then we moved into Plan B. From pieces of conversation I picked up, Plan B was indeed to sink the ship.

"Should have named the mission Neptune Calling," I quipped.

Angella did not think that was funny and told me in no uncertain terms to concentrate on the mission. The only problem was, I *was* concentrating. Especially now that the transfer launch was approaching the *Irisl Bijar* which had been freshly painted in anticipation of its public arrival into Laguna Madre, USA. Its name was also now spelled in Persian script beneath the English, leaving no doubt as to its Iranian heritage.

A ladder was lowered over the side and four mechanics went up ahead of us. After much debate, a woman had been added to the work party so that Angella would not draw undue attention. It seemed like a good idea at the time, but judging from the cat calls and whistles as the first woman made her way onto the deck, I had my doubts.

Angella and I started up the ladder. She put her hand over mine, squeezed for an instant and let go. For all we knew, we were being monitored by friend and perhaps by foe and there was no need to exacerbate the situation.

Once on deck we followed the other mechanics toward the engine room. The deck was empty of people just as it had been in the video we had studied. I stopped at the tool drawer where my knife had been hidden. Angella paused at the coil of rope where her knife had been positioned. I noted that neither of us had been searched upon boarding, but we could not have planned it that way.

The boat lurched, causing Angella to stumble. She fell to her knee and my first instinct was to focus on anyone around her who could cause trouble. She had timed her fall perfectly, allowing her to reach under the rope with no one in position to see her extract the knife.

I then bent and pulled the drawer open with my left hand, sticking my right inside to retrieve the kit.

My fingers touched nothing.

I reached further inside and moved my hand all around the small space.

Nothing.

I heard footsteps coming up the ladder from below and didn't know if it was one of ours or one of theirs. My question was answered when I realized the language was Persian. My hand moved frantically trying to locate the missing weapon, all to no avail. But even if I could find the knife, it was too late to bring it out.

I slipped my hand out, pushed the drawer closed with my knee and stood up, my back now to the drawer. Two crewmen appeared on deck, a bushel of potatoes carried between them. Cook's helpers, I concluded, the same on all ships. They walked past me barely noticing the foreigner aboard.

I again bent down, but before I could wrestle the drawer open again, a loud explosion sounded below and a bell began to ring. I could hear running feet going in every direction. This, I assumed, was our distraction. I quickly pulled the dog whistle from my pocket and blew as hard as I could. With the racket going on no one paid me any attention.

Angella came over close and said, "What's troubling you? You have your *I'm not in control look* on your face."

"Find your kit?"

"Affirmative."

"Mine's gone. Not good. Let's go over to the port side and get———"

Angella grabbed my arm. "Hear that?"

A dog was barking. It was faint, but real. The sound, more of a howl than a bark, was coming from the starboard side behind us about mid-ship.

We ran in that direction. But before we could locate the hatch to go down, the howling ceased. This time Angella did the honors and immediately the dog resumed its howling.

"Keep blowing, but maybe, not so hard," I suggested. "The dog's really reacting."

"Isn't that the idea," Angella called after me as we ran aft, "to find where he is."

"Don't want his ear drums to burst. He won't be any good to us if he can't hear. Besides, he's just below where we are. Hold for a while." We were almost to the stern of the cargo vessel and at the widest part of the boat. "I don't have a weapon, so you've got my back."

"Knives are not the best for this, but here we go."

It wasn't hard to find the dog. The poor animal was inside a cabin at the base of the ladder. The door was unlocked and when I opened it the dog was running back and forth between the cabin door and a large safe-like structure in the far corner.

As before, when the whistle stopped blowing, the animal stopped howling. But he continued his circuit, as if trying to have someone relieve him of the responsibility.

"Give me the explosive," I said, "and step into the hall."

A moment later I had the small putty-like ball in place. According to the briefing, this explosive created a shock wave that vibrated the container open instead of blowing it apart. We had been warned to stay clear of the wave, which was delayed by five seconds after ignition.

"Five," I called to Angella. "Four."

"Get out of there, Jimmy. Now."

I was on my way. Only I had paused to grab the dog.

"One."

It was too late to scoop him up so I dove for him, and caught him just under my left arm, my body mostly on his.

Whoosh.

The sound was not as bad as I had expected, but the hammering impact, followed by the violent air movement, pinned us both to the deck.

Fido was up before I was, again racing in circles.

"Jimmy," Angella said, stepping back into the room. "It actually worked. It's open."

She walked to the now open safe, the spectrometer in her left hand. With her right, she pulled out a carton of the medications from PAP. It looked like the same container we had last seen in Buenos Aires. The knife, I assumed, was safely tucked in her jeans belt.

"This stuff is off the scale!" she exclaimed. "The meter reads it all right. It's the A packet. Wonks guessed right. But the amount we're going to require to neutralize it is far more than we have, at least by two."

"We weren't briefed on that. We'll use what we have and attempt to reach operations for clarification. At least we'll cut down the potency by half."

During the time we were mixing the medications Fido laid quietly in the hall just outside the door, his snoot on his paws, watching us with bored interest. Once or twice the dog let out a yip, but for the most part remained quiet. Best of all, he had not been trained to attack us, which saved Angella from having to slit its throat.

The mixed medication cartons were piling up against the wall. We only had five more to go. Assuming there were no more safes, and there didn't appear to be based on the dog's action——or lack of action.

"Okay," I called to Angella, "we're done with the cartons. Got a few packets left. I'll go back and mix them in with the cartons we've already done."

"It's worth whatever we can do. But we're about out of time. Are we throwing this overboard or...or what?"

"If it had been completely neutralized, I'd just put it back in the safe and let them bring it in and dump it in the bay as they had planned. But now, with it being twice the strength our experts thought, I don't——"

Both of our mission timers vibrated at the same time. We had five minutes to wrap up, get on deck and over the side and into the launch. "Decision's made," I said. "This is going over the side out here. The SEALs can recover it. Ten trips up to the deck should do it."

Before I finished talking, Angella had piled four cartons on top of each other and was lifting them off the floor. They were more bulky than heavy.

I joined her and we raced up onto the deck, deposited our loads and returned several more times until all of the cartons were piled neatly along the railing. The surprising part was that we had not encountered anyone moving about.

"Almost finished," I said to Angella. "Over the side with this stuff and then over we go. We'll have to trust they'll pick us up soon enough."

"They'll retrieve the boxes before they retrieve us. We might be in the water a while."

"If Captain Boyle had his way, they'd forget about us. We'd be in the water a real long time."

"Not so fast," came an all too familiar voice from the doorway. What the hell you two doing?"

Angella and I turned to face the speaker.

Standing behind us, a Sig Sauer pointed at my chest, was my son Les, his face still puffy, but his eyes hardened in fury.

FIFTY-SIX

"Les," I said, "what have you gotten yourself into? Put that gun down."

"You're the person who doesn't belong here! You and your lady friend! You always get in the way, don't you?"

The words spit out of his mouth with a vengeance I had never before seen Les display. The hate on his face was palpable——and frankly, frightening.

"I was hired to protect the drug shipment," he said, his tone softening slightly, but his face still contorted in rage. "Couldn't exactly tell you that over dinner, now could I? And for once in my life I will complete what I'm supposed to do. So get away from those cartons."

"Les, put the gun down for goodness sake! These folks want to...they want to destroy our country. They're enemies! You're in league with enemies, aiding and abetting!"

"I know what I'm doing! The United States is the aggressor! Not the other way around."

"You're confused. You're an American———my son! What's happened to you?" I had been inching closer and about to grab the gun when he stepped away. Up to this point, I had been concentrating on Les entirely. His sudden movement to the side made me realize Angella had worked herself further around to his other side and now he stood almost with his back to her, concentrating only on me. It was as if Angella was a bystander incapable of taking action.

"Now I understand what happened," Les said. "Took me a while, but I now get it. How you got aboard."

"Put that gun down. For heaven's sake, put it down. We are on the same side. You're not going to shoot your own father."

The gun was thrust even further in my direction and he now held it in both hands, almost as if making sure he couldn't miss. His hands were rock steady, his stance was professional. "I will if I have to," he snarled. "I have a job to do and nothing, nothing, will stop me! I must prove myself!"

"What is your job, Lester? What is so vitally important to make you turn against your own father? My God! To even suggest such a thing is unthinkable!"

"Making sure this medication gets into the bay. Kill every living thing so that the United States learns it's not so all powerful! The United States can't and won't control the world! I can control that! You're nothing but...but a hindrance to be rid of!"

His already puffy face was bloated even more, having turned beet red with rage. Keeping him talking was important. Angella needed to work her way slightly closer and at the same time retrieve her knife.

If I couldn't get my son under control, she'd have, at best, one opportunity to slash his throat. If she did what she had done the last time, and go for a secondary wound, she and I would both die at his hands. "Les, you said your job is important. But you weren't here when we came. Is there someone else in charge? Someone you should discuss this with?"

"No, I'm in charge. It's my job. I was called down to the engine room because they needed an interpreter for those inept mechanics. I figured it out! The mechanics and…and you are working…together. The U.S. government is worried. Well, good! They should be!"

"Please, Les, don't———"

"Shut up! No more talking. Step back away from those cartons."

I took a step back, not because I was abandoning the mission, but because I wanted to give Angella a cleaner trajectory to him.

Then I saw what I had hoped never to see again in someone's eyes. Pure hatred coupled with the emotionally vacant look of a psychopath. That explained the steady hands. Les, my son, was indeed about to pull the trigger.

"Les," I pleaded, desperate to get through to him, "please lower your weapon before it goes off. I see the hurt in your eyes and know you don't want to do this. Put the gun down before someone gets hurt." I was speaking not only to my son, giving him a reason to hesitate, to come down from his psychotic high, but I was also speaking to Angella. In one of our many training sessions we had decided that the phrase *before someone gets hurt* is the trigger phrase for a coordinated assault. From the time my fingers opened we were each to count five seconds. If, on the count of five, the situation had not been resolved, I would make a sudden movement in a direction away from her. She would then attack with deadly force, using whatever means she could muster.

What Angella could not see, and what I now realized all too clearly, was that Les had made up his mind to shoot. Five seconds was not an eternity. The gun started to move upward toward my head even before my silent count reached three.

Something moved off to my side causing Les to scream, "Where the hell have you been, you stupid mutt? What the hell good are you?" His eyes had focused on the dog who had selected this moment to come bounding out of the hatchway onto the main deck, its ear pain forgotten, its tail wagging in friendship.

Les's gun fired, blowing the dog's brains over the deck and sending the dead animal crashing through the railing and over the side.

Les's gun moving off to the side, coupled with the silent count reaching five, propelled me forward toward him. He was no longer my son, but a psychotic killer who had to be stopped at all costs.

Angella also moved into action. The knife came out and she heaved herself toward Les's neck.

I was in mid-air, my head about to slam into Les's knees, when my brain finally processed the facts. It's amazing to me how slow time actually moves in these situations. Maybe time doesn't actually slow down, but the human processor ticks faster. However it works, a lifetime does indeed pass before your eyes in an instant.

My body was already below the gun when it turned downward to focus on me. Angella's body slammed into Les's shoulders with a force I didn't realize she could muster. Then my head and shoulders drove him into the rail hard enough to hear metal snap.

The next gunshot was deafening, as if it had been discharged against the side of my head. The three of us were going down in a heap together. For what seemed an eternity we all lay on the deck. I could hear nothing.

I hadn't felt a bullet pass into my body, but sometimes with gunshot wounds it takes a while before the body sounds the alarm. The fact that Angella also was not moving did not bode well. Not for the first time, I prayed for her.

I reached up to secure the gun and my hand hit warm blood. Not just a trickle, but a gusher was flowing above me. I was on the bottom of the pile. Angella was on top. Between us lay a dead body, its head severed almost from ear to ear.

FIFTY-SEVEN

Other than two of the cartons breaking open when they hit the water, the rescue operation came off as planned. We were delivered to the Coast Guard Station on South Padre Island. Camp South was now off-limits to us.

The SEALS, following orders, had immediately separated Angella and me and had admonished us to say nothing about the operation. I had been told Angella had sustained some bruising when she landed in the water on top of a drug carton. The statement had been terse and to the point. I knew nothing further about her condition.

I was painfully aware that trauma injuries were subjective and that a bruise to a SEAL could be anything from a slight nick to missing body parts——and most likely was tipped toward the latter.

I needed to talk to Angella about the death. I wanted her to hear from me that she had performed as expected. Options had been taken out of her hands.

I looked up, expecting to see Angella, but instead Tiny was framed in the door behind Sylvan Jacobs. "Just the two I wanted to see," I said. "I suppose you've been briefed?"

"If you're asking about what transpired on the *Bijar*, most certainly," Jacobs said. "Sorry for your loss, Jimmy. It couldn't be prevented."

Before Tiny could say anything, I responded, "Let's not talk about that now. We were estranged, as they say. I need to concentrate on the mission."

"Mission's over for you two," Tiny informed me. "Like it or not. But if you need to wrap your mind around something, try this. A major international furor is building over what went down. To put it in technical terms, the shit's hit the fan! All hell's broken loose!"

"What the hell! We stopped major contamination of our waters! And that's causing a flap? What's the world come to?"

"Politics———as usual. Welcome to my world."

"Good thing we didn't sink that crate," Jacobs volunteered. Then he added, "This operation cast us in a bad light. We need widespread support for the sanctions on Iran and this just shot that all to hell! Iran may be backward in much of what it does, but in this operation it was masterful. Played us like a child's toy. They managed to put us on the defensive and at the same time put Israel on the firing line, while also driving a wedge between us and our only real friend in the Middle East. Palestinian rocket attacks have dramatically increased and Israel's hands are tied. We can't afford to respond with this going on."

"We protect our shores and this is what we get. The world is nuts!" I was pacing the room, growing angrier and angrier by the moment.

"In politics, it's not facts, but opinion that counts. Manipulate opinion and you control your destiny. Right now we're being played big time." Jacobs paused, fished out his cell phone and held it up. "Want to see what the world is seeing, try this."

There Angella and I were, clear as day throwing cartons of what is characterized as toxic chemicals into the Gulf of Mexico.

"Keep in mind," Jacobs reminded us, "Those are the toxic drugs the world believes came from Israel. Nothing we have said has changed the narrative. The United States and Israel working together. It's hard to refute video evidence."

"The fact they were in sealed containers doesn't count? The fact that we were trying to render the drugs harmless means nothing?"

"The world's gone visual," Tiny replied. "Might as well manufacture TVs without speakers for all the good all that talking does. As Sylvan said, this was well-orchestrated. And the U. S. is taking the rap."

"So, we're the bad guys."

"If the costume fits——"

"Feels like it was tailored to fit. How's Angella?"

"Superficial injuries. She'll be along in a few minutes. She's broken up over what she had to do. Taking it hard."

"She did exactly right. If she hadn't done what she did, there is every likelihood that one or both of us would not be here today. Not to mention the United States would now be held hostage. Or worse, the Gulf of Mexico would be the Dead Sea."

"Not if they sunk that tub," Jacobs volunteered. "I understand they were only moments away from pulling the trigger——so to speak."

"Correction," Tiny injected, "trigger was frozen. President refused to give the order. Preferred further negotiations."

"Further reason why Angella did the exact right thing," I said, struggling with the fact we were now on the hot seat for saving ourselves. I heard the mental chain saw stop and watched helplessly as the limb we were on crashed to the ground.

"You'll need to tell her," Tiny said. "You need to be sure Angella understands. That's all she's focusing on. Killing your son."

"Angella will be fine when this all settles. I have no doubt about it." Changing the subject, I said to Tiny, "Speaking of my son, you started working on this a while back, but we need to approach it from another angle. Something's wrong here. I don't think that was Les out there."

"What's troubling you?" Jacobs asked. "You certain it's not classic denial? Wishful thinking?"

"Perhaps. Where Les is concerned, I've been known to deny the obvious. But here's what I have. Timing. The original video showing the drug transfer had Les involved. We now know that video was shot before Les came to visit me. That, and Les just doesn't like dogs. What would he be doing with a dog?"

"Continue,"Tiny said, "that's not new news. And he did shoot the dog, didn't he? Also, he could have come down early and just not called you. That's the way I see it. Sorry."

"I'm thinking it was Sal, both in the video and on board the *Bijar*."

"Wishful thinking. You don't want to accept that your son is———was———a psychopath. Angella confirmed the look on his face———in his eyes. According to your report, the kid showed no emotion about killing you. In fact, from the video of him shooting the dog and then turning the gun back on you, and from his speech patterns, several profilers have pronounced him psychotic."

"Whoever it was, was psychotic. I agree. But we know Sal fits that description as well. Too bad the body wasn't recovered."

"One of those mysteries. Our surveillance shows you and Angella throwing the cartons over the side and then going over yourselves. The body was left on deck. About five minutes later a deckhand picked it up and took it below. What happened then is anyone's guess. Nothing was found when Customs boarded an hour later."

"Someone threw her overboard. What about her half-brother, Touchy?"

"Ig the Pig's gone missing as well," Jacobs replied. "There's reason to believe he was aboard, but we can't confirm. He wasn't there, as far as we can determine, for the immigration process. But, frankly, that's nothing to take to the bank."

"You have something in mind?" Tiny asked, "I mean about finding your son."

Tiny usually spoke with a smile, even when delivering bad news. Now his lips were set hard, his words clipped. His eyes spoke volumes. He was humoring me. I said, "Go with me on this. I live off my hunches, and if I might say so myself, they serve me well."

"At your service," the big guy said, "your wish is my command."

Jacobs winced, but said nothing. He looked away, as if he didn't wish to be part of the conversation.

"I had you looking for the boat Les was injured on."

"Found no trace. We contacted every company we could find. No injures to your son were reported——and no one would acknowledge anything off the record."

"He wasn't injured. Not if my theory is right, he wasn't."

"Look, Redstone, we even checked the crew manifest of every fishing boat up there. We know your son's work history ever since he arrived in Alaska. Jacobs can bring up the FBI file, if you want to see it. The last time your son worked was last spring. He made good money, but he hasn't worked——not in the fishing industry that is——for almost a year."

"Hear me out. I should have thought of this sooner, but things moved so fast I...anyway, he's working under a different name. Manhyme, or Comings, or whoever is orchestrating this, got to him, probably several months ago, and enticed him to work under a different name. Fixed him up with a Social Security number, the whole nine yards. He's up there. I just need to find him."

"He hasn't called you——or his mother. We checked."

"Part of the deal. Sign on for a fixed time. High pay. Maybe a windfall. Deal is he can't tell anyone, including his parents, where he is."

"And you know that because he shot the dog?" Tiny said, finally losing patience. "Cut me a break. By your account, he hates dogs."

"Not to the point where he'd shoot one. It was that imposter, Comings, I'm telling you. I saw the look in her eyes!"

"You're pretty certain, aren't you?"

"Here's another fact. I thought——we all thought——that Angella going to Argentina without me was because they wanted her down there for something. They did. It was to kill her. I assumed they were after me with that break-in at the hotel the first night we were there. But I had that wrong. They needed me alive and back in South Texas, so they could show me on the boat with my son. Pin the U.S. to the drugs. They were after Angella, wanted her out of the way."

"Pieces fit, but still far out."

"Just find my son. Or...or I just thought of another way to prove my theory. My guess is that Interpol agent Holland is now among the missing. She and Sally may be one and the same. If she's gone missing then we can assume Angella dispatched Sally and not Les."

"You've gone too far, Redstone," Tiny said. "And what about the Wolf?" A smile spread across his broad face, "She in it also?"

"No need to get nasty. I think Comings killed Holland and took her place years ago. Or, Holland invented Comings and went rogue. Should be easy to figure out. Just find Holland and prove me wrong."

"Actually," Jacobs said, a slight smile on his face, "Kagan suggested that same theory an hour ago. We're on it. Hey, speaking of the devil, here she is."

Angella had entered the room and was standing tentatively just inside the door.

Tiny swallowed her up in his arms and Jacobs touched her on the back. Jacobs then said, "You two need some alone time. I have stuff to work on."

Tiny, following Jacobs' lead said, "I'll get started circulating Les's picture among the fishing fleet, but I'm not holding out much hope. This will take a while, at best."

"Les's picture?" Angella asked. "Why in the world———"

"Tell you later," I said, pulling Angella close to me. The sadness in her eyes didn't allow me to fool myself into thinking I could erase all that had happened in a few moments.

"Oh, Jimmy," Angella said, "I keep thinking it'll get easier, but it doesn't, does it? I'm so, so, very sorry. I could have———"

"Afraid not. You did it exactly right. If we ease up, they've got us. It's like a basketball game. You're up twenty points, you coast. Then it's the last second and the other team throws in a three-pointer at the buzzer. You lose."

"That's exactly how I feel. We work our butts off and…and… this is what we get."

"It could have been worse. They could have brought the whole toxic load in——and Sally with it."

Angella pulled away, before I caught myself.

"Sally?" she said. "What's Sally got——"

I told her my theory. As I did so I watched the sadness in her eyes deepen. I reached out for my lover, but she held her ground. "You did just the right thing," I again said. "She had a gun. You had a knife. Deadly force was exactly right."

"But…but…Jimmy, even if you're right about Sally, at the time, I…I thought it was your son." She again looked away. "Everything happened so fast. I'm so sorry."

"I'm telling you, it wasn't——"

"All because you think he wouldn't shoot a dog! Jimmy you're not facing…stop trying to make it easier on me! Have you called his mother?"

"Not yet. Listen, Angella, I need you to understand, it's not just the dog. His eyes. Everything. Those were not his eyes!"

"Call his mother! She has a right to know what you know. Please, Jimmy, call——"

The door opened and in came Sylvan Jacobs. From his demeanor he had come to deliver bad news. "Sorry, Redstone, but your theory on Holland isn't holding up. She just climbed off a plane in Buenos Aires. On her way to visit Plevin in the hospital. He took a turn for the worse and they won't release him. She's alive and kicking."

"Positive?"

"She might still be an imposter, but if Comings had her neck slit then even I know it's not Comings."

I kicked the table leg, prompting Angella to say, "I'm sorry, Jimmy, really I am. I'll never accept——"

"It wasn't Les," I shouted. "You hear me, it wasn't Les!"

Angella put her arm around me, but said nothing.

Jacobs took the opportunity to slip out of the room.

Within two minutes he was back. His eyes told a story, but I couldn't decipher what was on his mind.

"Prelim tox reports are not good! In the last hour alone, ten thousand man-o'-wars have been found dead. They're in the bay as well as in the Gulf. Dolphins are agitated, possibly sick, to say the least."

"All that from the few containers that broke?"

"They're afraid it'll get a lot worse before it gets better—— assuming nothing else was dumped."

"They're jellyfish," I said. "I don't know much about jellyfish, other than they sting when you touch them. What's the big deal?"

"Jellyfish and man-o'-wars are not the same. Man-o'-wars float at the surface," Angella said, "and hang down under water. No means of propulsion from what I remember. They can't swim, so they can't get out of the way."

"Right on. They're the first indicators of what's to come. From what I heard," Jacobs said, "tons of them will wash up on the beaches in the next twenty-four hours."

"I'll take those over dead dolphins or sharks any day," I said.

"I agree," Jacobs continued, "but that Francese character over at the lab claims dolphins will begin washing up soon enough. He doesn't hold out much hope to save them."

Angella was about to say something when Tiny burst into the room, his demeanor that of a circus ringmaster. "Angella and Jimmy, this is your lucky day!"

"How come I always feel I'm about to be…let's just say, abused…when you say that?"

"You and Angella are scheduled as guests of the State Department at a press conference." He checked his watch. "Actually, they're gathering in the parking lot now. They are only waiting for the satellite link to come up. It'll be just a few minutes. They're attacking this crisis head on."

"What do they have in mind, throwing us in with the dead man-o'-wars?"

"Not exactly," Tiny said, "but can you say thrown under the bus. Actually, footage of the dead jellyfish has gone viral. Someone called the Dolphin Whisperer posted video on YouTube of them piled knee deep further up the coast. TV stations from here to Alaska are broadcasting the image."

"I suppose I'm being blamed for dumping the contaminated drugs overboard."

"We can't very well tell the world that SEALs were down there. Afraid you're it."

"Better than being tossed out of a plane," Angella commented, apparently not happy at being forced to relive for the public what it felt like to slit someone's throat. Especially when that someone was your partner's son. "I take that back. I'll take the plane."

"At least coming out of the plane," I responded, "there are a few possible positive outcomes. Parachute being one of them. With the question and answer stuff from a hostile public, nothing——and I mean nothing——good can come of it. The government has found a scapegoat and they'll ride me until my hide comes off."

"They're ready out there," Tiny announced. "Keep in mind they know at least one person died, but the name of the deceased has not been released."

"Do they know...that...that I did it?" Angella enquired, her face going pale.

"I believe so, but not certain. Listen, I suppose I shouldn't say anything, and be sure to keep this to yourselves, but the Joint Chiefs laid out a plan they worked out with Israel to go in and take out the nuclear sites in Iran. The idea is to show the world the U. S. cannot be blackmailed."

"The President will never go for it," I said.

"It's politics my friend. And in politics anything is possible. Word has it that the President is favorably considering the plan. So you can work into your remarks that the tainted drugs were a result of Iran. That sets the stage for attacking them should POTUS give the thumbs up. Come, can't keep the public waiting."

Before walking through the door, I again pulled Angella close and whispered, "There's no good way to do this. Answer their questions honestly, but say as little as you possibly can. Don't volunteer anything. You can always punt and claim you can't say something because of an ongoing investigation."

"Is there an investigation?"

"There's always an investigation."

FIFTY-EIGHT

I wasn't prepared for the crowd. A small platform had been set up in the front of the parking lot and cameras and microphones were focused on us from every angle. The reporters overflowed the area with the excess being herded onto the helicopter-landing pad. The area behind the landing pad was lined with a myriad of trucks, their dish antennas pointing skyward.

A stench was prevalent, being blown in from the bay off to my right. I winced when I glanced in that direction. The alcove beside the Coast Guard station, normally blue-green was now a sea of iridescent blue. Dead man-o'wars washed back and forth in unison with the waves generated by boat traffic out in the bay.

Captain Boyle, his dress uniform sharply creased, his white hat with its black trim, low over his eyes, was speaking. He had dutifully reported that the *Irisl Bijar*, flying the flag of Iran, had requested assistance with a disabled generator. He had given the *Bijar's* precise latitude/longitude coordinates at the time of the distress call. Adding, "That placed the ship one-hundred-ten miles off the South Padre Island Coast."

Reporters were quick to copy that information into their ever-present notebooks. I knew the question of U. S. territorial limits would be raised, and I also knew Boyle would duck the question, claiming the United States was simply responding to a mayday on the high seas.

Boyle then said, "I have with me on the platform two of the mechanics, Jimmy Redstone and Angella Martinez, who were aboard the *Bijar* at the time of the explosion. "They are here to answer questions pertaining to the explosion in the engine room." He turned to me and flashed the only smile I have ever seen on the man's face. To the camera it may have appeared genuine. To me it was sinister with a touch of *got you now* thrown in. "Jimmy and Angella. The microphone is all yours."

I reached forward to adjust the mike. Tiny, towering over the crowd, caught my eye. He was trying to gain my attention, but I studiously avoided him. I wanted my mind clear to deal with the cameras. I began talking about the broken generator and how we boarded the *Bijar* to repair it. Then I said, "Ms. Martinez and I were———"

"Pardon me, Sir. I'm Harold West from *Southern Cross*. Isn't it a fact that you and Ms. Martinez are Agents for Homeland Security?"

"We are," I answered, following my advice to Angella to tell the truth. "Would you please hold the questions until———"

"If you are HS agents posing as mechanics that changes the story. Does it not?"

"I'm not at liberty to discuss———" My cell phone vibrated, followed by the distinctive tone reserved for critical communications from Tiny. I pulled the phone out and snuck a peek at the screen. It read: SEE THIS VIDEO BEFORE ANSWERING ANY QUESTIONS.

I brought the phone all the way up so that I could see what was troubling Tiny, saying to the audience, "Please excuse me for a moment. I must see this."

I shielded the screen from the bright sun light and hit the video play button. There, streaming across the screen was a high-resolution image of Angella and me just as Angella's knife impacted our attacker's throat. The camera, wherever it had been located, was centered on my son's face as death froze the agony forever.

I looked up to see Tiny holding a sign high over his head reading, ON LIVE TV!

"As HS Agents," the reporter pressed, "what were you doing aboard a flag ship of Iran posing as a mechanic?"

Before I could answer———or even think of an appropriate answer———to that question, another reporter, sensing a lamb at the slaughter, yelled, "Can you confirm reports that the dead person is your son?"

I swallowed hard. Cut and run is not my style. But for the first time since as far back as I can recall, I wanted to do just that. Disappearing from the face of the earth was what I had in mind. Angella's hand on the small of my back steadied me, giving me a moment to catch my breath, to form an intelligent answer.

I moved closer to the mike. "As you are undoubtedly aware, we had information that drugs———tampered with medications actually———were aboard the *Bijar*. It is our belief that Iran was threatening to dump the toxic material in U.S. waters if the United States continued its sanctions on Iran. In order to avoid a confrontation I boarded that ship to render those toxic materials harmless."

"With all due respect, Agent Redstone, you didn't answer the question. Was that your son who Agent Martinez killed?"

"The evidence...photographic evidence...seems to suggest that it was."

"By your answer, then, is it fair to assume you have doubts?"

"I have no doubts. None at all."

"Was it your son, then?" the reporter pressed.

There are several possibilities when it feels as though a horse is sitting on your chest. One of those possibilities is a heart attack. Another is a panic attack. I felt as though I was experiencing both.

I was numb, so whether or not I was experiencing physical pain I didn't know. The mental pain, however, was overwhelming.

I took a deep breath.

Then another.

Slowly the air began seeping back into my lungs.

I looked up, ready to answer the question. I would have to concede that, indeed, it had been my son. To say otherwise would cause me to reveal controlled information about Sally Comings and the military operation that had been mounted. That I had not been authorized to do.

Again, Tiny held a sign above his head. ANSWER YOUR PHONE

Anything to delay answering the reporters' questions. "Hi Dad," the voice, sounding like my son's voice, said. "I just got back from a gig up at the Aleutian Islands. Best fishing gig ever! Been out two months. I was paid a whole lot of money. I mean a whole lot. I don't need to work for a long time. Maybe never."

"Why," I managed to ask, "are you calling now? But thank God you did."

"I'm watching TV and I see you down there. I didn't think you'd answer my call with all those microphones around. Hey, this is real neat. But a few minutes ago they showed you and some lady on a boat down there in the Gulf. I was with you. The lady cut my throat! What the hell's that about? I'm up here in Alaska. You trying to tell me something?"

"I can't talk now. But no, I'm not trying to tell you anything other than——"

"Listen, Dad. I'm sorry I didn't call, but——"

"It's okay, son. It's okay. Just come down and visit. I'll send you a ticket."

"Dad. You didn't hear me. I'm rich. Really rich! One hundred thousand dollars rich! Money's in the bank and all. Is next week okay? We can go out fishing and sailing like me and you——and Mark——used to do. Hey, is he still stationed with the Coast Guard down there? Tell him I said hello."

Before I could answer, Angella's knee, hidden behind the podium, slammed into mine. Startled, I glanced up, and realized the cameras and microphones were catching my every word and expression.

The phone was dead when I put it back to my ear to say good-bye to Les.

I turned back to the microphones and I'm positive I heard the collective gasp all the way from Washington of the Joint Chiefs when they heard me say, "I am absolutely certain the person involved with the drugs and the person who died on the *Irisl Bijar* yesterday was not my son, but rather a person impersonating my son."

I looked up in time to see Tiny frantically running his finger across his neck in the universal "kill it" sign. Or maybe he was giving Angella instructions as to what she should do to *my* neck.

The reporters, sensing a story, rushed forward, their arms waving like school kids desperate for a potty pass. "Do you know the identity of the impersonator?" one of them shouted.

"Can't comment. It's all under investigation. Now if you don't mind, I have no further comment——other than to tell my son, who is watching on TV, I love him."

Other Books by David Harry

Jimmy Redstone / Angella Martinez Series

the Padre Puzzle
the Padre Predator
the Padre Paranoia

General Fiction

Standard Deviation

Thank You

A special thank you goes to Marvilyn Miller who painstakingly corrected misspellings, faulty punctuations and other no-no's that tend to creep into manuscripts. Thank you also to Jim Welton for his plot line comments and astute observations.

Communications

David Harry can be reached at david@davidharryauthor.com

For information on upcoming books and other items of interest, please go to http://www.davidharryauthor.com. You can follow David Harry on Facebook: davidharry; on twitter: david1harry and on his blog : davidharryauthor.com.